LAST
OF THE
LIVING

LAST
OF THE
LIVING

DAVID MOODY

The right of David Moody to be identified as the author
of this work has been asserted by him in accordance with
the Copyright, Designs and Patents Act 1988.

First published in 2014 by Infected Books
'Who We Used to Be' first published in 'Living Dead 2'
by Nightshade Books (2010)
'Muriel' first appeared in the SFX Zombie Special
by Future Publishing (2011)

A CIP catalogue record for this book
is available from the British Library

ISBN 978-0-9576563-3-8

www.davidmoody.net
www.lastoftheliving.net

www.infectedbooks.co.uk

Cover design by David Shires
www.theimagedesign.com

INTRODUCTION

I've been writing about the living dead for a long time. In fact, going back through my dusty records recently, I discovered the handwritten notes which became the very first draft of AUTUMN dated 1997. Whilst I'm still a huge fan of our undead friends, after six AUTUMN and three HATER books (not technically zombies, I know) I've feel like I've said all I wanted to say. It's time for a change of direction.

This collection represents my remaining zombie output. In fact, I'll go as far as to say this will be my last word on zombies for the foreseeable future. The stories printed here are unconnected, and each has their own 'rules of the dead'. I've included brief introductions to set the scene and give you a little background.

I'm still an ardent fan of the zombie sub-genre. The living dead are, as far as I'm concerned, the most adaptable and terrifying of all monsters. You can drop them into pretty much any situation with ease, then sit back and watch chaos ensue. And why are they still so damn frightening after all these years? I think there are any number of reasons, not least their physical closeness to us. I'm not talking about zombies being in the next room or right outside your door, I'm talking about how easy it would be for *us* to become *them*. The strongest survivor might last years, but they'll always be walking that delicate fine line between the living and the undead. A single scratch, one drop of infected blood, a bite that just breaks the surface of the skin... that's all that separates you from the end of the life you know and a hellish eternity spent walking the planet until your rotting body finally fails you. Grim, eh?

Let's hope when the zombie apocalypse begins (and admit it, we're all secretly hoping it happens), that you and I don't fall at the first hurdle. Like many of the characters you'll meet in this book, here's to us both becoming one of the LAST OF THE LIVING.

David Moody, September 2014

CONTENTS

THE COST OF LIVING

Sometimes a germ of an idea will embed itself in your brain, and the only way to get rid of it is to write it out of your system. In my experience, that usually does the trick. Occasionally, though, it might not go to plan. For any number of reasons, the story you end up with might not say what you wanted it to say, or you might go off in a different direction and, before you know it, you're back to square one.

That was what happened with THE COST OF LIVING. The initial idea came to me many years ago while I was writing the early AU-TUMN books. I tried to develop the story as an AUTUMN short but, because of the technicalities of my invented infections and the 'rules' of the AUTUMN world, it didn't work. So I put the idea to one side and planned to come back to it later.

Post-HATER, I tried writing the story again, and the result was a four thousand word short named PRIORITIES (which you'll find later in this book). It was okay, but it wasn't quite right...

Sometime later still, when I was asked to write a piece of seven-hundred and fifty word flash fiction, I again returned to this same idea, wondering if I could say more with less. Though the piece (also printed later in this collection) was well received, I still wasn't satisfied. It packed a decent punch, but the characters didn't have sufficient space to develop.

Looking back, I decided that the length restrictions I'd imposed on the different versions of the story were the problem, and I started again. This time I was just going to write without worrying about word counts or formats, until I was satisfied I'd told the story properly.

And I think I've finally done it.

GABBY
SATURDAY 9 MAY – 11:38am

And I'm just looking at him thinking, *did you really just say that?* 'It's a pair of bloody supermarket leggings, Stu, that's all.'

'No, it's three pairs of supermarket leggings. Do you really need three pairs?'

'Yes, I really need three pairs. They're comfortable. I've been living in leggings since the baby and mine are all worn out.'

'I get that, but three pairs? You know how tight money's been since we moved. I'm just thinking that—'

'I know exactly how tight money's been. It's all you ever talk about. The cost of living this, the cost of living that... you're like a broken bloody record.'

'Not in front of Sally, love.'

'You bought yourself a load of work shirts last weekend.'

'Yes, but that's different.'

'Different? How?'

Sometimes I just give up. He means well, but Christ, he does my head in. I don't give him any chance to answer, I just shove three pairs of leggings into the trolley and push it away. Give him thirty seconds and he'll have caught up and he'll be grovelling. I know how his mind works.

'I'm sorry, Gab,' he says, alongside me again now, arms full of baby. 'It's just I'm under a lot of pressure at work and I'm worried about money and—'

'And I know. You make it sound like I'm extravagant and I'm not. I don't want three pairs of leggings, I *need* them. Believe me, I'd rather not be shopping for clothes in the supermarket.'

'I know. Look, things'll settle down in a few more months. Once the Harvest project's done and dusted and the O'Rourke contract's finalised I'll get a decent pay-out. First thing we'll do is go into town and have a spend-up. We'll get Hannah and Sally kitted out, get Nathan the trainers he's on about...'

A drunk-looking woman comes through the automatic doors, straight across the front of the trolley, not looking where she's going. I almost hit her. 'Don't mind me,' I shout. She just ignores me, heading straight for the booze.

'Pissed before lunchtime,' Stuart says disapprovingly, shaking his head like a typical old dad.

'What time's Nathan's football training finish?'

He looks at his watch as if it's going to tell him. 'Half-twelve.'

'And what time is it now?'

'Quarter to.'

'Then we'd better get a move on.'

Shopping with Stu is a pain in the backside. Everything takes twice as long as it should. I do the food shop every week, but it's like a bloody adventure for him. I go straight for the stuff I always buy, but he's always looking for alternatives, trying to find a cheaper option. He's at it already with the bloody potatoes. 'But you can get two packs for three pound fifty. We'll save seventy pence if we buy two.'

'But we won't use two, will we? We won't get through both packs before they go out of date. You're not saving seventy pence, you're wasting twice that. Don't you get it?'

He's not convinced. I'm thinking he's about to start trying to tell me how I should cook more potatoes to make things cost-effective when Hannah starts grumbling for her bottle and Sally pulls me over towards the sweets. I'm glad of the distraction. 'Can I have some chocolate, Mummy?' Sally asks, and I can feel Stuart on my shoulder, ready to launch into another tirade, but I'm not having it.

'Of course you can, love. What would you like?'

I glance back and see him struggling with the baby, and the chocolate's chosen and in the trolley before he can protest. I push on to the next aisle before he can start.

Wait.

This doesn't feel right.

I can hear something.

You don't realise the normal soundtrack you hear in places like this until it's disturbed. The kids, the trolleys, the conversations, the music... they've all just been silenced. There's a weird, uncomfortable quiet now. Stu's noticed it too. We just look at each other and he shrugs.

Around the corner and into the next aisle and we see it. That drunk woman is kicking off. I try to distract Sally but it's too late and she's seen her. 'What's wrong with that lady, Mummy?'

'I don't know, love. Perhaps she's not well. Maybe she just feels a little bit sick.'

I look at Stu again, both of us instinctively keeping it light and airy so Sal doesn't get scared. This isn't good. I can still hear noise elsewhere in the store, but it's all dwindling down to nothing as more and more people become aware of what's happening. The woman's having some kind of convulsion it looks like, a full-blown fit. A couple of staff are trying to get to her but they're struggling to get through the onlookers and their massed trolleys and baskets. There's a PA announcement for the duty first aider.

'They don't need a duty first aider,' Stu says. 'They just need to hang her out to dry somewhere.'

There's a security man, a young girl and a slightly older guy around the woman now, trying to hold back the crowds. They're doing what they can, but they're just part-time folks here to stack shelves and stocktake, and I can see them all desperately looking for the first aider so they can pass the buck. To be fair, I'd be the same on their wages. Another woman in a supermarket uniform brushes past us and I see the young girl look up and make eye contact with her, immediately jumping to her feet and calling her over.

Believe me, I'm not one of those people who stands and stares at accidents. I make a conscious effort not to look when we see crashes on the motorway and get slowed down by all the other foul rubber-neckers. But the thing is, we can't move here. There are shoppers in front and behind now and we're trapped. The security man is trying to move people back to give the woman on the floor some space but it's not easy. He has to shout over the heads of the people at the front so that those near the back can move first, but there are still more people crowding into this aisle than there are going the other way. I doubt half of them even know what's happening. All the half-full trolleys make it virtually impossible to move, bunched up tight together. I pick Sally up and put her in my trolley with the shopping to get her out of the way. She protests, but a piece of chocolate shuts her up fast.

I can see the woman on the floor now through a gap that opens up in the crowd. Bloody hell, that's horrible. She's just lying there, facedown on the marble, mouth hanging wide open, eyes staring into space. I don't think she's conscious. Is she dead?

This is just like the reports we've seen on TV.

'We need to go,' Stu says, thinking the exact same thing. 'I reckon she's got it.'

He starts trying to move back, holding onto Hannah with one hand, pulling at my arm with the other. But there's no way out, not until a few more of these bloody idiots shift. Hard as we push back, they're still pushing forward.

Now the security guy's getting shirty, but he can't see we're stuck here. Someone has a go at him and I'm thinking this is going to get nasty if we're not careful. I just want to finish the shopping then get out of here and go pick up Nathan from football. I knew I should have done this yesterday. Bloody Stuart. If he hadn't insisted on coming with me today then we—

Wait.

A second ago I thought that woman was dead. Now she's moving again.

'See that?' Stu says, grabbing my arm even harder.

'I see it. But she was—'

'But nothing. I swear, she's got it. They collapse, then they get up again.'

There's a collective scream. Loads of people try to run when the woman moves suddenly. She rolls over onto her back, quick as you like, then starts clawing at the floor with her fingers like she's trying to get a grip. Even the first aider's keeping her distance.

'We need to go,' Stuart says, pulling me away. It hurts and I yelp with pain. I try to tell him to stop but he's as scared as I am. 'Fuck me...' he says.

The woman who'd collapsed has attacked the young girl in the supermarket uniform. She's got her pressed up against the shelves now and there are tins and packets of food flying everywhere as the girl tries to fight her off, but the woman's all over her. Bloody hell, even the security guard can't drag her away. She's got her arms and legs wrapped around the girl, their faces just inches apart.

Oh, God.

Now we're being pushed back faster than we can walk, everyone trying to get away at once. The woman's dragged the girl onto the floor now and she's on top of her. Jesus... she's vomiting into her face. Dirty brown gunk. It's blood or sick or germ-filled spit... Christ, that's foul.

I try to untangle the trolley. It's caught up with someone else's.

'Leave it,' Stuart says.

'But what about the shopping?'

'Pick Sally up and just leave it,' he says again. 'Now!'

STUART
SUNDAY 10 MAY – 1:14am

So the others are in bed but there's no point me going up yet. I know I won't sleep. Gabby went up early but I stayed down to watch a film. I sat through the whole thing, but didn't take any of it in. Too much on my mind.

What we saw in the supermarket was shocking. Sickening. There's been reports of similar things on the news over the last few days, but seeing it in the flesh like that was so much worse.

What we get on BBC and SKY is the safe, sanitised, watered-down version of events, the bits they want us to see. We're spared the gory details, and because it's what we're used to, we don't question it. They show endless footage of wars, but you hardly ever see any blood. You see all those cities in ruins, buildings crumbling, desperate people searching through the rubble... but you're always watching it from a safe distance. You can't smell it. You can't taste it. You can't *feel* it. All that changed today.

We didn't think anything of it when we saw the first reports. Just one or two cases... nothing much in isolation. There's a new disease doing the rounds every couple of months, and for all the panicked predictions, they never seem to amount to much. There was Swine Flu a few years back, Bird Flu before that, and then there was that virus they found buried in the Siberian permafrost that had been dead for thirty-thousand years but which some dick in a lab managed to bring back to life. But this season's killer syndrome of choice is different. It came after the annual flu surge and caught everyone unawares. Seems it was something in this year's mutation of the flu that opened the door to this new germ. The first epidemic paved the way for the next.

But back to the news...

I was sitting here with Gab and I remember the bulletin clear as day. They were talking about how this particular infection strikes its

6

victims all of a sudden. It literally knocks them off their feet. One minute they seem fine, half an hour later and they're flat on their backs in the middle of a supermarket aisle, apparently out for the count.

And this is where the TV version of events differs from what we saw today.

On the news they talked about infected people's salivary glands working overtime, constantly dribbling and drooling, some kind of involuntary reaction after they've lost consciousness. But I don't know... that's not what I saw today. I mean sure, she lost consciousness, that much was obvious, but it's what happened next that doesn't tie up. She attacked that poor shop girl and she was doing everything she could to get spit all over her. She was definitely conscious, and she was definitely hurling or drooling or whatever, *over* the girl. It was controlled, it was violent, and it was frightening as hell.

It doesn't add up.

And now I'm left sitting here on my own in the middle of the night, sleep the very furthest thing from my mind, thinking *why are they lying about this?* Don't people need to know? If these sick people are out on the streets, shouldn't somebody be telling us or doing something about it?

It's probably just me, blowing the whole thing out of proportion.

I'd like to know what happened to the supermarket worker who got caught today, though. Maybe she's all right tonight, maybe she's out drinking with her friends, trying to forget about the day from hell she's just survived.

But what if she isn't?

And what about the woman? Did they restrain her? How many more people could she have drooled over on the way from the supermarket to the hospital?

STUART

TUESDAY 19 MAY – 10:54am

I have the radio on as I work. It used to be a distraction that got me through the tedium of the day, now the work's the distraction. Concentrating on the stuff the boss tells me makes it easier to block out everything else. I think something big's going on here. Part of me thinks I'm wrong because no one else seems to be reacting, but then I look at the facts and I know I'm right about this. See, I think this should be the main headline, but they're treating it like an afterthought, squeezing in a mention between the local news and the weather reports.

I know I'm coming across like a conspiracy theorist here, but the mainstream media changed the way they talked about the infection a few days ago. I can't help thinking they're trying to make it look like less of a big deal than I know it is. They're still talking about isolated cases and extreme reactions, but if you dig a bit deeper and start looking at the unofficial news – people's Facebook timelines and tweets, all that kind of stuff – it paints a very different picture.

I can't do it here on the office computer, but I can see stuff on my phone. You look at some of the crank sites (at least I used to think they were cranks), all the sites for Preppers and the like, and they're all full of it. They're all saying the exact same thing. They're reporting huge numbers of cases. Well huge by comparison to the ten o'clock news, anyway. I found this report from a kid in Aberdeen. Something like what happened to the woman in the supermarket happened to a friend of his, apparently. How much of this was bullshit I don't know, but it made for pretty disturbing reading. He was talking about his friend having gotten sick after one of his sick relatives (who subsequently died or disappeared, I'm not sure which) had coughed up gunk all over him. He dropped in the middle of the street without any warning. A few minutes later and he was up again, literally spewing bile over anyone he could get close to. He puked up over more than ten people before anyone could stop him. Just one sick kid.

Thing is, if this is as bad as I'm thinking and this is how this infection spreads, then what's happening is scattershot, isn't it? One infected person could contaminate a whole street if they're not stopped and sedated in time.

I'm finding gaps in explanations, holes in stories, unexpected spaces where there should be information. And no one else is questioning it.

Right now, all this is little more than gossip. No one's sounding particularly worried, and that's strange in itself because people are usually happy to panic. Christ, I remember what happened after nine-eleven. I was on work experience in a law firm in the middle of the city centre, halfway up a twenty storey building. The days and weeks after the attack people were talking crap about how *friends of friends of friends* had been approached by an *Arabic-looking gentleman* at the train station, warning them to stay out of city centre high-rises. I remember the mild panic when someone spotted a plane circling, but it was just a light aircraft. If you looked close enough, you could see a logo painted on its tail. It was a bloody weather forecaster doing circuits for local radio, nothing more sinister.

People don't ever stop and analyse. They either ignore what's in front of their noses or jump to conclusions and make assumptions without realising what they're doing. Why would terrorists launch an attack on our office, for Christ's sake? Hardly a key tactical target, was it? And would anyone really have been so inspired by what they'd seen across the Atlantic as to want to fly a small plane into the side of a building in Digbeth? I doubt it. People can be so bloody stupid at times.

Now it's the reverse, though. Now I think something *is* happening, but people have got their heads buried in the sand because that's easier than facing up to what might be coming.

This started overseas. South Sudan had a head start on the rest of the world for once. On the radio now there's a report from the UN where some specially convened meeting is discussing sudden huge rises in the rates of infection in other parts of Africa. And my colleagues are still casually talking about the football and who got voted off the latest shite reality TV programme last night, because what's happening *over there*, isn't happening *over here*. Not yet. Not in the same kind of numbers, anyway.

But if you look back at reports from those other countries, I think you can see a pattern emerging. It all started the same way. I think it's only a matter of time.

STUART

Today's the day it changed. Today it stopped being something on TV I can just switch on and off when I feel like it. What's happening out there is serious, the implications vast. I've tried to keep it from Gabby and the kids because there's nothing they can do. I'll try to preserve their normality for as long as I can but, if I'm right, in the next few days their world will inevitably begin to fall apart. *Everything* will start falling apart.

I've been scouring the dark recesses of the Internet again, looking for information. Gabby thinks I'm looking at porn, because every time she gets close I shut the laptop case fast. I wish that was all I was doing.

I've found a link to a load of footage from South Sudan and other countries nearby. I've seen whole swathes of land left desolate with just the infected left there to roam. In one clip, it was taken live on a phone and streamed elsewhere, some guy stumbled into a village where there were twenty or thirty of them just drifting, looking like they were in some kind of trance, a weird malaise. But then, when they saw the guy who was filming, they stampeded after him, racing with each other like they all wanted to be the one to infect him. I was shaking when I stopped watching, because I know that's coming over here.

It's not just Africa now. Parts of Russia are the same, and India and Pakistan too. Now it's spreading across Europe, though you wouldn't think so if all you watched was the mainstream media. The rise in case numbers in those regions has been exponential, and I can't see how anyone thinks they'll get this situation back under control. It's just a question of time.

Gabby thinks I've got an off-site meeting this morning. There is one, but I'm not going. I've got more important things to do. I know she'll be out all morning. I wait until she's taken Nathan to school, then head out myself. Just have to hope that the schools are open and that they'll be okay. I'd rather we were all at home together, but I need the space. I need to do this.

I'm a few steps ahead of the game. I'm still questioning myself constantly, wondering if I'm overreacting, but I know in my heart I'm not. See, I've always known this part would be key to surviving the shit that's about to hit the fan. Most people are still going about their day-to-day business like nothing's changed, and I almost envy their ignorance. There's no avoiding it, though. Something terrible is coming.

I drive to the wholesalers we use at work and start doing the thing I've always dreaded. I'm stocking up for the apocalypse. Part of me feels like an idiot, like I'm the one who's got this wrong. I can see people looking at me, thinking I've lost my fucking mind, but all I have to do is picture the faces of my wife and kids to keep me focused and on task. They're all that matters. The lad on the till looks at me as if I've gone crazy. Who knows... maybe I have?

I load everything into the back of the car, then go straight back in again for more. This time even more of the staff have clocked what I'm doing. None of them are completely stupid, they're just not ready to accept that their old lives are coming to an end and that a much more uncertain future now lies ahead, if any future at all. This time as I work my way around the warehouse, I know they're all watching me. Half the staff are thinking *look at that fucking idiot.* The other half are thinking, *should I be doing that?*

I have to move fast. The development is at its quietest at this time of the morning and I reverse onto the drive of our house and unload everything into the garage, satisfied there are no prying eyes watching. It's almost too quiet. There's a guy in one of the small terraced houses across the way who says goodbye to his girlfriend then acknowledges me, but other than him I don't see anyone else. The development's only two-thirds built, but it doesn't look like many of the builders turned up to work today.

Now I head straight back out again, this time to the DIY store. It's no good getting in all those supplies and not taking steps to make sure the house is secure. I buy sheets of plywood, fencing, padlocks and chains, industrial-size containers of bleach and other cleaning agents. The teller puts everything through. She's polite enough, but I can tell from the look in her eyes that she's uneasy. Does she know what I'm doing? The combination and quantities of stuff I'm buying is a dead giveaway. She knows the axes aren't for cutting down trees, and this black rubber sheeting's not for lining a fish pond.

I get everything unloaded with just a couple of minutes to spare before Gabby gets home. It's only taken just over an hour. I'm still putting the last of it away when she pulls up on the drive with the kids. She doesn't have a clue why I'm here. 'What's wrong, love?' she asks me. 'Aren't you well?'

'I'm fine. How come you're all back?'

'Not enough teachers at Nathan's school so they closed it. Never mind that, Stu, why are you home? Don't tell me they've made you redundant? You said there was a chance...'

I shut the front door. Nathan goes up to his room. The baby's asleep and Sally's immediately occupied by the TV, so I sit Gabby down in the kitchen and try to tell her things how I see them. 'I think this is bad, Gab, really bad.'

'What?'

'The sickness. I think it's a lot worse than people are letting on.'

'Come on, Stu... are you for real? Something like this happens every few years. A couple of weeks' time and it'll all be forgotten and they'll be onto the next health scare. Honestly, love... this isn't like you. You've been working too hard. Do you need to take some time off? Maybe we should—'

'There's nothing wrong with me, Gab. For the record, I hope you're right. I hope I have got this wrong, but I don't think I have. Watch the news, read between the lines... they know what's coming, they're just not saying. They don't want people panicking.'

She closes her eyes and shakes her head. What's she thinking? Does she believe me, or does she think I've lost it? Is it easier to believe that than accept the truth? 'You're wrong.'

'I'm not.' I slide my laptop across the table towards her. 'Here, have a look. You have a look at what's happening in Russia, then go back a couple of weeks and see how it started there. Look at South Sudan and South Africa. Look at Chad and Nigeria. It's the same bloody pattern. A few isolated cases – like that woman in the supermarket, remember? – then more and more. Then it all changes in a couple of days. It spirals out of control.'

'But it's not out of control in Russia.'

'Just look at the news, Gab.'

She does what I tell her and her eyes widen when she sees the reports I was looking at earlier. Hundreds of cases have become thousands overnight. Maybe it'll be hundreds of thousands by this time tomorrow. Maybe it'll be more.

She shakes her head, shuts the laptop, and slides it back my way. 'This doesn't prove anything. It's just scaremongering. I'm more worried about you than anyone in Russia, love. I think you're putting yourself under too much stress. You're starting to sound paranoid.'

'I'm not paranoid. This is real, I know it is.'

She gets up and walks over to the kitchen window. She sees the pile of papers I've left on the counter; the receipts from this morning. She starts leafing through them, and I know exactly what's coming next. 'Stu... what the hell have you done?'

'What do you think?'

'I think you've blown our food budget for the next three months. Christ, love, we're struggling enough as it is. You're the one who's always lecturing me about the cost of living, and you go and do this?'

She's doing this on purpose, because fighting with me is easier than facing what's coming next.

'We need to talk about this, Gab.'

'Damn right we need to talk. Bloody hell, when I think of all the grief you've given me since we moved... all that bullshit about tightening our belts and cutting costs... then you go and do this? I give up. And you still haven't answered my question, why aren't you at work?'

'That's not important. What's important is trying to—'

'Not important! What if Ray finds out and you lose your job? What happens then? What happens if we can't pay the mortgage and feed the kids and... and why are you looking at me like that?'

'Sit down again, love, please.'

She refuses. I make her a coffee. Her face is streaked with tears. She dabs at her mascara with a tissue. 'I think you've gone crazy. Absolutely bloody crazy. It's just a flu virus.'

'It's more than that and you know it. The flu virus is a red herring, I told you that the day before yesterday. It's because of the flu virus that so many people's immunities are low, and that's why it's spreading so quickly. The hospitals are overcrowded... the whole health system is stretched to breaking point. Take Sally's booster jab, for example. When was the last time a routine appointment like that was cancelled?'

'Never,' she admits, thinking it over. Then she turns again. 'You're making huge assumptions, though. Just because it's happening in other countries, doesn't mean it's necessarily going to happen here...'

'It already is happening, love. Have you seen the news this morning? It's the exact same thing. Same as India. Same as China and Russia. And there are reports from the US and Canada too... They said it would never happen there, remember? As recently as last week they were saying they had it all under control... now look. There's no reason to think it won't happen here.'

'But they said we were safe. They said it wouldn't happen here. They said they'd be able to contain it and because we're an island they said there's no way it could—'

'We talked about this. It's always the same. What were the people on TV supposed to say before today? The truth's unpalatable sometimes, but we have to stay positive and look on the bright side here, love, because—'

'There's a bright side?'

'Yes, there's a bright side. We're ready for this and we're together. I'm going to do everything I have to do to keep this family safe. I won't let anything happen to any of us.'

I wait for her to say something, but she doesn't. She knows I'm right. She starts crying. I take her hand and hold her tight, then show her the garage. It's piled high with stuff, and for a second the sheer amount even takes me by surprise.

'Jesus...' she says under her breath, and I explain.

'Enough food to keep us going for a couple of months if needs be. Medical supplies for every eventuality. Water purification tablets, cleaning products, disinfectants, detergents... everything we're likely to need and a lot more besides.'

'What's...' she starts to say. She stops and composes herself. 'What's all the wood for? What are you making?'

'Not making anything. It's to help secure the house if we need to. Strengthen the windows and doors, that kind of thing. We might need to keep people out as well as keeping us in. I told you, I'm not taking any chances, Gab. You four are all that matters to me.'

Back to the kitchen. Sally appears from out of nowhere, face full of snot. I grab a tissue and wipe her clean. 'Hungry,' she says.

'I'll get you something,' Gab tells her. Sally watches as she makes her a Marmite sandwich.

'Mummy sad?'

Gabby wipes her eyes. 'Mummy's okay,' she says.

'Mummy sick?'

'No, Mummy's fine.'

STUART

WEDNESDAY 27 MAY – 11:52pm

And so it begins. The mainstream media has finally woken up to reality.

I've been following this story since late afternoon. A hospital in Manchester had to close their doors to new admissions. I'm not sure why, because there's no information coming out of the place. I presume it's overcrowded. Either that or it's damage limitation, something like that? Maybe they're trying to preserve the place because they know what's coming?

But people kept arriving. More and more people are getting sick, and huge numbers of them are obviously trying to get medical attention, even though from what I can tell, there's nothing any doctor can do for the infected. So crowds have been building up all around the place all evening.

Trouble threatened to break out several times, but it was about four hours ago that it really kicked off. The news cameramen filmed from a distance, not wanting to get close, but long-shots were good enough to show what was happening. The infected who'd been brought to the hospital were turning, immediately trying to infect those who were still free from the germ. It was like watching a riot: pockets of sporadic violence breaking out in the midst of this massive crowd of desperate people. It didn't take long for the whole area to be consumed by panic. People were breaking into the hospital, others were breaking out... it was absolute carnage. The cameraman abandoned his camera and left it filming the chaos – an unbroken long-shot of Manchester tearing itself apart.

Now, hours later, the streets are quieter. There are just infected left out there now. They wander around with their heads bowed, like they're in some kind of trance. Now and then something attracts their attention – someone unaffected, perhaps – and they chase after them in huge numbers.

And now the TV has cut to Downing Street. There's an old guy on screen, talking about the COBRA meeting he's just chaired, and I'm thinking, *who the hell are you?* He's not the Prime Minister or his deputy... I reckon this is some deputy's deputy's deputy, and I reckon he's probably all that's left.

We're well and truly fucked.

STUART

THURSDAY 28 MAY – 5:50am

This is the hardest thing I've ever had to do; the toughest decision I've ever had to make. I knew it was coming – I was ready for it – but that didn't make it any easier. It's time to seal us in. I just hope I'm not too late.

I sat up all night watching the news, watching the world continue to fall to pieces, and watching dumb fucking substitute politicians spinning the same old bullshit about how things would soon be brought under control, and that lessons would be learned and so on. All just empty words, empty promises. No substance. No facts. Just a smokescreen: a way of hiding the truth because everyone's finally beginning to realise the truth here is going to be fucking awful.

And then, about half an hour ago, the crisis outside got a lot closer to home. The sickness has reached our development. It was the family diagonally opposite, the ones with all the dogs in one of the smaller houses. I sat in the baby's room upstairs and watched from the window, one eye on Hannah, the other across the street. Fuck, I could taste their fear even from a distance. They're never coming home. I could tell from the way they bundled a few bags and their kid and the dogs into the back of their car and drove them away that they were evacuating. They're as good as dead.

And so will we be if I don't do this.

It hurts.

As I make my way around the house, trying not to wake the others while I check all the locks and cover the windows, I can't help thinking about our extended family and all the other people I'd love to help. Mum and Dad, Gabby's folks, Phil and his family, Sandy and her kids... the list goes on and on but I know I have to focus all my efforts on the five people in this house, and I have to believe the others will be doing the same thing, wherever they are. Dad'll be okay, I'm sure of that, and Phil should be all right too if he gets his head out of his arse in time. I sent him a message last night, but he hasn't replied.

I keep telling myself they'll all look after their own the same way I'm looking after mine. When I feel any doubt, guilt or remorse, I just turn it around. I ask myself, *who else is going to look after Gabby and the kids?* And the answer's simple. There's no one. It's all down to me.

I bolt and padlock all the doors. I keep all the keys locked away apart from one set that I'll carry with me. As soon as the others are awake I'll tell them what's happening. The kids will be scared but they'll soon realise that what we're shutting ourselves away from is far more frightening than anything else.

Gabby gets it. She stays in bed, Sally lying next to her, Hannah alongside in her crib. She looks beat. For a second I'm worried it might be the sickness, but I know it's not. She had all her jabs and I kept her from those friends who might have been exposed. She's barely seen anyone this last couple of weeks, and that was the right thing to do. She's just tired now, emotionally drained. We both are, but I make myself keep going.

Nathan's a different kettle of fish. He doesn't have a problem with not going to school, but when I tell him he can't go and visit his

17

girlfriend half a mile away, he gets nasty. They're just kids. It's his first crush, nothing serious. 'You're not going anywhere,' I tell him. Bloody kid's at the front door with his jacket and trainers on, trying to force the padlock. 'Do you know what's happening out there?'

'No,' he says. 'You've stopped us watching the TV, remember? You unplugged the satellite. I can't watch shit.'

'Don't use that kind of language with me, son.'

He kicks the door again, and mumbles something under his breath about me being fucking stupid or something similar. I let it go. He's scared. He's upset. We both are. We *all* are.

I need to make him understand. I'd planned to leave it a while longer, but we'll have no front door left at this rate. 'How much do you know, Nathan?'

'Not enough. Like I said, you censored the TV and I can't get anything online. Half my friends have stopped answering my texts.'

'There's every possibility your friends are dead.'

He stops fighting for a second and just looks at me. He laughs, then sneers, then turns back and starts booting the bottom of the door again. I pull him away, he shrugs me off. 'Leave me alone,' he says, doing what he can to not let me see the tears.

'Listen, son, I know it's never cool to do what your dad says, but this is one occasion you really need to.'

'But I need to go and see Jen. I need to know she's okay.'

It's just puppy love. He'll get over her. I don't care what happens to anyone else, but I humour him just the same. 'We have to believe that her family are doing the same as us, and if they do, in a few weeks' time, I'm sure you'll be able to see her again.'

'I'm not waiting a few weeks. I'm going now. She's only just down the road. I'll be back in an hour or so. I just need to know she's all right...'

'It's not happening.'

'But, Dad...'

'Listen to me, son, and listen very, very carefully. The disease that's doing all the damage out there is highly contagious and—'

'I'll stay away from everyone else. I'll run there and I'll run back. Jen's brother's cool with me going and I—'

'Her brother? Where are her parents?'

'Her dad moved out a couple of years back.'

'And her mother?'

He pauses before answering, and the hesitation speaks volumes. 'She's sick,' he eventually admits. 'She's in the hospital. I have to go and see Jen, Dad. She needs me...'

'You have to understand just how serious this is now, Nathan.'

He stops fighting and slumps back against the wall, barely managing to suppress his anger. 'I know, but—'

'I'm not sure you do. You see, I can't let you go anywhere, Nathan, because if you leave this house, I won't be able to let you back in again.' I can see that my words have shocked him. He looks at me, then looks away again. 'That's not an idle threat, son, it's a fact. If one of us gets sick, we all get sick, and I can't let that happen.'

'She's only round the corner...'

'No.'

His head drops. He finally lets go of the door handle. I put my arm around his shoulder and take him into the lounge. He sits on the sofa, deflated – beat, and I plug the satellite back in to show him what's happening out there.

'You need to see this, son,' I tell him. 'You need to understand.'

The first thing I see on the TV takes me by surprise. It hits us both hard. At some point during the last few hours, the BBC has disappeared. What we're seeing now is some kind of emergency broadcast, as terrifying as it is clichéd. Just a list of instructions on a loop, dos and don'ts, ten times more *don'ts* than *dos*. My mouth's gone dry, and Nathan's just staring at the screen. 'Is this for real?' he asks. I clear my throat and try to answer.

'Yeah, it's for real. You understand now, Nath? Look, I recorded a few news bulletins because I thought this might happen. I want you to see some of the things I've been seeing.'

'Why didn't you just leave the TV plugged in and let me see them anyway?'

'Because I care, that's why. Because I wanted to make this as easy as I could. If we do the right thing here, son, we'll get through this. You, me, Sally, Hannah and Mum... we'll be okay.'

I show him some clips from Manchester last night that I recorded. 'Why did you save this stuff?' he asks.

19

'So that we don't forget. It's important. We need to remember why we're having to do this.'

He just stares at the screen, open mouthed. I'm not stupid, I know he's probably seen some of this on his phone, but these are the edited highlights, for want of a better word.

I show him some stuff on the laptop. I swear I could have written the script for this next clip weeks ago. It's a report from outside a supermarket. Cut to inside, and the camera pans along empty shelves, then swings over to one corner of the strangely echoing store where people are fighting over the little food which remains. 'Have you looked in the garage recently?' I ask him.

'Tried to a couple of days back,' he answers. 'Couldn't get in. Too much stuff.'

'You see all those gaps on the shelves on the screen? That food's here. I saw this coming, Nath. I've got enough for all of us, and it'll last for a couple of months if we're smart and ration ourselves properly.'

'Rations?'

'It's got to be done. I'm not saying it's going to be easy, but I don't see we have any other option. But if we can get through this, we'll get through anything.'

On screen now is a camp that sprung up the day before yesterday. It's somewhere just outside London, I think, thrown together to cope with hospital overspill. 'Looks like Afghanistan,' he says.

'You're thinking of Syria, son.'

'Same difference.'

'Not really.'

It's pointless arguing about geography at a time like this, so I let it go and let him watch. He's right, though, this looks like the kind of thing we used to see on the TV news, endless reports from the war-torn Middle East. But this is somewhere in the Home Counties.

'Remember when we went camping a couple of years back and we stayed on that farm near all the wind turbines?'

'I remember.'

'This is just down the road from there.'

His silence speaks volumes.

This next clip makes me go cold every time I see it. I must have watched it a hundred times since I found it yesterday morning. It's like something out of a horror movie. It's an abandoned factory, I think, a massive concrete space in between a number of obviously derelict buildings, endless empty windows and doors. It's a morgue now, a disposal site. The entire space – and it must be a hundred metres square – is filled with dead bodies in bags, all laid out in lines. The camera operator is filming from on high. Smoke drifts, and the cameraman shifts focus to find the source. There's a bonfire. A fucking huge bonfire with searing orange flames. The dirtiest black smoke I've ever seen billows up. They change position and zoom in tight, the picture getting shakier the closer they get, pixelating and going in and out of focus. And then, in amongst the flames, there are faces. Fingers. Arms and legs. Hair curling up and burning away. Skin being peeled. Black holes where eyes used to be.

Nathan doesn't say anything. What's left to say?

Final recording.

'This is why we can't go out, son. This is what it's like out there now.'

The centre of London in chaos, footage taken from a helicopter circling overhead. Uncontrolled panic in the streets. A handful of soldiers try to maintain order, but they're fighting a losing battle. There are bodies everywhere, lives ended without warning, people's last moments spent in utter terror, face down in the stinking gutters. Buildings burning, fire spreading. Some still run for cover, but few reach their destinations. The entire world is dying.

And throughout it all, snaking through the carnage, hunting out those frightened few who remain somehow untouched, are the infected. Their movements are chillingly alien: staccato and unpredictable, stop then start, watch then attack. Unexpected jerks and sudden changes in direction, dead but for the germ which drives them on.

STUART

THURSDAY 28 MAY – 5:17pm

Over the course of the last twelve hours, hell has enveloped our neighbourhood. The family leaving in the middle of the night just gone was a pre-cursor to the full-blown chaos we've witnessed today. Now it seems everyone is fleeing their homes, and I don't understand why. What do they hope to achieve? Where will they go? Why this preoccupation with running? The safest thing to do – the *only* thing to do – is to stay locked away like us and wait. Going out there to-day... that's only going to put people in more danger, not less. I can understand wanting to get out of the cities and put some distance between yourself and the rest of the population, but if everyone else is running too, what good will it do?

I was worried there might be some kind of forced evacuation, that the authorities might round up those of us who haven't been infected while they try to decontaminate the rest of the country. Half the time I'm convinced I'll see tanks and troops driving up the road when I next look out the window, but I know now that's just nerves talking. I've heard explosions and I can see smoke drifting into the sky, but I think we're long past any kind of coordinated response. What's left of the news on the TV and online shows a country in chaos. I don't think there even are any authorities anymore. I've tried to find out what's happening in those countries where the infection began, but there's nothing coming out of them at all, complete radio and Inter-net silence. There are thousands of possible reasons why communi-cations might have been disrupted, but the most likely explanation is that all those places are gone. Nothing left. Dead. I managed to catch a snatch of an emergency broadcast on the old long wave, but it turned out to be a recorded message on a loop. It could have been running for days. And I found an old, old website with a list of web-cam feeds too; tourist spots, city centres, those kinds of things. That refugee camp or evacuation centre or whatever it was? Gone now. There was a camera left looking down over it; a black, burned out hole... no one alive.

It feels like the walls are closing in, like the world's getting smaller.

Gabby keeps asking me if we should be running too because ev-eryone else is, but I tell her again and again that this is the only way of surviving. Isolation is everything. I tell her to try and imagine the chaos on the roads right now. She doesn't know, but I've been think-ing about this day for longer than I dare tell her.

I never said anything to Gabby at the time, because she'd either have got angry or divorced me on grounds of insanity, but when we bought this house at the start of last year, I had disaster preparedness in mind. Of course the location, the number of bedrooms, the local school and facilities and so on were the main reasons for moving here, but I'd been feeling for a long time that we were overdue a disaster. That might sound overdramatic, but sitting here today and having watched the neighbours trying to cram what's left of their lives into suitcases and cardboard boxes and loading their cars, it seems I was right. To be honest, I thought it was more likely to have been some kind of terrorist attack or social unrest that caused all the damage, but whatever the reason, the end result is the same: the world as we know it is gone. Nothing's ever going to be the same again.

Our development was built on the site of a Victorian hospital. It was closed many years ago, and only a couple of the original buildings remain now. Despite it being in a relatively built-up area, the fact we're on what used to be the hospital grounds has a number of advantages. We're enclosed, for a start, the whole estate ringed by substantial metal railings. There's a single access road, and from the other end of that road the development is all but invisible, set behind a patch of raised grassland and a copse of trees which obscure most of the houses. Thankfully it's late spring. The increasing foliage decreases the visibility. And there are less than forty finished homes here anyway... from outside you'd hardly know there was anything here at all. Our house is smack-bang in the middle of it all, completely hidden from anyone looking in. Invisible from all sides.

When the time comes I'll block the access road if I have to; seal us off completely. We have everything we need to get through this: enough supplies, medication and water. Most importantly, we have each other. I'll sever our ties with the rest of the world in a heartbeat if it comes down to it.

The quiet this evening is unsettling. I hadn't realised how loud life was until it all stopped. The sounds have steadily reduced all day. Now there's nothing. Helicopters, panic, the occasional scream... the screech of tyres as more people left the development, the sounds of fighting and uncontrolled panic on the other side of the border fence, the last of the few overly-optimistic clean-up crews being over-run and giving up. It was a gradual quietening, but the silence now feels sudden. It's like they've all stopped trying at the same time, like they've given up together.

Maybe they have. Maybe we're all that's left now. But we can't be, can we?

And now the silence leaves me feeling dangerously exposed. This is something I hadn't bargained on. I mean, I thought I'd covered all bases, but I wasn't prepared for this. Now that everything's so quiet, any little noise we make is amplified out of all proportion. That's okay most of the time because Gabby, Nathan and me can keep our mouths shut when we need to, but it's not as easy with the girls. Sally's scared, and why wouldn't she be? How do you tell a three year-old that everything's going to be okay one minute, then that she can't talk the next? It'll take time, but she'll get used to it I guess. To be honest, I'm even more worried about Hannah. When she cries for her bottle now it's like someone's sticking pins in me. I imagine all the infected for miles around, turning and heading in this direction when they hear her. I need her to be safe and well fed, but right now it's equally important for her to be quiet. Isolation, remember? We can't risk being found.

There's no information coming in from outside now. The internet has slowed to a crawl and even when I do manage to get an update, it's already so old it's not worth reading. All the TV channels have gone, replaced by emergency broadcast music or, more frequently, empty black screens and silence. But it's crucially important that I stay abreast of what's happening, particularly in the area immediately around our development.

When we first visited this place, a couple of months before we agreed to buy the house, we left the sales office with a file full of stuff: brochures with floor plans of all the different house designs, leaflets about the locality and various financing schemes, and a map of the development. I've pinned the map to the garage wall and have been slowly marking it off. When people have moved out, I've crossed their house through. There are plenty I'm not sure about yet – all the houses we can't clearly see from ours, those which are unfinished – but I know which of the others are empty.

Clive and Christine Parish, that awful couple who lived at number one, were amongst the first to go. And since they cleared out (almost two weeks ago... off to stay with relatives up north until this all blows over, Gabby said she'd heard), all the houses between ours and theirs have emptied too. I take a chance and sneak out while Gabby, Nathan and the girls are occupied elsewhere, telling them I'm going to sort out the supplies in the garage again.

Christ, I don't like being out here. There's no one else around, but I feel like I'm constantly being watched. Either that or I'm about to be jumped, but I know from the unending silence that there's no one here but me. If there is anyone watching, they're too scared to show themselves. That's good. We keep ourselves to ourselves from hereon in.

I break into Clive and Christine's house easily enough: in through the side gate, then prise open a kitchen window the idiots left open on vent around the back.

I do a fast recce of the house, making mental notes of everything that might be of use in case they're not back before our supplies run low. There's not a lot. Bloody hell, it's just as I expected it would be in here. Hideously over-fussy. Every available windowsill and surface is covered in tat: little porcelain dolls, collectibles, glass ornaments, commemorative china plates... I always wondered who bought those bloody things. I used to see them advertised in the back of magazines, but I never actually saw any in the flesh until now. The birth of one royal, the death of another... they've got the history of the whole bloody family Windsor immortalised in garish crockery. Waste of time, money and effort. Makes me think about the royals, though. Don't suppose their lineage and blue blood's helping right now.

Anyway, it's not so much the contents of this house I'm interested in, more the view. Christine used to make a big deal about how she and Clive were the first people to move onto the development, crowbarring it into every conversation I was unfortunate enough to have with them. She was always going on about how the people in the sales office made a fuss of them, and how there was a bottle of champagne and a fancy box of chocolates waiting when they first walked through their front door. Fat lot of good any of it did them. Better common-sense and an escape plan than a box of fucking chocolates.

I head upstairs, because I know at least one of the rooms up here should give me a decent view of what's left of the world beyond the development. I'm in their bedroom now – more tat, more crap everywhere, all kinds of stuffed toys – but the view from here is as good as I'm going to get. I brought my binoculars with me and I can see right out through the trees.

Christ.

I almost can't bear to look, because it's worse than I imagined. It's hard to believe what I'm seeing, but there's a part of me that's almost relieved because I know beyond any doubt now that locking my family away from everything and everyone else was the right thing to do.

I remember seeing something on the news just before the BBC went to hell... something about how the virus or whatever it is that's caused all this has an inherent desire to spread. We saw it in the supermarket, way back when, but didn't understand what we were seeing at the time. Thinking about that day makes me catch my breath. So much has changed. What I'd give for the safe normality of life back then... But seeing one of the infected in the distance brings me back to reality. Damn thing looks lost, dragging itself along the street. What's it thinking? What's it feeling? Anything?

For a few seconds I'm struggling to remember what it used to be like out there beyond the development, because all I can see now is about half a mile of utter chaos. Litter blows across the street like tumbleweed, and there's a car on its side halfway up the road. I used to joke with Gabby that people must do that on purpose whenever the shit hit the fan, because there's always a smashed-up or burned-out car somewhere, no matter what crappy post-apocalyptic movie you're watching. But I know this isn't a joke, because through the spider-web cracks covering the windscreen I can see a bloodied face pressed up against the glass.

The pub down the way has all but disappeared; just a charred but still smoking ruin left behind like a scab. We used to like going there for a drink at weekends. Such a shame.

That damn infected fucker wanders lazily into view again. This bastard of a disease is spread through the transmission of bodily fluids: blood, sweat, saliva... even piss and shit I heard. Infection renders the victim brain-dead within a few hours... still breathing, still functioning on a very basic level, but no longer the person they used to be. Infected people are plague carriers, no more and no less, existing purely to spread the infection. I've been sheltered from the worst of it over the last few days, but I can see it happening right in front of me now. The sick are hunting out the living.

A bloke appears, running at speed. I can tell from the way he's moving that he's like us, not like *them*. It looks like he's been running for a while and he can barely keep going. He turns right, straight into the path of that infected creature I was just watching. He panics... tries to turn back and run the other way, but there must be one behind him too, because now he doesn't know which way to go. At least four of them converging on him at once. This poor sod looks exhausted... broken. He slips past two of them, straight into the path of another bunch of three I didn't see. They swarm all over him, and there's not a damn thing anyone can do to stop it. He knows it's over.

The attack – if you can even call it an attack – is over quick. They don't bite him, don't scratch, barely even fight... they just infect. Job done, they roll away again and leave him, no longer of any interest. He lies there helpless in the middle of the street, all but invisible to the infected now, drenched in their foul brown gunk.

And in my head now, all I can see are the thousands of helpless people who crowded into the overflowing hospitals and refugee camps we saw on the news: all herding together, waiting for the worst of the crisis to pass. I guess all it would have taken would have been for a handful of infected to get in. Maybe even one would have been enough to wipe them all out, perhaps just a single drop of blood or saliva... The fragility of it all is terrifying.

There's another one of them outside now, and seeing it helps me focus on the threat. I have to be on my guard here; can't let anyone or anything know we're still here. The thing outside – I can't call it a person anymore – hauls itself along the street listlessly and slowly, every movement taking effort it doesn't have. Its shoulders are drooped and its head hangs heavy as if its weight is too much for it to support. It's stripped to the waist, and because of its long, straggly hair I thought it was a girl at first. It's only when it turns around and I get a clear look at its naked torso that I see it's male. He's painfully thin, chest caved inwards, and he barely lifts his feet as he walks, just drags them along.

Then something changes.

He stops and looks up, sniffing the air, and even though I'm well away I instinctively move back out of the way in case it's me he's seen. Common-sense takes over again and I relax, because I know that even though it's impossibly quiet out there, I'm too far away to be seen or heard.

He's looking in different directions now, like he's listening out, and I think it's weird because a few seconds ago, this poor fucker looked like he could barely support his own weight. Now he makes his move, darting across the road, running with odd, unnatural loping movements like he's learning the controls as he goes. The lethargy has gone, replaced with ferocious speed. I know exactly what he's doing. He's hunting.

There's someone else like me out there, someone else uninfected. The bloke I saw being attacked just now is up on his feet again, calling to someone... screaming at them to go the other way. It's a girl, Nathan's age or thereabouts. She tries to outrun the infected thing that's nearest to her, but she looks even more exhausted than the germ-filled fucker close behind. It's relentless. The damn thing trips up the kerb and smashes its face on the ground, then just gets up and carries on after her like nothing's happened, barely even missing a beat.

The kid – and she's only a kid – looks like she's caught in two minds. She's making for the guy on the floor, but he's pleading with her to leave.

All the time I'm watching I'm thinking *I should help... I should do something...* but I know I can't, because if I risk going out there to help a kid I don't know anything about, then I'll put the people I am responsible for in danger. They need me, and I need them, and as hard as it is to accept, this kid is not my concern.

She stops and tries a half-hearted punch, but she's barely got the energy to keep breathing, never mind fight. Swinging her fist knocks her off-balance, and in the brief delay as she tries to steady herself, that infected bastard is on her.

And now *it* has become *they*.

There are more of them again, swarming from the shadows. I'm so distracted by their appearance and sheer numbers that I forget about the girl. They appear from out of nowhere, as if they were there all the time but I just couldn't see them: disentangling themselves from piles of rubbish, staggering out of open doors, throwing themselves out of windows to get to this poor, helpless kid and infect her. Others – some which I thought were corpses lying rotting in the gutter – are starting to move. It's like they're waking up, like they've been woken from their near-death slumber by the scent of someone uninfected.

A few attackers is now a herd of the fucking things. In the time it's taken me to process what I'm seeing, as many as twenty more of them are coming after the girl, fighting to be the one that infects her.

With these numbers, she doesn't stand a bloody chance.

She runs towards the development, and I hate myself for willing her to go the other way. The closer she gets, the worse I feel and the more I can see. She's looking back more than she's looking forward now, but the infected are coming at her from all sides, surrounding her... cutting off every escape route. She makes a sudden change of direction, then another, then another, but they're everywhere now and she knows it. There's nowhere left for her to run, nothing left to do... she slows down, then stops and she just stands there sobbing, beaten before they've laid a damn finger on her.

And then they're all over her.

One germ-riddled male leaps up from the middle of the oncoming crowd; a single unexpected movement that's more controlled than anything else I've so far seen. The infected man literally knocks her off her feet but he holds onto her shoulders and falls with her. She lands on her back, the sick man on top, pushing her down. She's trying to beat him off, but he's not fighting and that's the problem here. He's just *infecting*. She locks her elbows and holds him at arm's length, but all he has to do is just vomit and spit and drool all over her face.

In the silence of everything else, I can hear her. She screams and gags and wails all at the same time: a hideous, heart-breaking noise.

Then it's done.

The infected crawl away, retreating back into the shadows, leaving the girl just lying there on her back, sobbing, soaked through with that foul discharge. She wipes it from her face then rolls over and vomits, as much through fear and disgust than anything else, I guess. She gets up and tries to walk away, ragged clothes drenched like she's been caught out in the rain, but effort and resignation combine and she stops again and drops to her knees. There's another infected close by but it barely lifts its head, barely even looks at her. She's of no interest to them now. The girl just sits there, waiting for the sickness to take hold.

And all I can think about are Gabby and the kids. The thought of this happening to any of them is too much to even consider.

STUART
FRIDAY 29 MAY – 10:32am

We've barely moved since yesterday, barely even spoken. I told Gabby everything I saw from the neighbours' house, but she was frustratingly dismissive. I'm not sure she realises the full seriousness of our situation yet. The way she talks to the kids isn't right... going on as if nothing's happened, telling them it'll be like this for a little while, then things will get back to normal. I told her to be realistic and honest, but she said she was doing it for Sally more than anyone. It won't help in the long run.

Just over twenty-four hours and I'm already going stir crazy, cooped up with the family. It's just nerves, I reckon. I need to get things how I want them here. It's time to make some changes. I'm in the back garden holding the cat, and Gabby and the kids are at the window, watching my every move.

I spent a sleepless night thinking about all of this. I've told them what's going to happen and it's not gone down well. Gabby said I should do it when Sally's asleep, but I don't see the point. It's not like I'm going to kill the damn cat, just get rid of it. I feel bad enough already, but she's trying to make me feel worse. I don't have any choice and they have to understand that. Our lives might depend on it.

There can be no more waste. The longer we stay in isolation here, the better our chances, and I need them to see that. When I think about all the half-finished drinks I've thrown away over the years, all the wasted food... it makes me damn angry. I can't allow that to happen anymore. Our daily rations must be strictly adhered to, everything eaten, irrespective of taste and personal preferences. Gabby gets it, and I think Nathan does too, but Sally's going to be a problem. How do I explain to a three year old that she can't have anything else to eat today, or that if she doesn't eat what she's just been given, she won't have anything else until tomorrow? How do I pacify my daughter when she's crying for juice but she's used up her allowance and I can't risk giving her more? We've already clashed. She didn't want her meal last night. I told her *you eat it now, or you eat it stale tomorrow.*

And that's why the cat has to go.

There's no room for sentimentality here anymore, and there's no option: the cat *has* to go. He's a health hazard. It pisses me off... no one was that bothered about him before. It was always me who ended up feeding him and it was me who emptied the bloody litter tray or cleaned up the crap when the damn animal dragged something half-dead inside from the garden. Bloody Smudge. I won't miss him. I put him over the fence then glare at Sally when she starts crying again and banging on the kitchen window.

The cat will hang around for a few days I'm sure, then he'll get used to the idea he's not welcome anymore and he'll piss off. Cats are manipulative little bastards – you need them more than they need you. When he realises he's not getting fed, he'll find his food somewhere else. He's better off out here.

I felt like a heartless prick when I snatched Smudge away from Sally earlier, but I have to put emotions to one side and focus on the realities of our situation. The cat cost us food and water – albeit a small amount each day – but if you add it all up day by day, that small amount might make a difference. I don't know if cats are susceptible to the disease in the same way we are, but I have to assume they are. It'd be cruel to keep the animal locked up indoors, and it's too much of a risk to let him have free reign. Imagine if I went to all this trouble and effort, just for us all to be infected by something the damn cat dragged in. I've nailed boards over both sides of the cat flap.

Bloody thing's making a hell of a noise though.

He's in the garden behind ours, making that horrible deep wailing noise he does when another cat encroaches on his turf. I climb up onto the compost bin to shoo him away.

Jesus Christ.

The grass is overgrown here. I never saw the lazy sods cut it, but I'm pleased they left it now. The lady who lived here is dead in the middle of the lawn. It looks like foxes have had a go at her fingers. Smudge looks up at me then runs for it when I hiss at him, his tail slipping through the gaps between two bushes, disappearing into the unkempt flower-bed.

Back inside.

The others shun me like I'm some kind of leper, like I've got the bloody disease that's caused all of this, but I've got a thick skin and I can take it. It's a small price to pay. We've all just got to get used to living this way if we want to stay alive. Trouble is, we're all like the bloody cat. We're used to things being easy, to having everything our own way. Life is different now, and I have a feeling it always will be from hereon in. We might always be fighting, we might always be living on our nerves, surviving on a fraction of what we had before, but that's just how it has to be.

I tell Gabby and Nathan, but they're in no mood to listen. I try and explain that when we leave the house... maybe a month or two from now, perhaps... it'll be easier out there. Fewer people. More space. More supplies. Freedom. It's strange, but there's a part of me that's actually excited by the future. It's not going to be easy, I understand that, but it could still be *good*. We just have to make sure we're not dragged down by what's left of the old world first.

STUART

TUESDAY 9 JUNE – 11:14am

It's tense in here. The claustrophobia, monotony and boredom of our incarceration over the last couple of weeks is getting to all of us.

Mealtimes are the worst. I don't know who's being more difficult, Nathan or Sally. Reasoning with a fifteen year old is proving to be as hard as reasoning with a frightened three year old, but he usually sees sense in the end. Hannah's not letting us forget she's here either. Every time she screams for her bottle the noise cuts through me like fingernails scraping down a blackboard.

'I don't like soup,' Sally says, shoving her bowl away. I push it back. 'Don't want it.'

'Try and eat it, sweetheart,' Gabby says.

'Don't want it,' she says again.

'Try a little bit for Mummy.'

'No.'

'Come on, love, just eat half of it...'

'She eats all of it,' I interrupt. 'What is this, a bloody holiday camp?' I just look at Gabby, amazed. Does she not understand the seriousness of our situation.

'I just think...' she starts to say, but I'm not having any of it.

'We don't have the luxury of choice anymore, Gabby, in case you hadn't noticed. We eat what we're given now. All of us. Whether we like it or not.'

'But I don't like soup,' Sally moans, grizzling now.

'Tough. If you don't eat it, you go hungry.'

She starts full-on wailing. 'Go easy on her,' Gabby says.

'No. She has to eat.' I turn back to face Sally. 'You have to eat. Eat!'

She shoves it away again. 'Don't want this. Want chicken nuggets.'

I count to ten. I know she can't help it.

'Well we don't have any chicken nuggets,' I tell her. 'Daddy's already explained this to you time and time again... we don't have a freezer at the moment, love. Not since the electricity stopped working.'

'Mummy can make some.'

'Not without a chicken.'

'Or an oven, or the rest of the ingredients, or breadcrumbs, or fresh milk or butter or anything else...' Gabby adds unhelpfully.

'We get the picture,' Nathan says.

'Maybe I could have a look and see if I can find something else you'd like?' Gabby says to Sally.

'No, Gab, you won't. Bloody hell, have you not been paying attention? We eat what we're given, no questions asked.'

There's an awkward silence. Gabby looks down at her food. I hate myself for having to be so abrupt, but I don't know how else to say it. I'm at the end of my tether here.

The quiet doesn't last long.

'I want to go outside...' Sally says.

'Why can't we, Dad?' Nathan asks.

'You know why not. It's too dangerous. We don't know what's out there.'

'But there's nothing out there,' he mumbles. 'There's nothing left, remember?'

'We can't take any chances. We're not doing anything until we've blocked the road.'

'But everyone else is dead,' Nathan says. 'Dead or gone.'

'And so will we be if we're not careful.'

'Am I going to die?' Sally asks, and the innocence in her little voice is heart-breaking. Gabby squeezes her hand and helps her with her soup.

'We're not going to die, love. We're going to be just fine here.'

'Daddy's going to look after all of us,' I tell her.

But she does have a point. It's getting harder and harder for the five of us to keep going in the house like this. We're going to have to go outside eventually, aren't we?

'We can't go on like this,' Gabby whispers, and I know she's right.

'I need to be sure we're safe here. I'll go out later and have a look around the development. If it's as quiet as it looks, maybe we'll be able to risk going outside to secure the development.'

'You think it'll be okay?'

'Everything I saw and read about the disease said it was spread through contact with bodily fluids,' I tell her, keeping my voice low for the sake of the kids. 'So why not? The railings have kept people out. There are no infected in our back garden, are there?'

I don't tell her about the corpse in the garden behind ours.

'You said something about blocking off the road into the estate,' Nathan says.

34

'It's a *development*, not an estate,' Gabby corrects him, though the time for such distinctions is long gone. 'Estate sounds so...'

'Common?' he suggests.

'I didn't say that.'

'No, but you were thinking it. You're such a snob, Mum.'

'I'm not.'

'You *are*!'

'Stop picking on me,' she says, pretending to be hurt.

'Mummy's a snob, Mummy's a snob!' Sally sings playfully. Gabby glares at her for a moment, then shakes her head and breaks into a broad smile. That's the first smile I've seen from any of them in days. In the fortnight since we've been locked in here, come to think of it.

If going outside is going to make such a difference, then assuming it's safe, maybe that's what we should do.

Nathan wanted to come but I said no. Not yet. I explained that I'm just checking the rest of the development this afternoon. If everything's okay and as quiet as it seems, then he can help me block off the estate in a couple of days' time. Imagine how much of a difference that'll make to all of us. We'll use stuff from the building site at the unfinished end of the development.

I'm nervous but I don't let them see. I get myself ready in the shed. This isn't like when I used Clive and Christine's house as a look-out post, this is very different. I'm going door-to-door today, and I have to be prepared for all eventualities.

I put on the protective suit I use for decorating then tape up my ankles and wrists so there's no chance of contamination. The suit has a hood, and I cover my face with goggles and a mask. A pair of outdoor gloves I used to use when I creosoted the fences completes my ridiculous outfit. I might look stupid, but I know I'm safe.

Fuck, but this is terrifying.

I open the latch – it's so loud it sounds like someone cocking a gun, ready to fire – then let myself out down the side of the house. I look up and see them all watching me from an upstairs window, even though I've told them not to. I keep the felling axe I'm carrying out of sight, holding it close to my body. I told them it was to help me get into locked houses, but they're not stupid. They know why I'm

35

really carrying it.

I've memorised the layout of the development. It's pretty much a horseshoe shape, with a couple of cul-de-sacs leading off here and there. I'm going to work my way from house to house, checking if they're empty. I'm certain the vast majority, if not all of them are, but there are a couple I'm not sure about.

God, but it's so quiet out here. I can't hear anything. Admittedly the noise is muffled by the hood I'm wearing, but this never-ending silence is eerie beyond belief. No traffic. No voices. Just the sound of a plaintive dog in the middle-distance. The frightened hound's noise makes me catch my breath. The poor mutt sounds as scared as I feel.

I distract myself looking at each of the houses I pass. It's funny... back when we had neighbours, when the world was still intact, you automatically kept your distance and respected everyone else's property. At least, most of us did. There was that horrible dickhead who lived in one of the houses opposite – a proper geezer; all bullshit, attitude and swagger – he didn't care. I used to see him regularly walking over his neighbours' lawns to get to his front door or reversing onto their drives to turn his car around because he couldn't be bothered to drive the few metres to the turning point at the end of the grove. Insufferable arse. Wonder where he is now? Wonder *if* he is...?

And this house I'm outside now... he was another one. Objectionable dick. A proper show-off. I remember Christine gossiping about him once. A single man with no shortage of visitors. Apparently he'd made a fortune from a dating app for mobile phones... some kind of personality compatibility test or something like that, preying on the vulnerable with computer-generated bullshit and lies. He used to annoy me. Half my age, and absolutely dripping with cash. He had one of the biggest houses on the development and I doubt he even had a mortgage. I know it shouldn't have bothered me but it did because I've worked my arse off and done everything the right way since leaving uni, and it pisses me off when I hear about people hitting it lucky like that. It used to, anyway. Things have changed. I have to start thinking about this stuff in past tense now. Like I said, I did everything the right way and it's paid off. What good did the luck and all that cash do this guy? Not a lot, by the looks of things. I peer in through his lounge window, cupping my hands to block out the light. Christ, look at the size of that TV! It nearly fills the entire wall! But material possessions don't change material facts: this house is empty, devoid of all life. There's stuff all over the place, like he left in a hurry. Who knows where he is now? Chances are his life won't be as comfortable as he's used to anymore.

What was that? I stop dead, sure I heard something. It sounded like a door, but when I look around there's nothing and no one. I tell myself to calm down, my own heartbeat now the loudest thing I can hear.

I keep going, moving into one of the side roads now.

Another noise up ahead. There's definitely someone else here.

I remember the woman who lived in the house at the far end of the cul-de-sac just as she appears in the shadows of her open door. At first the light's so poor I'm not even sure there's anyone there, and my dirty safety goggles don't help, but then she trips down the step and almost falls and my throat becomes dry with nerves. Is she as scared as I am?

It's hard to tell what's happening here. Is she infected or clear? Her pale skin is heavily discoloured, like she's been living in squalor since all this began. I take a few steps closer, and she does the same, stepping out of the shade and into the light. Is she sick? Is she just scared? I try to talk but my tongue feels too big for my mouth.

I feel like we're staring at each other forever, but it can only be a few seconds. I can't see where the dirt stops and her body begins. Her flesh is mottled, her face hollowed out, eyes and cheeks sunken. And now I can see that she's hardly wearing anything, just a pair of brown-stained knickers. I clear my throat and try to speak to her.

'Are you okay...? I live just around the corner. Are you on your own here or...?'

She doesn't talk, but her actions immediately answer all my questions.

Her head jerks back twice, like she's choking on something, struggling to swallow it down. Then her chin twitches, her face in spasm, turned round so she's looking at me sideways. And then she starts to run, a sudden burst of frantic speed, legs pounding, arms flapping uselessly at her sides, brown drool spewing from her open mouth. I know she's beyond hope and that I should run but my legs are like lead and I can't move. She comes at me making a godawful moaning sound: a dry half-choke, half-scream and I know what I have to do, but I don't know if I can. I've tried to prepare myself for this moment, but I'm not ready...

I shove the head of the axe between her breasts, pushing her away, because even though I know what she is now and how dangerous this is, I don't know if I can do it.

She trips, legs folding in on themselves, and now she's on her backside in the middle of the road. But before I can react, she's at me again, lunging forward, and whether she has control of her movements or not, I know she's not going to stop until she's infected me. The woman lets out a sound that's like a sad sob, a low, sorrowful moan, and I don't know if it's the disease making the noise or her? Does she remember? Is she still alive in there, a prisoner of the infection?

I push her away with the end of the axe again, and in the few seconds of space, I make myself think what would happen if I was infected. I know I'd end up back at the house: either I'd walk home or they'd come out looking. Whatever, the end result would be the same. I picture Gabby and the kids like this woman, and my nervous fear evaporates. I keep telling myself, *I have to do this.*

This time when she comes at me, I'm ready.

I swing the axe around in a wide arc, the weight of the weapon increasing the force, and I gag with disgust when it sinks into the small of her back, clacking against her spinal cord. The dead-weight when she falls almost pulls me over with her, and it's all I can do to keep my balance and stay upright as I wrench the head of the axe out. And still she keeps coming, arms outstretched, fingers digging in the dirt to try and pull herself along as I move further away.

I lift the axe again and bring it down on the back of her head. It wedges into her skull, splitting the bone like an egg, and this time I lose control. I whip the facemask off and vomit everywhere, so much gunk flooding out of my body that, for a few seconds at least, I'm confident nothing'll get in.

Once I've got the mask back on and the sweats have passed, I check the rest of the houses, but I figure if no one's come out to see what's going on after I've just hacked a woman down in the middle of the street, then there's no one else left here, alive or infected.

I fetch some lighter fuel from home and set fire to the body. She's still moving as she burns.

I leave everything – my clothes, the axe, the goggles and facemask – in the back garden to be decontaminated later with bleach, and I go inside.

STUART
SUNDAY 14 JUNE – 10:03am

I've left it as long as I can before going outside again, but it's time. I've waited until I'm sure my activities last week have gone unnoticed. I get Nathan out of bed and tell him to get dressed. I knew he'd be like this: he's been moaning non-stop about wanting to go out but, now he's about to leave the house, all the macho bullshit has been dropped. He's as scared as I am.

'I'm not happy about this,' Gabby says as Nathan gets himself ready. 'He's just a kid, Stuart.'

'I'm well aware of that. This needs two of us though.'

'So I'll come out with you.'

'Don't be ridiculous. We've been through this already. We can't take the risk. What if something happens while we're out there? How would the kids survive on their own?'

'You're not making me feel any better.'

'I'm not trying to. Look, we're not going to take any chances. We'll roll a couple of cars down the hill to block the road, then use stuff from the building site to stop them getting through. An hour's work, tops.'

I can tell she's not convinced, but when Nathan appears at the top of the stairs she stops arguing. He needs this. I could probably do it on my own, but I want him there as back up. It'll help him get rid of some of that pent up anger and frustration. Christ, I remember what I was like at his age – all those hormones and attitude playing havoc with my head. And my life was easy compared to his.

I haven't told either of them about the woman around the corner. What's the point? Gabby will get upset, Nathan will be scared... it's only going to make an already difficult situation that much harder still.

Ten minutes later and we're standing on the green at the front of the development, hiding behind the trunk of one of the oaks like kids playing some kind of game. Except this is far from a game. This is as far from a game as you can get. We're both trussed up: me in my decorating garb, Nathan in a boiler-suit with the wetsuit we bought him for that diving break he went on last summer underneath. We've both got our faces covered. I've got my axe, he's got a baseball bat. We won't need to use them, I've told him, they're just to make us feel better. We can see everything from up here on the bank. And Christ, the world looks even worse than when I last looked out.

The road stretches away from the development. At first glance it's like the view I got that day from Clive and Christine's bedroom window, but everything's covered with an additional layer of dirt and decay. As we're watching, a single infected walks into view. 'Look at him,' I say, nudging Nathan. 'They look pretty docile when they're like that, don't they?'

'Pretty what?'

'Docile... harmless.'

'Suppose.'

'Told you it was bad, though, didn't I?'

He just nods, finding it hard to talk.

'We need to move fast and stay quiet while we're out here, right? Don't want them finding out we're here.'

'Right.'

'You follow my lead, and you do exactly what I tell you.'

'Right.'

'We're going to block the entrance with cars from the development, okay? We'll wheel them down. I'll push, you steer. Then once we've got a few of them in place, we'll use the machinery from the building site to bring pallets of bricks and sand and whatever else we can find over here. Got it?'

'Got it.'

'You ready?'

'Uh huh.'

'You're going to have to do better than that, Nath. I need you to be positive. I know you'd probably rather be anywhere but here right now, but you have to be focused and ready for anything. Understand?'

'I've got it.'

Even though his eyes are hidden behind his goggles, I can see how scared he is. Even up until last night he was giving it the *big I am*... telling me how nothing was going to bother him, how he'd be the one looking after me when we got out of the house. The wind's been well and truly knocked out of his sails.

It starts to spit with rain. The sky's a heavy grey overhead, and it's only going to get worse. It's like the clouds are giving up and falling, covering everything in their murk. Uncollected litter blows along the streets like leaves, an artificial, out of season autumn. There are bodies. Many bodies, most in differing stages of decomposition, some lying together but most lying alone. 'Don't look at them,' I tell him, but I know he already has. 'And whatever you do, don't touch anything. Not a bloody thing. If one of them comes towards you, don't do anything stupid. You don't try and fight because you can't win... just get the hell away from it fast. You understand?'

'I understand.'

'Good. Let's do it.'

There are three cars parked near the first houses up the hill. I take a chance and find the keys to two of them. I won't risk starting the engine, but it'll be easier to do this if the steering lock is off. I get Nathan to sit in the driver's seat, make sure he knows what he's doing and where to put the car, then I lean in, take off the handbrake, then go around to the back and push.

And it works. Beautifully.

The car glides down the hill, picking up speed and running away from me, and he slots it into position perfectly, blocking more than half the road. He gets out carefully – quietly – like I told him, and runs back up.

We do the same with the second car.

Third time, with the width of the road fully blocked, he steers too hard and too late, and instead of coming to a halt alongside the first two vehicles, he ploughs nose first into the side of one of them. He gets out, keen to let me know he's okay. But it's not him I'm worried about.

'I'm fine,' he says as we meet near the bottom of the hill. I grab his arm and spin him around to show him what I've seen. Infected. Only a handful of them, but we both know one is too many.

'I'm going over to the building site,' I tell him.

'What do you want me to do?'

'Keep out of the way. Stay at the top of the hill. You've done your bit, son.'

'But, Dad...'

'But nothing. Do as I say.'

He doesn't argue, he just turns and walks away, shoulders dropped and head down.

I have to move fast now. The nearest edge of the part of the development that's still a building site is some fifty metres away. There's a digger-like machine with an extendable crane – I think it's called a tele-handler or something similar – that I'm going to use to finish the barricade. I fetched the key from the site office earlier.

The machine starts first time, a deep, belly-shaking grumble that's more intimidating than I expect. It's not that the tele-handler's too powerful, it's just so bloody loud. I used one of these at college once and it all comes back to me quickly. I manage to pick up a pallet of bricks and get it down to where the cars are, but I lose it as I'm trying to place it, and instead of laying it on top of the first car we moved, I drop it.

The noise is deafening.

When I look up, the road on the other side of the blockade is filled with infected.

No time to piss around. I drive back again and fetch another pallet, but by the time I get it into place a couple of the infected are already trying to get across. I manage to drop the bricks on one of them, and it's sickening and exciting in equal measure.

Third and fourth loads go without a hitch. As I'm trying to manoeuvre the fifth pallet, though, I see that two of the infected have managed to get through. I jump out of the cab and grab my axe, then

42

have to get out of the way fast when a car comes rolling past. Nathan's behind the wheel. Silly little fucker. I'll berate him later, though, because right now there's more work to be done. More through luck than judgement he's managed to steer into the path of the infected stragglers and has wiped them out. He gets out of the car and I grab his arm. 'Don't get anywhere near the blood, remember?'

He pulls his arm away. 'I know what I'm doing, Dad.'

'We'll see about that.'

Back to the tele-handler. I drop the bricks then turn around and head back for more. Nathan's already pushing another car down the hill, right over the grass this time, not even bothering with the road. The steep slope works to our advantage and the car picks up a huge amount of speed with minimal effort. I wait for it to thump into the back of the others, then lower a massive bag of sand onto the roof of one of the first cars we shifted.

There are no other accessible cars on this side of our blockade, so I concentrate on using the tele-handler to build things up, using the metal fork at the end of the long hydraulic arm to lift up the end of different vehicles to try and flip them over. It works well, and with a few more minutes of noisy effort, the barricade has been massively strengthened.

I look around for Nathan. Can't see him. Must be back on the hill.

I reverse back, then drive forward again at speed, faster than this thing should probably be driven. With the arm down I slam straight into the side of one of the vehicles we moved, shunting it further into the others, but when I try to reverse back out again, I'm stuck. I can drive the tele-handler away, but if I do, I'm worried I'll pull the blockade open and give the infected a way through. I get out and run around to the front to try and release the arm.

Shit.

It's properly stuck here.

The arm's smashed through the side of the first car, but in doing so I've disturbed another car on top, and that one has dropped down, trapping the arm good and proper.

I sense a flash of movement behind me. Must be Nathan. I spin around to ask him to help, but it's not him. It's one of the infected. I try to run but I trip and now I'm on my back, looking up. It's on me before I can get up.

The infected drops down onto my chest, surprising me more than hurting me, and I instinctively grab its wrists but I know it's not going to be enough. I try to wrench its arms around so it can't get its face close enough to infect me, but it just keeps fighting. Its eyes are vacant... dead... no emotion, no sign of life. It pulls its head back on its shoulders like it's going to butt me, and when it throws its neck forward all I can do is roll over to one side. I feel – but I don't see – its face smack into the ground with a soft, wet thud. And straightaway it's up again! Fucking thing is up again... blood and broken teeth mixing with the deadly drool flooding from its mouth. And I can see another figure close behind now, with more of them getting even closer... what have I done?

The infected bastard on top of me lifts what's left of its head again, ready to strike—

—and a swipe from a baseball bat virtually decapitates it.

There's germ-filled blood everywhere. My suit is covered and I start to panic but the gaffer tape seals have held.

And it takes me a couple of seconds to realise I'm no longer under attack. The few infected close enough to be a problem have been hacked down. Is there someone else here? Another survivor like us? I get up and look around and see Nathan swinging his baseball bat wildly. There are several fallen infected around his feet. Can't tell how many, it's just a tangled mass of body parts, broken limbs overlapping.

What the hell does he think he's doing?

'I told you to stay out of the way,' I shout at him, grabbing his shoulder and spinning him around. He lifts the baseball bat again, thinking that I'm another one of them.

'You'd be dead if I'd done what you told me.'

No time to argue – there'll be plenty of that when we get back to the house. For now we need to just finish the job we came out here to do. The few infected that made it over the mass of cars and building materials have been dealt with. It seems that even though I got it stuck, I blocked the flow with the tele-handler after all.

I grab Nathan's arm and drag him back up onto the green. I turn around to get a better view, and immediately wish I hadn't. There are huge crowds coming our way.

'Why so many, Dad?'

'Because there's nothing else. No one else out there. I think we're all that's left now.'

We stand and watch as the diseased crowd on the other side of the blockade grows. And I can hear them now. I hadn't noticed it before, but they all moan. It's a horrible, sad noise – it sounds like the last gasp of the people they used to be, trying to escape. Individually it's nothing, but the more of them there are, the louder it'll get. It's a ghastly, unnatural noise, and it fills the air.

'They're calling to the others,' Nathan says, and I just look at him.

'Bollocks.'

He just shrugs. 'I reckon that's what they're doing. They're making a noise so others know we're here.'

I don't think he's right, but I don't want to take the chance. We've taken enough risks already this morning. 'We should get back to the house.'

'It's not strong enough.'

'What?'

'The barrier. They'll get over it. Shouldn't we try and make it stronger? They're not going to give up easily.'

I point towards Clive and Christine's house – the nearest plot to this point. 'That house is definitely empty. We need to get whatever we can from in there and block all the gaps. Pile it up. Underneath too. We need to wedge as much stuff as we can find under the cars, stop them crawling under or getting over. Just stop them getting any closer.'

Between us we carry a sofa from the house and dump it. Then we head straight back again and fetch the next biggest piece of furniture we can easily move. Then again, and again, and again. Once we're done with furniture, we use whatever we can find to plug all the gaps, making sure nothing can get through.

It's hard work, physically and emotionally, and though we're both exhausted, by the time we're done we've a barrier that an army of fit people would struggle to breach, let alone the poor sick bastards out there.

'You see why I couldn't let you go out there,' I tell Nathan, struggling to make myself heard through the facemask. 'You understand why we have to stay here now?'

He just nods. Words aren't enough anymore.

Together we stand on the top of the bank and look down over the dead world. There are hundreds of infected out there now, dragging themselves through the streets towards the development from every visible direction, forming a vast, moaning crowd outside the development.

'They won't get through, will they?' he asks.

'I doubt it. We'll go home now, son and stay indoors. It's only the noise we've made that's brought so many of them out of the woodwork today. They'll disappear again soon enough. We'll be safe back at the house.'

I burn everything we took outside today in the garden of the house behind ours. I do it out of sight, and tell the others not to disturb me. I have to get rid of every potential source of infection. I don't want them seeing me put the neighbour's body on the fire.

STUART
TUESDAY 23 JUNE – 9:21pm

It was Nathan's birthday today. Poor kid. He understands, though, he gets it. He knows things have irrevocably changed and that stuff like birthdays and Christmas don't count for anything anymore. Gabby tried to make a fuss of him, but it felt hollow and forced without any gifts and with only our normal daily rations. 'It's weird,' I told her a couple of minutes ago once he'd gone up to his room, 'Sally and Hannah will grow up not knowing any different. Birthdays, parties, presents... they won't know any of it.' I told her we'd given the kids the best gift we could – life. That might have sounded like a cliché, but it was true. No other family has as much as we do now. I doubt there are many other families left.

It feels later than it is.

'Might as well go up,' Gabby says.

'We're getting old,' I tell her. 'You were a party animal when we first got together. The thought of you ever being in bed before ten...'

'That's what having kids does to you. Besides, there are no parties anymore, in case you hadn't noticed.'

'Times have changed. *Everything's* changed. We get up with the sun and go to bed when it gets dark now. That's how it used to be. That's how our ancestors had it.'

'Yes, but that's nothing to be proud of, is it? It's the twenty-first century, for crying out loud, Stu. We're living like we're back in the dark ages.'

'At least we're living.'

'Whatever.'

'You have to stay positive, love.'

'I'm trying. But is there any point?'

'I don't want to hear you talking like this, Gab. We agreed...'

'*You* agreed. I don't remember having any say in the matter.'

I don't rise to her bait.

The silence in the room is awkward. I don't know what to say to her at moments like this, and there seem to have been more moments like this than ever recently, certainly since Nathan and I sealed us off from the outside world. I've told Gabby over and over that it won't be much longer now. Once the infected have all gone, by the end of the year at the latest, I reckon, then it'll be safe for us to leave here again. Six months or so. That's not too bad. We've been here for six weeks already.

'What are we going to do?' she asks. I feel my heart sink. She must ask me that same bloody question at least once an hour, and each time I give her the same bloody answer.

'We're going to carry on doing what we're already doing, love. We're going to survive. Maybe you should come with me tomorrow to Clive and Christine's house so I can show you what it's like out there.'

'I don't want to see it.'

'Well maybe you should. If you'd seen the things I've seen, the things Nathan's seen, you wouldn't even ask.'

'But what's the point?'

47

'The point of what?'

'Of putting ourselves through this?'

'What's the alternative?' I say quickly, trying not to let my anger and frustration show. It's not her fault and I have to remember that, but it's hard. 'Should we just have let the kids get sick and die? Should we have done the same as everyone else? I'm proud of what we've done and how we've done it. We've been through this a hundred times already... there is no alternative, and that's fine. It doesn't matter if there's nothing else out there, because everything we need is in here, don't you think? You, me, the kids... we're all that matters now. We're in the best place we can be, and I'm going to make sure we're okay.'

'I know that.'

'Do you? You don't sound so sure...'

'It's difficult, that's all.'

'I know it is.'

She holds her head in her hands. I pull her closer, and though she's reluctant at first, she soon softens and leans against me. The rest of the house is silent. Everywhere is silent. And these days the quiet is never ending.

'I still can't believe what's happened,' she says, her voice barely a whisper. 'A couple of months ago everything was fine... everything was great. Now this. Now it's all gone to hell.'

'No it hasn't. You have to stop this, love. The rest of the world might be gone, but we're not. We're still here... we're still strong.'

'I know, I know... I've been thinking about the future, though.'

'What about it?'

'I'm talking long term here—'

'I'm glad to hear it.'

'—and it frightens me. Say we do survive all of this...'

'We *have* survived it.'

'I know, but hear me out... say we manage to survive and we leave here and make a new life for the family somewhere else.'

'Sounds good.'

'And maybe it will be, but...'

'But what?'

'But what happens when we're gone? What happens when it's just

48

the kids left to fend for themselves?'

She has a point, and it's something I've already thought about. But there's no point looking that far ahead just yet. 'We'll prepare them. That's years ahead of us. And who knows, once we're away from here we might find other people who've survived like we have. Like-minded people. I don't think the kids will be alone.'

For a moment I'm gone, imagining what it would be like to have the entire planet to myself. Sure, it would be hard work, frightening, maybe, but what an opportunity...

'I just don't know how much more of this the kids can take,' she says. 'I don't know how much more *I* can take.'

'I've told you, love, stop talking like this.'

'And I've told you, I can't. It's on my mind constantly.'

I've been toying with an idea... do I tell her? I figure I should. It'll be good to give her something positive to focus on.

'Listen, I've been thinking... we know the development is secure now, so maybe we can start using the space we've got a little better. You and the girls might be able to go outside. Would you like that?'

'I'd love it. Honestly, Stu, you've no idea how much I've grown to hate this bloody house. When I think about all the effort and expense we went to to buy it and move in...'

'And it was worth every single penny. We're strong here, love, stronger than we would have been back at the old place. We're cut off from the hell outside now, and there's no way anything's getting in. In the next few days I'm going to start going through some of the other houses and—'

'You can't.'

'What?'

'You can't do that... you can't go breaking into other people's houses. What if they come back?'

She's really not grasped the full implications of what's happening here, has she?

'No one's coming back, love. They're all gone. There's no way back in here anyway, remember? And I've already told you, I'll do whatever I have to do to keep this family safe. There will be things we can use in other folk's homes. Supplies, medicines, clothes, fresh bedding...'

'Half the food in the garage has gone.'

'You haven't been taking extra, have you? Gab, I expressly told you how important it is to make sure we only use the daily allowances I put out. If we start—'

'I haven't taken anything extra,' she shouts, annoyed. 'I've been using the daily rations like you said, but they're running out. We've been here for weeks now.'

'I'm sorry, love. I didn't mean to jump down your throat. It's important that you and I both remember to only use—'

'I know, I know... I get it. For Christ's sake, you don't have to keep telling me the same thing. Every bloody day you tell me to be careful and not use more than I'm allowed. I get it. I'm not stupid. It's difficult, you know.'

'I understand, but—'

'You understand the practicalities, yes, but do you really appreciate the impact all this is having?'

'Yes.'

'Did you know Sally's wet the bed for the last five nights in a row?'

'You never said...'

'You never *asked*. You're too busy plotting and scheming to see what's actually happening here. Sally's scared. We're all scared. Considering the fact we're all shut away in here twenty-four-seven, Sally says she never sees you. She says whenever she asks you anything you just tell her to go away and find Mummy.'

'I'm busy.'

'I get that. But surviving's not just about making sure the walls are strong and that we've got enough food, is it?'

'No, but those things are crucial. Without them we're—'

'I know, but we have to have a reason to survive too, love. Otherwise we're just going through the motions. It's like being in prison.'

'I can't help it. What do you expect me to do?'

'I don't expect you to do anything. Why do you assume it's all your responsibility?'

'You're my family. You are my responsibility.'

'Funny, used to be *our* responsibility.'

'You know what I mean.'

'Yeah, I think I do.'

I don't know what she wants me to say. I'm doing everything I can, but this is an impossible situation. 'I can't just flick a switch and make it all better again.'

'Believe me, Stu, if there was a switch that could fix all this, I'd have already done it.'

The room falls silent. It's virtually pitch black now, utterly silent. I can't see, but I feel her shifting in her seat next to me.

'I was thinking,' she says, 'what happens when the food runs out?'

'I already told you, now we know the rest of the development's empty, we'll go through the other houses. I was thinking about this earlier... everything happened so fast, so unexpectedly... there's going to be plenty of stuff in people's kitchens. They'd have been well-stocked, like normal. There are enough houses here... if we can find even just a couple of days' supplies in each one, that'll be more than enough to keep us going for another couple of months. Imagine that, love, another couple of months without having to worry about food.'

'What about after that?'

'Things are bound to be better by then. We'll have almost reached that six month stage, won't we?'

'Suppose,' she says, but she sounds less than convinced.

'Look, maybe in the next couple of days we'll do what we were talking about. . . maybe if the weather's okay we'll spend some time outside. I think it'll be safe now.'

'That'd be good.'

'Do you have any idea what the forecast is for the rest of this week?'

I've asked the question without thinking. I hear her laugh, then she starts to cry. 'I'll put the TV on, shall I? Oh, and I didn't get a chance to get down to the shops to pick up your paper today.'

I reach out for her and hold her as she sobs. 'It'll be okay,' I tell her.

We sit in the dark for a while longer. I must have fallen asleep at some point, because when I put my hand out to find her, she's gone.

STUART
MONDAY 29 JUNE – 11:05am

Pissing rain has stopped us doing anything for almost a week. None of us have yet been outside, other than when I've gone out to collect the rainwater. We've got plenty now. I filled the bath. Sally's paddling pool is full outside too, and loads of pots and pans and buckets. It'll last us ages.

It's a beautiful day today though. It's warm and dry, not a cloud overhead. We have a slow start, then sit around the breakfast table, eating thin porridge that Gabby cooked on the camping stove. She made it with water. It's not the best, but it's warm and it's enough. I tell the kids it's important to make sure we have at least one hot meal each day. Sally has a paddy and throws her spoon on the floor, but I know how to deal with this.

'If you don't eat up, you won't grow to be big and strong.'

'Don't want to be big and strong,' she says, looking straight at me. 'Don't want to be anything.'

'Now that's just silly talk. Listen, how about this... if you eat all your breakfast, maybe Mummy and Daddy will take you for a walk.'

'What... outside?' Nathan says, his interest piqued.

'Well we could just walk around the lounge if you'd rather.'

'But isn't that—?'

'It's fine,' I tell him. 'It's been a couple of weeks since you and I were out there. I've been keeping an eye on the development and I've not seen any signs of trouble. I reckon if we stay close to the house and keep the noise down, we'll be fine.'

'I'll stay inside,' he says, surprising me.

'Come on, Nath... it'll do you good.'

'No thanks,' he says again. 'I've seen what it's like out there.'

'Suit yourself. Mum, Sally, Hannah and me are going out.'

'No.'

'Where will we go?' Sally asks.

'Oh, not far... we can take a ball out and play, okay?'

'Okay,' she says as she starts shovelling down what's left of her porridge.

'Come on, love, there's nothing to be scared of.'

Sally's standing at the end of the drive, the tips of her toes literally at the point where our drive ends and the pavement starts. We've been coaxing her for a couple of minutes, but she's holding back. I'm carrying Hannah. 'Come on, sweetheart,' Gabby says. 'Isn't it lovely to be out?'

'Don't like it.'

'Why not?'

'Too quiet.'

She has a point. I don't know if I'll ever get used to the lack of noise these days. 'Quiet's nice,' I tell her. 'Maybe it's not that it's too quiet now, maybe it was too loud before?'

'Don't like it,' she says again.

This is stupid. What's the point? If we're going to do this, we're going to do it right. I have an idea. 'What about Smudge?'

Her expression changes. Her face lights up. 'Is he still here?'

'He's a cat, he'll be here somewhere I'm sure. He's probably just hiding in the grass over there...'

I gesture over towards the green at the front of the development. When I look back, Sally's taken a couple of steps forward. She's on the pavement now, standing on tiptoes, craning her neck to see. 'Why's the grass so long?' she asks.

'Everybody's too busy to cut it right now,' Gabby explains. 'Lots of people are having to stay indoors like we are.'

She seems to swallow that. 'Daddy could do it,' she says. 'You could do it, couldn't you, Daddy? You haven't been to work for ages.'

'There's too much for me to do here, love. I don't have time to go to work anymore. Lots of things have changed.'

'I know. I don't like it.'

'You'll get used to it. We all will.'

She's let go of Gabby's hand now. She walks further from the house, crossing the road towards the green, and I signal for Gabby to let her. She has to explore on her own, has to find her confidence. Then she shouts for the bloody cat at the top of her voice, and I feel myself freeze. *Don't get angry. She can't help it.*

'Smudge!' she yells again.

'Don't, love,' I tell her, running over and crouching down in the grass so I'm at her level. 'Don't make so much noise. Cats have got amazing hearing. He'll know we're outside soon enough.'

'But...'

'But nothing. No noise, Sally, okay?'

'Okay.'

I leave her to it again and look back at the house, wondering if Nathan's coming out. He's upstairs, watching from the window. I gesture for him to come down and join us, but he won't budge. Oh well. He'll change his tune soon enough.

'You think it's all right to be out here?' Gabby asks.

'Sure it is. It's a good thing. I can feel the tension easing, can't you?'

'I guess...'

'It's good to get out of the house. Good to get a change of scene. You know, love, you've been talking all this time about how we're stuck at home, and that might be true, but we've got all this place too. We could have a house each if we want, not that I'd want that. But you see what I'm saying? It'd be good for Nathan to have more space, and for Sally and Hannah to have more room to play, don't you think?'

'I suppose.'

'You don't sound sure. Come on, love, you have to be more positive.'

'I'm trying... it's hard, that's all.'

For a second I think Sally's gone. I look around and see her walking further into the development. She's okay as long as she stays in view and doesn't go behind any of the houses or around the corner. I gave her a pep talk before we came out. I didn't want her finding what's left of that woman I had to deal with a few weeks back. I should have gone and done something with her remains before today but I couldn't face it. Maybe later...

Sally's back. She comes running over, a huge grin on her face. She grabs my hand and starts pulling it. 'Can we play, Daddy? Can we play?'

'Who? You and me?'

'No, silly... me and the little girl.'

'What little girl?'

'In that house,' she says, and she points to one of the other houses across the way.

'There's no one there,' I tell her. 'There's no one else anywhere around here now, love, just us.'

'Us and the girl,' she says, indignant.

I'm curious. 'Show me.'

She holds my hand and takes me over towards the house she was standing in front of. All the way I'm telling her how she shouldn't make stuff up, and how it's more important than ever that we're all honest because we're going to have to rely on each other for all kinds of things now and we're always going to... and I stop right in front of the house and look up at the window. That wasn't there before, I'm sure. I would have definitely noticed that.

I feel my pulse start to quicken.

One of the downstairs windows is covered in a mass of tiny handprints. There are smears of blood and grease everywhere, cross-hatched scratch marks where a kid's fingers have been clawing at the glass. I pick Sally up and hold her face close to my chest as I take another step forward.

'What's wrong, Stu...?' Gabby asks, startling me. I turn to try and stop her coming any closer. I try to tell her, but my throat's dry.

When I look back at the house, there's an infected kid's face staring at me. I stagger back, still holding onto Sally, almost tripping over my feet with the shock. I want to stop Gabby seeing this and getting any closer but it's too late. She knows something's up... she knows there's something here...

'Stuart, what's going on?'

I don't answer, just bundle Sally over to her and try to put myself between her and the window, blocking her way through. But all I can see whichever way I look is that little kid's ghastly face: her pallid skin, sunken eyes, the brown, germ-filled drool trickling from the corners of her twitching mouth.

'There's a girl in that house,' Sally says. 'I want to play with her.'

'She's not very well, love,' I manage to say. 'She can't come out.'

'But Daddy... I haven't got any friends anymore.'

And the emotion's too much now, and I can feel myself welling up. I try to explain to Gabby and hold her back but she just pushes past me to see for herself. And from here I realise she can see the body in the cul-de-sac, and I can feel everything unravelling...

'You have to listen to me, Gab...'

But no one's listening to anything I say now.

The dead kid in the house hammers on the glass. When she can't get out, she takes a run up and throws herself at the window. And again. And again.

Gabby's screaming. Sally's screaming because Gabby's screaming. And all I can do is stand and watch as what's left of this bloody kid walks back then throws itself at the window again and again and again.

'Do something?' Gabby shouts, but what can I do?

'Like what?'

'Make her stop.'

'How?'

She knows there isn't an answer and she turns and runs back to the house, Sally still in her arms. I stay there a few minutes longer, long enough to be sure the girl won't get out. The glass is stronger than her skull. She keeps throwing herself at the window until her head's just a mass of bloody pulp and she can't move anymore.

On the way back to the house, I see Nathan coming the other way. 'Get back indoors,' I tell him.

'Not yet. You need to see this.'

He looks scared, the expression on his face bordering on panic. I don't know how much more of this I can take today, but I do as he says and I follow him deeper into the development.

'What, son?'

'I've been watching,' he says. 'I need to show you. It's been going on for a while but I didn't think it mattered, then you went outside and it all went crazy.'

'What are you talking about?'

He stops on the green. 'This, Dad, look. I was watching with your binoculars. As soon as they heard Sally scream they started.'

'Who started?'

'Them,' he says gesturing.

Fuck me.

There are infected all around the front of the development. More than I can count. The longer I watch, the more I can see. They're coming from all angles, all converging on the barrier Nathan and I built to keep them out. Okay, so they're not here in massive numbers yet, but the potential's there.

'We need to get back indoors,' I tell him, feeling my legs weaken. 'As long as we're quiet and out of sight, they'll disappear, won't they?'

'They did before. Like I said, Dad, I've been watching. I snuck out a few times and checked.'

I should be angry with him, but I'm not. I'm relieved.

'So let's get back to the house. And we'll keep this quiet, okay? I don't want your mother and your sister upset more than they already are.'

'So what happens when Sally wants to play outside again?'

'We'll cross that bridge when we come to it. Come on, son, let's go.'

'Not yet, Dad. Wait. There's more.'

He walks, and I follow. He leads me through an open gate between two houses, then down the length of a back garden to the fence at the end. There's a metal tool-store in one corner. He gets up onto it and gestures for me to do the same.

'How long have you been coming out here?'

'Long enough.'

'For Christ's sake, son, have I been wasting my breath all this time? The risk of infection was—'

'I know about the infection, Dad. I *do* listen to you, even if you think I don't. I haven't taken any risks. I haven't touched anything. Not even what's left of the body around the corner. Did you do that, by the way?'

'That woman... yes, I did.'

'Sick.'

I think that's a complement, but it's of little importance now. I climb up onto the tool-store next to him, and look over. Immediately backing onto the fence here are the six-foot high metal railings around the perimeter of the development, and Jesus Christ, there are even more infected bodies here. There must be hundreds of them in total, crushed against the barrier, piled up in places with arms and legs and even heads pushed through the gaps like they're reaching out for us. I'm up on tiptoes now, looking directly down, and here they're almost impossible to distinguish from one another. I can't see where one ends and the next begins; just a solid, endless mass of diseased flesh.

'Like I said, don't tell your mother. I don't want her worrying more than's necessary...'

'It gets worse,' he says, though I don't know how it can.

This time he takes me way behind the back of our house and the houses behind, all the way to the copse of trees on the other side of the railings at the outermost edge of the development, as far from the barrier we built as we can get. Here too there are more bodies. It's like a truck-load of mannequins have been dumped behind the fence. Most of them remain motionless, but some are twitching and juddering. The longer I watch, the more they start to move. I think it must be a trick of the light, that they were moving all the time and I just didn't notice, but Nathan doesn't think so. 'They always do this,' he says.

'Do what?'

'Start waking up. It's like they know we're here. It's like they can smell us.'

'Bullshit,' I say, but I know he's right. There's a face I was watching, one cheek pushed into the ground, only half its vacant expression visible. I could have sworn it wasn't moving, but it is now. The one eye I can see is looking around, and its mouth is beginning to open and close, dribbling gunk into the leaves and dirt.

'Are they zombies?' he asks, and the question makes him sound like a child again.

'Depends what you mean by zombies. If you're talking *Night of the Living Dead*, something like that, then I don't think so. I don't think they're dead, do you?'

'No. They can't be. That wouldn't make sense.'

'Not much of this makes sense, Nath. No, I reckon the virus has slowed them down, maybe taken them to a point near death, and that's where they've stayed. When they see or hear us, whatever it is that's controlling them starts working again. It's all about spreading the infection. I still reckon in a few months they'll all be properly dead, if you get what I mean. By then it should be safe for us to come outside again.'

'But who says the germ dies when they die?'

I can't answer him, so I don't waste time trying.

There's a high bank in the trees behind the development. There are more infected up top, though Christ alone knows how they got there. They're not in any great numbers, but there's enough all the same. I don't know whether they're reacting to us, or reacting to the reaction of the germ-filled figures closest to us. A couple of them lose their footing and start falling down the bank and, bizarrely, others start throwing themselves down after them. It's surreal: an ex-human avalanche adding to the drift of flesh already pressed up against the railings. The damn things are unaffected by anything that happens to them. I see bones break as they fall down the incline, hear limbs snapping as they hit rocks and trees, but nothing fazes them. Their injuries go unnoticed. All they're interested in is getting closer to us.

'They're reacting to us being here,' I tell Nathan.

'No shit.'

'We have to get back to the house.'

'I'm sick of that bloody house.'

'Mind your language, son.'

'Mind my language? Come on, Dad... seriously? The world's dead, we're probably all that's left, and you're having a go at me for swearing? Fuck's sake.'

He's gone before I have chance to pull him back into line. I let it go this time. Getting to safety is more important than anything else.

STUART

TUESDAY 30 JUNE – 3:09am

The screaming starts just after three and I'm up like a shot, Gabby right behind me. Everything is pitch-black: black-out blinds and boards at the windows, all candles and lamps put out. We feel our way through the house to get to Sally. The place is like an obstacle course, stuff everywhere. She's sitting bolt upright in bed, still screaming non-stop. I try to hold her but she pushes me away. She's soaked through. Gabby has more success. I find a torch then light a lamp so she can see it's just us. And now the bloody baby's started. Hannah's screaming too.

'What's the matter, love?' Gabby asks her, holding her tight and stroking her head.

'It was that little girl,' she says. 'She wants to play.'

We don't go back to bed. I strip Sally's bed while Gabby settles her in ours. She's okay. It was just a dream, though I knew that anyway. I watched that kid smash her own head in trying to get at us. She's where we left her.

Gabby and I sit in silence downstairs. Maybe we know that any conversation will be difficult. Maybe there's nothing left to say. Eventually, she speaks.

'We can't go on like this.'

'We *can* and we *will*.'

'Just listen to what you're saying, Stu. Just for a second, stop talking and *listen*. Think it through.'

'I have.'

'I'm not so sure.'

'What do you mean by that?'

'What do you think I mean? Have we made a mistake here?'

'Don't talk crap...'

'I'm not.'

'You *are*. I'm doing what I have to do.'

'You're doing what you think you have to do. There's a difference. Is it all going to be worth it? All this effort, all this hurt... what are we trying to achieve?'

And I just look at her sitting across the room with her head in her hands, only her outline visible in the first light of dawn.

'For Christ's sake, Gabby, just listen to what you're saying. Think about the alternatives. Have you seen the infected? Can you imagine our kids ending up like that? Believe me, love, I've done everything

I can to protect you all from the very worst of this. Outside this development it's hell on Earth. We don't have any choice. We have to see this through.'

NATHAN

THURSDAY 9 JULY – 7:14am

My dad's a fucking idiot.

He doesn't have a fucking clue what's going on here. Fucking dick. He thinks I don't know what's happening, but I do. He might be able to stop Mum from asking too many questions, but I know more than he thinks. He's not the only one who can walk around the estate at night when no one else is watching. Prick. And he reckons *he's* going to protect *us* from the infected? Fuck's sake, I walked two steps behind him a couple of nights ago and he didn't even know I was out there with him. If I'd been one of them, he'd be dead.

He's got no fucking backbone.

He's not surviving here, he's just *hiding*. And I don't reckon he's ever going to come out.

It makes me fucking sick. You know, he comes out with all this survival stuff, but it's just bollocks he's seen on TV. Bear Grylls and all that shite he used to sit and watch for hour after hour on the Discovery channel. He just doesn't get it. There's a whole world out there, so why just limit ourselves to this place? I know it's the family home and Mum and Dad are proud of the house and everything, but it's a bit late for all that now. We'd be better off at the top of a tower block, I reckon. Or a prison... somewhere strong like that or maybe somewhere out in the country. Not here, though. Not in a normal house, pretty much right next-door to the city centre. Dad's always coming out with these clichés about thinking outside the box and seeing the bigger picture, but he's the one with tunnel vision. I read this book once about a bloke who built a bomb shelter next to his house. The nukes went off, and the house collapsed on top of the shelter, blocking his way out. Tried to tell Dad about it, but he was too busy rearranging the shit in the garage for about the hundredth time to listen to anything I had to say.

I've been watching the fences. I've been watching them better than he has. I know what to do.

There's a gap. Over the garage that belongs to the small house down by the offices near the front of the estate, then down between two parked cars, over a gate and I'm away. It's a kind of channel, and those sick fucks outside can't get through. They can't climb, can't jump... can't do anything but drag themselves around. I reckon I'll be okay as long as I keep moving. So I ripped a map out of this old road atlas Dad had, and I worked out a route that'll get me from here right into the heart of the city. There has to be other people there, other people like us who aren't infected. It's only a few miles. I can do it in a day. And if there's no one there, well then I'll just head out of the city and into the country.

As soon as I find other survivors, I'll bring them back here. I don't hate my family, really I don't, I just can't stand being with them right now, not like this. If I can get away from here then get back safely, if I can prove to Dad that there's hope somewhere other than this fucked-up, dead-end hole, then that changes everything.

Nearly two months we've been locked up here. Two months too long. I know they won't understand – they won't even listen – so I'm just gonna do it anyway.

I've been hoarding my rations for a few days so I know I've got enough to last until I find more. I bag it all up, then put on my wet-suit and all the other protective stuff I've got left, the goggles and the facemask... the whole deal. I even use tape to seal the gaps, just like he showed me.

I'm standing on the green now, looking at the excuse of a barricade me and the old man made.

Tell you something... it's fucking scary out here. I mean, I'm gonna do it, but I'm scared. That's good. I read this book about how being scared is a positive thing, how it keeps you alert and on the edge, and I'm going to have to be like that today and from hereon in.

No turning back.

The idea of staying here is worse than the thought of leaving.

I do it before I can talk myself out of it.

See, I was right.

I've been running for about quarter of an hour now, long enough to get over a mile from home, long enough to get used to the pace. My legs feel fine. It's really hot already, though. Going to need loads to drink.

I haven't seen any of them yet. Plenty of them dead on the ground, but none moving. Dad says the disease is only spread through direct contact, so as long as I stay away from the bodies I should be fine. There's gonna be loads of food around here, loads of places to shelter...

I don't know if I'm going the right way. It all looks different on foot. I used to get the bus this way with my mates, but I reckon I might have taken a wrong turn and not noticed. It's okay, because I know I'll end up in the city centre if I keep going this way, I'd just rather follow the route I planned.

Wonder what's happened to Mikey? He lived up here. His house was half way down that road I just passed. There's a part of me wants to go and see, but I can't. Too dangerous. He might be okay, but he's probably one of them now. Fuck me, that's a scary thought... thinking about Mikey all sick and twisted like that makes me feel really uneasy. I don't like it.

Remember those films? There was that *I am Legend* with Will Smith, remember that? Shit film I know, but that's me now. I'm the one who survived. I'm the last man on Earth. Always thought it would feel different to this though. It's kinda frightening. There's a lot of responsibility. No Mum or Dad around now. Just me. Everything starts and ends with me.

And I've definitely fucked up with my directions.

I was trying to go around the centre of Northfield, not through it.

Now I'm right in the middle of the place, right in the middle of all the shops, and I'm thinking I should go back and work out where I went wrong. I keep getting distracted 'cause there's loads of bodies here. I mean, I'm used to it and they don't bother me like they used to, but it's still weird seeing so many of them like this. You start giving them stories, start trying to work out who they might have been and what they were doing when it got them, wondering if you knew them or if they knew you...

I slow down, then stop. I get out the map and try to work out where I am. I remember Dad getting lost on the way to somewhere once and he said the first thing you've gotta do is stop. If you keep going, chances are you'll just get yourself more and more confused. A rare nugget of common-sense from the old man.

I wish all this had happened a couple of years from now, though. I'd have been driving by then. I mean, I could try and get a car going, but if I—

Wait.

What's that?

I look around, sure I heard something. Then I see a rubbish bin rolling around in the wind, and when it moves it makes the noise I heard. Shit, that was frigging scary. My heart's thumping. I need to calm down.

Hang on.

No, that's not right.

I need to get a grip here.

There's a body right in front of me, facedown on the pavement, head turned away, and I swear it's moved. But there's hardly anything left of it.

I take a couple of steps forward, trying to see if it was a man or a woman. It's weird how they all look the same now... all thin and scrawny and greasy and covered in dirt and shit and—

Fuck me!

The fucking thing swings its arm up and over like it's trying to swim. It doesn't look up, doesn't even move its head, it just digs its fingers into the tarmac and starts trying to pull itself along...

Fuck. Is it trying to get to me?

I take a couple of steps back and the sound of my boots on the ground seems to excite it. It lifts up its head, neck twisting in ways it shouldn't, and I know all it wants is to infect me. Its mouth hangs open and thick brown spit starts dripping out all over the place. It's like its mouth's watering, like it's hungry.

Shit. There are a couple more of them starting to move now. I shouldn't have stopped here. There's one up ahead that definitely wasn't there a few seconds ago. It's standing upright, head twitching, and even though I don't think it can see me, I know it knows I'm here.

Breaking glass.

There are two of them in a shop across the way. One's gone arse-over-tit and managed to fall through a window, and the fucking thing's almost cut itself in half. Its innards are everywhere and I think I'm gonna be sick. But I can't. I can't throw up in this mask and I can't take it off, so I just try and breathe slow and stay calm, but it's hard because the other one is coming my way, its feet slipping in the cut-up one's spilled guts.

Another one tries to get up but its legs are fucked. They're fucking useless and I know I can outrun them, but that's not the point.

They're everywhere now... everywhere I look. Coming at me from out of nowhere. One minute there's nothing, then there they are. There's a mound of rubbish that's built up outside the front of the bank Mum and Dad used to use. And I don't see it until it starts moving, but there's one crawling out of the litter now. It's like the fucking thing's been hibernating in a nest... waiting for someone like me to come along...

The door of a shop flies open with a creak and a scrape. Three of them trip out into the light and start coming for me. Another one appears from an alleyway.

I can do this. Just need to stay calm and keep moving.

Like I said, I know I can outrun them. I'm walking now, and already I'm leaving them behind. I'm still in control here. I'm better than them. I'm stronger than them. Even though I'm scared, I'm still in control. A few seconds' hard effort and I'll be away from here and I'll have left them for dust.

One distracts me when it lunges, and I trip on a kerb I didn't see. I'm on my hands and knees before I know what's happening. I try to get up again but something's got hold of me. When I look back I see one of them right behind me, lying in the road, holding onto my boot. Fucking thing's weak, pretty much falling apart, but it's hanging onto my frigging boot like it's the most important thing in the world. And I know all it wants is to make me sick like them. Nothing else matters.

I kick the fucking thing in the face and start running again, weaving around several more. I keep my pace steady, 'cause steady is fast enough and I don't know how long I'll have to keep this up. Should I turn back and head home? Was Dad right? When I look back over my shoulder, I know I don't have any choice but to keep going.

The road behind me is full of infected, like some sick, germ-filled army. It's like something straight out of a zombie movie, but it's a thousand times more frightening 'cause this is real.

I stick to the Bristol Road 'cause this was the way the bus used to take me into town and I know it pretty well. I reckon I could probably find my way along the side streets, but I'm not taking any chances.

I look back and they're still coming. Doesn't matter how far I run, if they still see me, they'll just keep coming.

Up ahead there's a building site where there used to be a college. The gates are locked but I manage to climb over and down the other side. I snag my trousers on a nail and that makes me panic again, because there's only these few layers of clothes stopping me from getting infected. I just have to be careful. *Don't panic. Take it steady. Don't panic.*

My guts are churning so food's the last thing I want right now, but I know I'll need to eat and drink sooner or later. Thing is, can I risk taking off my facemask? I know Dad said it was just the fluids that carry the infection, but how do I know he's right? What if I breathe it in if I get too close? We didn't get sick back at the house though, did we? I'll just have to make sure I'm not around any bodies when I eat. And I'll have to check I haven't got any of their shit on me too.

This place was going to be a massive old people's home, some kind of retirement village. There's big billboards up everywhere with pictures of old folk. Some parts look almost finished, other sections are just concrete and scaffolding skeletons. It looks like a prison from here, and I think that's a good thing. Maybe I can stop and wait for the crowds to disappear? I look back through the gate to check and they're still coming for me. It's like they're moving in slow motion. Their slow speed makes it more frightening, not less.

There's a site office: a load of metal cabins stacked on top of each other. I'll look in there. The door's half-open. There might be some food or water, maybe a vending machine, something like that.

I go to open it but one of the infected comes at me from out of nowhere. How the fuck did it get in here? It comes at me fast – too fast – and all I can do is grab hold of its wrists. I bend its elbows back and lock them, stopping it getting any closer, but I don't know what else to do. It's not as strong as me, but the fucking thing won't stop squirming. I'm remembering all the films me and my mates used to watch and I'm thinking *this should be fucking easy... just go for its head...* but it's not that simple. Its head keeps jerking back and there's brown gunk running down its chin. I think it's trying to spit. It knows it's not close enough and it's trying to spit germs at me instead.

All I can do is shove it back into the site office. I push it into the dark room and it ends up on the floor in the corner, arms and legs everywhere. I'm only watching for half a second but it's already up and coming at me again, moving with impossible speed now. I pull the door shut in its face, keeping hold of the handle, and I feel it throw itself up against the door again and again and again. It knows I'm still here, but it can't get out.

I just wish the noise would stop. I bet you can hear it for miles.

Feels like I've been gone for days, but it's only been a couple of hours. From up here on the roof I can see for miles. Parts of the city centre have disappeared. There's dirty smoke in the air above where the tower blocks used to be. The place looks completely dead.

The infected are still here. The one in the Portakabin is still making a hell of a noise, but I don't think that's the only reason they keep coming. I don't know if these are the ones that followed me from Northfield, or if this is a new crowd that's sniffed me out.

And I'm lying up here on my belly, looking down over the edge of the roof, and even though I know they can't see me, I know they know I'm here. The weird, fucked-up way they move makes it hard to work out how many there are, but that doesn't matter. All it takes is one – one drop of blood or spit or vomit – and I've had it.

STUART

THURSDAY 9 JULY – 11:37am

'What do you mean, he's not in his room?'

I just look at Gabby. Is she losing it?

'What do you think I mean?' she says. 'He's not here. I've checked his room, the garage... everywhere. I looked out all the windows...'

'And he was definitely inside last night?'

'I checked on him when Sally started screaming.'

'And?'

'And what? He was in bed, wide awake, just looking up at the ceiling.'

'And he didn't say anything?'

'Like what? By the way, Mum, I'm going to run away in the morning?'

'Don't back-chat me, Gabrielle. This isn't the time.'

'And don't belittle me.'

She turns her back on me and storms out of the kitchen, Sally at her side and Hannah in her arms. I get dressed to go out, putting half my stuff on in the utility room, the other half when I'm outside. That bloody kid. He'll be hiding out in one of the other houses, I know he will. I'll crucify him when I find him. Selfish little shit.

No sign. No sign of him anywhere. I've torn this place apart, checking every house. Most of them are still locked and he doesn't have any keys, but I haven't found any forced doors or broken windows.

He's hiding from me. Little bastard. He's playing games. He's probably watching me right now, enjoying putting me and his mother through this. I'll give him hell when I find him.

I walk around the full perimeter of the development, checking the fence. He wouldn't be stupid enough to have damaged the fence or the blockade we built together would he? I don't know what's going through his head right now, and even if he does want to give me grief because he's stuck here, I don't reckon he'd do anything to put the safety of his sisters or his mother at risk.

There are more bodies than ever around the outside of this place now. Piled high. Dead but for the germ which keeps bringing them ever closer towards us.

I head back for the green and I shout out for Nathan. The noise is a risk, but I can't not do it, can I? When he doesn't answer, I return to the house.

He thinks he's got one over on me. Bloody stupid kid.

STUART

THURSDAY 9 JULY – 6:19pm

'Daddy,' Sally says, tugging my arm, 'there's a man at the door.'

My blood runs cold.

Is it Nathan? Is it one of the infected?

It's neither.

I hang back at the end of the hallway, watching the shape on the other side of the frosted glass. Who the hell is this? I don't recognise him. Where the hell did he come from?

'Aren't you going to answer it?' Sally asks.

I crouch down so I'm level with her and I whisper. 'Go upstairs and find Mummy.'

'Mummy's upset about Nathan,' she says, whispering too now.

'I know. Go and make her happy, there's a good girl. I'll see what the man wants.'

I watch her all the way up the stairs. She looks back and I gesture for her to keep going.

He's gone. Where is he?

Fucker's having a good look around.

I see him moving in front of the living room window, checking out the house, trying to see where we are. How does he know we're here? What's he after? Is he just trying his luck, looking for supplies. Christ, the supplies. I have to stop him before he goes anywhere near the garage. We've not got enough to last ourselves. I'll be buggered if anyone else is getting hold of any of our stuff.

Nothing else for it. I'm going to have to go out there.

I slip into the kitchen, moving quietly. I start to put on my protective gear but when I hear him at the door again, banging on it now, shouting through the letter box, I know I don't have any choice. I grab my axe then run around the side of the house, ready to defend what's mine.

He's still standing at the door, bending down and looking through the slot. He doesn't even know I'm here. How the hell has he survived so long?

'Move away from the house,' I tell him. He panics and spins around and starts moving towards me, mouth opening and closing, tears running down his cheeks, hands raised in submission. I hold the axe up ready to hit him, even though I don't know if I can.

'Please,' he says, sobbing. 'Please don't...'

'Move away from the house,' I tell him again, and I gesture for him to move to the middle of the front lawn. He does what I tell him. Christ, he's in a state. His clothes look like they haven't been changed in weeks, and his beard and hair haven't been touched. He keeps pulling up his trousers. Skinny bugger looks like he's lost half his body weight. If I didn't know better I'd think he was infected. Wait... I think I recognise him. Is he that slacker from across the way? The one who never went out of his house? 'What do you want?'

'Have you got any food you can spare?' he asks, his voice so weak it's hard to make out.

'No.'

He sobs again. 'I ran out a couple of days ago. I don't want much. Just a little...'

'No,' I tell him again. 'How did you know we were here?'

He points at one of the other houses. 'I live at number twelve.'

'But I checked all the houses. I knocked your door.'

'I know.'

'And you didn't think to answer?'

'Too scared.'

'So you've been locked up in there all this time?'

'Yeah... I heard you and I saw you outside a few times... I didn't know if it was safe to come out. I thought you might get sick and I didn't want to risk it.'

'Who else is with you?'

'Just me.'

'What about your family?'

'My girlfriend's dead.'

'Where?'

'Not here. She died way back. She was in the hospital. I'm on my own now. You're my only hope now. There's no way back in or out since you blocked the road.'

Fair point. I look up at the house and see Gabby looking down. I try and get her to move back behind the curtains. I don't want this guy knowing how many of us there are here.

'I'm sorry,' I tell him again, 'I'm not giving you any food. Like I said, I don't have enough for my family.'

He turns his back on me and starts walking away. Fucker looks emaciated. He doesn't even have the energy to lift his feet, just drags them along like one of the infected.

Then he stops.

'I know where your kid went.'

'What?'

'I saw him earlier...'

He stops again and makes proper eye contact for the first time. What's his game?

'Tell me where he went.'

I curse myself. My voice sounded more desperate than I intended, and he knows it. I can see him thinking through his options now, a little life back in his eyes.

'Give me some food. You give me food, I'll tell you where the kid went.'

Fuck. What choice do I have? But wait, what difference does it make? 'Why should I? What am I supposed to do about Nathan?'

He shrugs. 'I don't know... but I know I'd have to do something if I was in your shoes. I mean, I couldn't just sit there and do nothing if I thought he might still be alive out there. There's nothing I can do for my girlfriend, but your kid's only been gone a few hours. You could still catch him if you wanted.'

'You watched him leave?'

'I know what he was wearing, what he was carrying, which way he went... I've seen *everything* these past weeks.'

I do what I can to hide what I'm thinking. Don't want him to think he's got any advantage, any kind of hold over me. 'I don't want you near my family,' I tell him.

'And I don't particularly want to go anywhere near your family. I just want something to eat.'

I look up at Gabby, still visible at the window. I can tell by the way the curtain shifts that Sally's with her too. What do I do? My family is the most important thing here, and this guy knows it.

'You stay away from here, understand?'

'Like I said, I just want—'

'You go back to your house. Wait there. I'll bring you something.'

Amazingly, he does as I say.

'What's happening?' Gabby asks. I'm in the garage, bagging up a little food.

'Stay upstairs and keep out of sight.'

'Who is he?'

'A neighbour.'

'And he's been here all this time?'

'It looks that way.'

'But why? Why didn't he let us know he was here. Why didn't he—'

'That doesn't matter now. Just go back upstairs and stay there. I'm going to get rid of him.'

'What do you mean, get rid of him. Wait, Stuart, does he know anything about Nathan? Does he know where he's gone? If he can tell us anything then—'

'He doesn't know anything. He's full of shit. He's sick. Deluded. I'm giving him this stuff to keep him quiet. He won't bother us again.'

'I don't like this, Stu. I think you should—'

'I think you should do what I told you. Go upstairs with the girls and stay there. I'll be back in a little while. Keep out of sight.'

Back outside, this time wearing all my outdoor gear. I don't know what this guy's place is going to be like. I've got my axe too, just in case.

I head straight over, pulse racing, and he's in the doorway waiting before I get anywhere near. He looks surprised, seeing me in my full garb. But if he's as desperate as I think he is, he won't react.

He lets me straight through and I go inside, holding the axe where he can see it. Don't know if I'll use it, but I don't reckon he'll take any chances. He's apologising about the state of the house, but I'm too busy to listen, checking all the downstairs rooms. It's a crying shame – this place would have been quite nice when he first moved in, but it's wrecked beyond repair now. The dirt in here is engrained and I can taste a foul stench in the air even through my facemask. It sticks in my throat. He's been cooped up here on his own for weeks. The downstairs toilet is overflowing with shit.

He shuts the front door, and that makes me feel uneasy. 'Leave it open,' I tell him, but he doesn't.

'It's okay... I'm not going to try anything, I swear. I'm just relieved you're here. I've been watching you for ages, but I was too scared to make contact until now. It's only seeing your lad that made me come and see you.'

'I don't understand why you didn't do it sooner? Can't believe you've been here all this time.'

'I didn't know how you'd be. You've been perfectly reasonable. I thought you might be a little unhinged, given the circumstances.'

I don't tell him I thought the same thing. I still think that, actually.

'So which way did he go?'

He gestures for me to follow him upstairs. 'I've spent most of the time around the back of the house,' he tells me. 'I thought it was more sensible. I know those things outside can't see me from the back of the house.'

This place is vile. The floors are covered in litter. His bedroom, the room we're in now, is like some kind of filthy nest. The covers are badly soiled. I can't even see the carpet. 'How did you let yourself get in such a state?'

He seems to take offence. I shouldn't have said that.

'I lost my girlfriend, remember? There's just me here. Didn't seem any point keeping the place nice.'

'Yeah, but there's nice and there's *nice*, isn't there? This isn't healthy, mate.'

He just laughs at me. 'Strikes me the whole world's not that healthy anymore.' He turns to the window, moving crap out of the way so he can get close to the glass. He points at a gap. Some kind of alleyway down by the offices adjacent to the development. 'He went out that way. I heard him climbing over the fence. It was about half-seven this morning, I think. Bugger woke me up.'

'And which way did he go?'

'I haven't got fucking telescopic vision, you know.'

'What was he wearing?'

'Full garb like you. And he had a rucksack. Now what did you bring me? I'm fucking starving.'

I give him a couple of scraps. We can't spare any of this, but I needed to know what he knows. 'Here.'

'This all? You're taking the piss.'

'I'm not. I've got a family to look after.'

'Half a family. The boy jumped ship, remember?'

'Don't push me.'

'I'm sorry, man,' he says, and he genuinely looks like he is.

He's wolfing down the food.

'How long's it been since you've eaten?'

'Couple of days,' he says between mouthfuls. 'I had enough to last until now. I thought about breaking into some of the other houses, seeing if there's any food there, but I didn't want to do it on my own. We could do it together if you like. We could both do it and split the difference.'

That stuff – if there is anything in the rest of the estate – is mine. Mine and my family's. 'I already checked,' I tell him. 'There's nothing. I cleared most of the houses out a while back.'

He nods thoughtfully, still chewing. 'Oh, well.' He sounds resigned, accepting. 'That's all of us fucked then.'

'Looks that way.'

'What about your kid?'

'What about him?'

'You going after him?'

'Maybe.'

'I reckon he'll be all right, you know. He looked up for it. Well prepared.'

'You think? I'm not so sure.'

'All the more reason why you should go.'

And leave you here with my wife and daughters? I think but don't say. I know I couldn't go now, even if I wanted to.

I turn to leave. 'Stay here,' I warn him as I go back downstairs. 'Keep yourself to yourself, and we'll do the same. Right?'

'There's no need to be like that...' he starts to say as he follows me down and I stop, turn around, and pin him up against the wall.

'You keep away from my family, got it?'

'Got it,' he says, and I can feel him shaking with nerves. Fucker doesn't have the strength to fight me even if he wanted to. I let him go and he slides down the wall, sitting in a heap in the crap at the bottom of the stairs. I slam the door behind me, but it's open again before I've even made it to the end of his drive.

'I mean it,' I tell him, pointing the axe in his direction. He holds up his hands... capitulates.

'I get it, I get it...' I walk away and he shouts after me. 'I just want us to be mates. I'm Dean, by the way...' But I just keep walking.

'I can't go out and look for him.'

'Why not?' she says, tears streaming down her face.

'Think about it logically. Use your brain, love, like Nathan should have. He could have gone anywhere. The chances of me finding him are next to zero.'

She's screaming at me now. 'So that's it? You're just going to write Nathan off? Leave him out there to die?'

'Listen to me – I don't have any option.'

'Fine then, I'll go.'

'Don't be stupid.'

'Don't call me stupid, I'm not stupid. I can't just give up on our son like you can.'

'It's not about giving up on him. The best thing we can do is wait here and hope he comes home. And anyway, I'm not going anywhere now we know there's someone else on the development.'

'I can handle him. I'll just—'

'You'll just what? You'll just invite him in, make him a coffee and explain nicely that it's probably for the best that he stays away? For fuck's sake, Gabby, get a grip.'

'I wouldn't do that. I wouldn't let him in.'

'You *would*. I know you better than you know yourself. It's a harsh new world we're living in now, love. The old rules don't apply. We have to be hard to survive, cruel even. That's why that fucker over the road can go to hell, and that's why we're not going after Nathan. He made his choice. If he wants to act the big man, then he has to take the consequences too.'

'But, Stu—'

'But nothing. Don't argue with me. You know I'm right.'

STUART

FRIDAY 10 JULY – 6:23am

What happened yesterday changed everything. Nathan's gone, this Dean person has revealed himself... we're in the same place, facing the same issues, but it feels like nothing's certain anymore. There's a new urgency to everything, and I have to get to work. I'm up early, creeping around the house so I don't wake Gabby. I think I've done it, but as I'm about to go outside, she startles me. She's in the door-way, looking like a ghost in the low light. 'Shit. You scared the hell out of me, love.'

'Where are you going?'

'Outside.'

'What for?'

'To start checking the other houses. I should have done it weeks ago.'

'Why now?'

'I need to see if there's anything worth salvaging out there.'

'Yeah, I get that, but why now?'

'Isn't it obvious? Because of *him*.'

*

The first few houses don't take long. Dean's house is way over to the left as you look out of our front door, so I go right. I start with the houses I know he can't see, houses I've given the once-over to before, houses I know are definitely empty.

I figure there'll be something I can use to carry stuff in each house, and for the most part I'm right. There's a house the same design as ours but with the reverse layout and horribly decorated inside. I find a decent stash in the kitchen. I reckon this is where that really fat couple must live. Gabby was always pointing them out. He had one of those mobility scooters, and he didn't look any older than me. It's a sad state when you let yourself get in that kind of condition. Mind you, I'm starting to think I might have gone too far the other way. I was shocked at how thin that Dean was yesterday, but when I catch my own reflection in a mirror in the hallway, I have to look twice to be sure it's me. Even with all this kit on I'm half the size I used to be.

I could do with that mobility scooter now to help me carry this stuff to the house. I dump it all in next door's garden where I know Dean won't be able to see me. I'll come back and sort it all later when it's dark. I've come across plenty of people like him before now. Self-ish. Only thinking about themselves. Fucker would take all our stuff and not think twice about it. He'd see my kids starve just as long as he's got a full stomach. He waited like a coward until I'd made the development safe, and he was quick enough to help himself yester-day...

Thinking about my kids makes me stop again. Nathan. I wonder where he is, what he's doing...? Is he still alive? Is he infected? I wish he hadn't run, but a part of me understands why he did it. I might have done the same if I'd been in his shoes.

I could do with him here now, though. The work is physical and hard, too much for one person.

There's less in the next few houses. It's taking me a lot longer to do this than I was expecting. I didn't count on getting so tired so quickly, nor on having to keep looking over my shoulder, watching out for Dean. And if it's not him, it's *them*. From time to time I can see them on the other side of the metal railings. There's no way they can get inside, but they keep on trying. Even those at the bottom of the crush of diseased flesh keep reaching out for me, stretching their hands and arms between the posts.

I've built up quite a pile of food next door now, but I'm going to have to stop. I'm exhausted. Hungry. But at least I managed to get a few treats. A couple of cans of beer and some spirits... some chocolate for Sally. We'll eat well tonight. It'll be good for everyone. It'll help calm Gabby down and settle her nerves. More to the point, it'll settle my nerves too. I've managed to find a few books and a couple of board games for Sally, and a baby toy or two for Hannah. I don't allow myself to think about where the original owners of these things might be. I properly scared myself a while back, imagining an infected baby crawling over the massive drifts of dead flesh which surround the development. I force myself to focus on the future. I think ahead to a few more months from now when they'll probably al¹ have withered down to nothing, and a couple more months later still when winter will take hold, when what hasn't rotted away will have frozen. We'll be safe then.

There are three more houses 'til the end of this row. I'll just check them, then go home and shift everything from next door's garden into ours. Then I'll sort the garage. That's enough work for one day.

Christ, I'll sleep well tonight.

STUART
SATURDAY 11 JULY – 1:37pm

I sit up quick, then lie back down again. Fuck me, my head... What the hell happened?

I remember as soon as I smell the booze. The stench of stale whiskey makes me gag. My stomach's flipping over.

'So you're awake,' she says. Gabby's sitting on the chair in the corner of the bedroom, reading a book and watching me. 'I told you you shouldn't have drunk so much. I said it'd affect you, didn't I? You've barely drunk anything for the past few months. Half a bottle of malt whiskey's enough to knock anyone off their feet.'

'What time is it?'

'Just gone half one.'

That takes a couple of seconds to sink in. Half one in the morning, or the afternoon? The curtains are closed, but there's light trickling in through the gap between them. 'Jesus, how long was I out for?'

'Catching up on all the sleep you haven't had in weeks, I reckon,' she says.

'How long?'

'You were out like a light just after eight last night. A bomb wouldn't have woken you. I was starting to get worried.'

For a couple of seconds longer I just lie there, soaking up her words and waiting for my guts to stop swilling. This feels almost normal. Strange. It's like the morning after a work's do. Then reality starts to return...

'Any sign of Nathan?'

'No, nothing.' She pauses. Is there something she's not telling me? She catches my eye then looks away. She opens the curtains slightly, pretends she's busy. Then she drops the bombshell. 'That man was here again. Dean, was it?'

'What? I told him to stay away.'

'Yeah, he said that.'

'I hope you told him to piss off.'

'Not in so many words.'

'What did he want?'

'He wanted to know where you were, actually.'

'Why?'

'How am I supposed to know? Anyway, I did exactly what you said, I told him we didn't want any trouble, and asked him to keep himself to himself.'

'And?'

'And he did.'

'And where did you say I was?'

'I told him you were sleeping. Don't worry, I didn't tell him about the booze. I just said you were feeling a bit fragile.'

I get up fast, then regret it. But I have to keep going. I make it to the toilet, then throw up everywhere. Jeez, I really can't take my booze anymore.

'I'll go and get some water,' Gabby says, and I hear her leave the room.

I make myself get dressed, then clean up when she brings the water. Then I go straight to the garage and check the supplies. Thank God for that... everything's just as I left it last night. If that bastard sets foot in here... so help me, I'll tear him limb from limb. I'll feed him to the infected on the other side of the fence. Little shit. Who does he think he is, coming around here?

I need to tell him.

I need to put him straight.

He answers the door as soon as I start hammering on it, like he was waiting for me. 'Morning, Stu,' he says, and that wrong-foots me.

'How do you know my name?'

'Gabby told me,' he says, looking all innocent. But innocent is the last thing he is. I can see it in his eyes. Fucker's playing with me. 'She's lovely, your wife. You're a very lucky man.'

That's enough. Have to show this cunt who's boss. I grab him by the neck and force him back into his house, all the way down his hall until we hit the kitchen door and can't go any further. 'You stay away from my house and from my family.'

'I was just trying to be neighbourly... we're all stuck here together... I thought we could help each other out.'

'Forget it. The only way you can help me is by staying away. Got it?'

'Got it...' he says, and I can tell from the expression on his face now that he really has. I let him go and he falls at my feet, still cowering. Weedy little bastard.

I've already wasted enough time today. Since I'm out now I figure I'll empty a few more houses. Even though I slept for hours I'm still tired. I don't feel at all well, but I'll make myself do this anyway.

I manage to check a couple more homes before the effort gets too much and I go back. There's always tomorrow. No sense peaking too soon. I'm in this for the long haul.

But I can still see that fucker watching me from his upstairs window.

STUART
SUNDAY 12 JULY – 10:02am

I feel much better today. Refreshed. Ready.

Physical work stops me thinking about Nathan, stops me worrying about him. He's been gone three days now. I half expect to find him hiding in one of these houses, though I know in my heart that he's long gone by now. Wish he hadn't done it. Wish he hadn't gone.

I found a good haul in the first house I cleared out this morning. Stacks of stuff. Some tins of food and other stuff that's in date... packet mixes, jars of sauces, that kind of thing. Should last us for a few days, and I reckon if I can squeeze a few days out of each couple of houses, then that should keep us going for a couple more months. Gabby keeps on at me, keeps asking what we're going to do after that. Bloody woman's getting like a broken bloody record. She knows what I'll tell her. Same thing I always do: another couple of months and everything'll look completely different. Fewer infected, and those that'll still be here will be in a far worse state. The world'll be ours for the taking.

I've been able to get in most places easy enough. This next one is easier than most. The back door has already been forced. They're all looking much of a muchness now. Have I been here before? Can't remember. It looks familiar, but I don't recall leaving a door open like this. I would have remembered, wouldn't I? Could it be Nathan? I check the house at double-speed, running from room to room, wondering if my son's here, if all the worry has been for nothing. I know before I've finished that he's not here, of course, but just for a second I allow myself to dream I've found him. I wouldn't be cross, wouldn't be angry. The kid's acted like an idiot, but I can't hold that against him. We've all been under incredible stress since the beginning of May.

No sign.

I'm standing in the kitchen, and it's only now that it hits me. I definitely haven't been in here before. Someone has, though. Some fucker has already cleared this place out. The cupboards have been emptied, everything taken, and I know it was recent because there are obvious signs. Dust has been disturbed. There's a wrapper on the floor that looks fresh, not sun-bleached like everything else. The rest of the kitchen is relatively clean, but there are crumbs all over the worktop.

Dean.

The fucker's found his confidence. He locked himself away for weeks on end, only to finally emerge once he'd seen me and my family outside, once he knew it was definitely safe. I'll show him. Bastard. This is *mine* now. This is for *my* family, not him.

I head for his house. I'm going to kill the little shit.

I run from one side of the development to the other, and now I see all sorts of signs that he's been more active than he should have been. There are a couple more front doors open, scraps of rubbish blowing in the wind... a fucking huge rat runs across my path and I stop dead, because I don't know where it's been or where it's going. What if it's infected? Can rats carry the disease? Has that dumb bastard left scraps around to encourage them?

I hammer on his door and try to get in but it's locked. I kick it and beat it, but it's strong and I can't break it down. I'm knackered. Exhausted. Soaked with sweat. I'm not feeling great. It's all I can do to keep standing, but I have to try and look the part, because I know that frigging weasel is watching.

'What's wrong, Stu?' he says, and I look around for him. Can't work out where he is.

'Come out here, you cunt.'

'Bloody hell, mate, that's a bit strong.'

I look up and see him hanging out of one of his bedroom windows.

'Get down here, you shit. And I'm *not* your mate.'

'What's the problem?'

'You've taken my food. My family's food.'

'No I haven't. It's as much mine as yours. It's neither of ours, if you want to get particular about it. All belonged to the neighbours.'

'It's *mine*.'

'You're being very unreasonable, Stuart,' he says, and the patronising tone of his voice just makes me want to kill him. I try to open the door again, but we both know it's not going to happen. We both know he's safe up there. Fucker.

'Come down here,' I scream, and now I'm kicking the door, throwing myself against it. I take a few steps back then run at it, determined to get inside. Then again. And again. And again. And all the time he's up there looking down at me. Cunt.

One more.

I step back again, and someone grabs my arm. I spin around fast, thinking it's one of the infected. But it isn't. It's Gabby. 'Come on, love,' she says, trying to pull me away. 'Come home.'

I pull myself free and keep kicking at the door. Again, she drags me back.

'Leave me alone.'

'Come on, love,' she says again, and this time I stop. I don't want either of them to see, but I'm fucked. I can't keep going. I go back to the house with her because I don't know what else to do.

'He's right, you know,' she says when I explain what's happened.

'I know that technically he's right, but things have changed in case you hadn't noticed, Gabby. The world's a different place now.'

'I get that, love...'

'Do you? Do you really? I'm not sure you do. I don't want the stuff that's in other people's houses just to spite him, I want it because you, me and our kids *need* that food. Now do you get it? It's all well and good standing there like some prissy churchgoer, taking the moral high-ground, but what good's that gonna do Sally and Hannah when the food finally runs out? I'm not exaggerating here... you might think he's got some entitlement, some kind of right to share, but he hasn't. Things are different now. He's killing our kids and I'll do anything I have to to keep you and the kids safe. You hear me, Gabby? *Anything.*'

STUART

MONDAY 13 JULY – 1:02am

He's spent the whole day at his window, watching out for me, and I've waited just as long, watching him watching me. Watching him *thinking* he's watching me, anyway. I slipped out through the back and went into one of the other houses facing his. Fucker's been looking in the wrong place.

And I'm scared and I don't want to do this, but I know I have to. The things I said to Gabby have been running round and round my head since we spoke. *He's not just taking care of himself, he's killing our kids.*

He's been out of sight for almost an hour, and I reckon that's it. He's sleeping, he must be. Time to move.

I head straight for his house, axe in hand, and before I have chance to talk myself out of it, I smash the front door lock. It takes two more strikes before it gives way. I kick it open.

He's downstairs before I'm inside. Look at him, useless piece of shit. He stands there in front of me in a grubby vest and dirty shorts and all I can think is *this filthy little cunt thought he mattered more than my kids.*

'Stuart... what the hell...?'

'What did I tell you?' I say to him, and he shakes his head and screws up his face like he doesn't understand. I pull my facemask down. 'What did I say to you about the stuff in the other houses?'

He backs away down the hall, arms raised. 'Come on, Stuart... let's talk about this sensibly.'

'I tried that earlier.'

'But you didn't, mate... you *didn't.* You just told me how it was going to be, you didn't give me any chance...'

'And that's just how it is.'

'But that's not right. That's not *fair.*'

'Again, that's how it is. I've got responsibilities, Dean. Those people in that house over there, they're counting on me. You don't get that, do you?'

'I do, I do...' he says quickly, still cowering. 'It's just that...'

'Just what?'

'Just that I don't see they're more or less important than me, that's all.' He pauses, but I can see he's got more to say. He needs to think very carefully here because he's on the verge of making a monumental fuck-up. 'I get that they're your family, mate, I really do... and I wouldn't want to do anything to harm them... but put yourself in my shoes for a sec. What about me?'

'What about you?'

'I need to eat too, mate. I've made it this long... I'm not just going to roll over and give up now.'

'Then maybe you should look elsewhere for food.'

'I've as much right to be here as you.'

And now I'm stuck, because he's got a point. Before all of this happened I used to be a reasonable guy. I'd talk and negotiate and do everything I could to see another person's point of view. But this is different. The whole damn world is different now, what's left of it. 'The old rules don't apply anymore,' I tell him.

'We can work together...'

'I reckon we're already past that point.'

'Think about it... You don't look so good, Stu. You're tired... what good will you be to your kids if you burn yourself out?'

He's playing games, trying to trick me. 'Shut up, Dean. You had your chance.'

'I meant what I said, mate, we could work together. Two heads are better than one and all that... think how much easier it'll be if we helped each other out.'

'It's not going to happen.'

He stands a little straighter, like I've given him an ultimatum, or he's about to give me one. 'So what are we gonna do? Because I'm not giving up what I've got, Stuart. The stuff that's in this house is mine, and I'm not giving it up, not for you, not for no one.'

'I'll take it.'

'And I'll take it back. Come to mention it, I might help myself to whatever it is you've got stashed away in your garage. By your logic I could have that too. I saw you yesterday, scurrying about. Truth be told, that's why I did what I did. If you'd kept quiet, I probably wouldn't even have come out yet. I'm a survivor, mate, and I'm gonna keep surviving, no matter what it takes.'

'Not at the expense of my kids.'

'No sign of your son yet?' he asks, and that stings. 'You see, I think your lad had his head screwed on right, maybe better than both of us. He knows there's nothing left here, that we're just playing a waiting game. We can't win, you know. None of us can. Maybe your lad's the

85

only one who stands a chance. Then again, maybe he just got sick of being ordered around by a fucked-up control freak like his old man?'

I lift the axe and go at him, but the bastard barely moves. His eyes barely flicker. 'I could kill you,' I tell him.

'Yeah, but you won't. If you were the man you think you are you'd have already done it by now.'

The axe is raised, ready to swing. 'I was giving you a chance.'

'Bullshit. You don't have the nerve. You know, I've seen blokes like you come and go before now. You think you're the big *I am*, dontcha? Think you're a cut above the rest of us. I used to see you driving around the estate, looking down your noses at folks like me who didn't have a house the size of yours. I saw the way you used to look at that flash fucker with the Jag, the one younger than both of us. You're a weak, spineless, middle-class cunt. You're too scared to die, and that's why you've got your family banged-up in here.'

He's almost sneering now, and I can't work out the logic. Has everything that's happened fucked with what's left of his brain? Does he have a death wish? 'I'm giving you one last chance,' I tell him. 'Shut yourself away and stay here. You can keep the food you've already taken, everything else belongs to me and my family.'

'And I'm supposed to just accept that, am I?'

'Seeing as I've got the axe and I'm blocking your way out, yes.'

'You're bullshitting again, Stu. See, you're the one backed into a corner. A real man would have rolled up his sleeves and started fighting by now. You're too middle-class for your own good. If you really are the man you think you are, why don't you just do what you have to do?'

So I do.

I bring the axe down hard. It glances off the side of his head and buries deep in his shoulder. He just looks at me, eyes full of surprise, then looks down at the head of the axe stuck in his flesh. I pull it out again, but it's sunk so good I almost pull him over.

'I told you. I told you not to fuck with me.'

He starts crying, and the pitiful noise cuts as deep as my blade, making me realise what I've just done. But I can't leave this unfinished. He looks up at me, eyes wet with tears, and I hit him again, right on the crown of his head this time. The impact sends shockwaves running through my hands and arms. It makes me feel sick to my stomach. It's a relief when he drops, but now he's just lying at my feet, looking up at me, his mouth opening and closing like he's still trying to speak, still trying to argue his point.

I had to do it. I keep telling myself I had to do it.

'It's your own fault,' I say to him. 'You made me do it.'

But I can't leave him like this.

Don't know what else to do.

Now I feel guilty, like I've made a mistake, like I could have found a better way...

Think about Gabby and the kids. He was taking food from their mouths.

I bring the axe down one more time, right onto his chest... his heart. Bones crack. His breathing's all I can hear now. Rasping. Laboured. He tries to say something, and I can't stand the noise. I hit him again.

There's a noise behind me. I spin around and see Gabby in the doorway. 'I was worried,' she says. 'You woke me up. I saw you over here. Is something wrong...?'

I try to stop her, but she pushes me aside. And even though there's hardly any light in here, she sees all she needs to see. She screams and I drop the axe and run after her, catching her when she's halfway back to the house.

'I had to do it, Gab...'

'Get off me,' she yells, and in the dark I lose my balance. She races away and I try to get up but I can't.

The nausea comes hard and fast.

I'm on my hands and knees, vomiting in the gutter. Everything is completely silent. All I can hear is high-pitched whistling in my ears: the pressure of knowing what I've just done.

I retch again, then spit what's left into the overgrown grass. I get back up, my hands shaking and numb, heart pounding.

I stop again before I get home and my legs buckle under the weight of what just happened.

Hannah?

I hear the baby scream, and I look up and see Gabby coming out of the house again. She's got Hannah over her shoulder and she's holding Sally with her free hand. Looks like she's trying to carry a bag or something heavy too... where the hell does she think she's going?

I try to stop her but she just pushes past, side-steps me and ushers Sally out of the way. 'Where're you going?'

Still no response. She half-walks, half-runs away from the house now, heading down towards the front of the development and the road Nathan and I blocked off. What the hell does she think she's doing?

Now Sally's crying, and Hannah's screaming, and the girls' noise is filling the air. Doesn't she realise what effect this'll have?

'Gabby, stop,' I tell her, but she doesn't. She keeps marching. She's never been this far from the house before. She doesn't know what it's like... 'You can't go out there.'

And then she sees it.

The moon's still up, revealing more of the outside world than any of us want to see. Much of the land around the development is in shadow, and my mind starts to fill in the blanks, imagining huge masses of writhing infected. Gabby's still trying to get closer. I can't let her. I run forward and grab her shoulder but she brushes me off. Then I make a grab for one of the kids but Gabby snatches her away. She changes direction, moves towards the railings around the estate, then she stops.

The smell here is unbearable. The kids are still crying. A sliver of moonlight illuminates a patch of ground close to Gabby's feet and she looks down, then staggers back. There are hands stretching out through the gaps between the railings. Dead arms trying to get at us.

She's stopped now. She's a little calmer.

'You can't go out there,' I tell her, and I try to take Sally's hand. Gabby just looks at me.

'Stay away from me. Stay away from the girls.'

'But Gab, I had to do it.'

'You didn't have to do any of this.'

'I did it for you and the kids.'

'What the hell happened to you? Just stay away from us, Stuart.'

STUART

A noise wakes me up with a start. I sit up and listen, but it's nothing. Probably just an animal... It's nothing to worry about, and I put my head back down.

I'm three houses down the road from home. Gabby still won't let me back in, won't even talk to me. I have to give her space and time to understand that I did what I had to do, that I did it for *them*. I keep trying to tell her, but she's just not ready to listen. I stood outside the house yesterday and shouted through the bloody letterbox to try and make her see, but she's too caught up with the events of the last few days to be able to think logically about the long-term. If – when – she calms down and thinks this through, she'll understand. I've made mistakes, sure, but who wouldn't under this kind of pressure? *Look around*, I keep telling her, *how many other people are in as good a position as us? How many other families are left alive?* She knows the answers, she's just not ready to accept everything yet.

Shit.

There's that noise again. Much closer, this time. What the hell is it? I'm worried it's Gabby, trying to take the girls away. There's no way she'll get out of the development, but it's the damage she'll do trying to get out that I'm concerned about.

I'm up and out of someone else's bed before I can think. I stumble down the stairs, confused by the layout of this house. It's the same as ours but reversed, and I turn the wrong way at the foot of the stairs, heading for the back not the front. I realise and turn back, going over onto my ankle and cursing my stupidity.

The light outside is grey. I can already see movement out front. Is it Gabby? Is it one of the infected? I push my way out, still hobbling, then stop.

It's neither.

It's Nathan.

'Dad...' he says and he starts coming towards me. He's ripped off his facemask and goggles, and has stripped his wetsuit down to his waist. He's dripping with foul gunk. All I want is to reach out and grab hold of him and hug him and tell him everything's going to be okay.

But I can't.

'Don't, son. Don't move.'

'What?'

'Stay exactly where you are.'

'But, Dad...'

'Please, Nathan, just listen to me. You might be infected.'

Now Gabby's outside the house. She comes bursting out of the front door, running towards him.

'Nathan, love,' she shouts. I head her off, almost have to rugby tackle her. She tries pushing me away but I won't let go.

'You can't, Gabby. We can't risk it.'

'What the hell are you talking about?' she says, still fighting.

'He's been out there for almost a week. He might be infected.'

'Don't be stupid... look at him. He's fine, aren't you, love?'

Nathan takes a couple of steps forward, then stops. 'Dad's right, Mum,' he says. His voice sounds sad... resigned. 'It's not worth the risk.'

'But...'

'Honestly, Mum,' he says, doing his best to reassure her, his teeth chattering with the cold. 'I'm just happy to be home. I don't care if I have to spend the rest of my life stood out here, I'm just glad to be back.'

Gabby stops squirming, but I still don't let go. And, for the first time since the incident with Dean, she softens towards me. I know she'd rather be holding our son, but she holds me instead.

'Nathan, I'll go inside and get you some clothes,' I tell him. 'Strip off what you're wearing and go into that house there.' I gesture at the house I've been sleeping in. 'There's some food in the kitchen. You'll need to stay there for a couple of weeks, just to be sure.'

'Isolation?'

'Yeah, something like that. Just long enough so we know you haven't got it.'

'I don't think I have. I was careful.'

'I'm sure you were, son, but you understand, don't you?'

'I understand.'

*

The morning passes in a haze of speed and unexpected optimism. Nathan's return has lifted the mood and given us focus. I stand outside in the early summer heat and burn his clothes.

It's mid-afternoon, and he's been sleeping solidly since he got back. Gabby's playing with the girls on one of the patches of grass. They're watching the birds overhead and looking for shapes in the clouds. Nathan's at the downstairs window of the house now. He calls over to me. Gabby sees him and comes across too, carrying Hannah. Sally's close behind.

Nathan's still stripped to the waist, and it's a shock to see him in broad daylight like this. He's always been in good condition, always looked after himself, but he looks thin and dishevelled now. I can see his ribs, like a POW picture from World War II. I try not to let my surprise and sadness show. He opens the window slightly so we can talk, locking it on vent.

'You okay, son?'

'I'm okay.'

'Want to tell us what happened out there?'

He doesn't answer at first, and I don't want to push him.

'Come on, love,' Gabby says. 'It might help.'

He starts crying. He tries to act the hard man and hide the tears but it's no use. He can't stop. It's a couple of minutes before he's composed enough to talk. Christ, this is so hard... all I want to do is go in there and hold the kid, to tell him everything's going to be okay. I look at Gabby and she looks at me and I know we're both as worried as each other.

Nathan calms down eventually. He clears his throat. 'I'm sorry... I shouldn't have gone. I shouldn't have done it...'

'That's okay,' I tell him. 'I mean it, Nath. You did what you did, and nothing's gonna change that. I think maybe you had to go through this. The important thing is you're back here now. We're all here. All of us together again. All safe.'

He looks at me, then looks away.

'It was horrible out there...' he starts to say. He stops again, still struggling to pull himself together. 'It's so much worse than what we saw on the edge of the development, Dad.'

'In what way?'

'It's never-ending. It never stops. There are infected bodies everywhere, and as soon as they know you're not like them, they come for you. When they don't know you're there, it's like they're just drifting... peaceful. I almost envy them 'cause it's like they're in a trance, like they don't feel anything. I swear though... doesn't matter how sick they are, how weak... once they know you're there they just keep coming. I saw things that should have been dead – half-bodies, ones that had been crushed or burned, stuff like that – but they were still coming after me. You remember that Pied Piper story? I was like that. Wherever I went, loads of them followed me.'

'So where did you go?' Gabby asks him.

'Into town to start with.'

'Into town? Bad move. Why didn't you go the other way out into the country?'

Gabby just looks at me and I bite my tongue.

'I panicked, I guess. I thought it made sense to stay around buildings and look for places where there might be food or other survivors. I got into Northfield before I realised it was a mistake, but by then I couldn't just turn back. I had to keep going.'

He stops, and I can see the effort it's taking to remember. 'Go on, son.'

'I was looking ahead for places to stop, covering small distances so I was only outside for a few minutes at a time. Even though they don't stop, these things, they're slow too. You can outrun them if you have to... as long as there aren't too many, and as long as you know where they are.'

'What do you mean?'

'I stuck to the main roads,' he explains. 'That way I had a better idea where they were – either in front or behind. This one time I ended up on a roundabout in the middle of a shopping centre – Castle Square, I think it's called – anyway, they were coming at me from all sides... I nearly didn't get away. Still don't know how I managed it...'

He stops talking, his voice fading as he recalls the hell he's just been through. I know this is hard, but I also know he needs to do this. It's important. It's therapeutic. I can only imagine the things he's seen. 'Keep going, Nathan.'

'I found a couple of big supermarkets. There was a massive Asda at the bottom of a hill and I thought about staying there. I took what I could, but I ended up dumping most of it. I know how stupid that sounds, but I didn't know what else to do. It was too heavy to carry. It slowed me down. And I couldn't risk taking off my mask when I was out there, so I couldn't eat or drink much. To be honest, I was too scared. I made myself eat a couple of times but I ended up throwing most of it up again. I swear, if the nerves don't get you out there, the stink will. And if it's not the stink, it's what you see... It never stops. Everywhere you look there's death and disease. Everywhere...'

He's gone again. Drifting back into a trance-like state.

'You don't have to do this now, love,' Gabby says, pressing her hand against the glass.

'I want to, Mum,' he says, and the strength I see in my son's face is inspiring. I'm proud of him. He clears his throat again and continues. 'I got lost. I just kept running and I didn't know where I was going.'

'Did you see anyone else?' I ask. 'Any other survivors?'

He shakes his head. 'No one. There's no one else left anywhere, Dad, just us.'

'Jesus.'

'So I kept going, 'cause I didn't know what else to do. I kept running, thinking I'd see a road sign or something else I'd recognise. So that's what I did. It was really hard. It kept getting harder. All the time I had bigger crowds of them following me, and even though I knew they wouldn't catch me, they just kept coming.'

'How did you find your way back?'

'Don't know, really. I must have run in a massive loop, I reckon, 'cause I ended up back on the Bristol Road and I just followed it home. This time yesterday I thought I was dead. I thought I was never going to see any of you again...'

'It's okay, Nathan,' Gabby says, her palm against his, still separated by the window. 'Everything's going to be all right.'

'No, it's not,' he says, and I sense he still has more to tell us.

'How did you get back, son? Once you'd reached the development, how did you get back inside?'

'Same way I went out. There's a gap...'

'By one of the offices?'

'Yeah, how did you know?'

'I spotted it. Figured that was how you did it. But how did you get back?'

'Over the roof of the security building. There's a truck on the other side of it we hadn't seen before. I managed to get through most of the bodies and up onto the bonnet. Then I just climbed up onto the roof. It was like running through water. Like raw sewage. Some of them are falling apart.'

I try not to get fixated on the horror outside, because I'm trying to focus on other details. 'Did they see you?'

'Sure. Of course they did. But it's okay... Like I said, they won't be able to get over the way I did.'

'And you're certain of that?' Gabby asks, looking as uneasy as I'm feeling.

'Yeah. Completely sure.'

'Good.'

'The Bristol Road was definitely the worst bit,' he says, sounding a little calmer now. 'It's so wide and so straight... I just had to run for it and hope I'd got enough energy left to get back here. I nearly didn't make it. I couldn't stop, couldn't turn around. There were so many of them following me...'

'How many?' I ask him.

'It's impossible to tell. They merge, you know? They all look the same and you can't tell how many are in a crowd because they're all—'

'Hundreds? Thousands?' I interrupt.

'Go easy on him, Stu,' Gabby says. 'He's been through a lot.'

'This is important. How many?'

'Too many,' he answers, his cockiness returning, almost bragging now. 'I didn't stop to count. You've never seen anything like it. The whole Bristol Road was full of them for as far as I could see. All the way back towards Northfield. Thousands of them, I guess. Maybe tens of thousands. Why?'

My legs feel like they're about to give way. I tell Gabby to go back inside and to take the girls, and when she starts to argue I scream at her until she runs to the house in tears. Nathan's yelling at me too, banging on the glass for me to listen to him, but I can't hear anything anymore. Nothing's sinking in. I run towards the entrance to the development, not knowing what I'm about to find.

I climb up onto the barricade, standing on the tele-handler I used to block the road more than a month ago. I don't want to look, but I know I have to. I have to know how bad things are.

And when I do look out there, I wish I hadn't.

Ahead of me for as far as I can see are the infected. It's like an endless sea. The road, the cars, the burned out pub... everything's obscured by an incalculable number of disease-ridden bodies. Nothing but plague victims cramming themselves ever closer to the development. And the few spaces which remain between them are filling as I'm watching, more and more of them edging ever closer. And they'll keep coming. I can see it now, clear as day. We're the only ones left, Nathan said, so they'll keep getting closer and closer and closer. When there's no room here, they'll spread out around the sides, and before long they'll have surrounded the whole development. I understand what he was saying about their numbers, because it's impossible to tell how many there are. All I know is that, in the absence of anyone else, every plague victim for miles around will drag themselves here. He's brought the whole damn world to our doorstep.

Gabby's waiting for me back at the house. 'What is it?' she asks. 'What's wrong?'

I try to tell her, but the words won't come.

'It's okay though, isn't it? You said we're safe here. You've always said we're safe here. They won't get in...'

'Don't you get it? They're infected. Even when they're all dead, even when they've rotted down to almost nothing, the whole area around this place will be toxic. Mile after mile after mile of poison. We'll never get away from here now. Nathan's cut us off. It's not about the infected getting in, Gabby, it's about us never getting out.'

STUART
TUESDAY 18 AUGUST – 11:40am

I tick the eighty-second day off the calendar I've drawn on the garage wall. Almost twelve weeks since lock-down. A month since Nathan came home.

That's it. We're done. The last of the supplies. The very last house on the development completely emptied. There's enough to last another week. Maybe ten days if I forgo some of my rations. Trouble is, I don't think I can. I'm so hungry all the time. But I have to try. The kids must come first. All three of them are malnourished. Hannah's half the size she should be. She still looks like a new-born. It's like she stopped growing when all this began.

I give Gabby the food for the day. I half-expect the kids to come running when they hear us in the kitchen, but they don't. They don't have the energy to run anymore. We spend all our time in the lounge and that's where they are now. Nathan's lying on the sofa, reading the same story to the girls that he's already read a hundred times or more.

'You look tired,' Gabby says to me.

'I am.'

'Funny how exhausted we are, when all we do is sleep.'

I pull her closer to me. It still catches me out when I hold her like this. She's changed so much. So little weight. Her spine is more curved than it was, her arms much thinner. Her breath rattles. Her smell has changed also... no more perfumes and crèmes, just her natural scent. It reminds me of the smell of an old-fashioned sweet-shop, like how my grandma used to smell. And Gabby's hair... brittle like straw. It breaks my heart. I know how much she used to love her hair, how she always used to keep it in such lovely condition.

'I need to get on,' I tell her.

'Get on with what?'

'Checking the supplies... ordering the stuff in the garage...'

'But there's nothing left in there, love.'

'I want to be sure. I need to double-check.'

'You did that yesterday.'

'I know, but I might have missed something.'

'Just stop. Come and sit down. Come and be with me and the kids.'

'I will, I will... I just want to go through the bins, check I haven't missed anything.'

'Will you never stop, love?'

'No, Gab, I won't.'

GABBY

MONDAY 24 AUGUST – 5:35pm

Today's the day. Barely any food in the garage. So little left.

'Do you know what day it is today?' I ask Stuart. He just looks at me, blank, so I answer for him. 'August bank holiday.'

He's been dozing again, and it takes him a while to respond. 'That's right,' he says. Bloody hell, he sounds about seventy. 'Weren't we going to go away? Didn't you want to take the kids to Cornwall this week?'

'We could still go,' I tell him. 'Hop in the car, drive down to the coast...'

He starts to laugh, but the laughs quickly turn to coughs. Soon his noise fills the whole house.

So tired. We're all so tired.

Stuart thought I didn't understand. He didn't think I realised how serious our situation was, but I knew right from the start, same as he did. We just had a different way of dealing with it is all, a different point of view. He's always been the practical one, but it's not always about being practical, is it? I don't think he thought I pulled my weight, but I've worked just as hard as he has through all of this. I'm the one who looked after the kids and answered their impossible questions. The one who cooked and cleaned and kept the house as normal as I could. The one who saved half their food each day and shared it out between the children. I'm as tired as he is. I was supporting the family in different ways, that's all.

I'd just like a break. I'd love to just switch off from all of this for a while. Nathan told me about the infected again this morning, about how when they're not hunting, they're just *drifting*. He says it's like they haven't got a care in the world, like nothing matters to them.

I got angry yesterday when I caught Stuart in the garage again, divvying up our already meagre rations into smaller piles still. I said *it's the same amount, love, doesn't matter how you share it out*, but he just got all defensive. He kept asking me what else I expected him to do, and I said I didn't expect anything, that he'd already done enough. I told him he didn't have to keep trying to take all the responsibility. He said he did. I don't think he'll ever listen.

All things considered, I think we've probably got enough food for another week. We might make even it to the beginning of September. That's sad. Such a shame. It's the kids I feel for most of all. At least Stu and I have lived a little. Still, if your fate's sealed, I'd struggle to think of a better place to go than at home, surrounded by the people you love the most.

We've all been sitting together in the lounge this morning, a brief illusion of normality. We still sit around the TV, even though it's been dead for months. When I half-close my eyes and relax, I can almost imagine this is a normal day like the ones we used to have. Nathan's found some batteries and has managed to squeeze a little life out of a handheld game he used to love. Sally's playing with her dolls, with occasional help from Hannah. Stuart's in his armchair, trying to read a book but struggling to stay awake.

The moment feels perfect, but desperately fragile. This won't last long. I think if I could bottle and preserve these feelings, I could live off them for years.

It's definitely time.

'Who's hungry?'

They all look up when I ask the question, surprised. After having to save every crumb, every morsel for weeks on end, it's shocked them all that I'm actually offering food.

'Gabby, what...?' Stuart starts to say, immediately concerned. I put my hand on his.

'It's okay, love. I know I shouldn't have, but I kept something back. I thought there might be a day when we'd like a nice family dinner together to help keep our spirits up, and as it's a holiday, I think it might as well be today. That okay with you?'

He looks like he's about to cry. 'Yeah... that's fine. That'd be lovely.'

'What is it, Mum?' Nathan asks, looking up from his game.

'Some meat and vegetables. All out of tins, I'm afraid, but I've got a bit of gravy powder left and some herbs and spices. I think I'll be able to rustle up a decent stew.'

'I don't like stew,' Sally grumbles.

'You don't like anything. You'll eat it if you're hungry enough.'

I leave them bickering and go into the kitchen, enjoying their noise. I shift some of Stuart's crap out of the way, then give the camping stove a quick wipe over and start cooking. I've had this planned for a while. Almost as long as we've been shut away here, I think.

The smell quickly fills the house, and it's heavenly, like the Sunday roasts we used to love. Another wave of nostalgia washes over me. The kids are laughing now. It's wonderful to hear, but heart-breaking too. So sad that this is just a fleeting reminder of what we used to have all the time, what we used to take for granted.

No one notices me nip outside.

Whether they like stew or not, no one's complaining. Even Hannah's managed a few mouthfuls. That should be enough, I hope. I laid the dining table like we used to. Sad that a simple thing like a family meal with hot food feels like such an extravagance now. It feels like fine dining. I would have gone upstairs and put on a dress, if the stairs weren't such a climb, and if I had anything that still fitted.

The meal tastes good, even if I do say so myself. So good that no one notices.

By late-afternoon, we've all got it. I make up beds in the lounge, telling the kids they'll feel better in the morning, but knowing they won't. They won't feel anything. That's what I planned.

I close my eyes and imagine myself drifting.

Stuart looks frightened. I lie down next to him and hold him tight, feeling his life draining away as fast as mine. It's hard for him to speak, but he manages a few words. 'What... what did you do?'

'I did what I had to,' I tell him. 'I love you, Stu. You worked so hard to keep us all safe, but we both know we're long past the point of no return. We knew it would get us sooner or later. We wasted so much energy. We should never have fought so hard.'

'But...'

'I thought it would be better this way. I've seen those things beyond the fence. They're free and out of pain, we're not. Seems to me the infected have a better life than we do now.'

He squirms, his guts beginning to spasm, and I hold him even tighter.

'It was the only thing left for me to do, love. Think about it... the infection is our last way out of this nightmare. I took some blood from one of them and added it to the food. We've all got it now. It's done.'

I kiss his forehead. He's burning up, soaked with sweat.

'It's for the best,' I tell him, and I hope he can still hear me because I really want him to understand. 'You see, love, there always comes a point when you just have to face facts, don't you think? There's no way out of this for us. This is the best option, our *only* option. It's funny, you were the one always banging on about the cost of living, and I always said it didn't matter, because we'd always get what we needed. But you just couldn't see it, could you? I was never talking about pounds and pence. When the real price is hidden, love, it's impossible to make the right decisions. Sometimes, it's just too high a price to pay.'

PRIORITIES

There are more than a thousand corpses outside the house in Baldwin Close, and at least as many more again dragging themselves towards the mouth of the cul-de-sac. They come because they know there are survivors here. Even now, almost a month after the beginning of the end of everything, there's no let up. They are relentless. They never tire. They just keep coming.

Inside number nine live Stuart and Gabby Parker and their seventeen year-old son, Nathan. They haven't set foot outside for almost thirty days. There's no question, they've done spectacularly well to survive this long. In fact, if you were to start at their house and search outwards, you'd have to travel more than thirty-two miles before you found anyone else still alive.

STUART

What time is it?

I open my eyes and look around. It's almost light. The alarm clock says six-thirty, not that it matters anymore. I lean across and check on Gabby. She's still sleeping. I don't want to disturb her. Her breathing is light and shallow and I carefully slide out of my side of the bed. Christ, it's cold in here. I take my clothes to the other end of the room and get dressed.

The rest of the house is colder still. I pass Nathan's room and pause outside the door to listen before heading downstairs.

Morning rituals.

You've got to have a routine. It's vital. My only purpose now is to keep my family safe inside and keep the outside out, but we'd never have made it through the first week if I hadn't been so organized. Regimented, almost. I check all the downstairs doors and windows are secure, pausing in the front room to look out across the drive. It's clear but I can see the bodies on the other side of the blockade. When the shit really started to hit the fan, I blocked the entrance to the house with our cars and a couple of my business vans, parking them end-to-end. The barricade's holding firm for now. I thought a few of them might have been able to slip through or under but, so far, it's kept them out.

Fetch the daily rations of water, food and fuel from the garage, then lock and double-lock it again. With the cars out on the road, I've used the space in the garage to stockpile supplies. As soon as I heard what had happened to the bodies in London, that the dead were rising and the infection was spreading, I knew this was going to kick-off big-time. I've never had much faith in government emergency plans and the like and as soon as they started telling us everything was under control, I knew it really wasn't. Everyone else seemed content to sit at home and watch the unthinkable happening on TV. It was easier to watch from a distance than to look outside and accept it really *was* happening, I guess. I took advantage of their malaise to get out and get stocked-up. I bought two van loads of food home from the cash-and-carry and paid for them through the business, figuring that if this really was the end, then no one was going to bother chasing me for invoices and credit card bills anymore. I reckon we've got another month's worth of stuff left in there, maybe six weeks if we're careful. After that, who knows?

I split the food into three piles for Gabby to prepare today's meals – breakfast, dinner and supper. It's important we stay strong and well-fed. I put out three small bottles of water, one each. I'll leave Nathan's outside his room later.

I'm going to have to change the gas cylinder on the stove later so that Gabby can—

Oh Christ, here it comes again.

This is a morning ritual I could do without. My stomach's cramping with pain, so bad I'm doubled-over. I've had this every morning for the last week or so. I haven't told the others – don't want to worry them. I can't afford to get sick. I know Gabby would cope without me if she had to, but she'd struggle.

I use the downstairs toilet so they don't smell anything, but I have to stop when I'm only halfway there and hold my guts again. What the hell is this? Is it just sickness or nerves or something more serious? I barely get onto the toilet in time.

I can handle the diarrhoea and the sweats, it's the impact on our resources that's the real concern. I have to drink more water so I don't

102

get dehydrated and use more water to flush, and I've already had to start on next week's toilet paper and bleach allowances. But I don't have any choice. They need me. I have to stay healthy and strong.

Gabby looks tired.

'You okay, sweetheart?'

She nods and nibbles the corner of another biscuit. I almost have to force her to eat these days.

'I'm fine.'

'You've got to stay strong, love. We all have.'

She nods again.

'Have you spoken to Nathan this morning?' she asks.

'Not yet. Don't want another argument like last night.'

'I know, but you need to talk. Poor kid's not—'

'Poor kid's not seeing the bigger picture. Poor kid's not considering what's at stake here. He's old enough to understand and I need him to cooperate. If I lost my temper every five minutes and did whatever I wanted to without giving a damn about anyone else, we'd be screwed right now. We probably wouldn't even be alive.'

'I know, love, I know.'

'He needs to grow up fast.'

'He's just a kid.'

'I need him to be a man.'

'Just try and talk to him, Stu, will you?'

I need to keep this family together so I do what she asks. I always try and do what Gabby wants. I knock the door then push it open. Nathan's sitting on the end of his bed. He doesn't even look up at me.

'You okay, mate?'

He grunts something and throws a tennis ball against the wall then catches it. I choose my words carefully so I don't fire him up. He keeps bouncing that bloody ball. Every time it hits the wall or bounces off the floor I cringe at the noise it makes. He knows as well as I do what effect it'll have on those bastard things outside. I can see them through a gap between the boards across his window. There are hundreds of them out there, thousands even, all crammed into our cul-de-sac. We're safe here, but there's no point him winding them up unnecessarily.

'Nathan, just stop throwing the ball for a second, please. I want to talk.'

He catches it and holds it.

'What?'

'Look, I just wanted to say, I understand why you did what you did last night. It's just that—'

'No you don't,' he says, bouncing the ball again. 'You don't understand anything. You haven't got a bloody clue what's going on here.'

'Keep the noise down, son. They'll hear you.'

'They won't. They can hardly hear anything. Bloody hell, they're dead, Dad. Remember?'

'Mind your language, sunshine. Just because—'

'I can say what I want.'

'While you're in my house you'll—'

'What you gonna do?'

'What?'

'You gonna ground me? Take away my TV? Stop my allowance? Face it, Dad, you're all out of options so just piss off and leave me alone.'

'Don't you dare talk to me like that. Have some respect.'

'Respect? I'm supposed to respect you? Don't make me laugh.'

'If you don't shut up I'll...'

'You'll what? You won't do anything, Dad, because you're a fucking coward. That's why we're trapped in here. You're hiding because you're too scared to face up to what's happening outside.'

'That's rubbish and you know it. You know we can't go out there. You're just being difficult for the sake of it. When I was...'

'Keep your voice down, Dad,' he sneers. 'They'll hear you, remember? Don't want to upset the neighbours.'

'You little shit. If it wasn't for me you'd be...'

I don't get to finish my sentence. Gabby pulls me away and pushes Nathan's door shut.

'Stuart,' Gabby shouts from the kitchen, 'come here quick. They're in the garden.'

Damn, she's right. My legs go heavy with nerves when I see them out there. Looks like the fence between next door and next-next door has collapsed and some of them have managed to get through. A couple have found the hole in the hedge at the bottom of our garden. Shit. I knew I should have blocked it up... What the hell am I going to do now? There's still only a handful of them on our lawn but where one of them leads, hundreds more usually follow. I run upstairs to the bathroom to get a better view and Gabby follows. She looks down over my shoulder.

'What are we going to do?'

I can't answer. Can't think straight. Can't risk going outside.

'We'll wait,' I tell her. 'Maybe they'll keep going? What if I go out there when it's dark and make a hole in the fence on the other side? I could try to shepherd them out.'

'But they're getting closer, Stu. We have to do something.'

'If we go outside then they'll know we're in here. That'll be the end of it. They'll never leave us alone. They'll keep coming until—'

'Get rid of them and block up the fence,' Nathan says from behind us. Didn't realise he was there. 'Five minutes and we could have the place cleared. Come on... Jeez, just look at them. They're useless. They don't stand a chance. If you leave it we'll be overrun.'

'Did you not hear me? We can't risk going out there. It's too dangerous.'

He turns his back on me and goes back to his room.

NATHAN

Dad's not listening. Dumb bastard, he's too scared to go outside. Why can't he just admit it? We all know it. He's just trying to save face and all Mum does is pander to him. I've had enough of this bullshit.

The back door's secured with a padlock and chain but I know where he keeps the keys. He thinks he's so smart, but I've known about the little metal cash-box at the back of the bottom drawer since I was a kid. I'm outside before he's even made it downstairs.

I just stand there for a second, breathing in the air. It smells foul – full of death, decay and disease – but at the same time it's fresher than the recycled hot air and bullshit that's filled the house for too long. I grab a felling axe – one of the so-called weapons Dad's left lined up and untouched for weeks – then head out. I should have done this a long time ago...

The first one looks like it used to be a woman, but it's so fucked up it's hard to tell for sure. It's an absolute fucking mess, all charred and burned down one side, its clothes melted and fused into its flesh. One side of its scalp is covered with long, greasy hair; the other side's bald and raw, skin shrivelled and dry. It lurches towards me, skidding in the muddy grass, and I swing the axe around and virtually take the fucking thing's head clean off its shoulders.

Christ, that felt good.

Next one up used to be a big bastard. Its massive body is saggy and pear-shaped now. Gravity's dragged its insides-out and its stomach and legs are swollen. It tries to go for me but it's so bloody slow it's untrue. I just side-step it and watch it stagger past. It keeps moving for another three or four steps before it even realises I've gone. It tries to turn around but I'm too fast and I bury the head of the axe in its spine. It drops to the ground, legs paralysed. Still moving but going nowhere fast.

The last two dumb fuckers are still stuck down at the far end of the garden. I hardly look at the third one as I hack it down. The fourth is stuck, its tattered jacket snagged on a broken branch. Stupid thing leans forward and tries to reach out for me with numb, grabbing hands. There are no more of them about, so I don't kill it for a second. I walk right up to it – as close as I can get without it reaching me – and stare straight into its face. There's nothing there. Not a bloody flicker of emotion. I can't believe we've let these things take over. I know it's the infection that's done all the damage but I still reckon I could get rid of hundreds of them and not even break a sweat.

I lift up the axe then swing it down and crack the skull of this one open like an egg.

'The fence,' Dad shouts. At least he's made it outside. Chicken-shit is still at the other end of the garden, though, hiding in the shadows of the house. 'Block it!'

'You block it,' I shout back, though I know it's all down to me.

I could wait for him to come down and do it himself but the place would be full of corpses by the time he'd psyched himself up, and I can't be bothered with all this pointless pissing about.

The metal swing and climbing frame I used to play on when I was a kid are still here, despite the fact they haven't been touched in years. I pull the climbing frame over onto its side and drag it through the long grass. I wedge it into the gap the bodies came through. That'll hold the fuckers back. They don't have any strength. They're like Dad: weak and powerless and pointless. The similarities are remarkable. They're out there, we're stuck in the house. We're all as dead as each other.

What the hell's he doing now? Mum's trying to pull Dad back inside but he's standing over the fat corpse, ready to spear its head with a garden fork.

'Go on then,' I tell him. 'Do it.'

'Keep your voice down,' he says, looking up for a second. He swallows hard and shuffles his feet like he's getting himself into position. The corpse is still moving. It reaches out with a numb arm. Dumb, dead bastard.

Mum tries to pull Dad away again.

'Come on, Stuart, leave it. Let's get inside.'

I stand my ground, and the fact I'm watching seems to really piss Dad off. He lifts the fork higher but I know he won't do it. He hasn't got the balls.

'Go on, Dad,' I say again, egging him on. 'Put it out of your misery.'

The corpse reaches out for him then over-balances and flops onto its back like meat on a butcher's slab. It looks up at dad with cold, dead eyes. It probably can't understand why the useless fucker hasn't done anything yet.

'You're full of shit,' I tell him. 'If you weren't such a coward we wouldn't be stuck here now.'

Tired of waiting, I stamp my boot twice on the dead fucker's face. The massive corpse twitches and shakes, then lies still.

'Don't go in the house with those boots on,' Dad shouts after me as I walk away. 'Gabby, don't let him take anything infected inside.'

*

107

'I know it's hard, love, but think about what you're saying...'

'No, Mum,' I tell her, '*you* think about what *you're* saying for once. He's kept us locked away in here for almost a month and for what?'

'We're still alive,' she says, wiping away a tear and hoping I haven't noticed.

'You call this living? This is barely existing. This is no different to what those damn things are doing outside.'

'Your father has done all he can to keep us safe. He's made sure we've got enough food, he's kept the house heated, he's kept the place secure.'

I try not to shout because it's Dad I'm angry with, not Mum. 'All he's done is prolong the inevitable. Doesn't matter if we've got enough food for another day, another week or another year, when it's gone, it's gone. What are we gonna do then?'

'By then things might be better. There might be other people who—'

'Just stop and listen to yourself, Mum. You're repeating his bull-shit and you know it. Things aren't going to get any better, no matter how long we leave it. We're just waiting to die here.'

'Don't say that...'

'It's true. Stand up to him, Mum. Show some backbone. He won't listen to me, but you've still got a chance.'

She shakes her head and my heart sinks. Mum would have been twice the person she was if she'd put Dad in his place a long time ago. He's a stupid old bastard, stuck in his ways. He's stayed still while the rest of the world has changed. Even now I can hear him downstairs in the garage yet again; checking, double-checking and triple-check-ing the supplies and helping himself to a little extra while he's there. I know what he's up to. He knows as well as I do that we've only got a few days left. He talks about weeks, but he's fooling no one.

Deep breath. Tell her what I'm planning.

'Mum, I'm leaving.'

She starts to protest but it's like I've punched her in the stomach and all she can do is open and close her mouth like a fish, not saying anything.

'You... you can't...'

'I can't stay here. I checked this morning and there are nowhere near as many of them out behind the house. I reckon I can get through them.'

'But you just can't...'

'I'm going to try and find other people like us, then I'll come back for you.'

'No, love...'

'And even if I don't come back, your supplies will last longer without me. I'll find stuff outside. There will be loads out there.'

'But what about the disease?'

'I'll be okay. You've seen how slow they are. As long as I'm careful and I don't hang around, I reckon I'll be fine.'

'When?'

'First thing tomorrow.'

GABBY

You try and do the best by everyone but sometimes you can't do right for doing wrong. I told Stuart about what Nathan was planning – I had to – and the inevitable fight followed. I'm stuck in the middle between two unstoppable forces on a collision course and I don't know what to do for the best. Whatever I decide, someone gets hurt.

Nathan's right about Stuart, though. He's gone and got us trapped here and I can't see a way out. There are too many of those things outside the gates now, and the way he parked all those cars and vans means we can't get away easily. I lie awake all night, every night worrying about what we'll do when the food runs out. I keep my eyes closed when Stuart wakes up. I don't want him to worry. He's got enough on his mind.

But Stuart's right about Nathan too. He's a typical teenager – as bloody-minded and impulsive as his dad was when we first started going out together. It doesn't matter how hard I try to make him see someone else's point of view, he won't listen. He's stubborn and he's made his mind up and that's all there is to it. I could spend all night talking to him but it wouldn't make any difference, he'll still leave in the morning. But I know, his dad knows and, I think, *he* knows he won't last five minutes out there. There are millions of bodies outside – millions of them! All it takes is for him to come into contact with just one and he'll be infected. I can't stand the thought of him walking around out there like them, all alone. I saw it take so many of my friends when this all started. I thought Stuart might have caught it last week when his stomach started playing up, but I know that was just nerves. He should have told me.

'Need any help in there, love?' Stuart shouts. I can't help smiling to myself. As practical as he thinks he is, he's never been any use in the kitchen. Couldn't boil an egg!

'No thank you, love. It's ready now.'

I glance in through the open door. Nathan's listening to music on his headphones and Stuart's compiling another one of his endless lists of all the food we haven't got left. He makes me laugh! He thinks I don't know, bless him. He's been helping himself to extras since we first locked and bolted the doors.

'Here we are...'

The smell of the hot food is strong enough to make them both stop and look up. I hand them their bowls and they stare at the stew like it's the first hot meal they've had in years, not weeks. Stuart looks from the bowl, to me, to Nathan, then back to the bowl again.

'Bloody hell, Gab... where did this come from?'

'You're not the only one who's good at stockpiling, Stu. I've got my own supplies. It's only tinned meat, but I've been holding it back for a special occasion. We've all had a tough few days and I thought this might help.'

It seems to have done the trick. Nathan's taken off his headphones, Stuart's put down his pen and they're both tucking in. It's lovely to see them both eating so well. For a minute I just sit back and watch them.

And it only takes a minute.

Nathan drops his spoon and clutches his gut. This is the bit I've been dreading.

'Mum... I...'

He rolls over to one side, falls off his chair, then starts writhing on the floor. I'm so busy watching him that I don't see it take Stuart. He grabs my wrist, squeezing so hard that I yelp with pain.

'What's... happening...?'

I don't know if he can hear me, but I owe it to him to explain.

'Whatever we do, love, we're already dead. We've all known it for weeks, but both of you are too stubborn to accept it. I had to do this. I didn't have any choice. At least this way we get to stay together. No more arguing, no more worrying about supplies...'

Nathan screams in pain and thrashes around on the dining room floor. Then he stops and lies completely still. Stuart relaxes his grip on my wrist and slides off his chair too. He convulses for a few seconds, then stops.

'Think about it,' I tell them both as Nathan slowly starts to reanimate, 'this is the best option for all of us. The *only* option.' I take a deep breath then swallow the biggest mouthful of food I can manage. I chew it quickly and force it down, desperate not to waste my last few seconds. 'I took some blood from the bodies in the garden and added it to the food. This way we stay safe, we stay at home and we stay together...'

The first wave of pain shoots through my stomach like an electric shock and it's all I can do to stay upright. I try to force more stew down but I can't even hold the spoon...

Hard to keep talking. Have to try. Need them to hear this.

'I had no choice. It's my job to... keep this family together.'

Baldwin Close is empty. There are no survivors here now, and the huge crowd of bodies has disappeared. There's hardly any noise, very little movement, no sign of life...

Just three corpses remain inside number nine, isolated from the rest of the dead world. Safe. Together.

THE COST OF LIVING
FLASH FICTION VERSION

We wouldn't have made it to the end of the first week if it hadn't been for Stuart. I used to criticise him for being so anal: so pedantic, always penny-pinching. He was always going on about the cost of living. It was bloody infuriating.

But his attention to detail was what saved us. When everyone else was running around terrified out there, fighting over the last loaves of bread on supermarket shelves and stepping over the bodies in the aisles, we were safely locked away.

Stuart saw this coming. Smartarse even modelled it on his bloody computer. He showed me how the outbreak would inevitably become an epidemic, then a pandemic, then something worse. Typical bloody accountant. No emotion. He went out to the cash-and-carry with the business card and brought back enough food and bottled water to fill the garage. When everyone else finally caught up and started realising the end really was nigh, he'd already cleared out the DIY store and got everything he needed to make the house secure. By the time we'd locked down, the rest of the world was in utter chaos. The germ spread through any direct physical contact, so we cut ourselves off from absolutely everyone else.

Six weeks, four days. That's how long it's been.

We survived on adrenalin to begin with, living on our nerves. The girls were more upset about the cat than anything else, but Stuart was right, she was a contamination risk and she had to stay outside. After the first couple of weeks it all went quiet out there – too quiet. The screaming, the helicopters, the gunfire and the engine noise gradually all stopped. Then there was nothing.

The next weeks were harder, but we kept ourselves busy keeping the kids distracted, checking and re-checking the house was secure and rationing the supplies. Stuart said he'd worked out how much food and water we'd need each day, and that we had enough for a couple of months if we were sensible. I asked him what happened after that. He didn't have an answer.

We knew we couldn't think about anyone else, even if we wanted to. A woman tried to get in once. Don't know how she found us. It was hard leaving her out there, listening to her screaming. I took the kids upstairs and tried to keep them occupied. Stuart stayed down on the other side of the door, just in case she got in. Her body's still on the driveway.

The girls and Stuart are really struggling now. I can't let them see that I am too. We're all doing our best, but I don't know how much more we can take. The garage is half-empty, and we don't have any way of getting more food. We can't risk going out. We're fighting all the time now. Last night things came to a head.

'We keep doing what we're doing,' he said, tears streaming down his face. 'We ration the food even more, and we wait.'

'Wait for what? There's no one else left. And what about the kids?'

'What am I supposed to do?' he screamed at me. 'I've done everything I can for this family. I've kept us all alive.'

I held him as he sobbed. 'I know... I know...'

'I know I've built us a prison here, but it was the only option...'

I did it this morning while Stuart and the girls were still asleep.

I'd been keeping some decent food back, and I cooked the best meal I could with the little I had. Something I knew they'd all like. They ate every scrap, and for the first time since this started, they were all happy: bellies full, nightmare outside temporarily forgotten.

It took about an hour for it to take them. Hannah first, then Sally, then Stuart. I took what I needed from the infected body on the drive, and added it to the food. And that was that. A little bit of pain, a short burst of fear, then it was over. Far better than the alternative... the hunger... the panic... waiting for the inevitable.

And now, as I sit next to their still warm bodies and finish my food, I look at them all and remember how much I love them.

Sometimes, Stuart love, the cost of living is too high a price to pay.

ISOLATION

I'd always planned to write an AUTUMN story called KING OF THE DEAD. In it, a typical AUTUMN survivor (i.e. very ordinary and flawed) who'd been living a pretty thankless and miserable life, would find their position unexpectedly changed for the better by the zombie apocalypse. The story didn't make the original version of AUTUMN: THE HUMAN CONDITION, but I always intended to go back to it.

In 2010 I met with a film director from Colchester, Will Wright, who'd seen the AUTUMN movie and who was interested in adapting an AUTUMN story for the screen. I put together a screenplay based on KING OF THE DEAD, retitled it ISOLATION, and we worked on refining the story for a couple of years. Along the way the AUTUMN association was dropped and the rules of the dead were adapted to suit the intended short movie format: as with AUTUMN, almost all of the population dies one morning, coughing and spluttering and spitting up blood, only to rise again a day or so later. In ISOLATION, though, the living dead are immediately vicious and attacking, unlike the slow-burn build-up of AUTUMN.

Will and I (and, later, Toby Bowman) did a lot of preparatory work on the screenplay. Unfortunately, for a number of reasons, the project stalled. There's hope, though, that like one of the living dead, the ISOLA-TION movie will eventually be resurrected.

This novella is based on my original screenplay, revised somewhat to suit the page rather than the screen, and given a wholly different ending. As with all of my zombie stories, ISOLATION is about the living, not the dead. The end of the world forces both Keith and Anna – two lonely, broken people – to look at who they've become and try to figure out how they can survive. As you'd expect, the results aren't pretty.

DAY ONE

It's early. Too early. There's little movement in Ashton Grove save for a cat mooching through a torn bin bag, looking for food. He stops when he hears a car with a knackered exhaust race past the end of the grove. At this time in the morning, with everything else so quiet, it sounds like a Formula One car heading for the pits mid-race. The cat legs it, following a well-worn path around the edge of a wildly overgrown lawn then scrambling over a fence.

Ashton Grove is asleep. Save for the kid upstairs in number eighteen who's still playing Xbox and hasn't yet gone to bed, and the guy who lives on the third floor of the maisonettes who works permanent nights and has only just got home, barely anyone moves.

Except Keith.

He's up and out of bed before the alarm clock, but he's been awake much longer. Keith doesn't sleep so well these days. He'd go and see the doctor about it, but the doctor would only laugh or tell him to pull himself together, and anyway, when would he have time to make an appointment? Between his job and everything he has to do here at home, Keith doesn't get a second to himself. Apart from at night. At night he gets all the time he needs and more besides. Too much time, if anything. At night he can't switch his brain off long enough to sleep.

No one ever comes in this room but Keith. It's a bedroom stuck in a moment; frozen still when his life was irreparably changed. His faded duvet cover is from a long-forgotten kid's cartoon movie, and the headboard of his bed is plastered with spare world cup football stickers. Not the last world cup, or the one before that... these players, with their dodgy, dated haircuts and awkward forced smiles, represented their countries the time before that. Or was it the Euros? Some other championship altogether? Keith can't remember now. It doesn't matter anyway.

He stumbles to the bathroom for a shower, pausing by the door to stick the corner of a handwritten sign back down. KEEP OUT OR ELSE, it says. He made it when he was twelve. He stuck it under the porcelain plaque (which says KEITH'S ROOM, next to a picture of a castle) that Mum bought for him on holiday that time, and he's never got around to taking it down.

Keith opens the living room curtains and light floods into downstairs. He looks around and surveys the damage. A few crushed beer cans, an empty bottle of scotch... and in the middle of the debris is

Dad. He's facedown on the sofa where he spent the night, dead to the world, zombie-like. Keith tiptoes around his old man, not wanting to wake him because every second Dad's asleep is an extra second Keith has to himself. He puts the bottle and cans in the bin, picks up the framed photograph Dad fell asleep clutching, then checks he's still breathing. It's okay. He's always still breathing. *One day...* Keith thinks, then he curses himself, momentarily eaten up with regret for allowing himself to think that way.

He's standing in the kitchen now, watching his reflection in the window, drinking tea and eating a piece of toast he doesn't want but is forcing himself to finish. The garden's got overgrown all of a sudden. Mum would have been disappointed, but he thinks she'd understand. Keith's struggling to keep on top of everything right now. He makes plans to try and get out there and cut the grass at the weekend if he gets a chance. It all depends on everything else...

There's a clattering noise and the scrape of a chair on the lino behind him. Keith turns around and his heart sinks when he sees that Dad's awake. He slumps down at the table, looking into space. Keith fetches him a can from the fridge and opens it, then lights a cigarette. Dad smells the smoke and sits up straight, suddenly perked up. Keith puts the cigarette into his shaking hand and fetches him a dish to use as an ashtray.

Keith's all done up for work in his suit and tie now. He's standing in front of the mirror by the front door, combing his hair. He straightens the picture of him, Mum and Dad on the beach in Cornwall that time they went away and stayed in Mum's friend Pearl's caravan. Bloody hell, he loved that holiday. It was more than ten years ago now, but he remembers it as if it was yesterday: the sea, the sun and the sand... the freedom. Back then he could do what he liked, when he liked. Maybe he'll go back there one day. That'd be good. You've got to have something to aim for, haven't you?

He finishes his hair and pockets his comb, then looks back towards the kitchen again.

'I'm off now, Dad. I'll be back at the usual time. I'll get something for dinner while I'm out. Have a good day...'

He thinks all this stuff but doesn't bother saying any of it. There's no point. Dad's out cold. Dead to the world.

The vast open-plan office where Keith now works is a hive of noise and activity. The company employs more than two hundred staff here, spread out over several floors, each as busy as the one below and the one above. Some departments deal directly with clients, banks of operators taking call after call after call, cross-selling this and up-selling that. Other departments work alongside the field-based national sales teams, providing high-class admin and customer service support to clients with a perceived high net value. Some teams are what the company refers to as 'back office processing'. They do all the work that has to be done, but which should be invisible to the customers. *If the customer knows we're there, then we're not doing our job right*, Gloria, Keith's boss, is always saying. *It should be like we don't exist.*

Keith's job is essentially just data entry. He transposes information from a 'Know Your Customer' form directly onto the company's core computer system. He has a challenging rate-per-hour processing speed to achieve, and an equally challenging accuracy ratio, but then again, so do the rest of the department. Thing is, he's never going to hit his target today if he carries on like this. All around him his colleagues' fingers are flying across their keyboards, but he's just staring into space, watching his inert reflection on his computer screen, following the floating company logo screensaver with his eyes as it randomly drifts around.

A sudden flurry of movement startles him, and he instinctively nudges his mouse to bring his workstation back to life and make it look like he's been working. Darren, a work experience kid who's only been here a week, stops by Keith's desk with his trolley and drops a wedge of new 'Know Your Customer' forms into Keith's still half-full 'in' tray, then takes the few forms Keith has processed from his almost empty 'out' tray.

Keith starts to focus on his work now, prodding his keyboard with his index fingers, wishing he could type faster.

The phone shared between him and the next desk rings. Keith's on a roll now, several fields already completely filled, and the last thing he wants to do is stop, so he ignores it. It rings and rings, and he senses everyone looking at him, thinking *just answer the bloody phone*, but

Shelly's sitting as far from it as he is, so why can't she get it? He's on the verge of relenting, just about to move, when she finally picks it up. He tries to make it look like he was going to answer, but he can tell from the expression on her face she's not buying it.

'Good morning, Data Processing Support, Shelly Martin speaking, how can I help?'

A pause. Keith listens to the gaps, trying to work out who, what and why.

'Oh, hi Gloria. You okay?'

Another pause. Shit. It's the boss.

'Yeah, I'm not too bad, thanks,' Shelly says in answer to another unheard question. Keith's straining to listen now he knows who's on the line. 'I know, I heard about that, Gloria. Real shame. You were always saying something like that was going to happen eventually.'

Keith's still banging away at the keyboard with two fingers, trying to focus on his work but being distracted by the phone call. He feels Shelly's eyes on him and he senses Gloria's getting to the point of the conversation, small talk over and done with.

'Yeah, he's here,' Shelly says, and Keith's worst fears are confirmed. This call was meant for him. He knows he should have just answered it. Bloody idiot.

Just keep typing... just keep working...

'Sure, love. I'll tell him now.'

Shelly hangs up. Keith still doesn't react at all outwardly, though his heart's thumping and his mouth's dry. The pressure too much to stand, he finally relents and looks across.

'Gloria wants to see you,' Shelly says. Her voice is completely different now. He can't tell if she was sucking up to the boss, or if she's dumbing down to him.

'I'll just finish this KYC then I'll—'

'She wants to see you now, Keith. I wouldn't keep her waiting if I were you. She doesn't sound best pleased.'

Gloria marches from one end of the seventh floor to the other, Keith lagging behind, struggling to match her pace. This is the walk of shame. Generally, when you see someone being taken this way by their manager, you know they're in trouble.

Meeting room two. Everyone's watching.

She holds the door open for him. He squeezes past and goes inside. She dwarfs him. Bold and brassy, over-confident, over-dressed and over-made-up, she stinks of cheap perfume and coffee breath. She drinks espressos from the vending machines, permanently wired. She's not the kind of person you'd pick a fight with, not if you had any sense. Keith thinks he'd rather take his chances with ten blokes than one Gloria.

The meeting room is long and narrow. A large rectangular conference table takes up almost the entire floor space. There's a single small window at one end, but the blinds are drawn and the room's filled with unforgiving electrical light instead, harshly illuminating everything, leaving no place to hide. Keith sits down as directed, but Gloria's too angry. She paces around the table, massaging her temples. Keith watches her every move but keeps his head down, not wanting her to see.

'Have you got any idea how much shit you've caused, Keith? How much unnecessary re-work?'

Nothing. What does she expect him to say?

'Jesus Christ... it wouldn't be so bad if this was the first time we were having this conversation, even the second... but I've lost count of how many times I've had to bring you into this room.'

Keith knows exactly how many times, but he's not saying.

'You know, I thought you'd excelled yourself when you screwed up that file for Jenna Sallis, but that was nothing in comparison to this. You just don't get it, do you? You don't understand how your inefficiency impacts on the department and on the business as a whole, how it impacts on *me*. This ain't rocket science, Keith. This is basic, day one induction stuff.'

He looks up and catches her eye. She's at the opposite end of the room now, as far from him as she can get. He clears his throat. 'I'm sorry, Gloria. It's just that things have been really difficult recently and I—'

'Don't think I'm not sympathetic, Keith,' she interrupts, sounding decidedly *un*sympathetic, 'but we've been through this already. I've given you more than enough chances. I know you've been through a shitty time at home, but that excuse is only going to get you so far.

It's wearing very thin.'

'I didn't realise those forms had been dealt with. Gill said she'd done the security checks and I thought they were okay to process because—'

Another sentence goes unfinished as she jumps down his throat. He's starting to think there's no point even trying to get her to see his side.

'Don't you dare try and pass the blame onto Gill. Christ, I don't know how you have the nerve to sit there and say that.'

'I'm not saying it's her fault, I'm just—'

'Bloody hell, Keith, a team member like Gill is worth ten of you. If you take account of all the re-work your mistakes have caused, you're working out at about a third of an effective person a day. You understand that? You were never particularly fast, but your rates-per-hour right now are pathetic. Most people get quicker the longer they're in a job. You're getting *slower*. This is no one's fault but yours. You need to start taking some responsibility here.'

And all Keith can think is *don't talk to me about responsibility. You're not the one who had to change his dad's trousers last night after he pissed himself. You're not the one who has to cook, wash, clean, shop and do everything else because his old man is so fucked up with booze and remorse that he can barely function.* He just thinks all this, of course, doesn't dare say it. He just listens instead and takes everything she throws at him. Again.

'I'd put you on a development plan,' Gloria continues, barely pausing for breath, 'but I think we're past that stage now. At the end of the day, your job boils down to simple data entry. It's a piece of piss. You copy what's on the paper onto your screen... how much easier could it be? You have to really try to screw things up as badly as you have.'

'I know. I'm sorry. I'll change, Gloria. It won't happen again.'

'That's what you said last time.'

'But I mean it.'

'You said that last time too. Look, I'm sorry it's had to come to this, Keith.'

'Please, Gloria... Like I said, I thought Gill had done the security checks and I assumed—'

'Stop trying to blame other people,' she screams at him. 'This was *your* fuck-up, no one else's. You're the problem here, but you're still trying to blame everyone else. Frigging incredible.'

'Please don't swear at me.'

'Don't swear at you?! Way I feel right now I'd hit you if I thought I could get away with it. You're infuriating, you know that? You're a miserable, scruffy, sour-faced little sod. And thanks to you Mike Parker thinks I can't manage my department because bloody Doreen Phelps went straight to him with a complaint instead of me. Have you got any idea how that makes me look?'

Keith genuinely feels terrible – honest he does – but what can he do? He'd apologise again, but that'd only make things worse.

Gloria's exasperated. She's closer now, staring straight at him. He's still looking down at the table, too nervous to look up because he thinks he knows what's coming next.

'We've reached the end of the road here, Keith,' she says, confirming his suspicions. 'Like I said, we're out of options. No more last chances.'

'I don't want to lose my job.'

'Then maybe you should have thought about that before today,' she shouts, immediately angry again. 'You should have done something the first time I put you on disciplinary, or the second, or the third. Instead you just sit there snivelling, feeling sorry for yourself, blaming other people when you screw up. You can work until the end of the month, then you're done here. And don't even bother trying to...'

Her voice trails off like she's lost her train of thought, and this time Keith looks straight at her because he knows something's not right. He looks around, figuring there's someone at the door or some other interruption, but there's nothing and no one else: just him, her, and these four grey walls.

Gloria swallows, and it hurts. Keith can see the pain etched on her face. She rubs at her throat like she's trying to dislodge something, then she coughs and tries to talk again. 'Sorry... I think I need to get...'

Gloria can't breathe. She's stunned. Frightened. Fucking terrified. For a few seconds there's an uncomfortable malaise: Gloria confused and in increasing pain, Keith just staring at her, helpless. But as the clock ticks, the inside of Gloria's throat starts to swell rapidly, soon blocking her airway. She's suffocating, and there's no immediately obvious reason why.

Her air runs out.

And then panic.

She slams herself back against the wall, legs almost giving way, face flushed and eyes bulging. And as she desperately tries to suck more oxygen in, involuntary muscle spasms force everything back out. She falls forward onto the table, showering everything with splashes of stringy spittle and blood. Keith recoils, shoving his chair back and almost falling himself, then heading for the corner of the room, trying to get as far from his dying manager as he possibly can. Because she *is* dying, he's already certain of that. He doesn't know what's happening or why, but he knows she doesn't have long and he doesn't know what to do.

She falls to the ground with a sickening thud, catching her jaw on the table on the way down, then thumping the back of her head hard against the wall. Keith edges closer. He looks under the table and he can see her body twitching; all arms and legs, a hopeless tangle of limbs. Crimson blood is dribbling from the corner of her mouth, spilling onto her cream blouse and pooling on the terracotta carpet. And then he sees that she's still watching him. She doesn't have any control over her body now – she can't move, can't talk, can't breathe – but her eyes are still following him, silently imploring him to do something to help her... *anything*.

It's almost a relief when her eyes roll up into her head and her eyelids flicker half-shut.

And for a few seconds longer, Keith's just standing there like an idiot, thinking pointless, stupid, unhelpful thoughts. *The last thing Gloria saw was me... the last thing she saw was me doing nothing to help.*

Numb with shock, it's almost half a minute later before Keith starts to consider the implications of what just happened.

They'll think I did this...

He dives for the door, not sure whether he's going to get someone to call an ambulance or just run like hell and try and get as far away from this place as he can before anyone finds Gloria. He hesitates. The meeting room is silent now, and the idea of staying shut away in here with his dead boss is somehow almost preferable to going out there and facing the music. He even considers hiding under the table with her. He'd try the window, but he's seven floors up.

Get help or run?

In the end it's academic. He does neither. Because when Keith eventually goes back through into the main office, what he finds there is even worse than the nightmare he's left behind. He struggles to process what he's seeing, because it's not just Gloria who's dead, it's all of them. He walks through the inexplicable chaos, looking from side to side, stepping over sprawled limbs and avoiding the gaze of frozen faces which seem to demand answers he can't give. There's no noise now, save for the low electrical hum of the office and the air conditioning whir. Even the phones have stopped ringing.

What the hell happened here? Is it going to happen to me?

He spins around with a start when he hears something, assuming death's about to creep up on him too. His pulse is racing, heart thumping like it's going to explode, but it's nothing: just a pile of those bloody 'Know Your Customer' forms which have overbalanced and slipped out of someone's tray and spilled onto the floor.

Keith's soon back at his own desk. In some ways knowing everyone else is dead makes him feel slightly better, because he can't be expected to try and help all of them, can he? It was different when it was just Gloria and him in the meeting room; all the responsibility was his. He doesn't feel so bad about leaving her now. He's still scared – no, not scared, absolutely fucking terrified – but a little better all the same.

He knows he can't stay here. Shelly's on the floor under the desk next-door, the phone grasped tight in her death-grip. He picks up his jacket off the back of his chair and logs out of his computer like it's the end of his shift or he's just off for lunch. He even signs out on the timesheet by the door. He doesn't know why he does it – it's just instinct, he reckons, force of habit. Just nerves.

After fetching his coat from the cloakroom on sixth, Keith waits on the landing for the lift. Mike Parker – his boss's boss – is dead in a doorway behind him. Keith's thinking *should I be panicking?* But he's not. Not yet. It must be shock. He's sure the panic will come in time. He just hopes he can get somewhere safe before he completely loses it. That's if there is anywhere safe anymore.

When the lift doors slide open, there's a woman Keith doesn't recognise stuck inside. Her face is pressed up against the mirrored wall, but there's no breath, no condensation... He imagines the power failing and being trapped in this small metal box with just a corpse for company, and he decides to take the stairs instead. The long descent gives him a few more precious seconds to try and get his head around what's happened here.

But whatever it is, it's happened everywhere.

The world outside the office has just stopped; frozen in an instant. Keith thinks it's like someone's clicked their fingers and made everyone fall asleep, like one of those freaky end-of-the-pier hypnotists, but on a massive scale.

The traffic is all over the place. It's like the drivers all took their hands off their wheels at the exact same time and just let their vehicles drive until they hit something and stopped. One car's gone right through the window of the pub opposite where Keith works, the place where his colleagues often go for lunchtime drinks. The car's bonnet is almost touching the bar like it's waiting to be served. Elsewhere, a bus has clipped the kerb and is leaning over to one side, resting against the wall of a building like it's had one too many. There's a car on its roof in the middle of the road, and a corresponding hole in the railings of the bridge overhead.

There are traces of life seeping away wherever Keith looks. Blood oozes from the cut neck of a man who's gone through the windscreen and died half-in and half-out of his car. The bonnet of the truck Keith's leaning against for support is still warm. A cash wagon outside a bank is stuck in reverse, engine still running. It emits a shrill alarm and an automated voice on a loop warns Keith (and only Keith now) that he should use *caution... this vehicle is reversing...*

Keith doesn't have the first idea what's happened here, and right now he has very little desire to find out. He just wants to get home.

There's a twenty-nine bus just short of the place where Keith usually catches it, but there's no point waiting today. It hasn't moved since everything stopped, and it's not going to be going anywhere soon. In a daze, barely even aware of what he's doing, Keith walks the few miles home. Everywhere he goes he sees corpses. Hundreds of them. Thousands. It's frightening to think how many of them there must be. He tries to imagine all the ones he can't see. He looks at houses, shops, schools and offices, and pictures them all full of dead people.

And in all this time, he never once stops to ask himself *what did this?* Or *why not me?* He thinks more about why he's avoiding these questions than about the questions themselves. It's because, he decides, it doesn't matter. What difference does it make?

His unease is increasing now he's on familiar turf. The closer he gets to home, the more nervous he becomes. He walks down Shenley Fields, past the dental surgery, and makes even more of a concerted effort to ignore the endless bodies lying around here because he thinks he might know them. Okay, so he might not actually know them, but he'll probably have seen them about. It's the same on Barnes Hill, and again when he finally reaches Ashton Grove. It's as quiet here now as it was just after six this morning when he got up, maybe even more so. That mangy cat's still about though, still hunting for scraps, appetite undiminished by Armageddon (because that, Keith decides, is what this is). It watches him from around the corner of next-door-but-one's fence. Keith doesn't much like cats – and they don't much like him – but he calls out to it just the same, because it would be nice to have some company. It gets spooked and runs the other way.

Gordon's dead.

It shouldn't surprise him, but it does.

Poor old Gordon – the gentle old chap who lived opposite – is lying in his porch in his pyjamas, blood everywhere. Keith makes himself look, because for a second he's not sure if the same thing happened to Gordon as everyone else, or if he's met some other kind of horrible fate. There's such a lot of blood down his front, crusted over his white stubble. He wonders if he should try and help him, but he knows there's no point. The same goes for the guy sitting dead in his car outside his house – Vijay, Keith thinks his name was. And the young mum with the kid who died coming out of the flats...

Keith thinks he hears something, then he calls for that bloody cat again, then he makes himself stop, because he knows these are just delaying tactics. He's just doing what he can to avoid going into the house.

The postman has died on Keith's doorstep. He's on his belly, undelivered letters clutched tight. Keith has to drag him out of the way slightly so he can get to his front door. Christ, he's heavy. Keith's had plenty of experience of moving dead weights like this, though.

Key in the lock, he pauses and takes a deep breath. He looks around once more – just to convince himself that what he thinks has happened really has happened – then goes indoors. He shuts the door and leans up against it, his eyes adjusting to the dark inside.

'Dad? Dad... are you here?'

It's a stupid question, because Dad's always here.

Keith takes two steps further down the hall, then stops. He can see his dad now, and he immediately feels an unexpected sense of relief. He'd got it into his head that he'd find him stuck somewhere – in front of the TV, probably, or in the toilet – but Dad's exactly where he left him this morning, slumped over the kitchen table.

Problem is, that was several hours ago.

Keith walks into the kitchen, then shakes Dad's shoulder. Is he dead or drunk? It's hard to tell. Dad looks the same... smells the same. The booze-stink masks everything.

'Dad?'

Keith remembers the time just after they lost Mum; that time Dad drank all kinds of shit and had to have his stomach pumped. He was like this back then: cold to the touch, breathing so shallow it could hardly be heard. But Keith knows in his heart that this is different. After everything he's already seen today, how could it not be?

And even after everything he's been through with Dad these last few years, after everything that happened and all the damage he did, all that hurt... Keith still holds his father tight and sobs when he finally accepts that he's gone.

Keith's head is all over the place. He thinks he's crying for himself more than for Dad.

The littlest things frighten Keith most of all today. He didn't even realise the TV had been left on until hours later. It wasn't until he'd been upstairs and changed and was walking past the living room door that he noticed it.

The BBC news channel is like a reflection of the dead world he walked through to get home this morning: a rectangular, screen-sized microcosm. Like everything else, it all looks much the same as it used to, but indelibly wrong... changed forever. There's the reassuringly familiar desk and studio set being shot from the usual angle, the morning's headlines continuing to scroll and the clock in the bottom corner of the screen still keeping perfect time, but the newsreader is dead. All he can see is the top of her perfectly coiffured head and one hand which she must have stretched out over the edge of the desk when it – whatever *it* was – caught up with her and ended her life along with everyone else's. Everyone else except Keith.

The longer he's stuck here at home, the more he thinks about the situation and the less sense it makes. *Why me?* There's no rhyme or reason, and he knows there's no point looking for answers either because he won't get far when there's no one left to ask. Christ, he's asked enough impossible questions over the years and got nothing back but abuse, why should it be any different today?

Keith's social circle has never been particularly wide, and these last few years he's felt the circumference steadily reducing to little more than a full stop. That feels strangely appropriate today. There's just him left. Period. Still, he does what he can to make contact with the rest of the world (because surely there must be a rest of the world out there somewhere?). He calls all the numbers in the old family phone book, even some of Mum's friends he hasn't heard from in years, but doesn't get through to anyone. He tries all the contacts in his mobile (his brick, Shelly from work used to call it. *Remember Shelly...?*), but doesn't get to speak to anyone. He almost leaves a message after the tone a couple of times, but there doesn't seem to be much point. He knows no one will reply.

Things aren't getting any better.

Things aren't actually getting any worse, to be fair, but without anyone to talk to or look after, Keith's nervousness is increasing by the hour. More than anything he wishes he could do something about Dad, because he keeps seeing him sitting there at the table in his usual pose and it's freaking him out. But he struggled enough with his booze-addled old man when he was alive, so tonight he doesn't think he has any chance moving him.

And it is tonight now.

It's getting dark out.

Despite the fact that barely anything has happened for hours (not since *everything* happened first thing), the time has evaporated quickly. Keith's relieved the power's still working so he can keep the lights on (it's usually gone off by now in the few horror movies he's seen). He eventually plucks up enough courage to drape a blanket over Dad, then goes upstairs and shuts himself in his room.

It was hard enough sleeping before all of this, but tonight it's impossible. Keith lies on his bed, fiddling with an old transistor radio he's had since he was a kid, listening for voices. He gets the occasional burst of static noise, but not a lot else. Well, what did he expect? If anyone else has survived this, would they really be spending their time broadcasting into the ether in the vain hope someone's listening? He doesn't think so. He thinks they'll be out gathering supplies and banding together with other survivors like they do in the films. Either that or they'll be hiding in their bedrooms like he is, too scared to do anything else.

Maybe I'll try again in the morning...

He gets up and goes to the window, teasing open the curtains just enough so he can see out. All the other houses are dark, no lights on inside. The street lamps are working, though. He almost wishes they weren't, because the only thing they illuminate are the bodies.

DAY TWO

Keith wakes up with a start, lying on top of his bed, fully dressed but freezing cold. He checks his alarm clock and sits up quickly, thinking about work and how he can't afford to be late again after the grief Gloria gave him yesterday.

Then he remembers everything else.

He perches on the edge of his mattress, wondering if he should look outside or just lie down again and try and get back to sleep. If he stays here in his room he can pretend none of it happened, can't he?

And then the decision's taken out of his hands, because he hears something moving downstairs. No hesitation now, he runs to the landing and peers down. It's Dad. Bloody hell, it's Dad! He's in the hall. Keith can't believe what he's seeing. He watches Dad get all the way to the front door, then he seems to change his mind and turn around, heading back towards the kitchen again, probably looking for his booze or fags or, most likely, Keith.

Keith runs down to see him. They've had their differences, sure, and there have been times Keith's wanted to smother him with a pillow in his sleep, but this isn't one of them. Right now he's just relieved that Dad's okay and he's no longer alone.

Dad's in the kitchen now. It's definitely beer he's after. He catches his hip on the corner of the table – no doubt still half-pissed from yesterday – then walks to the sink and stops, unable to go any further. The blinds are closed and it's dawn-dark in here. 'Dad? Dad... you okay?' Keith asks.

For the longest time (just a few seconds, but it feels like forever) Dad doesn't respond. Then he slowly turns around, struggling in the enclosed space, clumsily pirouetting on leaden feet. This lack of grace is nothing unusual. Keith knows he just needs a nicotine or alcohol pick-me-up.

Keith flicks on the light to dispel the gloom, and now he's the one who freezes.

Dad's still dead.

It makes absolutely no sense, and it all sounds ridiculous, but he knows he's right. The old man's face is a death-mask. Expressionless. His chin and chest are stained scarlet with traces of yesterday's dried-out spittle and blood.

Keith panics, and Dad reacts. He seems to come alive when he clocks Keith watching. He throws himself straight at his son.

The kitchen table comes to his rescue. Dad collides with it again, and it gives Keith a couple of seconds' grace. Numb with shock, he slams the kitchen door in his father's face, then feels his father's face slam into the kitchen door.

Keith staggers back down the hallway, the house filling with dead Dad's noise as he tries to escape his kitchen prison. Not knowing what else to do, Keith runs back upstairs to his room and shuts the door and blocks it with a chest-of-drawers, hoping the ancient 'KEEP OUT OR ELSE' sign outside does the trick and keeps his old man at bay.

When he opens the curtains to let in more light, what he sees outside is terrifying. Dad's not the only one who's on his feet again. They all are (apart from George across the way who can't seem to get up and the postman who's still on his belly). The rest of them, though, are all mobile. Those same people who spent almost the entire last twenty-four hours lying on the ground – those *dead* people – are up and about again. And to make matters worse, one of them has seen him. A tattoo-covered corpse who worked in security and lived further down Ashton Grove just happens to look up at the exact wrong moment and makes dead-eye contact with Keith at the window. The man immediately changes course: staggering back towards the house now instead of staggering down the road. And others start to follow.

What the hell is going on?

The death of everyone yesterday was hard enough to handle, but what's happening now is just impossible.

Keith pulls the curtains shut and sits under his desk, covering his head with his hands as the dead begin to hammer on the door downstairs.

He's out.

Shit.

Keith knows from the way the noise in the house changed just now, that Dad's managed to get out of the kitchen. It's taken a while, but there's no question he's on the loose now. Maybe he just dropped his hand on the handle by chance, or maybe he opened the door intentionally... however it happened, he's roaming free downstairs. And the more noise Dad makes, the more the other dead folks outside seem to react. Keith creeps back to the window and teases the curtain open slightly. Bloody hell, there's a crowd of them out there now. There must be more than twenty.

What do I do?

The simple answer – the easy answer – would be to stay here in his room, but that's not going to help him in the long run. And soon the decision seems about to be taken out of his hands, because he can hear Dad getting closer. He's heard him crawl upstairs in a drunken stupor enough times to recognise the sounds of hands and knees on the staircase; the slips and thumps and groans when he loses his balance.

Can't stay here.

Keith feels like he's on the top floor of a burning building, the fire climbing fast, the first flames already licking at his feet. He bursts out through his bedroom door and runs straight into Dad who's coming the other way, almost at the top of the steps. More through luck than judgement, they collide at speed and Keith manages to send his old man spiralling back down. He watches him fall over and over, eventually clonking his head on the floor at the bottom, and for a second all the fear disappears and he's left feeling concerned.

I just pushed my Dad down the stairs...

Shit. He's going to be in so much trouble.

But that's the least of his concerns, because the noise and commotion seems to have had two serious side-effects. First, Dad's getting back up, and he looks angrier than ever. Second, the crowd on the front step is getting riled. Dead hands thump against the door, desperate to get inside.

Noise makes noise makes even more noise.

It's a vicious circle: the more of a din the dead make, the more noise Dad makes, and *vice versa*.

Keith knows he has to move. He runs down and jumps over Dad's outstretched legs, but trips over one of his feet and hits the deck hard. He's winded, and before he can get up and get moving again, Dad grabs hold of him. Keith scrambles to his feet, dragging Dad up with him. Dad's weight shifts unexpectedly and the two of them collide, glancing heads. Keith shoves him away, and though Dad's brain still clearly retains a modicum of control, it's like he's operating on a two second delay, everything working slower than it should. Keith takes advantage of the delay to push him away again.

But he's pushing him deeper into the house, and he needs to send him the other way.

Keith grabs his dad's shoulders once more, then spins him around through one hundred and eighty degrees. He reaches past his father and snatches at the door handle, pulling the front door wide open.

Fuck. Really bad move.

Although all operating on a similar dull delay to Dad, a crowd of bodies stand poised to flood into the house. Keith has no time to think, he just runs straight at Dad and shoulder charges him out, managing to shift most of the dead out of the way at the same time, and just managing to let go and grab hold of the doorframe at the last moment, stopping himself from falling out onto the street with the mass of corpses.

Keith reaches out for the handle and pulls it shut, but the door won't close properly. He tries again, the seconds ticking and the bodies approaching, but it's no good – there's something in the way. He looks down and sees the postman's outstretched hand in the door jamb, fingers mangled and broken but still moving. What does he do? He helplessly tries to pull the door shut a couple more times, feeling the bones of the postie's hand crunching and breaking every time he does it, but he knows this isn't going to work.

The other bodies are *really* close now. There's an old woman in a blood-stained nightie who's so close he can smell her. Keith screws up his eyes then bends down and lifts the postman's sleeve to swing what's left of his deformed hand out of the way, but it's too little, too late.

The dead woman crashes into the house, her unsteady progress accelerated by the impact of several more dead things which collide with her from behind. And then there's Dad. Whether he knows what he's doing or not is debatable and irrelevant – like it or not, he's coming home. More precisely, he's coming for Keith, and Keith knows it. He backs away down the hallway, desperate to keep some distance between him and *them*. He glances at the staircase but immediately dismisses that idea because he knows if he goes back up there, he won't be coming down again. The ground floor of the house is rapidly filling and he knows if he goes up, so will they. It's the same with the lounge: one way in, no obvious way out.

There are so many of them now that they're fighting to get inside, literally pushing each other out of the way to get to him. But the woman in the nightie is at the very front of the queue. She raises her arms in a classic undead pose and he catches her hands and tries to push her back the other way. She glares at him with cold, milky eyes and opens her mouth wide, brown drool trickling down her chin, dripping all over her already stained nightwear.

Keith knows he has to go if he wants to stay alive. And he also knows there's every chance if he leaves here now, he won't be coming back. Of all the horrific things that have happened over the last twenty-four hours, leaving home hurts most of all. He's never lived anywhere but here. Some would say he's never lived.

He forces the dead woman back the other way, recoiling from the feel of her cold, pudgy, putty-like flesh, then slips the clutches of another dead pensioner and runs into the kitchen. He shuts the door and drags the table across to try and block it, then pauses. *Am I sure about this?* When the weight of dead flesh in the hall manages to force the door open slightly, shunting the table back across the kitchen floor, Keith knows he has no choice. He lets himself out through the back door.

It's pissing down with rain. He runs down the garden, his trousers and trainers soaked from the overgrown wet grass. One last look back at the house, one final chance to remember, then he's gone.

He slips out through the back gate and creeps along the alley-way to the main road. Then he stops again. *Shit.* There are more of them here. Not crowds of hundreds or anything like that, but more than enough all the same. He watches them. They obviously don't yet know he's here. They're milling around like slow-moving, fidgeting kids who can't keep still. He tries to plot a route through them, because he can't stay here all day, can he? But on the other hand, what else is he going to do? Where can he go? It's only now that the full enormity of what happened here is starting to sink in. How widespread is this 'problem'? He wonders if he might be able to find someone in charge... some authorities or military-types to take him somewhere safe along with all the other survivors (because there must be other survivors, right?). The fact he's heard nothing and seen no one doesn't give him much hope.

For the second time in less than twenty-four hours, his world has been completely turned on its head. He stands there, getting soaked by the freezing rain, trying and failing to make sense of everything. *So let's get this straight*, he says to himself, *everyone died yesterday, now they're still dead but walking around, and I've just lost my house and everything in it.* Things are going from bad to worse. Keith sighs with resignation and leans back against the fence, and part of it that's been recently patched up gives way. He shifts with a start, figuring the whole fence is about to go over, and his sudden panicked noise and movement is enough to alert all of the dead in the immediate vicinity to his position. They definitely know he's here now.

For a half-second he remains completely still, wondering if inactivity will be enough to fool them into thinking they were wrong, but it's clear it won't. They're already homing in on him from all directions: twenty-odd random trajectories all converging on him. He looks the other way and sees more of them coming along the alleyway towards him from behind the houses near his, and Keith knows all he can do now is run.

And he runs and runs, too afraid to stop.

He knows his way around this area well – it's the only place he's ever lived – but good local knowledge doesn't make a whole lot of difference this morning, because the panic and the fear and the persistent heavy rain combine to leave him virtually blind. He's not planning on trying to get to anywhere specific right now, he's just trying to get away from *them*. Trouble is, they're everywhere. All of the bodies he walked past yesterday are mobile again, and every last one of them, without fail, turns and lumbers towards him when he gets anywhere close. It doesn't matter where he goes or how fast he runs... he knows there will be more of them waiting for him wherever he ends up.

Past the end of the road his junior school was on (*can't go there*) then along the road where Craig, his mate from Cubs used to live. Past the house where Mum's friend Margaret lived (*wait, was that dead Margaret at the window?*) and now Keith's going round in circles. A series of right-hand turns and he's heading back towards home again, and as much as he'd love to go back there, he knows he can't.

The smell of death out here is getting worse, the rain amplifying the stink. He's taking in deep breaths, and he doesn't know how much longer he can keep this up. He hasn't had to run like this for a long time. He's already tired and he has a killer stitch. He's going to have to stop soon.

But he can't.

They won't let him.

As long as he keeps moving, he'll just about be okay. He's not particularly fast, it's just that they're particularly slow. They don't seem to see him until it's almost too late and he's virtually on top of them, but as soon as they realise he's there, they attack. They swing their fists, swiping at the air with clumsy hands, then stumble after him in slow-motion pursuit.

He can't be completely alone, can he? He glances up at some of the places he runs past, hoping he'll see someone else, someone who'll shout down to him and help. There are plenty of faces at the windows, but they're all dead, all trying to get out.

The shops.

It comes to him in an instant. *Why didn't I think of it before?* It's the sensible place to go – if there are any other survivors, surely they'll head there too? Just a little further now...

He takes a corner at speed – reinvigorated momentarily – and runs headfirst into a bunch of them lumbering in the opposite direction. He's on his back in a puddle in the gutter before he knows what's happening, and they're on top of him before he can do anything about it. But they're so lethargic and useless that they can't co-ordinate themselves well enough to attack. They simply pile on, one after the other, like they're playing some stupid playground game. And the weight and the bulk of those falling on top prevents those closest to him at the bottom of the heap from doing any real damage. With a little kicking and squirming, Keith's able to wriggle free and crawl out from under the scrum, sick with the stench of the dead things, leaving them all behind. The effort is almost impossible to sustain now but he keeps moving because he doesn't have any choice.

Another sharp corner. This time he stops and checks. He has a few seconds of breathing space – just a few, but it's just enough. He peers around the end of the wall and sees clear passage to the supermarket he knows well. It's where he gets his dinners and Dad's booze. The building and the precinct in front of it are an ugly slice of abrasive, angular 1970's concrete design, but right now it looks like the most beautiful place on Earth. One last push, one final burst, and he'll be inside. He pushes away from the wall and runs, aware of shapes closing in on him from all angles, then smacks into the automatic sliding glass doors. Not so automatic this morning. Not sliding, either.

Keith looks back and sees hordes of the dead advancing towards him. No surprise. Half of him thinks *I should just give up and let them have me.* The other half thinks *shit, I'm too scared to die...* He digs the tips of his fingers into the metal groove between the two halves of the non-automatic doors, hoping to prise them apart. He doesn't want to look, but he can see the mirror images of the rapidly approaching bodies in the glass. Four or five of them at least, their reflections looming large. He knows there will undoubtedly be more if this takes much longer.

With a hard shove and a grunt of effort, he manages to force his fingers between the doors. Another shove, and the two halves judder then separate by a couple of inches, just enough for him to get his right arm through. And once his arm and one shoulder's in, he uses the bulk of his body to open the doors enough so he can slip through.

And he's inside.

The doors are on some kind of resistive mechanism, because the moment he's made it to the other side, they slide shut again like a snapping monster's maw, but not before one of the dead is almost able to follow. The corpse of a lanky, long haired guy who looks a little younger than Keith is trapped now: head, shoulder and one arm inside, everything else left out in the rain. Thankfully, it doesn't have the strength to do anything about its predicament. It constantly stretches and strains to reach Keith, but he's standing just out of range and there's nothing it can do. Still panting hard with the effort of the run and the terror of the moment, Keith slides down the wall and sits there on the floor looking up at the dead kid, motionless. He has a grandstand view now as more of the creatures begin to crash into the glass, still trying to get to him as if they're unaware there's anything to stop them. In the space of a couple of minutes there are so many of them that almost all the visible light has been blocked out. It's like someone's drawn the curtains.

It's all too easy to slip back into routine in a place like this. Keith casually pushes a trolley around the supermarket like he does a couple of times most weeks, looking for all the things he usually buys.

The power's down here. He doesn't know if it's just this store that's affected or if it's more widespread. That explains the problems he had getting inside, he thinks. It's strange being in here without the lights on. Alien. It doesn't look right. It's usually so bright and unforgiving – banners advertising this deal and that deal, buy one get one free, lowest prices guaranteed... that kind of thing. It doesn't matter, because everything's free today, he realises as he fills the trolley with cans of food, bottles of drink and other stuff. He doesn't know what he's going to do with it all, mind. He has nowhere to take his shopping. Maybe he'll just stay here for a while longer and build himself a nest.

Oh, but it's great to be distracted.

He's had so much to think about since yesterday, so much crap spinning around inside his head, that to switch off like this momentarily is bliss. He's no closer to understanding any of what's happened, no closer to knowing what's going to happen next, but right now none of that's as important as clearing his mind and finding some guilt-free and pressure-free headspace.

As long as he focuses on the interior of the store and doesn't look outside, he's okay. He's not felt like eating much since yesterday, but he's suddenly aware that his stomach's growling angrily. He takes a bag of his favourite crisps from a shelf and shovels the contents into his mouth, then eats another, washing the snacks down with a bottle of Coke. Then chocolate... then cakes. Honestly, there's so much stuff in here he'd happily eat. Okay, so a lot of it will go off soon, but there's plenty that'll stay good for a while longer yet. At the back of his mind are a few dark thoughts (*Will I have to pay for all this? What happens when all the supermarket shelves are clear?*) but he manages to keep them at bay with more food.

Christ, having this much personal space is a novelty. It's been a long time. He stops near a wall display of paperback books. Keith's always loved reading, he's just never had the time. *Maybe that'll change now, now that Dad...* No matter what he thought of his old man, he can't yet bring himself to reach that sentence's inevitable end. *Can't believe he's gone...* Has he gone? Another thought strikes Keith now, and he wonders whether this is just a shock-induced sugar-rush. He finds himself wondering if what happened to the rest of the world really has happened, or if it's just him? Is he the only one who's changed? It all seems so preposterous, so far-fetched... *I mean, zombies for fuck's sake. Zombies!* He feels stupid just thinking the word.

Most of the books he's looking at are easy-reading, mass-market titles which sell by the bucket-load. This stuff has never really appealed, but there's a first time for everything, isn't there? He avoids the thrillers and the crime novels and picks up a slice of cliché-filled chic-lit instead, more because of the nice-looking girl on the cover than for any other reason. He flicks through the pages and stops at a sex scene, eyes wide. Bloody hell, he had no idea they wrote books like this... it's pretty much just text-based porn! Then he turns his attention to a fashion magazine and ogles the scantily-clad Photo-shopped models adorning the glossy pages. This feels so wrong, inappropriate even given what's happened to the rest of the world, but in the absence of everybody else but him, who cares?

The dead checkout girl comes at him from out of nowhere.

She knocks him flying. Smashes him against the side of a rapidly defrosting freezer then grabs hold of him with her cold, dead hands and drags him down. He's on his back in a puddle of water with her on top, seeping blood and gunk all over him. She forces a fist full of icy fingers into his mouth, like she's trying to pull explanations out from his innards. He's gagging on the taste of her rotting flesh. He can't breathe, can barely move... he tries to fight but all he can see is her. The familiar green and white of her uniform is stained with discharge.

He thinks *this is it, I'm dead,* and he struggles to get a grip of the reanimated corpse now on top of him, but the frigging thing won't keep still...

I'm fucked. I blew it. I'm history...

And then she's gone.

She's lying alongside him now, on her back but still thrashing wildly. He ducks for cover, rolling away to one side as someone swings an aluminium baseball bat through the air and splits the dead girl's face in two.

Keith's too scared to look up. Curled into a foetal position on the wet floor, gasping for breath and stinking of death, figuring he's next. He pictures the killer, but everything he imagines is wrong. He thinks he's going to be facing some huge, muscle-bound mother-fucker – all attitude and swagger – but he's not. He hears the baseball bat clatter as it's dropped to the ground and dares to look.

Standing over him is a young girl. She's short and pretty, wearing the latest gear, hair all tied up nice, wearing loads of makeup and chewing gum at speed. But all of this is irrelevant, because all Keith can focus on is the pistol she's pointing into his face. The end of it is wavering, probably because of the weight, not because she's nervous. She looks cool as anything. 'Don't move a fucking muscle,' she says. He won't.

'I'm not dead.'

'Prove it.'

'I'm talking to you, aren't I?'

She thinks it through... he has a point. She waves the barrel of the gun like she's seen them do in the movies, gesturing for him to get up. He starts to move but slips in the blood and water. When he looks down he sees he's put his hand in a puddle of something that's spilling from a crack in the dead checkout girl's face. Between the gore and the smell and the defrosting food and the nerves, he can't take it. He drags himself up onto his feet then leans over and empties the freshly filled contents of his stomach into one of the freezers, adding to the foetid stink.

'Nice,' she says, watching as he wipes stringy spit and vomit from his mouth with the back of his sleeve. 'Guess that proves it.' She looks him up and down disparagingly. 'What's your name?'

'Keith.'

'I'm Anna.'

'Do you know—?'

'What's happened? No. You?'

He just shakes his head. There's an awkward few moments of silence, then she starts to walk away. 'Wait.'

'What?'

'Where you going?'

'Home,' she says, like that's the dumbest question she's ever been asked. She keeps walking.

140

'Wait,' he says again, and she reluctantly does. 'You're the first person I've seen. Don't you think we should stick together?'

Annoyed, Anna gestures for him to follow her, and he does. She takes him back to the front of the store where the dead hordes are still packed tight against the glass. 'You did that,' she says. 'Fucking amateur.'

'I know, I'm sorry... I didn't mean to. They were chasing me and—'

'I can't afford to take chances. Can't afford to get stuck with someone who can't look after themselves.'

'It won't happen again...'

'Not until next time.'

She walks back into the supermarket, aware he's still following. She can understand why he'd want to stick with her, but she's struggling to think of any good reasons why she should stick with him. She leaves him standing over another body that's had its head caved in with the baseball bat.

'I really think we should stay together,' he shouts after her. 'It makes sense. Safety in numbers and all that.'

'I've got a gun and a baseball bat,' she tells him. 'Can't see how havin' you hanging around's gonna make me any safer.'

'I can cook,' he says, clutching at straws. 'I've bagged up loads of stuff back there. You keep us safe, I'll keep us fed.'

She thinks about it. It's a decent offer. She's been too busy trying to stay alive to think about food. Keith edges closer, not wanting to let go of the one fellow survivor he's so far found. He thinks he needs to stick with this girl. He thinks she can handle herself.

'Suppose it's worth a try,' she says, and the relief on his face is visible. 'You do what I say though, right?'

'Right.'

'I don't reckon you'd last long on your own anyway.'

They slip out of the back of the supermarket. Anna leads, Keith follows, overloaded with stolen shopping packed into those heavy duty 'bag for life' carrier bags they have at the tills. She thinks that's really funny in the circumstances, but Keith doesn't appreciate the joke. He steps out but she gestures for him to wait. 'Too many of 'em.' They press themselves back against the wall. As long as they stay still, they're ignored.

The handle snaps on one of the bags Keith's carrying, sending tins of food rolling everywhere. The noise isn't bad, but with the rest of the world so quiet, it sounds as loud as thunder. He instinctively starts trying to pick everything up, making even more noise, but she pulls him back.

'They can hear us,' she whispers. 'Ain't you worked it out yet?'

Keith's so scared he can hardly breathe. He's happy to do whatever this girl tells him because he's fucking terrified and she clearly knows what she's doing. He thinks she must know far more about what happened than he does because she clearly gets it: she knows what to do, what to say, how to act... she called him a fucking amateur a few minutes ago, and he thinks she was right.

The crowds are thinning out again.

'You ready?'

He tries to answer but can't. He just nods.

'Follow me then,' she says.

And he does, because right now, not following her would proba-bly be the stupidest thing he could do. She moves like a pro – sprint-ing across empty spaces when gaps appear in the lifeless multitudes, ducking down and weaving between bodies which are moving in different directions, holding back when too many of them get too close... He's already breathless and soaked with sweat but she still looks perfect: cool as fuck with the pistol held ready at her side.

'Where'd you get the gun?' he asks when they stop again and crouch down behind a wall of wheelie bins full of garden waste.

'Found it.'

'Where? You don't just find something like that.'

'Dead policeman.'

'You're kidding me.'

'Do I look like I'm kidding?'

'Didn't think police carried guns around here.'

'Well this one did.'

'You know how to use it?'

'It's a gun. You pull the trigger. Jeez.'

'Got any bullets.'

'Got plenty. Now shut up.'

'Sorry.'

'Remember, move slow like them. They don't see you as good if you move like them.'

'Okay.'

They creep along the front of a row of houses together. Keith knows this area well. Home's not far, but he keeps having to remind himself that home's not home anymore. He used to walk this way back from work sometimes. Funny how it looks like it used to, but feels completely different. He feels nervous, like he shouldn't be here, like he's trespassing.

Anna starts down an alleyway but he's not sure. 'Wait.'

'What's the problem?'

'There's nothing much down there. This just goes to the park.'

'I know.'

He follows her again, and the unexpected isolation they find within the alley is welcome: tall fences on either side form a shield and the curve of the pathway means that, for a while at least, they can't see the beginning or the end of the passage. Keith decides he'd be happy to just stay here, but Anna's got other ideas. When they reach the end she looks up and down the street then runs out into the open. It's a twenty-or-so metre dash to the park gates, and Keith's left with no option but to run after her. There are even more bodies here, all converging in the way they inevitably do now, but Keith and Anna have relative strength and speed on their side. Anna reaches the wide, grey metal park gates and slides the bolt across. Then she waits.

'What are you doing?' Keith asks, nervous. He's standing right behind her, arms aching, still overloaded with looted supplies. He looks back over his shoulder and sees the nearest of the dead things are just a few metres away. And the gap's closing.

Anna's toying with him now, enjoying herself. She keeps him waiting a few seconds longer – just that little bit too long – then opens the gate and pushes him through the gap.

They're so close Keith swears he can feel the tips of dead fingers brush down his back. He goes further into the park then stops when he realises Anna hasn't yet followed. He puts down his many bags and turns back to look for her. The gate's closed again now, and she's standing on the right side of the barrier, just out of reach of the dead.

They clatter repeatedly against the metal, a forest of arms reaching through the many gaps for her. She soaks it all up, like she's getting some kind of perverse pleasure from the adulation of the crowd.

Keith hasn't been to this place for years, even though it's less than a mile from home. He used to come here all the time with his mates after school. They'd spend virtually the whole of the summer holidays here, building dens amongst the trees and kicking their way through the meandering stream which cuts the park in two. He reckons the park is about a mile wide, its perimeter probably about three miles. There's a long straight path which runs down into its heart, and not a lot else. In all this time it's hardly changed...

Anna brushes past and picks up a couple of bags, leaving Keith with the bulk of them to carry. He picks everything up, struggling with the weight and the awkward bulk of it all, then runs to catch up. 'Why here?'

'Why not?'

'I could give you a hundred reasons. There's nothing here for starters.'

She stops again and just looks at him. 'Ain't that the best reason of all?'

But Keith's wrong. The park isn't completely empty. Christ, he probably walked this way a thousand times before and never noticed. Right at the very heart of the place, at the central point where all the footpaths converge, is a house. A tiny little bungalow, easily accessible, yet hidden from prying eyes by thoughtfully planted trees. He assumes it's where the park-keeper (back when they used to have park-keepers) used to live. There can't have been anyone staying here for years...

Anna opens the door and goes inside. 'What d'you reckon?' she says proudly.

Keith's not sure. He stands in the doorway and looks around, his eyes adjusting to the dark. The place is so small he can pretty much take a full guided tour just standing in one spot. One large room, it looks like it was last decorated about thirty years ago and it smells damp. There are black marks on the walls, wallpaper curled and peeling. The council must have been using it for storage since the last parkie moved out, because there are tools and chemicals and all kinds of other stuff stockpiled in the little galley kitchen. Keith dumps the bags of food in the only space he can find.

Anna's clearly made herself at home here. There's a space she's claimed as her own directly under one of the windows in the living area. There's a sleeping bag and a pillow on the floor, and some rubbish lying scattered around. Junk food wrappers, a few empty drinks cans, couple of magazines... She sits on her bed and leans back against the wall and looks at him. He's still standing in the doorway like a spare part, dripping with rain. He doesn't know what to do with himself.

'Don't say a lot, do ya?'

He tries to talk but he can't. It's too much. Now that they've finally stopped running and panicking, now that there aren't any dead bodies immediately hounding them, the inexplicable reality and sheer helplessness of his situation is beginning to bite hard. His lip starts to quiver and the more he tries to hold his emotions in, the harder it gets. He's standing there in front of her now, a grown man, crying like a little kid. She shakes her head and opens a can of cider.

'I don't...' Keith starts to say. 'I don't know...'

But the rest of his words remain unspoken.

Anna, looking embarrassed, remembers the stash of food they brought back from the supermarket. She starts mooching through the nearest bag. 'I'm frigging starving, I am,' she says. 'I'd kill for a KFC.'

'Dad's dead... What am I gonna do?' he asks. She just looks at him, then tears open a packet of biscuits with her teeth.

'They're all dead. Cryin' ain't gonna bring any of 'em back.'

Despite everything, by late-afternoon things are starting to feel almost normal – as normal as they can be after an inexplicable cataclysmic event; as normal as they can be when you find yourself sharing an abandoned house in a municipal park with a total stranger. Keith mumbles something about trying to get a fire started, and he goes out to fetch wood.

The rain's finally stopped. Keith finds a wheelbarrow around the side of the bungalow and he pushes it towards the trees. The ground is boggy and soft, and it frequently gets stuck. Once there he starts picking up fallen sticks and branches, much of it too wet to burn. Anna turns up a few minutes later. She drops a log into the wheelbarrow, and the sudden noise makes Keith's heart skip a beat. He didn't know she was there. 'Bloody hell. What are you doing?'

'Calm down,' she tells him. 'Fuck's sake.'

'Don't creep up on me like that then.'

'I wasn't creeping up. It's you what wasn't listening. I said you was a fucking amateur.'

Keith takes Anna's log out of the barrow and throws it back into the undergrowth. 'Too big,' he explains. 'And it's wet. It'll never burn.'

'What, you a Scout or somethin'?'

'Used to be.'

She sniggers, and he ignores her.

It doesn't take long to fill the barrow between them, though the work ratio is about seventy per cent in Keith's favour. 'We need to get this stuff dry,' he tells her. 'And we should sort it too. Different thicknesses.'

Anna's not listening. She's leaning against a tree, watching him. 'So where was you?'

'What?'

'When it happened? When they all started dying... where was you?'

'At work,' he tells her, and for a moment he allows himself to dwell on a succession of horrific memories he's consciously blocked out until now. Gloria, all the people he used to work with, the neighbours, Dad... Fortunately she's making enough noise and talking enough crap to distract him again.

'I slept through it,' she says. 'Bad, eh? I'd been out drinkin'. Can't remember what time I stopped, but when I woke up everyone was dead.'

'You slept through the end of the world?'

She laughs. 'I know. It's mad, innit!'

'It's all mad.'

He starts pushing the barrow back towards the bungalow, grunting when the wheel sticks in the mud again.

'Anyway,' Anna says, 'who said anythin' about the end of the world? I'm still here, you're still here... how can it be the end of the world if us two are still alive?'

She has a point, of sorts. He doesn't want to labour it, but she clearly does.

'You can't tell me you never dreamed of somethin' like this? About having the whole world to yourself...?'

'Maybe, but we haven't got the whole world to ourselves, have we?' He gestures up towards the park gate at the top of the hill. Even now, several hours later, there's still a sizeable crowd of bodies gathered there.

Anna opens the bungalow door and Keith tries to get the wheel-barrow inside. It's tight. It should just about fit through if he gets it square-on, but he's having trouble bumping the wheel up the step. He reverses a little and tries again, but doesn't hit it quite right and smacks the door-frame. He has another go, but still can't do it.

'Come on,' Anna says, cold and bored and tired of waiting. 'Get a bloody move on.'

He has another attempt and almost gets the barrow inside. He glances back over his shoulder when Anna starts moaning again and he panics. There's a body. It's close. Where the hell did it come from? Anna can tell from his face that there's something wrong, but by the time she turns around to look, the dead man is already upon her. He tries to grab her shoulders but does little more than shove her forwards instead and she smashes face-first into the outside wall of the bungalow. She manages to turn around and locks her arms to stop the creature getting any closer. Heavy and aggressive the corpse might be, but the dead aren't particularly strong and she easily holds him back. The dead man squirms and shifts constantly, and as his head swings from side to side, she sees Keith waiting behind, watching anxiously.

'Do somethin', you fucking idiot!' she yells at him.

But he can't.

He's paralyzed with fear again, not knowing how to react, not sure if he can. He goes to grab the dead man, then bottles it at the last second. He can't bring himself to make contact with his dead flesh. It turns his stomach... unnaturally coloured and cold, broken veins and bruises, swellings where the lack of circulation has allowed blood to pool rather than pump...

Anna's getting tired. The dead man isn't. She catches Keith's eye again. 'FUCKING DO SOMETHIN', YOU PRICK!'

Deep breath. He puts a hand on each of the dead man's shoulders and pulls him back. His rotting brain can't keep up with his legs and they buckle beneath him. He's lying in an overgrown flowerbed now, still trying to fight, still looking for Anna, and she's fucking furious. She doesn't stop to think, she just stamps on his upturned face again and again. Keith gags at the sound of crunching bone, and then again at the sight of black blood and mucus and Christ knows what else. Anna's still stamping, but enough damage has already been done. The dead man is dead again.

Panting with anger and effort, she turns her frustrations on Keith.

'I'm sorry...' he mumbles. 'I didn't know what to do. I just—'

'How hard can it be? They're already dead, you fucking idiot.' She pushes him out of the way and goes inside, stopping long enough to hurl a couple more insults in his direction. 'You're absolutely fucking useless. How did I end up gettin' stuck with a loser like you?'

It's dark now. Late. They're not sure how late, but it doesn't matter. It's only been a day and a half since the end of the world, but their old routines are already redundant. *It didn't take long,* Keith thinks, and he remembers all the years he was a slave to his watch.

He's managed to find enough dry wood to build a fire in the hearth. Anna wouldn't let him use any of her magazines to get it started, so he had to use the chic-lit paperback he picked up at the supermarket. It's a pity. He was looking forward to reading that.

He's cooking some of the food they collected this morning (*Was it really only this morning? Feels like a lifetime ago...*), desperately trying to make amends for his pitiful performance earlier. The warmth, the light, and the crackle and pop of the flames helps them both to relax a little.

Keith's got a tin of beans on the boil in the embers and he's found some meatballs. 'You got a can opener?' he asks.

'Nope.'

'Great. This stuff's useless if we can't get into any of it.'

'We can get one.'

'I'll start a shopping list, shall I?'

'Don't take the piss.'

'I'm not. I'm serious.'

He abandons the idea of meatballs and finds something else to cook instead. He's hungry now, really hungry, and he can tell by the way Anna's been edging closer and closer that she is too. She looks younger in the dancing light. Her hair's all messed up now, her lipstick faded.

'Never liked meatballs anyway,' she says. 'You know what they make them from?'

Trick question? 'Meat?' he answers rhetorically.

'Yeah, but d'you know what kind of meat? It's all the spare stuff. All the bits no one else wants. All the guts and innards. The bollocks an' all that.'

'Is that right?'

'Yep. I saw it online. An' I saw this photo on Facebook once of a loaf of bread what had a dead mouse in the middle of it. You see that, Keith? It was disgustin'.'

Keith just looks at her and shakes his head. He hopes she'll take note of his lack of response and be quiet for a while, but she's too busy talking to care.

'It's good not havin' nothin' to do, innit?' she says. 'I mean, I never done a lot, anyway, but now I can do whatever I want. I can go anywhere, do anything...'

Christ, she's annoying. 'Don't you ever stop? Just listen to yourself, Anna. The rest of the world is dead out there, in case you hadn't noticed.'

'Course I noticed.'

'Doesn't it matter to you?'

She shrugs. 'Not really.'

'Not really?' he repeats, barely able to believe what he's hearing. 'Not really? What kind of a heartless bitch are you?'

She just shrugs again. 'Can't help it.'

'My dad's dead... Everyone's dead...'

'I'm not,' she says. 'You're not.'

'Might as well be.'

'Go and kill yourself then, miserable prick.'

'You're not interested in anyone but yourself, are you?' he asks, and he takes her lack of response as a resounding *no*. 'Have you thought about the implications of what's happened? What happens when we run out of food? What happens if there are more of those things out there and they get more aggressive? What happens if one of us gets sick or if we both get ill because of all the germs and flies when they start rotting? What happens when—?'

'Give it a rest,' she shouts, interrupting angrily. 'No point worryin' about any of that shit 'til it happens.'

'You're so bloody naïve. You scare me.'

'I done all right so far,' she mumbles.

Keith stirs the beans with a spoon, then picks up the hot can with a pair of pliers and empties it into two bowls. He starts eating but he's not as hungry as he thought he was. He's not hungry at all, actually.

'It's like one of them films,' Anna says.

'What are you on about now?'

'Them zombie movies. It's like one of them.'

'Is it?'

'Yeah... *Dawn of the Dead* an' all that. You see it?' She looks at him but doesn't get any reaction. 'Come on... there's two versions of it. You must'a seen it.'

'Nope.'

'*Night of the Living Dead* then? That's the first one. It was black and white. I seen it online.'

'I don't have a computer.'

'No computer? What, was your dad a paedo or somethin'?'

Keith instinctively jumps to Dad's defence. 'He's got a drink problem, that's all. He's not a paedo.'

'What about your mum?'

A pause, then 'She's been gone a few years.'

'Had enough of the drink?'

Another pause, then he forces an answer. 'Something like that...' He tries steering the conversation back into safer waters. 'What about that other film... *28 Days Later*, was it? Something like that?'

'Oh, man,' she says, more animated, 'scared the shit out of me, that did. You see it?'

'No.'

'Anyway, they weren't even dead in *28 Days Later*, just sick. I checked enough of them bodies outside to know they was all dead. I thought they was, anyway.'

Mention of the bodies gets Keith thinking again, and he starts to doubt himself. Sitting in here with Anna, isolated from everything else, the things he's seen since this all started seem impossible.

'They can't be dead... How can they be moving if they're dead?'

He didn't mean to ask the question out loud.

'Dunno,' she answers. 'It don't make any sense.'

'Maybe they're not dead. Maybe they are just sick? I should go home tomorrow and try and find Dad and then—'

'Don't be a dick,' she interrupts. 'Like I said, it don't make any sense, but that's just how it is.'

Keith wipes more tears from his face, hoping she'll think it's just the smoke from the fire getting in his eyes. He clears his throat. 'What about *I am Legend*?'

'That the one with Will Smith an' his dog?'

'Kind of.'

'I didn't like it. You see it?'

'No. I read the book though.'

'People say books is always better than films, but I like films more. I get bored reading books.'

He just looks at her and smiles to himself. 'Anyway, *I am Legend* is about vampires, not zombies.'

Anna laughs out loud... almost too loud. The noise makes Keith feel uncomfortable but she can't stop. She's rolling around the place, bean juice dribbling down her chin. 'Vampires! Now that's just stupid.'

When she's finally quiet again – and it takes a few minutes for her to fully calm down – Keith summons up enough courage to ask the question that's been on his mind since he first got here. 'What are we going to do?'

She's got her answer ready. She switches straight back from dizzy kid to apocalypse survivalist mode in a heartbeat, her face deadly serious. 'We're gonna stay here. We're gonna sit this out.'

'Sit what out? Things aren't going to get any better. Christ, everyone died yesterday, do you seriously think things are going to improve?'

'We'll be okay, you and me. I'll keep us safe, you look after the dinners, right?' She grins, but she's semi-serious. 'We'll be all right here. We're safe from everythin' else.'

'Yeah, but isolation's not always a good thing, is it?'

'It is from where I'm sittin'.'

'I'm not so sure...'

'I *am*. Like I said, we're safer here than out on the streets or in your house, ain't we? But we're still close enough so they'll find us when help arrives.'

'You think anyone's going to come and help us? Wouldn't they have been here already? No, I reckon we're all that's left.'

'We can't be,' she says, but she doesn't have anything with which to back her statement up and she knows it.

DAY THREE

It's barely even morning, but Keith's already up and about. He's never been one for sleeping in, and right now he's finding it impossible to sleep at all. He was just getting comfortable after hours tossing and turning on the floor, when his bladder started to ache. It's taken him another hour to pluck up the courage to do it, but he's finally outside the bungalow now, looking for a decent-sized tree to pee up. That's just about all there is in this place: trees and grass. When he looks around he finds it hard to believe this little oasis of greenery existed so close to where he lives... where he *used* to live. The fading darkness blurs the detail of everything outside the immediate area. From here Keith can see very few signs of the outside world – a few grey rooftops, a couple of electricity pylons, and a huge block of flats which rears up out of nowhere on the outermost edge of the parkland.

The relief when he finally starts to go is immense. He leans against the old tree trunk with his free hand as he empties his bladder. He's concentrating so hard on the steaming stream that he doesn't hear the uneven, squelching footsteps behind him, nor the rustle of branches as one of the dead tramples through the undergrowth to get to him. He shakes himself dry and turns around just as the hideous thing lurches at him, arms outstretched in a clichéd ghoul pose. Its face is terrifying in the half-light; skin dry and eyes bulging, mouth gaping open.

'Fuck!'

The ground is sodden after yet another heavy downpour during the night, and Keith's over on his backside looking up before he knows what's happening. He shouts for Anna but she's either still asleep or she's got her headphones in because she's not coming. He tries to back away from the advancing cadaver, hands and feet slipping in the mud, unable to get any traction, all the time still screaming out for help.

She's not coming.

Now you know how I felt, he imagines her telling him, thinking back to how useless he was when that body came at her yesterday after they'd been collecting wood.

The corpse has a nightmarish appearance. It's still recognisably male, still recognisably human, but the certainty is beginning to fade. Its skin is slipping like loose-fitting clothing; saggy jowls and dark bags under its eyes. It's leaking. Keith can't tell if its rainwater, blood or something else entirely, but with each lurching step it takes towards him, something liquid dribbles from an open wound under its gut.

You're on your own, Keith.

He looks around and sees there's another one coming. Knowing he's dead if he doesn't do something fast, he reaches out and uses a sapling tree to haul himself upright, then runs at the first body. He drops his shoulder and charges into it, screwing up his face at the thought of what he's about to collide with.

Wow. He didn't expect that. Either he doesn't know his own strength or he's underestimated the weakness of the dead body, because the damn thing is near folded in two and sent flying by the force of impact. It skids along the ground, rolling over and over, and then, when it tries to right itself again, one foot slips down the steep and greasy bank of the stream. The corpse can't get its balance.

It falls backwards, toppling into the water with an unnatural lack of noise (sure, there's a splash and a little thrashing, but no screams, no cries, no protest...). Keith walks forward and peers down, watching it flounder in six inches of murky water. *If these things are so helpless, why am I so scared?* But there's no doubt he is still scared, because when the other one starts getting close, he turns tail and sprints back towards the bungalow.

Anna's half-dressed when he gets inside. Her top's off, everything on show. She starts to cover herself up, then thinks *what the hell...* Keith seems more embarrassed than she is. He looks away fast, then remembers the danger outside and quickly closes the door. He leans against the wall and peers around the edge of the window.

'What was all the shoutin' about? Jesus, Keith,' she laughs, 'look at the state of you.'

'It must have seen me.'

'You was in the middle of a park havin' a piss up a tree. Course it saw you.'

'You were watching? And you didn't come and help? Didn't you hear me shouting?'

'*They* heard you, I know that much.'

Shit – there are two more of them now. The corpse of an over-weight woman, half-wearing a bright red raincoat, half-dragging it behind her, is heading straight for the bungalow.

Anna, fully dressed now, is standing at the window in plain view. Keith tries to drag her away but she angrily snatches her arm from his grip. 'Fuck off. Get your fuckin' hands off me.'

'Get down. Get out of sight.'

'Why?'

'Because she'll see you, that's why.'

The dead woman's definitely picking up speed now.

'She already has, I reckon.'

Keith's spotted another one – number four. It's harder to make out than the others because it's dressed in brown and black and they're starting to decay now, their skin turning a putrid grey tone. They're blending into the background, blending into one another. It's like a kind of camouflage. 'I thought you said the park was safe. I thought you said you locked all the gates.'

'All the gates I could find,' she answers.

'What's that supposed to mean?'

'What do you think? It's a park, dummy. There's bushes an' trees everywhere. There was always gonna be a few gaps where they might get through.'

'So what do we do?'

'Shut up and stop panicking?'

'I'm serious.'

'So am I. Jesus, Keith, you're like a bloody old woman.'

The female corpse half-dragging the red coat smacks into the side of the bungalow. Her head rocks back on her shoulders with the force of impact and she butts the window with the ensuing recoil, leaving a greasy smear the way birds do when they fly into patio doors at speed. It's enough to make her stagger back a few paces.

Now it's Anna's turn to grab Keith. She pulls him down and they sit together on her bed beneath the window. 'All we need to do is stay quiet,' she tells him, whispering now. 'It's easy. Just keep your voice down, stop cryin' like a girl whenever they get close, and they'll bugger off and leave us alone.'

'And you reckon it's that simple, do you?'

'I know it is.'

He does what she says for as long as he can stand, but within a few minutes nerves have got the better of him and he's up on his knees, peering over the top of the windowsill. 'They're going,' he says, surprised, watching the corpses stagger away.

'Told you, didn't I?'

Keith stands and starts nervously pacing the room. 'I think we need to go,' he announces. 'Find somewhere better to stay, somewhere safer.'

'You can if you want. I'm stayin' here.'

'But we're too isolated here. We need to find out what's happening to the rest of the world and—'

'There's fuck all happenin' to the rest of the world,' she tells him, voice firm, more serious. 'We *are* the rest of the world now, in case you ain't noticed.'

'But don't you think—?'

'Just trust me.'

'Trust you? I don't even know you. I don't know anything about you.'

'So? Does it matter? I don't know nothin' about you, either. I don't know about your paedo dad, or if you're a paedo...'

'Piss off.'

'Point is, it don't matter now. Who you was ain't who you are.'

He's struggling to decipher that nugget of bullshit. 'What?'

'What I mean is, our old lives are gone, ain't they? None of it counts for nothin' now. Same goes for them dead fuckers out there. Look at them, then look at us. We're better than them. We're stronger than them. We're in control now, Keith, so long as you don't lose it and fuck everythin' up.'

The world has become something of a vacuum. What little sound there is travels far and fast. It might not seem like much, but raised voices, a few screams and shouts, the noise of an incessant body being dealt with... all these things combine to make more of a noise than you'd probably imagine.

Although there are parts of the perimeter of the park which are relatively easy to breach, the dead are struggling with anything but the most basic of physical movements. Their coordination and control is severely lacking. They don't instigate, they only react. They follow the herd.

The geography of this particular area is interesting. It's relatively flat, and predominantly residential. Many of the homes were built in the late fifties and early sixties and the layout of the roads within the estate is surprisingly uniform. This means the dead tend to move in the same general direction. Take the main gates of the park, for example, where Anna stood yesterday morning and preened herself in front of the masses when she first brought Keith here. Rather than turn and leave, those corpses that followed them here have continued to loiter, perhaps sensing the survivors are still nearby. And as more have subsequently arrived, so those nearest the barrier have become stuck: wedged between the gate on one side and the unsteady stream of new arrivals on the other.

Whatever the reason, there's quite a crowd building up here.

And it's not just the dead who are interested.

Smoke drifting up from the bungalow chimney, large numbers of corpses, the occasional raised voice... all these things are of real interest to anyone watching.

And people *are* watching.

The rest of the day disappears in a haze of nervous contradictions. It's like that first day all over again, Keith thinks: each individual second feels like it takes an eternity to pass, and yet now it feels like the light is fading way ahead of schedule. It can't be sundown already, can it?

As the bungalow gets darker, the fire gets brighter. Keith occupies himself by cooking and trying to sort their stuff into some kind of order. Anna watches from her bed. She can't wait for him to finish their food. She's starving. She's been pigging out on junk all day and she's ready for something warm.

Earlier this evening they made a run to the stream for water, bringing as much back as they could in flowerpots and watering cans taken from the park equipment. Keith glances over at Anna as an empty bean tin half full of water starts to bubble in the embers of the fire. He thinks she looks different again tonight. Her face is grubby from the smoke. She looks younger than she did when they first met in the supermarket. 'You're not wearing any makeup,' he says.

'So?'

'You were plastered in it yesterday.'

'So?' she says again. 'Perv.'

'I'm not a perv. Just think it's weird.'

'What's weird?'

'Why you'd make an effort to look nice just to go out looting.'

'It's not 'cause I was out lootin',' she explains, 'it's just 'cause I knew I wasn't gonna be sittin' in here all day. Didn't know who I was gonna meet out there. Anyway, you're just a bloke. You wouldn't understand.'

A body stumbles past the bungalow window, startling Keith. It's just a shadow, gone in a heartbeat. He remembers what Anna told him and holds his breath and holds his nerve. He peers out through a gap in the curtains, just to be sure it's gone. Even though they're thin and old, the curtains are good enough to keep the light from the fire inside and seal the darkness out.

The water's finally boiling. Keith sees that it's ready and uses it to make two Pot Noodles. Anna's eyes are wide. 'Beef and tomato or chicken curry?' he asks.

'Curry,' she answers without hesitation, and suddenly she's like a kid on Christmas morning. She waits impatiently for the processed food to be ready, stirring it and prodding at it incessantly with a plastic fork, watching him for cues, then she tucks in. She sucks up a long noodle and laughs as sauce flicks everywhere, splashing up her nose and across her cheek. 'You'd make someone a good mum, you would.' Keith doesn't react at first, and she's not sure why. Has she said something she shouldn't? 'I'm serious,' she says. 'Your food is lush.'

'It's a bloody Pot Noodle,' he tells her. 'You add boiling water and you stir. Nothing difficult about it.'

'Yeah, but you need to know how much to put in and when. You have to know how long you gotta leave it for an' when to add the sauce.'

He just looks at her, surprised by her naivety. 'The instructions are printed on the side of the pack.'

She nods and looks. He's right. She never noticed that before. No wonder she never made them right.

She eats some more, then asks a question that's been on her mind for a while. 'What happened to your mum?'

The question comes out of the blue. Unexpected. Hits him hard. 'She died.'

'Yeah, I guessed that much,' she says, still slurping noodles. 'How?'

'Jesus, Anna, you're not big on tact, are you?'

'What?'

'Don't worry about sparing my feelings or anything like that.'

She laughs again. 'You serious? Take a look outside. Everybody's dead, not just your mum. Get over it. Don't make no difference what happened to her now.'

'You think?'

'I *know*. So how did she die?'

'I don't want to talk about it.'

'Something to do with your dad?'

'Yes, if you must know.'

158

'Was it his fault?'

'Depends who you're asking.'

'I'm asking you. Did he murder her?'

'Grow up. Maybe you should ask someone else.'

'There ain't no one else.'

He thinks she might have got the message and given up by now, but not this girl. He busies himself with his food, avoiding eye contact. She continues, undeterred.

'So is that how you learned to cook then? Your mum died an' your dad started drinkin', so you was left to do all the dinners.'

'Something like that. Like I said, I don't want to talk about it.'

'Maybe you should...'

This is the point where he'd probably get up and walk out, but that's not an option tonight. He's stuck here. Stuck here with Anna and her bloody incessant questions. He puts down his food, frustrated. 'Maybe if I knew a little more about you I'd be more inclined to share?'

She's awkward now the boot's on the other foot.

'Nothin' to tell.'

'There must be something? Where were you when all this happened? Who were you with? Who have you lost?'

'I told you, I was asleep. I'd been out on the lash.'

'Who with?'

'My mates.'

'Who?'

'Just some girls. Oh, an' Josh, my boyfriend.' She scrambles around her bedding and finds a phone which she turns on. She searches for a photo and throws it over to Keith. There's a picture of a boy on the screen. Good-looking, trendy... everything that Keith isn't. His opposite, in fact. Anna explains: 'We was just hangin' around, nothin' special. We was just havin' a few cans and a bit of a laugh, that's all.'

Keith passes the phone back. 'What happened?'

'What do you think happened? Can you see anyone else here? Think I should send them a text and get them to come round?' She rolls over onto her side, facing the wall. 'They're dead. Like all the others.'

'I'm sorry,' he says, embarrassed, and he leaves her to her memories as he makes them both a drink.

DAY FOUR

Anna's snoring like a bloody elephant when Keith wakes up next morning. She's so loud, in fact, he wonders if her noise might have been what woke him up. He's slept a little better, though he still seems to wake up more tired each morning than when he fell asleep. He gets up quietly, so as not to wake her, and checks all the windows. It's all clear outside, as far as he can see. There's one body tripping through the distance, a dead kid, he thinks, but that's all. He decides to risk going out – he doesn't have a lot of choice – but he finds a much nearer tree to pee against this morning.

When he gets back – relieved in more ways than one – he looks around the cluttered park-keeper's bungalow dejectedly. The thought of spending another day trapped in this cramped and chaotic place is depressing. His mood worsens when he thinks even further ahead, because he can't see an easy way out of this. Right now it looks like it's him and Anna and these four walls from hereon in.

But maybe he could do something to make the place a little more bearable?

He starts tidying up. He made a token effort last night before the lack of light stopped him, but this morning he decides to really go for it. Anna's untidy nest has slowly spread from under the window to halfway across the floor, and he starts respectfully moving some of her stuff, not wanting to disturb her or invade her limited privacy (not least because he knows she'll give him a load of verbal abuse if she catches him near her things). He picks up food wrappers and puts them along with other rubbish into an empty carrier bag, then folds up her discarded clothing and piles it all neatly. Maybe he should do a wash later? He can heat up some water, use a bucket from the council stores, find some soap... his own clothes are filthy. But then he stops himself. He's slipping back into his old routine, taking responsibility and looking for jobs to do. What does it matter now if he's covered in mud and dried blood from the corpses? Who's it going to offend?

And then, lying under a pair of panties and a lone sock, Keith finds the gun. She's left it there like it's a toy, and that scares him as much as the gun itself. He clears a space around it and just looks at it for a moment, trying to decide what to do. He's almost too afraid to touch it. He's never held a gun before, not a real one, anyway. He gingerly picks it up by the grip, holding it at arm's length like it's toxic. The weight takes him by surprise.

'Put it back. It's mine.'

Christ, she scared him. He almost drops the gun. His heart's thumping.

'Sorry... I was just cleaning up. I found it on the floor.'

'I put it there. Give it back.'

He hands it to her and she takes it from him and puts it under her pillow before rolling over and going back to sleep.

Anna wakes up with a start. She sits up and looks around, feeling like she's been picked up and dropped into another park-keeper's bungalow in another park: one that's immeasurably cleaner and tidier than the one in which she fell asleep.

'Bloody hell...' she says.

'I got sick of living in a pig sty,' he says, before adding, 'I didn't mess with any of your stuff, just tidied it up a bit.'

'Looks great. Don't look like the same place.'

'Amazing what a bit of effort can do, eh? A bit of elbow grease.'

'You what?'

'Never mind. Doesn't matter. Look, I found a bike chain and a padlock. It'll make the door more secure.'

She nods, disinterested, then wipes the sleep from her eyes, stretches and yawns. 'What's for breakfast?'

'Whatever's left. We're running out of stuff.'

'We should go and get some more then.'

Keith was expecting her to say that. Cleaning up the bungalow really helped him realise how little they've got, but he's not keen on the idea of leaving here. He thinks he'd rather starve. 'It's too dangerous out there... there's still a massive crowd up by the gate.'

'Then we'll go out another way.'

'It's too risky. I don't like it.'

'You don't like anything. Okay then, we'll just stay here an' go hungry.'

'That's just stupid...'

'So you want it both ways? What are we supposed to do then, dumbass? 'Cause if we don't go out and get more food, we're fucked.'

'You think I don't know that?'

'I dunno what you think.'

'There'll be thousands of them up by the shops now.'

'Says who? If you and me aren't there, why are they gonna hang around? They'll just disappear again.'

Damn, he thinks, *she has a point.*

'Problem is, Keith, you're a coward.'

'Piss off,' he says quickly, even though he knows she's right.

'You do all the easy stuff, all the cooking an' cleaning, stuff like that, but when things get tough, you go to pieces.'

'That's not true,' he says, backpedalling furiously.

'You just wanna keep your head down and let me take all the flack.'

Keith's quiet now, searching for options and come-backs, but knowing there probably aren't any. He was distracted cleaning the bungalow – he actually *enjoyed* it – but now he's forced to face reality again, the familiar sickly nervousness has returned. He's straight back in hell.

And then, an idea. An alternative. A compromise.

'There are houses out there,' he says, pointing out the window. Anna gets up, hopping around in her sleeping bag, too cold to get out.

'Where?'

'Look... over there, behind the trees. See?'

When the gusting wind shifts the branches she sees the roofs of a line of houses. 'So what you sayin'? We just break in?'

'I guess so,' he says, feeling about as certain as he sounds. 'Don't see what choice we have. It's a better option than the shops.'

'It's not like they'll miss their stuff if they're dead,' Anna adds, thinking out loud.

'Thanks for that.'

'S'true, though.'

It might well be true, he thinks, *but it's not helping.* 'We should go later,' he says, looking for excuses again, delaying tactics.

'How much later?'

'This afternoon.'

'You're kiddin','' she says. 'What's the point of waitin'? I'm starvin'. We should go now.'

And she's already getting dressed before he can protest. She drops the sleeping bag to her feet and steps out of it, barely clothed. She knows Keith's watching, but cares less than she should.

Nervous doesn't even come close to describing how Keith's feeling right now. Scared is a little more accurate. Completely fucking terrified is much more like it. He's regretting this; cursing himself for even mentioning the houses and wishing he'd kept his dumb mouth firmly closed. But he also knows she's right. That wouldn't have done either of them any good in the long run. There's no doubt they have to do this, and they'll probably have to do it again before long.

The two of them walk across the park together. There's no cover here, no shelter or protection, just open grassland. Anyone could see them, if there was anyone left looking. There are no corpses nearby, and Anna reckons if they can't see any of the dead, the dead can't see them. That's what she hopes, anyway. Keith's not convinced by her logic, but it makes him feel a little better too. The morning gloom is helpful. Everything looks grey; a light mist covering everything. 'Perfect horror movie weather,' Anna says.

There's a copse of trees to get through, then a fence. They've figured they need to steer clear of 'official' park entrances, because that's where they expect to find the dead in large numbers.

The grass here amongst the trees is longer, full of ferns and weeds, soaking the bottom of Keith's jeans. He thinks about trying to find some replacement gear while they're out, though the idea of wearing a dead man's trousers definitely doesn't appeal. Anna's really struggling in her Converse and cut-offs, still dressing for appearances, not for the conditions. She's done her hair and put makeup on again. He thinks she looks good. He'd tell her, but he doesn't know how.

The trees here are young and spiteful: head-height branches constantly whipping at their faces. Keith thinks maybe the trees are trying to help... trying to protect them from the danger elsewhere? Or maybe they're doing the exact opposite. Maybe they're doing everything they can to stop them ever leaving the park, holding onto them like grabbing hands.

Keith's so nervous he can hardly think straight.

If only we'd ended up somewhere other than this park...

If only I hadn't screwed up at the supermarket...

If only I'd managed to get Dad out of the house so I could have stayed there...

So many regrets, all of them pointless, none of them helpful. It's just nerves talking, but the nerves seem to be talking all the time these days. Shouting more than talking, actually. *Screaming...*

They finally make it to the fence. There's no conversation, because they both know what they have to do. Keith edges along one way, Anna the other. He finds a way through first. A couple of slatted boards are missing, and another is loose. He pushes it away, cringing when it cracks like a gunshot, then squeezes through the gap.

And now they're standing directly in front of the first of the row of houses they saw from the bungalow. This is a street Keith's passed the end of hundreds of times – it's only a few roads away from home – and yet he's never been down here. It makes him realise how restricted his life used to be: wake up in the same bed each day, see the same few people, take the same bus to work, and then do it all again in reverse when the work's done. It looks different here to how he expected. The same design of council house to his, just arranged slightly differently – two long rows facing each other on either side of the street with a wide, grass-covered central reservation between them.

'Come on,' says Anna, teeth chattering with the cold.

Keith just stands there, thinking *it's funny how perspectives change.* All the time he was stuck in the bungalow in the middle of the park, all he wanted to do was escape its walls. Now he's actually made it out, all he wants is to go back. He tries to focus on the task at hand: getting in, getting what they need, then getting out as quickly as possible. But it's hard focussing on anything when you're this damn scared.

There's a dead body up ahead, coming slowly down the road towards them. There's no urgency about it, and somehow that makes it appear all the more threatening. They both watch it for a few seconds longer than they should, transfixed by its awkward gait. It's like it's trying to learn how to use its own body again. It's another bloody paradox: this thing looks barely able to coordinate its own arms and legs, and yet there's absolutely no question about its intent. Keith and Anna both know if they stand here much longer, they'll be in a shed-load of trouble. They have to move. The approaching cadaver has unknowingly forced their hand.

Breaking and entering.

This is all new to Keith, but obviously not to Anna. He tries the front door but she's already several steps ahead of the game. She tries a couple of ground floor windows, then scrambles up and over the side gate, feet kicking wildly as she reaches the top and drops over. A second later and he hears the bolt, then the latch. She ushers him quickly inside.

The back garden is clear. They check all the windows for any obvious bodies stuck indoors, but don't see anything untoward. It looks like no one was in when *it* happened. Anna raps her knuckles on a patio door and waits a while, just to be certain. She holds her breath, expecting one of them to come lurching out of the shadows and flying towards her at any moment.

The side door's locked, but there's a window that's been left open slightly. Anna reaches her slender wrist inside and is able to get to the handle and open it fully. Keith helps her up, struggling less with the effort and her weight, and more with the sudden awkwardness of this close physical contact. He's got his hands all over her backside now, holding her steady as she wriggles inside. She makes some dumb, inappropriate comment about how she hopes he's enjoying having a good feel, but he ignores her. Sex is the very last thing on his mind right now. He couldn't get it up if he tried (and he has absolutely no intention of trying).

There's a long wait while Anna roots around inside, trying to find the keys so she can get one of the doors open. When she finally reappears she finds Keith on his hands and knees, looking under the gate to see if that damn body has made it this far down the road yet.

She just looks at him lying down there with his face pressed against the paving slabs. She's wondering if he's finally cracked. 'Keith, you prick, come on,' she hisses. He gets up and brushes himself down.

'Just get stuff we can use,' he tells her as they go inside. 'You check the rest of the house, I'll do the kitchen. Start with downstairs.'

'Yes, Mum,' she says without thinking. He glares at her but bites his tongue, then starts ferreting through cupboards and drawers. He finds a load of Tupperware and a stash of carrier bags. He thinks they should take their time and take everything useful from this place. It's five minutes to the bungalow and back. They can risk making a few quick trips.

Anna leaves the kitchen like a girl on a mission, but she's really not. She waits until Keith's out of sight, then slows the pace dramatically. She wanders through the lounge, running her fingers over dusty surfaces, picking up nick-nacks then putting them down again, disinterested. A couple of things catch her eye, but there's nothing much worth taking. What did Keith expect her to find here anyway? Is he thinking about shifting a sofa or an armchair or some fancy ornaments to make the bungalow look nice? The only thing she'd bother with is the massive flat-screen TV in the corner. It looks like a really good one. It's bigger than any TV she's ever had, that's for sure. But there's no power in the bungalow, and there's no TV on anymore, remember? Even if she did manage to get it over there and plugged in, Keith would only start stressing about the noise and the light. He's like an old woman. He's always having a moan about something.

She meanders upstairs, taking her time, wondering who might have lived here. She thinks it's sad she didn't have a house like this. Maybe she could now? Okay, so it's not that big and it definitely ain't the poshest of places, but there's a nice atmosphere in here... *a good vibe*. She feels safe. Warm. Protected. She thinks about maybe trying to persuade Keith that they should both move over here. Either that or she could just move in on her own. She doesn't know how she feels about living on her own, though. She's getting used to having Keith around. She feels like she's been on her own long enough.

Considering it's only a few days since everyone else died, the house actually *feels* dead. Anna's not entirely sure what she means by that... it's hard to explain. It's like the life has been sucked out of everywhere. It's as cold inside as it is outside. A window on the upstairs landing has been left open and there's a massive water stain on the carpet. There's none of the usual noise she remembers from houses like this (though it has been a while)... just an unending silence. Apart, that is, from the din Keith's making down in the kitchen. She hears him curse when he knocks a load of stuff over, and she giggles at the noise.

There's nothing in the bathroom worth taking save for a little makeup which she shoves in her pockets. The main bedroom's not much better... it's all *Grand Designs* – all wood and metal, proper posh. She opens another door and glances into a boy's room. It's small and square and it stinks the way teenage boys do (did?). The football scarf and the posters of naked women are all she needs to see and she's out of there as quick as she went in.

She finds herself in a young kid's bedroom next. It's a little too juvenile for her tastes, but she appreciates how much the little princess who lived here's parents must have loved her. She can almost hear her talking to them... *I want this wallpaper, Daddy, and I want a desk like this and a table like that and a TV in the corner and a computer so I can talk to my friends whenever I want to...* Anna thinks she sounds bitter, but she's not really. Jealous, perhaps. Disappointed. Just upset that no one ever did anything like this for her, that no one cared enough. Daddy might have, but Mummy wasn't even sure which one of three blokes he was.

She's distracted by a poster on the wall when the dead kid attacks her. It's the teenage brother of the little darling who's room this was, but that's irrelevant because he doesn't live here now, he just *exists* in this place. He's gangly, clumsy, decaying and aggressive as hell. He hurls himself at her and the impact takes her completely by surprise. She hits the side of the bed face-first, then bounces off and onto the floor. She's lying on the carpet now looking up, all the wind knocked out of her, and the creature falls on top of her before she can even scream for help.

But, downstairs in the kitchen, Keith already knows something's wrong. The noise of Anna hitting the deck echoes through the whole building and though he's scared, though his heart's racing, he's already running up the staircase to get to her.

He doesn't expect to see this, though.

Anna's lying there with that thing forcing itself on top of her... like it's *violating* her. He wants to help, but the fear is too great and he's rooted to the spot, just watching.

Anna writhes in panic and disgust beneath the hideous dead kid, but he's such a weight she can hardly move. She tries to yell out for help again but there are dead hands all over her face, feeling her skin, rubbing against her tongue and teeth, pressing her eyes... She's having to breathe through her nose, her mouth full of icy fingers. When one unfeeling hand shifts unexpectedly, she tries to call out but manages only a choked sob.

That noise is enough.

It galvanises Keith and forces him into action. He knows he has to act, because Anna's all he's got. The thought of living in this dead new world is bad enough, but the thought of doing it alone is unbearable. He needs her, and she needs him. That realisation has more of an impact than he expected and he lunges forward angrily and grabs a fistful of the dead kid's lank, curly hair. It's so greasy and tainted with decay that the limp brown strands start to slip between his fingers like they've been covered in oil, but now that he's finally doing something, now that he's finally made contact with the corpse, he's not going to stop. He puts his hand under the boy's jaw, feeling his teeth grinding involuntarily, then drags him away.

Anna gets up and scrambles out of the way. She's left sitting in the corner of the room, knees pulled up to her chest, crying like a kid half her age.

Keith's stuck with a squirming corpse to deal with.

So he does.

Even though the body's arms and legs are thrashing wildly, its movements are purely instinctive and are barely controlled. It doesn't even try to defend itself when Keith screws up his fist and punches it in the face. It doesn't even seem to notice, either. It rides the blow, head slamming against the side of a small dressing table, then just rights itself like nothing happened. Keith takes this indifference as a personal slight. He's sick and tired of being ignored, sick and tired of being the expected underdog. He's had years of being treated like a bloody door mat. Even now, when there's only one other person left alive as far as he's aware, this dead bastard is treating him with the same kind of contempt he got from Dad and the people at work and everybody else. It's time to put an end to it. It's time to take control.

He knows kicking and punching just isn't going to cut it though.

There's a lamp on the corner of the dressing table with a heavy ceramic base. He picks it up and tries to swing it at the corpse's head, forgetting the cord's still plugged in at the wall. He wrenches out the flex, then tries again. The right-angled corner of the square lamp base digs deep into the corpse's left temple, almost becoming wedged. The corpse stops, appearing stunned for a moment, then continues fighting.

Keith hits it again, the base glancing off the side of the dead kid's skull this time.

And again, swinging wildly and cracking the boy's cheek bone, over-pronounced due to the onset of decay.

Once more, slamming directly down like he's cracking an egg.

Each time he makes contact, the creature's face becomes a little more deformed. Ice-white flesh is increasingly being obscured by slow dribbles and steady floods of lumpy, semi-coagulated black blood. In frustration (because the damn thing's not yet rolling over and giving up) Keith rips the shade off the lamp, smashes the bulb on the edge of the dressing table, then shoves the jagged remains of the bulb and the metal fitting deep into the corpse's left eye. He pushes harder and harder, feeling it sink deeper and deeper in until it won't go any further.

That does the trick.

Keith lets go and the dead kid slumps forward, gunk pouring out of the savage hole in his face, dripping chunks into his lap. Anna runs for the door, jumping the body's outstretched legs. Keith catches her wrist and pulls her back. 'What the hell were you doing up here? What the hell were you doing with that thing?'

She snatches her arm free and runs on.

She's back at the bungalow before he's even left the house.

When he finally gets back and shuts the door – three trips later, loaded up with armfuls of stuff each time – he barely talks to her, can

169

barely bring himself to look at her. He keeps himself busy by putting everything away; everything in its right place.

'Keith...' she says, his silence making her feel increasingly nervous. He doesn't immediately respond and she tries again. 'Keith...'

'What?' he yells, irritated, trying to secure the door with the padlock and chain.

'Aren't you gonna talk to me?'

'What's there to say?'

'I'm sorry if I fucked up. I was just tryin' to—'

'Just trying to do what?' He finally stops messing and stands in the middle of the room and looks straight at her. 'Come on, explain... what exactly was it you were trying to do back there? You were supposed to collect useful stuff, that's all. It wasn't bloody difficult.'

'I was looking for stuff...'

'So what did you find?'

'Nothin', 'cause I was about to go and look when that thing—'

'Bullshit,' he interrupts. 'That's just crap and you know it. You were dicking about. Same as you're always dicking about. I'm the only one who actually does anything here.'

She just stares into space, searching for words. She's angry at the tears she can't stop. Or maybe the tears are because of the anger? She doesn't know. Can't think straight.

'But you wouldn't have got nowhere if it weren't for me. I saved you in the supermarket, remember? I brung you here...'

'You saved me?' he repeats, voice incredulous. 'You *saved* me? I'll admit, I wasn't firing on all cylinders back then, but all you did was drag a corpse off me and smack it around the head. I'd have done it if I had to.'

'But you didn't have to. I done it. *I* done it.'

'You should have heard that thing in the house before it got anywhere close,' he tells her. 'You were distracted.'

'But you never heard it neither,' she says. 'We didn't check properly.' They both know that's a valid point.

Keith's about to speak again when one of the dead things crashes into the bungalow door. It takes him by surprise, but he's quickly over the shock. He watches it. It's on the other side of the glass now, dead eyes fixed on his, pointlessly pawing at the window with lifeless hands. *Stupid fucking thing.* He knows it'll never get in.

'Thing is, Anna,' he continues, voice no lower, winding up the corpse outside, 'I reckon you're gonna be a fucking liability. You think you know what's going on here, but it's just a fucking act. I can see it now. You're just—'

He pauses when a second dead body crashes into the side of the building and he yanks the curtain across to block the corpses out, irritated by the interruption and the lack of privacy.

'—you're just a kid,' he says. 'You're nothing and you're nobody. If I wasn't here, you'd be screwed by now. You'd be starving. Either that or you'd be dead.'

'But when I found you—'

'When you found me I was a frigging wreck, I know that, but it was just nerves. I'm over it now.'

'But in the supermarket—'

'In the supermarket I'd have been all right. And that's the difference. Upstairs in that house just now, you were in real trouble. I don't reckon you'd have got away if I hadn't helped.'

'Not true. I was about to get rid of it. It took me by surprise, that's all. I just—'

'This is what it boils down to,' he interrupts. 'You need me a hell of a lot more than I need you.'

'But Keith...'

He's had enough of her now. He paces around the room but there's no way out, no escape. He's trapped: trapped in this little box with this little kid. And he still doesn't even know anything about her. He has a flash of anger-fuelled inspiration and grabs her phone from where she left it next to her pillow. He switches it on and waits for it to start up.

'Leave it,' she says, and she tries to take it from him but he's got height on his side and he holds her at bay. He turns his back on her and walks away, leaving her sobbing in the corner.

'If you're not going to tell me anything about yourself, I'll get what I need from this instead.'

He starts trying to navigate the phone, all fingers and thumbs. He's not used to touchscreens. He sees a camera icon and presses it, then cycles through her photos. There are a few more pictures of her flashy boyfriend, but none of her. None of anything he recognises.

'Not my phone,' she says and he turns around and looks at her, confused.

'What d'you mean?'

'I said it's not my phone. I found it.'

'So your boyfriend...?'

'Just some kid. Don't know him.'

He drops the phone on her bed. 'So I'll ask you again... who are you, Anna?'

'Does it matter?'

'It matters to me.'

She folds her arms across her chest and stares dead ahead like a scolded kid. 'I lived with my sister, up near Princethorpe.'

'And what happened to her? Do I need to ask?'

'I don't know.'

'What do you mean, you don't know?'

'I ain't been back there.'

Now he's even more confused. This doesn't make sense. He thinks back to when she first brought him to this place... he remembers how it looked and smelled... how it felt lived in, borderline homely. The pieces start falling into place. 'How long have you been living here?'

'Few weeks,' she mumbles, almost embarrassed. 'About a month.'

For the first time in a long time, Keith senses she's finally being honest. 'So what happened?'

'How long you got?'

'Forever, it looks like.'

She half-smiles, then her face drops again. 'She was always treatin' me like a kid. I know what I'm doin' though... I ain't stupid.'

Keith's a little calmer now. He wants to tell her she is stupid – sometimes – but he doesn't. 'I know.'

'And she's always like *be in by this time, do this, do that...* I couldn't take no more of it. So I stopped doin' what she wanted and what the rest of them wanted, and started livin'. I started doin' stuff for myself, fuck the lot of 'em.'

'Ironic.'

'What's that mean?'

'It's funny... you start living and everyone else dies.'

'Can't see nothin' funny about that.'

He doesn't bother trying to explain.

'I do know how you feel, though,' he tells her.

'Doubt it.'

'I do. More than you'd expect.'

'How so?'

'Because I used to get the opposite. I just wanted to dick around and do what I wanted, but I never could. I was always too busy with work, and when I wasn't at work I was looking after Dad.'

'You ain't got neither of them now.'

'I ain't got nothing now,' he says, mimicking her lousy diction.

'You still got me,' she says quickly, and he's not sure how to take that.

'So how old are you, Anna?'

'Nineteen,' she answers quickly. Too quickly. Keith might be a little green, but he's not that stupid. She knows from the look on his face that he can see through her. 'Sixteen,' she admits. 'Almost.'

'Bit young to be living on your own, don't you think?'

'I'm doin' all right.'

'Yeah, I can see that.'

'So how old are you, then?' she asks him.

'Nearly twenty-one.'

'Bit young to be such an old man.'

She has a point.

'So where do we go from here?'

'Don't see there's anywhere to go. Just stick here, I reckon.'

Keith's not sure if that thought excites or depresses him. If he's honest, he's not sure of anything anymore. He looks outside again and sees that the two bodies have become disinterested and have wandered away. He remembers what happened in the house just now, and that makes him focus again. He knows he can't afford to allow himself to become distracted. Anna needs to know he's in charge.

'If you're staying here, you do what I say, okay?'

'If *I'm* stayin' here...? This is my place, dumbass, remember?'

'Things are changing.'

'Says who?'

'Says me. See, I've spent far too long looking after other people, and I'm damn well not going to tie myself up in knots looking after you. I'll cook, I'll clean, but I'm not your fucking babysitter, right?'

'I already told you, I'm not a kid.'

'You're not even sixteen years old, so technically you are.' She glares angrily at him, stewing. He likes that. He knows he's starting to get through to her, that he's learning how to deal with her better now. 'You hungry?' he asks.

She nods her head. Can't bring herself to answer. Again, he smiles inwardly. He knows food is her Achilles Heel.

'I'll cook us something. Did you remember to get a tin opener?' She shakes her head this time and readies herself for another torrent of abuse, but it doesn't come. He's playing with her. 'Thought as much,' he says, grinning. 'Good job I got one then.'

He goes over to the kitchen space – well ordered now, as clean as it can be in the circumstances – and collects all the things he needs. He makes a fire (he's graded the wood into different thicknesses) and lights it. He uses pages torn from one of her magazines to get it started, and as much as she wants to protest, she doesn't. She knows there might not be any more issues published, but all the magazines she could ever want are out there somewhere.

DAY FIVE

When Anna wakes up this morning, she sees that Keith's on his way out the door. She panics and sits up fast. 'You leaving me?'

'Where did that come from?'

'Dunno,' she says, feeling foolish. 'What's wrong?'

'Nothing's wrong.'

'Then where you goin'?'

'To fetch some water.'

He leaves the bungalow, carrying a number of pots and pans they took from the house yesterday.

Keith's starting to think they might be all right here, as long as he can keep Anna under control. And he will. He knows he will. He'll make her behave if he has to.

The more he thinks about it, the better he's starting to feel about this place. It'll definitely do for now. He's realised that making quick scavenging trips out to other houses nearby like they did yesterday might be enough to keep them stocked and supplied here for a while longer, at least until things calm down and the dead stop being such a damn nuisance. He reckons they will, eventually. And as long as they remain invisible to the bulk of the dead population until then, they should be okay. There's only two of them. How much stuff will they really need to stay alive? Enough food and water, fresh clothes, a supply of decent books... for the first time since everything fell apart, Keith realises he's actually starting to think slightly longer term.

He collects as much water as he can carry from the stream, then turns back towards the bungalow. In the short time he's been outside, grey light has begun to seep reluctantly across the scene, brightened by the merest hint of autumnal morning sun on the horizon. It's good to be out in the open again. He thinks back to this time last week and remembers where he was: queuing for the bus in the rain, heading for work but already knackered after sorting Dad out first thing.

The only visible movement comes from the bodies still gathered around the entrance to the park. They remind him of crowds being held back by security, waiting to be let into a concert arena or the January sales. They're a damn nuisance, he knows that much. Imagine how much easier life would be if they didn't have the dead to worry about? Everything would be completely different if it was just him and Anna. He longs for a time when his first thought every morning is *what do I want to do today?* Not *what do I have to do?*

He can see the body Anna dealt with on that first afternoon when they were out collecting wood. Christ, he was such an idiot back then, absolutely bloody useless. From here the corpse looks like it's being absorbed back into the landscape. Its feet stick up like mounds of weeds. A stiff arm twists up like a fleshy sapling. And, for the first time, rather than think *thank Christ Anna did that*, Keith now thinks *I've done that too, and I'll do it again if I have to, as many times as necessary...*

He leaves the water outside the bungalow then drags the body out of the way, well away from the building. He's worried it'll soon start to stink. He pictures hordes of angry, buzzing flies keeping him awake at night, and imagines a stench like the smell he remembers from Dad's all-night benders, when he had to chuck out his bedding and hose the old man down after he'd thrown up or shat himself or both. He wipes his hands on the grass while he catches his breath.

He doesn't want to go back inside. Not just yet. He looks around the park again, checking for other bodies on the lethargic prowl. He sees one or two of them, tripping through the undergrowth, staggering aimlessly through the slowly lifting gloom, but they're of little concern to him now. *How things have changed*, he thinks. He can't believe he made such a bloody fuss before. He'd have been inside by now, trembling in the shadows, waiting for them to disappear. He can't understand why he used to be so weak, why he was such a coward? He should have been like this version of Keith from the start. He thinks he should have been like this version of himself for a long time. Maybe the pre-apocalypse world would have been more bearable if he'd acted this way and shown a little backbone sooner? Whatever, he's glad to have found himself at last (and yes, he's well aware of just how pretentious that sounds).

Using the last of the dawn shade as cover, Keith decides to explore a little more of his environment. It strikes him how naïve he was to simply follow Anna into the park-keeper's bungalow without question, never once stopping to consider what else might be here, or if there was a better location nearby.

It's been a long time since he's been this deep into the park... a lifetime, almost. There's little to see. There's a children's playground which looks eerie in the shadows. In fact, he can hardly bear to look at it. A swing moves slightly in the breeze, and a roundabout slowly spins as if the ghosts of dead kids are playing on it. And Keith knows there will be literally hundreds of dead kids within the few miles surrounding this place. He almost scares himself into heading back inside with such thoughts, but he stops because he knows he has far more about him than that now. He's a bigger man than he used to be. A better man.

He walks around the perimeter of the park now, taking care to keep a short distance in from the very edge to avoid attracting the attention of the bodies on the other side. He can see them out there, moving constantly. The way they drag themselves around – resigned, weary – reminds him of the daily commute he used to hate so much. *Used to*. It feels good to be able to think like that. He's so relieved those days are over. These poor fuckers, they're still trapped like he was. They'll never escape... they'll never get away.

A couple of corpses spot him through the trees and immediately change direction, but there's no real threat here. They've no common-sense, these dumb, dead things. Now three of them move together like a gang or a lynch mob, trying to get to him across a dense thicket. But it's clear they're not going to get through. It's clear to Keith, anyway, if not to them. They just keep trying... relentless, pointless.

He looks up at the tower block in the near distance, its top few floors barely visible through the morning murk. *That'll be a good place to look for supplies*, he thinks. *A hundred or so homes, all stacked on top of one another. Imagine how much stuff will be in there...* But then he thinks about all the dead tenants and other inhabitants of those hundred or so homes, and he thinks he might take a rain-check on that idea. He stares up at the building for a few seconds longer, convinced he saw a flash of light in one of the windows, some movement. It was probably nothing. Just one of the dead trapped in its apartment, he decides. Either that or a momentary glimpse of the morning sun straining through the clouds.

Back towards the centre of the park now, and the outline of a dilapidated block of changing rooms looms between the trees. He remembers this place being built when he was a kid, but he never actually saw anyone use the building for its intended purpose. He slowly circles around it, checking it out. There are padlocks on the doors and spray-paint on the windows. It looks pretty solid, though. He thinks maybe they could move into this place if the bungalow becomes too cramped. Or maybe *he* could use this place? A man-cave, isn't that what they call it? There's a metal spiral staircase welded to the outside wall. Two storeys. He thinks how much of an advantage it would be to have a base up there instead of down here, though he realises as well that getting back down might prove to be a problem if too many of the locals became interested in his whereabouts. For a few minutes he just stands there looking up at the side of the silent building, daydreaming. *There you go again, Keith*, he says to himself, smirking, *thinking about the future like you've got one...*

There's a MURG here he doesn't recognise. This never used to be here. This used to be a paddling pool, or a bike track or something like that. He didn't even know things like this were called MURGs until just now. There's a sign at the entrance which explains everything. It's a *Multi-Use Recreation Ground*, apparently. Just a fancy name for a fenced-off five-a-side football pitch/basketball court. He pushes the wire-mesh gate open and it squeaks then scrapes along the ground, filling the air with noise.

Keith walks right into the centre of the court. When he looks back, he sees a football that's been left behind. For a moment he's too busy thinking about who might have left it here, who might have been the last kid to kick it, that he doesn't do anything else. Then he snaps out of it quick and starts playing with the ball. He passes to nobody, then sells a dummy to nobody else, nutmegs a third person who isn't there... Christ, team games can be awful lonely these days. But what the hell – it's just good to be occupied.

He traps the ball near the centre spot and eyes up a free kick, picturing a wall of imaginary defenders and a goalkeeper who isn't there. Then he shoots. He's not wearing the right shoes for this, but his shot's pretty impressive nonetheless. He gets the ball to curve but it doesn't dip as he'd hoped. It clatters against the mesh fence above the goal, filling the air with noise.

Not bad, he thinks, *but not that good, either.*

He retrieves the ball and turns towards the other goal now, taking a shot from three-quarters of the way down the pitch, sending it just wide. And he doesn't hesitate. He chases after it again, and once again he shoots, enjoying the sudden physical exertion and the distraction of football.

And again.

And again (and this time he actually scores!).

And again.

And this time he hears the wire-mesh rattle before he's kicked the ball.

Keith's got company.

He knows he's not alone now, that the opposition have finally turned up to play.

It looks like it was probably about his age when it died. The corpse is the remains of the kind of kid who used to intimidate Keith, back in the old world, back in the old days. He has a shaved head, too much cheap gold jewellery, and he's wearing grey jogging bottoms and a sweatshirt that's very heavily stained with seepage and decay. But he's nowhere near the threat he would once have been: all his swagger replaced by stagger. A useless, vacuous dumb fuck.

As the dead thing walks towards him, it inadvertently kicks the ball, sending it spinning off to the side, then ricocheting off the wall and into the goal. Keith laughs involuntarily. He's impressed! He recovers the ball and dallies around the dead kid. He's playing with him, taunting him, and the corpse is not best pleased. It swipes at the air with clumsy hands, missing Keith every time. But then either Keith misjudges or the corpse strikes it lucky, because his outstretched dead fingers make contact with the back of Keith's head.

And now Keith's fucking furious.

It's bad enough that this foul creature should end up in *his* MURG in *his* park, but to have dared make contact like that is unforgivable... it's not on at all. Does he know who Keith is? It's very possible, given the close proximity of Keith's home, that he knew who Keith *was*, but things have changed now. Neither of these two men are who or what they used to be.

At the other end of the wire cage they're in, Keith has spied a lump of wood. It's the shape and size of the kind of wooden posts that used to hold up estate agents' signs. How it got there he has no idea, but that's not important now. Keith knows it'll suit his purposes perfectly. He boots the ball straight at the dead kid, hitting him in the nuts and totally confusing him, then jogs back and picks up the wooden post.

This time when he turns back around, the MURG doesn't look like a MURG to Keith anymore. It's more like a gladiatorial arena. Keith almost begins to wish there were a few hundred more dead fucks on the other side of the fence to watch this, because he knows it's going to be good. He passes the wooden post from hand to hand, getting used to its shape and size and weight, then moves in to attack.

In his head he tells himself he's going in for the kill, but how can he kill this thing when it's already dead?

No matter.

He swings the wood around hard and fast, making brutal contact with the side of the dead youth's head, almost ripping his right ear off completely. The power of the strike is astonishing: the body spins around and around, twisting its legs around itself like a corkscrew then falling down hard. He hits its sprawled legs repeatedly, feeling bones break with every fresh blow. Keith knows he's already done more than enough damage to neutralize the threat but, the thing is, the damage he's done is *nowhere* near enough. He needs more. He needs to hurt this monstrosity. He needs to take advantage of this situation and beat the dead kid to a pulp to help release all the pent up anger and frustration that's been building up inside him like a cancer these last few days and weeks... these last few years.

And Christ, it works.

The kid is on the ground in front of him now, trying to get up, oblivious to the fact its legs are completely useless. It's unable to understand what just happened; unable to understand *anything*. Numb fingers claw at the asphalt, hands opening and closing, gripping at nothing. It's almost up on one shattered knee when Keith strikes again. Another savage blow to the head, this time almost wrenching its lower jaw clean off. Lumpy blood and brown, tooth-filled drool spills out from the ragged hole in its face, and a wide spray of the noxious stuff arcs across the floor of the MURG when Keith hits it again. And again. And again. And he keeps hitting the damn thing until he's panting with effort and can barely feel his arms.

Jesus... look at the state of that.

There's hardly anything recognisable left above the creature's shoulders. Wide splashes of vivid gore slice across the ground.

And, not for the first time, Keith thinks *I did that*. And it feels good.

'What do you reckon?'

'I reckon he's a fucking nutter.'

'He's just a kid.'

'Just a fucking crazy kid.'

'So what do we do?'

'We wait. Don't want to risk him going off on one and doing that to one of us. We'll bide our time. We can see enough from up here.'

Keith marches back to the bungalow. When he gets there, he sees the water he left outside has gone. He lets himself in and sees that Anna's up. 'I brung the water in, Keith.'

She's trying – and failing miserably – to get a fire started in the hearth. She looks him up and down, then returns her attention to the fire.

'Got a problem?' he asks, annoyed.

'You're covered in blood.'

'So? I got rid of another body that got too close. Jesus, Anna, how many matches have you used?' The number of spent matches he sees scattered around angers him. Damn kid's trying to light thick branches without using kindling or anything like that. 'What the hell are you doing? You'll never get it going like that. Don't you know anything?'

'I'm sorry... I brung the water in an' I wanted to make us a drink.'

'You *brought* the water in, not brung.'

'Sorry. I just wanted to help.'

'The best way you can help is by keeping out of the way.'

She slides back across the floor to her bed, hurt. He feels a twinge of regret, but then thinks *no, she has to understand. This is serious. We're not playing games here.*

'I was just tryin' to help,' she says again, sounding half her age.

Grumbling to himself as he works, Keith has the fire lit in no time. He scribbles down *matches* on a piece of paper he's been keeping. She calls it his shopping list. He calls it *essential requisitions for next trip out.* He knows which sounds best.

She watches him, doesn't take her eyes off him. She wonders if asking questions is a good idea when he's in this kind of mood, but she wants to know. She *needs* to know. 'Where you been?'

'Outside.'

'I know that,' she says quickly, tongue loosening again and temper getting the better of her. 'If you ain't in here then you're outside. *Where* outside?'

'Around and about.'

'Around the park?'

'Parts of it,' he explains, starting to feel slightly less annoyed now. He sits down and sets a tin of water in the fire to boil. 'I had a look around the fence, just to see what it's like out there.'

'And?'

'And there's no change. They're still dead, still here. Still wandering around the place like empty-headed idiots.'

She sniggers at his turn of phrase, then remembers herself and becomes more serious again. 'So why did you have to fight one of 'em?'

'It was in the way.'

'That what all that noise was? Sounded like you was playin' football.'

He doesn't react. He's too busy remembering. The killing of the already killed is beginning to feel unexpectedly therapeutic. Keith didn't feel scared out there today. He didn't feel afraid. He felt *alive*.

'But if we stay quiet, they disappear. You don't have to go killin' them just 'cause you feel like it.'

Keith stares into the flames. His thoughts are brighter now, clearer... as vivid as the fire. *Actually, Anna,* he thinks, *you're wrong. I can do whatever I want.*

There are more bodies in the park this afternoon. Keith wonders if their presence here is something to do with the noise he made earlier, massacring that kid. In the strangest way, he's almost glad they're here.

He stands at the window in full view, and one of the dead marches across the park with something approaching a real sense of purpose, its speed quickening the closer it gets to the bungalow. He's waving at the damn thing now, trying to get its attention.

'What the hell you doin'?' Anna asks, concerned.

'Cleaning up,' he tells her.

He picks up a shovel he found in the council stores, then makes for the door, a man on a mission.

'Don't go out there,' Anna says. 'Please.'

'Back in a minute,' he tells her, and he's gone before she has a chance to argue.

There's a moment of hesitation when the cold air hits him. It's bright outside, but the temperature drop is still significant. Nerves threaten to get the better of him as he watches the advancing cadaver, but the insecurities soon disappear because Keith knows things are different now. *He's* different. He remembers what he did to the body in the house yesterday, and then to the dead kid in the MURG early this morning... *Did you see what I did? Did you see how I hurt them, how I showed them who's boss?* Actually, he doesn't know if they can feel hurt, but it makes him feel good to believe that they can.

There's another corpse that's even closer. He hears it before he sees it; the rustle of soiled clothing dried by the sun, accompanied by a breathless groan as its movement forces air from its arid lungs. He looks this one up and down, spending time getting to know it before getting rid of it once and for all. *Who were you?* There's something familiar about the shape of its face and its colouring, but then again, that's probably because they're all starting to look the same now, death bleaching away their individuality. It reminds him of someone who used to be on TV... or is it someone from work? Or was it a neighbour? Doesn't matter.

Keith swings the shovel at its head and it makes contact with a nauseating, sonorous thud. The body remains standing, but it stops like Keith's pressed pause, then just drops. Christ, that was easy. Too easy. Keith's elated. *They can't touch me!*

Incredibly, there are six more dead bodies here now. Keith thinks he should maybe be feeling nervous, but he's not at all fazed. One of them wraps its arms around him from behind; he literally shrugs it off then turns around and buries the tip of the shovel in its rubbery gut. A few days decaying has seriously weakened its skin and Keith gags with disgust and jumps with excitement at the same time as an oil slick of putrefying innards spill out over its feet. It's like slashing a carrier bag bulging with week-old butcher's offal.

Getting rid of the rest of the rancid crowd is equally straightforward. What was all the fuss about? A swipe of the blade here, a full-force parry there... the fight – if you can even call it a fight – feels desperately one-sided in all but numbers. Within a couple of minutes it's all over bar the shouting, and Keith stands there breathless, surrounded by the remains of his kills.

The carnage is hard to comprehend, chunks of flesh spread around a wide swathe of grass, transforming the formerly pedestrian park into a bloody battleground. It's frightening how easy this is becoming. The nerves reduce with each new kill. Fighting never used to come naturally to him, but this is different. It's scary, but he's almost beginning to enjoy it now.

Will I get in trouble?

He's starting to feel nervous now... worried. He looks around, wondering if there will be repercussions because of what he's just done? If some kind of order is ever restored to the world, will he face the consequences of his actions? He's genuinely anxious for a few seconds, but then he realises it's okay. *They're all dead, Keith*, he reminds himself. *There's no one left to give you a hard time. It's just you and her now, no one else.*

And he needs *her* to understand how things are going to be from hereon in.

It's late. The atmosphere in the bungalow has been tense all afternoon and evening. Anna doesn't know what to say to him anymore. She hopes he's going to calm down again, be more like the Keith she first brought here, but the harder she tries, the more she seems to piss him off. She tries to make a drink again, but only succeeds in spilling water and putting out half the fire.

'You silly cow,' he says, trying to save the flames.

'Sorry...'

'Just sit down and get out the way. I'll make the drinks.'

'I was just tryin' to help.'

'You keep saying that, but when are you going to realise, you're not actually helping me. I'll do this, you just sit there and do whatever it is you do.'

'I'm glad you're here,' she says after a few minutes have passed. 'I know I'm a pain... but you make it okay.'

'You mean I cook for you? I keep you warm and make you tea?'

'Yeah, but that's not all. I like having you around.'

'I just make it easy for you,' he says without thinking. 'You're like my dad was.'

'How d'you work that out? I ain't nothin' like your dad.'

'You are. You're another dead weight. Someone else for me to carry.'

'Honest, Keith, I'm not... I'm different.'

'How?'

'I helped you, remember? I showed you this place.'

'Yeah, thanks for that,' he mumbles sarcastically.

'But we help each other. We need each other.'

He just looks at her. He knows he's being harsh, but he thinks it's about time she heard this. He needs to get her into line. 'I reckon you need me. I'm not so sure it's reciprocal.'

'Recipro-what?'

He shakes his head, irritated by her ignorance. 'What I'm saying is, I don't need you like you need me.' There's no point being subtle with this kid. He has to say it how he sees it.

Anna's face changes. There's a tear which she wipes away fast, determined not to let him see (though he clearly already has). He can see her thinking: her brain cycling through the limited options available to a dumb teenage kid trapped in an empty house in the middle of a park almost a week after the end of the world.

'I can help...' she says, sounding as desperate as she suddenly feels. 'You can give me jobs... I can do stuff... fetch stuff.'

'Really? Remember the house, Anna? That was a simple job – in and out – but you still managed to screw it up.'

'It wasn't my fault...'

'Then whose fault was it?'

'It won't happen again.'

'I won't be there to bail you out if it does.'

She thinks again, looking for ways to justify her position here. 'I can fetch food and water.'

'So can I. Anyway, the wood you collected was all wet. Either that or it was too thick.'

'Yeah, but I know now. I never done it before. I'll get it right next time... You can learn me how to do this stuff.'

Christ, her ignorance is really beginning to grate on his nerves. 'I can *teach* you,' he says, correcting her. 'It's not *learn* you, it's *teach* you.'

'You can teach me then.'

'Why should I? I already know what I'm doing. You never listen, anyway. I'd just be wasting my time.'

'But we've got loads of time...'

'That's hardly the point.'

The discussion ends abruptly, but she continues to watch him intently. He's messing with the fire now, prodding the flames with a stick. She met this woman at a barbecue at a pub once who said that *men can't help messing with fire...* and she thinks about how Keith's a typical bloke really, and she readies herself to play her trump card because it's all she's got left. She raises herself up onto her knees next to him and unbuttons her top. She thrusts out her slight chest, then reaches behind to undo her bra.

'Don't,' Keith says. 'Put yourself away. Silly little kid.'

'But there's things we can do, Keith... things we can do to pass the time. I can make you feel good...'

Keith shakes his head then gets up and moves away. Weird thing is, today he already feels good.

DAY SIX

It's late morning. The early mist has long since burnt away and the sky above the bungalow is a clear, faultless blue now. Although not particularly warm, the sun bears down uninterrupted. It's a glorious day. Picture a post-apocalyptic future where the dead outnumber the living by thousands to one, and you'd never have pictured a day like today.

Keith's started another fire now, but this one's outside. He spent a little time earlier piling up all the body parts he scattered yesterday, and he soaked them in fuel he found in the tank of a lawnmower that'll probably never get used again. He's sitting on a park bench a short distance from the bungalow, staring into the flames and watching flesh, bone and clothing being steadily reduced to nothing. *It's funny*, he thinks, *how it all looks the same in the end.* All reduced to carbon. Same colour. Same texture.

He knew starting such a large fire would be a risk, but it was one he was happy to take. He knew it would attract more bodies too, but what he didn't count on was the strangely cleansing effect it's having on their surroundings. The flames and the constant crackling, spitting and popping noises have acted like a call to the faithful, and more corpses than ever have begun to drag themselves towards the fire from all directions. He's not concerned. It's nothing he can't handle.

Anna sits at the other end of the bench, a little wedge of space between her and Keith. She has her hands buried deep in her pockets and though she's chattering with the cold, she's not complaining. She doesn't want to do anything to upset him. It's hard, though, because she really doesn't like being out here like this. If she could spend all her time locked in the bungalow with the windows and doors blocked, she thinks she probably would. She thought she'd got the measure of this fucked-up new world, but she feels like Keith keeps moving the goalposts.

She watches one particular corpse. She's had her eye on it for some time now. It was stuck for a while; the collar of its coat caught on an overhanging branch like it had been hung out to dry, but it's managed to wriggle and squirm free now. It's somehow lost its trousers too, and that should be funny, but it isn't. It's directly opposite them, right on the other side of the park, right on the other side of the fire, and it's coming their way. Sure, the bonfire's right between them, but Anna's convinced it's them it's locked onto, not the flames.

Step by stumbling step, the body gets closer. It's almost reached the fire now.

Keith glances back over his shoulder, startled by something, and when Anna tries to turn around and look at whatever he's looking at, he grabs hold of her arm and mouths a silent *no*. She senses movement, and then freezes. She remains perfectly still as yet another dead body – a little girl in a gingham school dress, half her height – stumbles past *en route* to the flames. A few seconds later and what's left of the kid is facedown in the flames. The fire is drawing them here from all directions like a beacon.

But that other damn body is still coming their way.

Anna's becoming increasingly agitated, and Keith can sense it coming off her. He understands why, though, because this particular corpse definitely is looking past the bonfire now and is staring at them. In fact, it doesn't even seem to see the heat haze, the smoke or the flames. Maybe its eyes are particularly good, or particularly bad? It's not reacting in the same way as most of the others. Anna starts to shuffle away, edging further along the bench, trying to move back towards the bungalow, but Keith won't let her. He's got her wrist now, and he's holding it tight. Too tight. 'Stay here,' he tells her. 'Don't fucking move.'

'But I want to go inside,' she moans, the gap between them and the corpse continuing to rapidly decrease. 'I'm scared.'

He won't let go. She tries to fight a little longer, but quickly realises there's no use. He's far stronger than she is and, more than that, she knows the more noise and movement they both make, the more chance there is of other bodies losing interest in the fire and coming their way.

She relaxes slightly when the half-naked body is caught by the leg by something. Keith almost laughs out loud because it tries to keep moving but can't. Either its foot has gone down a pothole or another corpse has managed to grab hold of it... whatever the reason, it's being held up right on the very edge of the bonfire, and although dampened by decay, what's left of the creature's skin and clothing has quickly caught fire. They watch as flames begin to lick up its bare legs, then wrap around its torso and arms, its coat catching light with unexpected speed. And within a few more desperately brief moments, its face has been consumed by fire; all hair shrivelled away to nothing, skin cooking like pork.

But the fucking thing's still coming.

It's somehow managed to free itself now, and it's moving towards them again. Surely it can't still see or hear them... how does it know? Anna begins to squirm again, desperate to get away, but Keith's grip continues to tighten and she stops fighting because she knows the more she struggles, the more he's going to hurt her.

Getting closer.

She thinks it reminds her of the cover of that album... the one that social worker had a poster of on his office wall. Was it Deep Purple? No, Pink Floyd, that was it. *Wish You Were Here.* A guy in a suit, shaking hands with a man on fire. Dad rock. The momentary distraction of searching for the name provides a welcome respite, but it's over as quickly as it began and now she's brought crashing back into this surreal reality again, wishing she was anywhere *but* here.

The burning body is still coming, trampling the ashes, more fire than flesh now. How does it keep moving? Why?

Anna tries once more to get away – a token effort. It's so close she can feel the heat from the burning corpse now, but Keith remains impassive and unimpressed, his grip on her wrist still painfully tight.

And then the body finally drops, the fire damage too severe. It sinks to its knees, then tips forward and plants its face in the grass, wafting a wave of heat and smoke and roast meat stink towards them.

Keith relaxes. Anna doesn't.

All is calm.

It's dark now, the fire outside reduced to embers.

Normally Anna would be spouting rubbish by now, boring Keith by pointing out all the inconsequential things she's found in her inconsequential magazines, but not tonight. Tonight she's silent. Subdued. Scared. Tonight it's Keith doing all the talking while she cleans up the dinner scraps.

'We'll get a few more fires going tomorrow,' he tells her. 'Key places. Key points around the edge of the park. It'll help us keep the numbers down, give them something else to focus on other than us.'

'Okay.'

'You were right about this place. We'll definitely stay here. Having this much land around it means we're pretty safe as long as we don't do anything stupid. We'll clear out a few more houses in a couple of days, get ourselves properly set up. If we're gonna do it, we might as well do it right, don't you think?'

She doesn't answer. She's looking into the ashes of the fire, remembering what happened earlier.

'Are you even listening to me?'

'Course I am, Keith.'

'Then what did I just say?'

'You're gonna start more fires.'

'After that?'

'Getting more stuff?' she tries hopefully.

'Clearing out more houses. Christ, Anna, you've really got to start paying more attention.'

'Sorry.'

'If you want to stay here and stay alive, you're going to have to listen to what I say and do exactly what I tell you. Got it?'

'Got it.'

Keith sits back and watches her, quietly relieved. He thinks they might actually be starting to get somewhere here. For the first time in his life, he's in complete control and, just as importantly, she's starting to understand how things are going to be.

DAY SEVEN

Keith's up first again next morning (no surprise). At first he doesn't move. He just lies there in his makeshift bed, listening intently, because he can hear something. It's something he wasn't expecting. There are footsteps outside the bungalow, but they're not the clumsy, barely coordinated footsteps of the dead. There's someone else out there. Someone else still alive.

His eyes are tired and full of sleep. He blinks several times and rubs them, then looks for Anna, trying to move as little as possible in case whoever's out there is looking in. She's still there, lying in her sleeping bag under the window, dead to the world (so to speak).

Keith continues to listen. He hears whoever it is try the door (*thank Christ for the padlock and chain*), then sees them move past the window. The curtains are drawn, so they can't look in. He hears them walking around the edge of the small building, following the sound of their footsteps as they complete a slow circuit. And then, after a couple of minutes which feel like an eternity, the footsteps start to fade. Assuming there's just one of them outside, it sounds like they're finally leaving.

Is it safe?

He gets up and looks out of the window, crouching down and

teasing up one corner of the curtain. And then he sees him. He's over by the remains of yesterday's huge fire, kicking through the ashes and the blackened bones, no doubt trying to work out why there's a burned out heap of body parts in the middle of the park.

What do I do?

Keith's intimidated by the appearance of the man (and he can tell by the way he moves that he's definitely a man). He's all done up in standard survival gear: dressed in black from top to toe, a facemask covering his eyes, mouth and nose, carrying some kind of long blade. He can see the man trying to piece together what might have happened here.

He's coming towards the bungalow again.

Keith presses himself hard against the wall, the way he used to when the dead got too close. The intruder rattles the door again, but the padlock and chain are holding and he won't get in. Keith shoots an anxious look over at Anna, thinking *don't wake up...* And, thankfully, she doesn't. She's still asleep under the other window. He's relieved she chose a position where she's hidden from anyone (or anything) outside looking in.

Keith waits, and it feels like forever until he hears footsteps trudging away again. He watches the unknown survivor disappear, heading off towards the trees. He has a feeling he'll be back.

But there's no question of Keith going out to speak to him. That doesn't cross his mind, not even for a second, and his reticence surprises even himself. Why wouldn't he want to make contact? Why is he hiding away from one of the only two other living people he's seen since this nightmare began?

The survivor outside retraces his route through the park the way rats follow the same trail around overgrown gardens. Has he been here before? Whatever he's done or hasn't done, wherever he's been or why, Keith's just relieved that he's gone. Other people present unwanted connections with the old world he's left behind. Keith doesn't want to go back to that. He's always struggled with other people, always been unable to fit in alongside everyone else. But here... here in the park, everything's different. It feels safer here, despite all the obvious dangers. This is Keith's Garden of Eden, where he calls the shots. He's in charge here, no one else, and that's how it's going to stay.

Two men and a woman are out on a balcony, looking over the park from the eighth floor of the block of flats. It's high enough here to be able to see over the tops of the trees and across the entire park.

'Well?' one of the men asks when the black-suited survivor returns.

'Just two of them, like we thought.'

'And?'

'And I already told you, he doesn't want to know. He thinks I didn't see him.'

'What about the girl?' the woman asks.

'I didn't see her today.'

'So what do we do?'

'Exactly what we said we'd do.'

When Anna wakes up, Keith tells her nothing of what he's seen this morning. She doesn't need to know. It'll only complicate matters unnecessarily. Much as he doesn't want to admit it to himself, there's a part of him that's jealous of the survival-suited intruder. Maybe jealous is the wrong word... intimidated, perhaps? Whatever the reason, the close encounter is bugging him. It's disturbed him, spoiled the moment, and he's not in a good frame of mind. He's losing his temper with Anna again. She keeps pressing him... trying to work out why he's acting so weird.

'Have I done somethin' wrong?' she asks.

'No.'

'What then?'

'Nothing. Just leave me alone, Anna. Go and get on with whatever it is you do around here.'

He's used that dismissive line on her before. It stings just as much second time around.

The atmosphere is unbearable in here, inexplicably tense. Anna wishes she could just open the door and leave but she knows she can't. Apart from the fact the dead world's bloody dangerous out there, there are more physical restrictions preventing her too. Keith's got the door locked permanently now, and he keeps the key in the pocket of his jeans at all times. She'd climb out the window if she thought she could, but there's too much uncertainty. Would he let her back in? Right now she wouldn't be too bothered if he didn't, but she can't afford to take unnecessary chances. She has to look out for herself, doesn't she? Christ knows, she's been doing it long enough.

Her stomach flips with nerves when he moves suddenly. He finishes the coffee he made a while back (they're down to two cups each per day until they can get out and loot some more), then ties his boots, tucks in his grubby shirt and picks up the shovel. She knows exactly what he's doing, but she still asks anyway. 'Where you going?'

'Where d'you think?'

'But do you have to...?'

'There are more of them out there, Anna. Don't you get it? I need to keep their numbers down. Can't let things get out of control here.'

And before she can argue – not that she would – he's gone. He opens the door and goes outside, locking it behind him.

There are three bodies in the immediate vicinity, all coming his way. *Is it wrong that I'm starting to like doing this?* He feels a little uneasy at the fact he's beginning to enjoy hacking down the dead and disposing of their remains. It makes him feel powerful. Vindicated. Justified. Christ knows he needs to feel that way. He's waited long enough.

'Please, Keith...' Anna yells from an open window, but it's clear he's not interested. He's not even listening. He's focused now, all his attention directed towards the nearest of the bodies.

When Keith was young, there was a man who used to come around to the house to see Mum. Mr Chapman, his name was. This corpse looks just like him. It's not Mr Chapman, of course, because he died years ago, and he probably looks a hell of a lot worse than this week-old cadaver now lurching towards him. The corpse is wearing a suit and tie, and its neck has swollen so badly that the tie has tightened like a noose. It would be cutting off its air supply (if it was still breathing) or its circulation (if its blood was still being pumped). Everything above its neck has swollen too. Its eyes are bulging and its jowls are sagging. Its oversized tongue is hanging from its mouth like a huge slug. Keith spends more time looking at it than killing it. A flurry of blows from his shovel and it's lying motionless at his feet.

One more for the next fire.

Keith thinks that this next corpse would have been quite a looker, back in the day, back before she died. She's still got a great figure, and if you look past the greenish tinge to her flesh and the nasty gash under her right eye and all the extra folds and creases where her body has become distended with gaseous bloat, she still looks pretty good. He almost feels bad that he's going to have to hack her down, but he does it just the same. He starts with one of his specialties: the shovel to the back of her head. He knocks her flying and puts his boot between her shoulders to stop her getting up again. He lifts the shovel blade up, ready to bring it down and sever her spinal cord, when he stops.

'Keith!'

Bloody Anna's calling him again. He turns around, ready to berate her and put her in her place again, but then freezes. There are two people standing in front of the bungalow, talking to her through the open window. All nerves gone, no time to think, Keith sprints back down to the house and positions himself directly between Anna and the others. 'Hey,' one of the survivors – a woman – says.

'What do you want?'

'We want to help.'

'We should go with them, Keith,' Anna says from behind him. 'There's four of them. They reckon there might be more. They're not far from here and—'

He pushes her back inside, then shuts the window in her face. Conversation over.

'We don't need your help,' he tells the intruders, because that's what they are.

'I was here earlier...' the man says.

'I know. I saw you.'

'...and like Jen says, we just want to help. There's so few of us left. We think it'd be better if we all stuck together.'

'We're fine,' Keith says, struggling to contain his anger. 'Thanks anyway.'

'You don't look fine,' Jen remarks, looking him up and down. He's absolutely filthy, covered in mud and blood and dried rot.

Keith's getting tired of this. Times past, he'd have struggled to hold his own in a conversation like this, but things have changed. He's changed. He's a new man now, a stronger man. He knows what he's doing. He pulls Anna's pistol from his back pocket, and the two survivors immediately begin to retreat, arms raised in submission.

'Take it easy,' the man says. 'We don't want any trouble. We were only trying to help.'

'And I already told you, I don't need your help. Fuck off and leave us alone. We're okay here.'

'What about your friend?' Jen asks, gesturing over his shoulder. Anna's frightened face is pressed against the glass, watching helplessly.

'What about her?'

'I don't think she's fine. I think she wants to come with us.'

'She's staying.'

'But don't you think—?'

'I said she's staying here,' he interrupts, and he takes a couple of steps towards them, gun still raised, pointing it from face to face.

They continue to back away.

'Okay, okay...' the male survivor says. 'We get the message. We're sorry. Didn't mean anything by it.'

'Keep going, and don't come back,' he warns, and he watches them 'til they're gone.

Back inside the bungalow, Anna's sitting in the corner sobbing. 'Why wouldn't you let me go...?'

'We don't need them, Anna. We're okay here.'

'But I wanted to go.'

'You're not going anywhere. You're staying here with me. You need me, remember? It's for your own good. You want to get through this, don't you?'

'Yes, but—'

'Then you do as I say. I'm in charge. Don't forget it.'

She nods and sniffs back more tears, but doesn't move.

She watches Keith intently now as he shoves the gun into his back pocket again and starts mooching through the council supplies. He's sure he's seen what he needs somewhere here...

And then he finds it. With a triumphant 'yes', he emerges from the chaos with a hammer and a box of nails. He uses them to secure those windows which open, then nails planks of wood and other scraps over the glass. He says it's to stop anyone getting in, but Anna knows it's more to stop her getting out.

Keith does all of this with a sense of calm, a fragile inner-peace. Because he really is in control now. For the first time in his life, what happens next is up to him.

And the first thing which needs doing is to get rid of those damn bodies. The arrival of those two intruders an hour or so ago really put the cat amongst the pigeons. He'd already started the morning's cull, but the interruption and associated noise meant that those bodies he didn't deal with were left to wander. They found their way to the bungalow (no surprise – his banging and Anna's crying didn't help) and they're not going anywhere. They frequently block out the light as they wander back and forth past the boarded-up windows.

'You don't have to kill them all,' Anna says, nerves mounting again as she watches him get ready. She's still in the corner, still not daring to move.

'We've been through this. The more of them I get rid of now, the fewer we'll have left to deal with later. And anyway, it's easy.'

'There's millions though.'

'I know.'

'But Keith, I—'

He's not listening. He's already on his way out the door. And Anna knows this is her moment. She gets up in a flash and shoves him out of the way, knocking him into one of the bodies as she tries to squeeze past and make a run for it. Keith runs after her, knowing he can probably out-sprint her, and knowing there's nowhere else for her to go. *Silly little bitch. What the hell does she think she's doing?*

He's as good as he thinks he is. Anna zig-zags across the park, ducking around three wandering bodies on one side and five on the other, while Keith sprints straight at her, just barging the dead away. The gap closes quickly.

Anna reaches the stream, but it's too wide to jump and she has to double-back, losing more precious metres. Keith reaches out for her but she slips him. She's more experienced than he is. He's never been done for shoplifting and had to make a run for it: she has. He's never broken out of a hostel and had to get across town on foot in the middle of the night: she has. He's never had to get away from blokes who've been following her since she got off the bus: she has.

There's a footbridge over the stream. She runs across, but trips on a crack in the concrete. She staggers on a short distance further, losing her balance more and more with each stumbled step, then goes down fully. Keith grabs hold of her and picks her back up, wrapping his arms tight around her. She kicks and squirms but he's not letting go. She screams, and the piercing noise deafens him and fills the air. 'Keep the noise down, for Christ's sake,' he tells her. 'You'll get us both killed.'

She knows there's no use fighting and she gives up, letting him carry her all the way back to the bungalow. He roughly throws her inside and locks her in.

'I'm doing this for both of us, Anna,' he says before he leaves her. 'I'm doing this to keep us both safe.'

And he shuts the door and secures it with the padlock and chain on the outside this time.

Right. Back to business.

He clears up the remaining mess outside quickly. Breathlessly. He's swapped his shovel for a pickaxe now, and the kills are easier than ever. It takes more effort to lift the pick than it does to dispatch the bodies. As long as he hits the head, the bodies go down. He laughs to himself as he butchers what's left of them. *It's just like all those movies Anna was on about, not that I ever watched them. Go for the brain...*

Anna watches through a gap between the boards across the largest window. And he knows she's there. He can't see her from this distance, but he knows she's watching and he puts on quite a performance. He needs to show her – and anyone else who happens to see this, dead or otherwise – that he's the boss. He needs them to know that right here, right now, what he says goes.

With all the rogue bodies mopped up, Keith marches up the hill towards the main gates, and stops a little way back.

Are you sure about this Keith?

He knows what he has to do now, and why he has to do it. He needs to get rid of more of the bodies. Doing that will leave everyone in no doubt that he's in charge, that they shouldn't mess with Keith. If they made a film of his life, Keith thinks, not that there's anyone left to make films (or even to watch them, for that matter), then they'd call it *King of the Dead*.

He stands in front of the rotting crowd outside the park with more confidence than he can remember having in a long time, if ever. He remembers Anna doing this when they first arrived here, and he understands why she did it now. It's a weird kind of power trip. It's a way of showing the dead what's what, of telling them he's untouchable.

'Morning all,' he says, chirpily. He's not expecting any response, and is surprised when he gets one. A wave of reaction quickly spreads through the maggot-infested ranks from front to back. Even though those furthest from him probably don't even know he's there, they react to the reactions of those in front. It spreads like wildfire.

Some of them try to grab at him through the railings, arms at full-stretch. He decides to save them the bother. Working quickly and carefully, he slides open the latch and opens the gate wide enough to let the first few through. He pushes the barrier shut again, getting it closed before the bulk of the dead masses can get any smart ideas.

About ten of them have made it into the park, and Keith immediately sets about them with the pickaxe. He swings the heavy garden tool around wildly, hacking the damn things down, and even if he doesn't manage to take out their brains, he at least makes sure he does enough damage to their spines or their legs to incapacitate them sufficiently so they no longer pose any threat. Vile creatures. *And that's all they are now*, he decides, *creatures*. There's nothing human about them anymore. He wonders if there ever was, because he's felt this disconnected from the rest of the human race for a long time.

With all of these corpses down, he works his way around them, finishing each of them off. Most can hardly move, but they react when he approaches. Some stretch up their arms, almost like they're pleading with him to put them out of their misery. And Keith's more than happy to oblige.

Panting, soaked through with sweat, he admires his impressive handiwork. Another batch of bodies reduced to next to nothing after just a few minutes effort. He's never felt this strong before, never had such power... A couple of others managed to get away when he first let them into the park, but that's not a problem: he'll deal with them later. He looks back at the bungalow and watches them amble awkwardly down the hill. There's a part of him hopes Anna's still watching, but he can't see her from here. There are a few more bodies, though. He sees another one stumbling out from a thicket the way they do, crawling then walking.

Time for more. He hasn't had enough yet. He can feel the tensions of the morning easing away.

Keith lets another group of dead things into the park, a few more this time. He's learning not to be afraid of people at last, and he's wondering why he ever was. He used to spend all of his time keeping out of everyone else's way before now, doing what he could to melt into the background and avoid being noticed. He always felt like he was pushing in the opposite direction to everyone else; going anti-clockwise while they all went the other way, what he thought was the *right* way. Why did he bother? Okay, so the rest of the human race is far easier to deal with in this miserable, pitiful state, but were they ever really as big a problem as he used to believe? If he'd shown a little backbone like this before they all died, would he have commanded more respect?

Remembering how he used to be makes him feel angry more than anything else. And Keith vents that frustration on another eight corpses.

Anna can't work out exactly what it is he's doing. He keeps disappearing now: vanishing under masses of groping arms and lumbering bodies, eventually re-emerging like something out of that bloody *Evil Dead* film she watched once and hated.

But he needs to be careful, because she can see something he can't. She'd shout and tell him, but she's trapped in here and anyway, it would only make things worse.

Much worse.

She doesn't know how it's happening or why, but there are crowds of bodies in the park now, many of them moving in from the opposite direction to where Keith's fighting. It's like a bloody army... hundreds of them. Are these things somehow communicating with each other now? Is this a coordinated attack? Are they responding to the noise Keith's making out there, or are they responding to something else entirely?

Whatever the reason, she knows she's dead if she stays here much longer. She starts hunting through the equipment the council left behind, looking for something with which she can fight her way out of this damn bungalow.

Keith's taking another breather, having got rid of the second lot of corpses in less time than the first. He looks down at his blood-soaked get-up and, not for the first time, curses his short-sightedness. He's been wearing the same clothes for days now. They were in a bad enough state before, but now they're appalling. He's soaked through with blood and other liquids (which are easier to identify through smell rather than sight). He's literally a bloody mess. A rank, rancid, bloody mess. He's thinking he'll take Anna out with him tomorrow to loot another house and get them both some new gear.

But not yet.

Right now he's still focussed on getting rid of more of these damn bodies, because he's starting to realise that if he can destroy a few more large batches, then the numbers around the main entrance to the park will have reduced, and that has to be a good thing, doesn't it? If they can think and feel anything – if there's any kind of cognitive thought still flickering through their dumb, decaying brains, then maybe they'll realise he's a big deal after all and find someone else to hound. Those other survivors, for example. Keith doubts the man and woman who trespassed here earlier would be capable of doing what he's doing right now.

As if to prove a point (albeit only to himself) he lets in the next batch of corpses. There's a definite surge forward when he opens the gate this time and many more get through than he intended. No matter. It'll take a little longer to deal with them than planned, but he's sure he'll get through all of them in time.

The first few go down as quickly as expected, though it's harder to see clearly what's happening now because there are so many of the damn things swarming all around him. They each try to rush him, as if they can't wait to be killed. The smell starts to affect him. He's panting with the effort of this physical exertion, each time sucking in lungfuls of rank, foul-tasting air, tainted with stale rot and must and other, even more repellent smells. The dead are criss-crossing in front and behind him, as many appearing to be herding towards him as those trying to get out of his way.

And then, through a random gap in the chaos, he sees something which blindsides him. At first he can't believe it. He stops fighting now and just pushes more of the dead out of the way when they get too close, letting them wander down the hill towards the bungalow. This is important. This is *really* important.

There's a dead face he recognises, pressed up against the park gate. 'Dad?'

He's not looked good for a long time now, but Dad looks so bloody awful this morning that Keith's not entirely sure it is him until he's had a chance to get closer and have a good look. He recognises the clothes he was wearing: the vest – stained more than he remembers – and those old trousers... they'd always been tight around his belly, but his distended gut has ballooned and he has a huge roll of pallid flesh hanging over his gusset now. His swollen skin is streaked with veins like cheese. It looks bruised. For half a second Keith's concerned, wondering how he got hurt, but the concern disappears fast. Keith just doesn't care anymore. To be honest, he didn't care much anyway. What he did, he did through duty, not love.

He walks away from the gate again, priorities conflicted, taking out a few more random bodies on the way. He notices quite a crowd building up near the bungalow now, but that's okay, he'll deal with them later. Right now, he thinks as he swings the pickaxe into the face of another corpse that gets in the way, he needs to decide what he's going to do about Dad. The one thing he knows for certain is he can't just leave him there. Don't get the wrong idea... he's not feeling sorry for his dead old man, he doesn't want to help him by ending his torment. Quite the opposite, in fact. He wants Dad to suffer for what he did to Mum. He wants Dad to suffer for making his life an empty, living hell for the last few years. In fact, he realises he wants to make his dad suffer because he did worse than that: he snatched Keith's life from him, stripped him of his freedom and choice, took away his real purpose and left him a zombie. Empty and vacuous.

Just existing. *For Christ's sake, why did it take me until the end of the bloody world to realise it?*

Keith thinks it's time to get his own back.

He deals with the last few stragglers of this particular batch which are still in range, just doing enough to incapacitate them now, not bothering with anything more final. They lie in pieces all around him, still reaching out with what's left of useless arms and broken hands, their bulging eyes staring at him, mouths opening and closing, forming silent screams...

Keith knows it's time. He yanks the gate open again and pulls Dad's body through, the useless lump of decaying flesh tripping and falling at his feet. He pushes the gate back then hauls Dad upright and the two of them finally face each other, man-to-man: one aware, the other barely even existing. It's like something out of an old Wild West movie. Keith passes the pick from hand to hand, and when Dad inadvertently lurches at him, he uses the end of the tool to push him away, laughing nervously as the old man rocks back on unsteady feet. Keith knows this could be over in seconds; a few well-aimed swings and swipes and that'll be the end of Dad. But that's not enough. That would feel strangely anti-climactic. He'd barely even break sweat. No, Dad deserves more than that. And when Keith thinks about Mum and all the damage Dad did, he knows he's going to get more too.

He uses the pick to start with. He hacks at Dad's legs, shattering his ankles and then both knees. After almost a week's worth of decay, his father's flesh can take nowhere near as much abuse as it did during life. Skin splits, bone splinters and sinews snap, and Dad's almost immediately down again. Keith rights him. His old man strikes a comical pose, reduced to half-height. He's in full view of the crowds outside the park, and that pleases Keith too. The nearest of them are just a metre or so away, and they rattle the gate with increased excitement as the one-sided battle continues.

Now the pelvis and hips.

Dad's flat on his back now, looking straight at Keith, unable to move from the waist down. His humiliation is almost complete. A couple more pickaxe swings and Keith destroys his shoulders too, and now the corpse can barely move at all. It would be so easy just to swing the pickaxe one more time and put it right through the middle of his face. The crowd's going wild behind him, and Keith's about to do it when he remembers.

The gun.

Keith does swing the pickaxe, but this time he brings it crashing down on Dad's ribcage, smashing right through his body and feeling the tip of the pick sink into the tarmac Dad's lying on. He can't go anywhere now, can't escape...

Keith takes the pistol from his back pocket and examines it. He's never fired a gun before, doesn't know how, but it can't be that difficult, can it? First time he simply aims and pulls the trigger, but nothing happens. Is there some kind of safety catch? He examines it again, running his fingers over either side, and he finds a latch and he's sure this must be it.

But before he can do anything, he hears someone shouting his name. And it's not Anna.

Keith spins around, and sees that the appearance of the park has changed dramatically in the short time he's been up here at the top of the hill. The open expanses of grassland are no longer open. There are hundreds of bodies here now, and from his unexpectedly good vantage point, he can see hundreds more approaching too. They're coming from all parts of the surrounding area, drawn here by the noise he's been making, no doubt. And yet they're not all coming for him. Most are converging on the bungalow.

And who the hell just called his name?

Whoever it was, they're shouting again. Keith picks out a group of figures moving with more purpose than the rest around the little building. It's the two survivors who were here earlier, and there are more of them here too. Christ, how many are there?

The fact the place is swarming with bodies is of little importance to Keith. He's more concerned that his precious little oasis of calm and space has been violated once again by these unwanted intruders. And, to make matters worse as he starts running down towards them, the fuckers are trying to break into the bungalow and get Anna.

'Get away,' he yells at them as he runs. 'Get out of here and leave us alone.'

He can already see Anna hammering at the glass as one of the trespassers tries to force the door. Christ, they've got metal cutters. They'll be through the padlock and chain in no time.

Keith throws himself at the woman survivor, tackling her to the ground, then picks himself up and runs at the next nearest of them. This guy's taking no shit, but Keith's a changed man now and he's not about to roll over and give up. He uses a nearby body as a weapon, charging into the disease-ridden creature and using it to slam the survivor up against the bungalow wall. The noise seems to excite the dead even more than before. They're closing in *en masse* now.

The bungalow door is opened by another survivor Keith can't get to, and Anna throws herself into the man's arms, sobbing with relief. There are bodies everywhere now, the nearest of them beginning to attack, but Keith barely even looks at them, because all he can see is Anna locked in an embrace with someone else. *His* Anna, holding another man. Why is she doing this to him?

'Anna...?'

'We need to get out of here, Keith,' she says, still clinging onto the other man. 'It's too dangerous. We have to go.'

'You're not going anywhere,' he tells her and he strides towards her and grabs her arm. When the male survivor he fought with moments earlier tries to pull him away, he reveals the pistol and shoves it into the other man's face.

Everything changes.

The survivors freeze and Anna screams at him to stop. The excitement of the dead rises to a new level as they react to the noise and movement, and they swarm like flies around shit. But wait, Anna's not screaming at him to stop. She's screaming something else. She's not even talking to him. She's talking to *them*.

'It's empty,' she's shouting. 'There's no bullets. I never had no bullets...'

And Keith just looks at the weapon in his hand. Useless. It looks the part, but serves no function. Just like him. He pulls the trigger again and again, aiming at face after face, but nothing happens.

The wind has been knocked from his sails. He looks from Anna, to the gun, then back again. He moves towards her, but a random body has other ideas and it crashes into him. He throws it to one side dismissively, then does the same with another. They're everywhere now... fucking dumb, dirty things.

And then another grabs hold of him, but this one has real strength. He tries to push it away but it has him tight in its grip and won't let go. Wait... What's happening here...?

'Keith,' the male survivor from this morning says, looking right into his eyes. 'We need to get you away from here, mate. You need to come with us.'

'Not going anywhere,' he says, and he pushes the man away. He tries to move towards Anna again, but the nearer he gets, the more she recoils. *She'd rather be with them than with me*, he realises. *She'd choose the dead over me now.*

And in a fit of barely controlled anger, Keith wrestles himself free then swings the useless gun around and uses it to club the survivor on the side of the face. The man yells out and staggers back, blood pouring from a gash on his forehead, and his noise appears to revitalise the dead yet again. Almost as one they change direction and head for him. His colleagues immediately see the danger and begin their retreat.

Anna's leaving with them.

Keith grabs the shovel from outside the bungalow and swings it at the nearest few cadavers, carving a path through the crowd. But it's too little, too late.

He can see the others looking up at the park gates where he's been fighting, and what he sees happening up there makes his legs weaken with nerves. He thought he'd closed the gates after dragging Dad through, but the sheer weight of dead flesh pushing from the other side has forced them open again. They've swung apart, and there are hundreds upon hundreds of corpses stumbling down the hill towards him now, gravity and the slope of the land combining to drag them all down towards the bungalow, an unstoppable flood of decay.

Too many?

For half a moment, he genuinely tries to weigh up the odds. *Can I do this? Can I get rid of them all?* But even in this terrified, deluded state, Keith knows it's hopeless.

'You fucking maniac,' he hears Anna shouting. 'Look what you did.'

And he does. He watches the advancing crowd, transfixed. And there's still a part of him that's wondering if this is an opportunity, not a threat?

'Last chance, Keith,' one of the survivors yells at him, their voice quieter now as they move away. 'Come on, mate. We need to go.'

But Keith's not leaving.

He starts to fight, because for him there's been nothing better than this place for a long time. He wants to reclaim it. He wants it back to how it was, how it used to be before these damn people turned up and messed it all up, just him and her. He was okay when it was just him and Anna. She was okay too. But now she's gone. He looks all around but he can't see her. He can't see any of the other survivors either, just more and more bodies everywhere.

They're all coming for him now. He thinks he's the only one left in the park. He has an image in his head of clearing this place again, then having the mother of all bonfires tonight when the job's done. When Anna sees the smoke she'll know he did it and she'll come back to him, he's sure she will.

'Wait for me, Anna,' he shouts, oblivious to the way his raised voice riles the corpses which surround him.

But, before he can get her back, first Keith has several hundred bodies to dispose of, maybe even more. Christ, they're still flooding in through the open gate. There are probably *thousands* here now.

Keith hacks at the nearest few, but the dead are coming thick and fast and a shovel and an empty gun just aren't going to cut it. He looks for alternatives, trying to remember all the stuff he kept inside the bungalow. He has a couple of knives, he's sure, and there was definitely a mallet there somewhere. And then there's what's left of the fuel from the mower... if he could get a big enough fire started, maybe the flames would just spread from body to body and the crowd would take care of itself?

He parries with the shovel, thrusting it deep into the gut of another corpse which he then manhandles back against the bungalow wall. He pulls the blade out again, a wave of putrefying innards spilling everywhere, then pushes past another glut of cadavers, grabs the bungalow door and forces his way inside.

There's got to be something here I can use...

The dead are trying to get in after him, but he can't afford to let them. He uses the shovel to block the door, wedging it under the handle. Now he's got time to think, space to breathe... he looks around the dark little building, trying to find weapons, but it's so dark in here compared to outside that it's hard to see anything. And before his eyes have even properly adjusted to the light levels, the dead have begun to clamour at the windows. All he can see are dead faces everywhere now, all those lifeless eyes staring back at him. The corpses try to scratch their way through the glass, and when that doesn't work they start banging. Soon the tiny building is echoing with deafening noise as scores of cadavers hammer on the walls.

Keith's still not scared. He's excited. *I can do this... Did you see how many of them I killed out there today, Anna? Did you see what I did to my dad?*

The volume of noise inside the bungalow is almost unbearable now. Keith leans back against a wall, feeling the dead hordes outside beating against it, and he uses the noise to fuel his desire. It's like a tribal rhythm – a constant, stirring noise like the battle drums of an approaching army. But he's still not fazed, not concerned. He knows he can do this.

Near his feet he finds a pair of rusty shears – a perfect weapon. He visualizes himself plunging the blade into the faces of countless attackers... slicing rotting flesh, impaling bodies... he pictures being back out there in the middle of the park surrounded by his many conquests, his enemies lying in pieces around his feet.

It's time.

He looks around the bungalow one more time before going out there. Anna's stuff is all over the place as usual, and he spends a couple of minutes putting it all back in order, ready for when she comes home. He holds one of her shirts up to his face and breathes in deeply. He can still smell her. He can still hear her voice... all the mispronunciations and grammatical screw-ups. Give him enough time, and he'll educate her right and straighten her out. She could really be someone if she sticks with him. She'll come around. Soon enough she'll realise how good she had it here and she'll come crawling back with her tail between her legs. That's what Dad used to say to Mum. *You'll be back...*

He's at the window now, standing on what was Anna's bed. His face at the glass is sending the part of the crowd gathered here into an absolute frenzy, but he just ignores them because he's looking beyond them out towards the gates where they continue to enter the park, their numbers undiminished.

It's going to be a long day. I might not get it all done. I'll probably still be fighting this time tomorrow...

Keith ties his laces and tucks in his shirt. He flattens down his hair and wipes mud and blood from his face. Then he stands and faces the door, weapon held ready.

He thinks about all the people at work – *if they could see me now.*

He thinks about his parents – *wish Mum could see how I stood up to Dad.*

He thinks about Anna – *hope you're watching this, Anna. I'm king of the dead!*

And he kicks away the shovel and opens the door, and within seconds the bungalow is filled with a tidal wave of dead flesh. And Keith's last thought as he's swept up and slammed against the back of the building, is how he hates people, and how he can't wait until it's just him and Anna again.

Won't be long. Wait for me, Anna.

They watch from the balcony of the flats. Five of them now. The park is an overcrowded mass of shadows and shapes, so many that it's no longer possible to make out individuals. It's like the entire place has crusted over: a single, rotten scab.

They see movement. A sudden surge of excitement. And they can tell from the direction the bodies are trying to go that something's happened near to the bungalow. It can only be Keith, and it can only be bad news.

'Sorry about your friend,' Jen says to Anna, laying a hand on her shoulder.

Anna just shakes her head. 'Fuckin' freak. He weren't no friend of mine.'

'But I thought...?'

Anna doesn't say anything. She takes her phone from her pocket – just a few minutes of battery charge left – and shows her a picture of Josh. Jen squeezes her gently, then leaves her to her thoughts.

WHO WE USED TO BE

WHO WE USED TO BE was written for John Joseph Adam's LIVING DEAD 2 anthology. I wanted to do something very different with this story, and decided to approach the zombie apocalypse from the opposite angle. In a nutshell, everyone in the world dies, only for them all to re-animate a few minutes later.

In his introduction to the story for the LIVING DEAD 2, Adams wrote: "Prominent atheist Richard Dawkins was recently asked if, since he did not believe in any sort of afterlife, he was afraid of death. He replied that he was not afraid of death – after all, the universe had existed just fine without him for billions of years before he was born, so why should it trouble him to imagine that it would go on existing without him for billions of years after he's gone? Rather, he was afraid of dying, because current laws compel dying patients to endure a torturous gauntlet of pain and suffering rather than letting them decide for themselves when to let go."

I wrote this story at the same time as PRIORITIES – the short story version of THE COST OF LIVING. It's the flip-side of that story, I think, and shares some thematic similarities. I deliberately used the same small family unit and had them ask the same kind of questions: How long do you keep trying? When is enough enough? When everything you value is at stake, what matters most to you and your family?

There was something beautifully ironic about the way mankind completely overlooked its own annihilation. Our society, for too long increasingly focused on the irrelevant, wasn't even looking in the right direction when more than seven billion lives were abruptly ended. Had anyone survived, they'd no doubt have been able to come up with a thousand and one half-baked, incorrect explanations: a mutated virus, terrorism, scattered debris from a comet tail, a crashed satellite leaking radiation... Truth was, even if by some chance they had stumbled on the right reason, it wouldn't have made any difference. And anyway, if anyone *had* been watching, then what happened next would have been even harder to comprehend than the sudden loss of all those lives. Just minutes later, as if each person's individual death had been nothing more than an inconvenient blip as trivial and unimportant as a momentary power-cut in the middle of a reality TV program, every last one of the dead got back up again and tried to carry on.

Simon Parker had been in his home office when it happened, poring fanatically over business projections. What he'd originally envisaged as an hour's work had, as usual, wiped out his entire Saturday morning. But it didn't matter. The work needed to be done. Without the business they could kiss goodbye to this house, the cars, the holidays... Janice and Cameron both understood. He felt bad that he'd left his son on his own for so long, but he'd make it up to him when he got chance. He knew Janice wasn't bothered. She'd just got back from shopping, arms laden with bags of clothes and other things they didn't need. Retail therapy kept her happy.

Simon mistook his death for a blackout. There were no choirs of angels or long tunnels leading towards brilliant white lights, no endless flights of heavenly steps to climb... Instead, his death came as a sudden, crushing pressure followed by absolutely nothing. One minute he was staring at the screen searching for a particular line of figures, the next he was flat on his back, looking up at the ceiling, unable to focus his eyes. He immediately began to search for explanations. A heart attack? An electric shock from a faulty power outlet? A physical manifestation of the stress-related problems his doctor had repeatedly warned him about? He tried to shout for Janice to help but he found he couldn't speak.

His sudden paralysis was suffocating and terrifying but, to his immense relief, it was also only temporary. With an unprecedented amount of mute effort and concentration, he finally managed to focus his eyes on the light fixture above him. Then he slowly turned his head a little. Then, with even more concentration and effort, he was able to screw his right hand into a fist and bend his arm at the elbow. He managed to draw his knees up to his chest and roll over onto his side. Then, having to will every individual muscle and sinew to move independently, he hauled himself up. No sooner had he stood upright when his center of balance shifted unexpectedly and he staggered across the room, stumbling like a new born animal taking its first unsteady steps in the wild. He tried to aim for the door but missed and hit the wall, face-first.

That didn't hurt, he thought to himself, panicking inside but unable to show it. Leaning back, he slid his hand under his shirt and pressed his palm against his chest. *Fingers must still be numb*, he decided. *Can't feel anything. Got to get help. Got to get to Janice.*

Leaning to one side until he over-balanced again, he rolled along the wall until he reached the open door and fell through. He staggered a few steps further then landed on top of Janice who had collapsed halfway down the hallway. Cameron watched them both from where he lay on his back at the very top of the stairs, with his head lolling back and eyes unfocused.

Both immediately suspected as much, but common-sense prevented Simon and Janice from accepting they were dead for a considerable length of time.

They had gradually been able to move around with a little more freedom and control and, between the pair of them, had dragged Cameron down into the living room. When the TV didn't tell them anything and the phone calls they tried to make went unanswered, Simon went outside to look for help. What he saw out there confirmed their bizarre and improbable suspicions.

When he left the house, Simon had braced himself for the expected sudden drop in temperature outside. He was only wearing a thin T-shirt and jeans – putting on anything else in his current ungainly state would have been too much of an ordeal – and yet he hadn't felt a thing. He hadn't felt the rain he could see splashing in the puddles around his bare feet, or the wind which whipped through the tops of the trees he could see behind the houses at the end of the cul-de-sac.

He'd originally planned to try and get to Jack Thompson, a retired GP who lived several doors down, but he hadn't even reached the gate at the end of his own drive before he'd lost his nerve and turned around. His hearing was strangely muffled and unclear, but a sudden noise over to his far left had been loud enough to hear clearly. He turned towards the sound, struggling with knees which wouldn't bend, hips which wouldn't cooperate and feet which were heavy as lead, and saw that Dennis Pugh, the pompous, odious property developer who lived directly opposite, was trying to drive his car.

Obviously stricken by the same mysterious affliction as Simon as his family, Pugh's bloated, unresponsive right foot had become wedged down on the accelerator pedal while his left foot had slipped off the clutch. With inflexible arms he fought to control the car as it careened forward at speed, clipping the low stone wall at the end of his drive then swerving out across the road and missing Simon's gate by the narrowest of margins. Simon watched as Pugh ploughed down Kathleen Malins from number seventeen before smashing into the back of a builder's van. Pugh half-climbed, half-fell out of the wreck of his car and staggered back towards his house, crimson blood dribbling down his gray face from a deep gash across his forehead.

Simon barely even looked at him. Instead, he watched Kathleen – one of Janice's circle of friends – as she tried to get back home. She was crawling along the road, badly broken legs dragging uselessly behind.

Safely back inside his house, Simon leant against the door and tried to make sense of everything he'd just seen. He caught sight of his face in the long mirror on the wall opposite and squinted hard to try and force his eyes to focus. He looked bad. His flesh was lifeless and pallid, his expression vacant and dull. His skin, he thought, looked tightly stretched over his bones like it belonged to someone else, as if he'd borrowed it from someone a size smaller.

Cameron sat in front of the TV while his parents had a long, difficult and surreal conversation in the kitchen about their sudden, unexpected deaths and their equally sudden and unexpected reanimation.

They had all stopped breathing but quickly discovered that by swallowing a lungful of air and forcing it back out again, they could just about speak. The Internet was still working – thank God – and they stood around Simon's laptop as he prodded the keyboard with cold, clumsy fingers. While most major news portals and corporate sites remained frozen and hadn't been updated, there was enough social network chatter to answer their most pressing questions: Yes, they were dead. Yes, it had happened to everyone, everywhere. No, there was nothing they could do about it.

The film that Cameron had been watching on TV ended and was

replaced with nothing. Simon returned to the living room, his legs tightening again, to see why the sound had stopped.

'Getting stiff,' Janice said. She was sitting next to Cameron, leaning up against him, unable to get up.

'*Rigor mortis*,' Simon wheezed as he fell into a seat opposite them, barely able to believe what he was saying. 'Won't last long. Read it online.'

'Scared,' Cameron said quietly, the first word he'd managed to say since he'd died.

'I know,' Simon replied, trying to focus on his son's face.

'We'll all just sit here,' Janice said, pausing mid-sentence to swallow more air, 'and rest. I'll get us some dinner later.'

Rigor mortis kept the family frozen in position for almost a whole day. For a time, they were barely able to speak, let alone move. In the all-consuming darkness of the long winter night, Simon stared into space, dry eyes unblinking, and tried unsuccessfully to come to terms with what had happened.

His family was dead, and yet he felt surprisingly calm – perhaps because they were still together and they could still communicate. Maybe the loss would hit him later. He tried to imagine how any of this could be possible – how their brains could even continue to function. He wondered: Is this strange state of post-death consciousness just temporary? Would it last as long as their physical bodies held together? Or might it end at any moment?

He tried to distract himself with other thoughts but it was impossible. Everything had changed now that they were dead. Janice's earlier words rattled around his head: her instinctive offer of a dinner he knew she'd never cook. He realized they'd never eat or drink again. He'd never again get drunk. He'd never smell anything again, never sleep or dream, never make love... For a while that really bothered him. It wasn't that he wanted sex – and even if he did, his sudden lack of circulation meant that the act was a physical impossibility now – what hurt most was the fact that that aspect of his life had been abruptly ended with such dispassionate brutality.

Silent, unanswered questions about trivial practicalities and inconveniences soon gave way to other more important but equally unanswerable questions about what would happen next. *What will happen to our bodies? How long will we last? For how long will we be able to move and talk, and see and hear each other?*

As the long, indeterminable hours passed, still more questions plagued him. He thought about Janice's faith. (Although he believed her regular trips to church each Sunday were more about seeing people and being seen than anything else.) Was there a god? Or had the events of the last day been proof positive that all religions were based on superstition and bullshit? Was this heaven – if there was such a place – or its unthinkable opposite?

He suddenly remembered a line from a horror film he'd seen once, and he adapted it to fit his own bizarre circumstance. *When there's no more room in hell, the dead will walk their living rooms, hallways, and kitchens.*

The next day, Janice had been the first to move. With a wheezing groan of effort she'd pushed herself up out of her seat next to Cameron – casting a disappointed glance at the large yellow-brown stain she appeared to have left on the cream-colored leather – then dragged herself upstairs on all fours. Simon went back to his office, leaving Cameron in front of the now lifeless TV. Simon needed to find answers to some of the many questions he'd asked himself last night.

He got lost on the still-functioning parts of the Internet. It took him a frustrating age to type and to move the mouse – he could barely hold it and click the buttons today – but he still managed to waste hours searching pointlessly as he'd regularly done before he'd died. He heard Janice crashing about in the kitchen, and her noise finally prompted him to move.

He checked in on Cameron as he passed the living room door. The boy looked bad. His legs and feet were swollen and bruised. His skin had an unnatural blue-green hue and one corner of his mouth hung open. A dribble of stringy brown saliva trickled steadily down his chin, staining his favorite football shirt.

'Okay son?' Simon asked, having to remind himself how to talk again. Cameron slowly lifted his head and looked over in the general direction of his father.

'Bored.'

'Just sit there for a bit,' he said between breaths as he carried on down the hall. 'Mum and I will work out what we're going to do.'

Janice's appearance caught him by surprise. In some ways she looked worse than Cameron. She'd changed her clothes and was wearing the dress she'd bought the day she'd died.

'Might as well get some wear out of it,' she said in response to his expressionless gaze.

'You look nice,' he said automatically, even though she didn't. *Always compliment your wife*, he thought, *even in death*. Truth was, the way she looked made him feel uneasy. By squeezing herself into such a tight, once-flattering dress, she'd highlighted the extent to which her body had already changed. Her ankles were bruised and bloated like Cameron's (because the blood which was no longer being pumped around her body was pooling there – he'd read that online) and her belly was swollen (most probably with gas from countless chemical reactions – he'd read that too). Her once-pert breasts hung heavy and unsupported like two small, sagging sacks of grain. She lurched into the light and, just for a second, Simon was thankful for the frozen, expressionless mask that death had given him and which hid his true reaction.

Janice looked grotesque. She'd covered her face in a thick layer of concealer which appeared even more unnatural than the jaundiced tinge of decay her skin had shown previously. She'd applied mascara (managing to coat her eyeballs more than her eyelashes), eyeshadow and lipstick with clumsy hands, leaving her looking more like a drunken clown than anything else. He didn't know what to say, so he said nothing.

'Just want to feel normal again,' she said. 'Just because I'm dead, doesn't mean I can't look nice.'

For a moment the two of them stared at each other in silence, standing and swaying at opposite ends of the room.

'Been trying to find out what's going to happen,' Simon told her.

'What do you mean?'

'What's going to happen to us. How bad things will get before...'

Janice moved unexpectedly. She didn't want to hear this. She headed for the dishwasher which she hadn't emptied since they'd died.

'Don't want to know...'

215

'Need to think about it, love. Got to be ready for it.'

'I know,' she wheezed. She squinted in frustration at the white china plate she held in her hand. It was dirty again now that she'd picked it up but she put it away in the cupboard anyway. 'How long will we have before...?'

'Depends,' he said, anticipating the end of her question, saving her the effort of asking it. 'Could be six months. Need to keep the house cool, stay dry...'

She nodded (although her head didn't move enough for him to notice), stopped unloading, and leant against the nearest cupboard.

'We're lucky really,' Simon said, pausing to take another deep breath. 'Six months is a long time to say goodbye.'

By mid-afternoon the street outside the house was an unexpected mass of clumsy, chaotic movement. More and more dead people had dragged themselves out into the open as the day had progressed. Simon thought he recognized some of them, although they were pale shadows of who they used to be.

What were they hoping to achieve out there? Surely they must have realized by now that the situation was beyond hope? *No one's going to help you*, he thought. *You can't cure death or make it any easier.* These people needed to get a grip and get back indoors. Some of them began to squabble and fight, unable to react to their impossible situation in any other way. Most, though, simply staggered around aimlessly.

Simon watched them all walking in the same clichéd, slothful way – shuffling and stumbling, legs inflexible, arms stiff and straight. That was one thing those horror film people got right, he decided. They were out by a mile with just about every other aspect of how they'd imagined the dead would reanimate, but they'd got the slow and clumsy zombie walk spot-on.

Zombies, he thought to himself, smiling inwardly (as he couldn't outwardly). *What am I thinking?* He cursed himself for using such a stupid word. He wasn't a zombie, and neither were Janice or Cameron.

Where *was* Cameron?

Janice was in the kitchen, still cleaning and fussing pointlessly, but he hadn't seen Cameron for a while. He tried shouting for him but he couldn't make his voice loud enough to be heard. The boy wasn't anywhere downstairs and Simon couldn't face the long climb up to check his room. He lurched into the kitchen.

'Where Cameron?'

Janice stopped brushing her lank, greasy hair and looked up.

'Thought he with you?'

Simon walked past his dead wife and headed for the utility room at the far end of the kitchen. Using the walls and washing machines for support, he hauled himself along the narrow passageway and looked up. The back door was wide open. The whole house would no doubt be freezing cold but, as they were no longer able to feel the temperature, humidity, air pressure, or anything else, neither of them had noticed. He squinted into the distance and thought he could see Cameron near the bottom of their long garden. There was definitely something moving around down there...

He went out to investigate, struggling to keep his balance through the long, wet grass. The shape slowly came into focus. It *was* Cameron, crawling around on his hands and knees.

'What the hell you doing?'

'Playing,' Cameron answered, still trying to keep going forward, unaware he'd crawled headfirst into an overgrown bramble patch. 'Lost ball.'

'Inside,' Simon ordered, leaning down and trying unsuccessfully to grab hold of his son's collar. Cameron reluctantly did as he was told. He reversed direction and shuffled back out, dragging spiteful, prickly bramble stems out with him which refused to let go. He stood up, fell back down when one of his legs gave way, then got back up again.

'What you thinking?' Simon demanded, managing to swallow just enough air to almost make his voice sound as angry as he felt.

'Fed up. Want to play...'

Simon grabbed Cameron's hand and dragged him back towards the house. He stopped and held the boy's discolored wrist up closer to his face. His paper-thin skin had been slashed to ribbons by branches and thorns. His ankles were in an even worse state. Flaps of flesh hung down over the sides of his feet like loose-fitting socks.

'Look what you done! Won't get better!'

Cameron snatched his hand away and trudged back towards the house, zigzagging awkwardly up the boggy lawn.

Simon's eyes weren't working as well as they had been earlier. It was getting dark, but when he looked outside it was still bright. The light was moving, flickering.

'Think it's... a fire,' Janice gasped, inhaling mid-sentence. 'House on fire. Over the road.'

He turned around to look at her. She was scrubbing at a dirty brown handprint on the wall, her barely-coordinated efforts seeming only to increase the size of the grubby mark. He noticed that she'd changed her clothes again. Probably for the best; several large, bile-colored stains had appeared on the white dress since she'd started wearing it. Now she wore only a shapeless, baggy pullover. He noticed that lumpy brown liquid was dribbling down the insides of her bare legs and splashing in a puddle on the carpet between her feet.

'What we going to do?'

Simon had been trying to think of an answer to that question all day, and he'd come to the conclusion that they only had one choice now – to barricade themselves in the house and try to maximize the time they had left together.

Earlier, when it had been lighter and he'd been able to see more clearly, he'd watched the chaos on the road outside with a mixture of fascination and unease. Their quiet cul-de-sac had become a seething cesspit of activity. There seemed to be a constant flood of people filling the street, marching incessantly towards nothing. (*Just like in the films*, he thought.) He remembered how he'd seen several of them trip and fall, only to be trampled down by countless others who were being forced forward *en masse* by the pressure of the swollen crowds behind. The street had become little more than a putrid, flesh-filled channel, ankle deep in places. But still they came, and still they fell. Stupid. Pointless. He was glad he'd had the foresight to have a gate installed across the drive. It made it easier to protect his family from the madness out there.

And what about Cameron? He'd caused irreparable damage to himself whilst on his own outside, and that had only been the beginning of his problems today. In punishment, Simon had sent him to his room, only for him to stumble back down an hour or so later, clutching his stomach. He'd fallen off his bed and had torn a deep gash in his side. Struggling to coordinate themselves, he and Janice had patched up their son as best they could. They packed out his gaping wound with towels, then wrapped virtually an entire roll of gaffer tape around his misshapen gut to keep the wadding in place. He now sat on a stiff-backed chair in the corner of the room, under orders not to move.

'What we going to do?' Janice asked again. Simon had lost track of how many times she'd asked him that. He couldn't remember how he'd answered, either. Even now he was struggling to hold onto his thoughts. That kept happening.

'Stay here,' he eventually answered. 'Open windows upstairs... make it cold. Block doors.'

'Go out,' Cameron grumbled from the corner, trying to pick a maggot out from a hole in his left leg just above his knee. The bones were sticking out of the ends of two of his fingers, making them as difficult to use as chopsticks.

'Not out,' Simon snapped, conscious that their conversation was beginning to sound primitive and almost totally monosyllabic.

'Yes, out!' Cameron said again. 'Bored here.'

'Can't,' Janice said, positioning her tottering, half-naked frame directly in front of what was left of her only child. 'Listen to Dad.'

'No point...'

'Go out and get hurt!' Simon yelled. 'Won't get better.'

'Already dead!'

Cameron's bizarre but factually correct response completely floored his father. His response, like many parents who lose an argument with their child, was to ignore him.

'You not going out. End of.'

The dark came again, then the light, then the dark. The family had barely moved in hours but, as dawn broke on the fourth day after death, Simon was forced to take action. When the bright sun was finally strong enough for him to be able to see out with his increasingly weak and useless eyes, he saw that the front of their house was surrounded.

He staggered to the window and squinted out. The number of dead people crammed into their crowded cul-de-sac had continued to increase. During the night just ended, the size of the crowd must have reached critical mass. The gate had finally given way and their block-paved driveway was now filled to capacity with rotting flesh. There were hundreds of them out there, faces pressed against *his* windows and doors. Furious and frightened, he hobbled over to one side and pulled the curtains shut.

'What matter?' Janice croaked from where she lay slumped in a puddle of herself on the floor.

'Outside,' was all he said as he limped past her and headed for the hall. Janice picked herself up and followed, her rapidly escaping, putrefying innards leaving a trail behind her. Cameron watched his parents disappear into the gloom of the rest of the house.

In the hall, Simon looked at the front door. He could see them moving on the other side. Barely able to coordinate himself, he purposefully collided with the coat stand by the mirror, knocking it sideways. It clattered down and became wedged across the full width of the door. Janice bent down and started to pick up the bags, coats, hats, and scarves which lay on the floor.

'Windows,' Simon groaned, already moving towards the next room. Janice followed, desperately trying to keep him in focus as he went into his office. She saw him grab at the venetian blind, trying to shut it with bloated hands. His stiff, twisted fingers became caught in the metal slats and he fell, pulling the blind down and revealing another mass of cold, emotionless faces outside. Janice tried to help him up but she couldn't. When he crawled away from her she dropped to her knees and tried to pick up the blind.

'Out!' he said, pulling himself back up, using the door frame for support. Janice, momentarily confused and disorientated, managed to work out where he was standing and shuffled towards his voice. Once she'd gone past him, Simon made a grab for the door handle, catching it with his fourth downwards swipe and pulling it shut.

They stood together in the hallway, leaning against each other, unsteady legs constantly threatening to buckle. Simon concentrated hard and made himself swallow air.

'Back door,' he said. 'Then safe. All blocked.'

He pushed Janice away so that he could move again. She toppled back then lurched forward, her face slapping against the wall like rotten fruit. Instinctively she took an unsteady step back and tried to wipe away the stain she'd left behind. She was still rubbing at it several minutes later when Simon limped back towards her.

'In,' he wheezed, his voice barely audible now. Together they crashed back through the living room door. 'Block up. Lock in.'

'Careful,' she said as he moved towards the bookcase adjacent to the door. 'My things...'

She began trying to pick precious items and heirlooms off the shelves – a trophy, a crystal decanter, a framed photograph of the three of them – but Simon wasn't interested. Summoning all the effort he could muster, he pushed and pulled the bookcase until it came crashing down across the living room door, trapping them safely inside. Janice stood and looked at the mess. Simon collapsed. He aimed for the sofa but skidded in another rancid puddle and ended up on the floor. It didn't matter. He was past caring.

They were safe. The house was secure.

After a while, he looked around the room. Something was wrong. He knew his eyes were failing, but he could still see enough to know that someone was missing.

'Where Cameron?'

Janice and Simon lasted another eighteen days together. They sat slumped on the floor at opposite ends of the living room for more than four hundred hours, longer than anyone else for several miles around, still recognizable when most others of their neighbours been reduced to post-human slurry.

It felt like forever: hour after hour after silent, empty hour, they sat and remembered who they used to be and how much they missed all they'd lost. Had they been capable of feeling anything, their eventual end would have come as a relief. As it was, more than a week after they'd died, first Simon and then Janice's brain activity dwindled and then stopped like batteries running flat.

By then, Cameron was long gone. He'd only lasted a day after escaping outside. His dad had been right about one thing: by staying indoors where it was cool and dry, the rate of his and Janice's decay had been dramatically slowed. But Cameron hadn't wanted to sit there doing nothing. In his one long day, he played football (after a fashion), made friends with a frog, chased a cat, tried to climb a tree, and explored that part of the garden that Mum and Dad didn't like him exploring. And even when he couldn't move anymore, when everything but his brain and his eyes had stopped working, he lay on his back on the grass and looked up at the clouds and the birds and planned what he was going to do tomorrow.

TIGHTROPES

We always assume the reanimation of the dead will herald the end of the world, but what if that didn't turn out to be the case? What if we had a get-out clause... a way of holding back the apocalyptic tides, even if only for a while? I'm sure there are many great stories to be written about living life alongside the undead. One thing's for sure, though, if it's not quite the end of days, it won't take long before people get used to having the dead around and absorb them into their daily routine. Before you know it we'll all be bickering about the same old things again, worrying about the stuff we always worried about, making the same mistakes we've made a hundred times before... TIGHTROPES was written especially for this collection.

The whole world feels like it's permanently balanced on a knife-edge. It could go either way. One minute there's calm, the next utter chaos. One minute there's smiles and laughter, the next screams.

And right here, right now, the screams have just started.

The fragile order has been destroyed by the sudden appearance of the dead infected man. He lurches out from the dark corner where his body previously lay undetected for hours, awaiting reanimation. Now he staggers out into the middle of the busy pedestrian area in the heart of town. The reaction of the crowds is unsurprisingly panicked and random, and yet still strangely uniform: they all do everything they can to get out of his way, running for cover until the sheer numbers of other people stop them getting any further, putting as much distance as they can between them and the germ-carrying freak now shambling towards them. The dead man seems confused by all the movement and noise, his decaying brain unable to fully process everything at once. He looks from face to face to frightened face... milky eyes never quite settling on any one thing long enough to focus. There are so many potential victims to choose from, so many to contaminate, so many to kill...

Of course, these aren't conscious decisions he's making. This isn't a career choice. These are instinctive reactions caused by the germ which laid dormant in his coagulating blood for the last eleven hours after an unfortunate chance encounter with the remains of a partially dealt-with corpse in a patch of scrubland this morning. Poor bugger was out walking his dog, minding his own business, when the stupid mutt dragged the dismembered yet still booted foot out from under a bush. The owner had panicked and tried to wrestle the boot from his dog's mouth, but had only succeeded in contaminating both of them.

The germ's in full control of the dead man's brain now, ordering him to attack.

There's a massive bubble of space around him, and it's an unexpected reversal of all the zombie movies these frightened people used to watch so avidly, because for all the panic and bluster it's almost like *he's* afraid of *them*. The living still outnumber the dead right now, and though the situation's precariously balanced, the human race is just about managing to cling onto control.

There's a simple reason why the dead haven't yet overrun us: this particular strain of dead flesh-reanimating disease has an Achilles Heel. It can be defeated (as long as you're bloody quick off the mark and don't waste a second). It can't be prevented, but it *can* be neutralised. As long as you can get your shot within four hours of being bitten, five hours tops, you'll probably be okay.

What's happening here in this busy city centre square is a small-scale reflection of what's happening to the world in general, a remarkably accurate microcosm. There's only one infected and if he's dealt with quickly and carefully, life will go on. If he's left to his own devices or overlooked for any reason though, we're screwed. The infection will spread exponentially. The human race is walking a tightrope these days, and there's a huge drop on either side.

The dead man makes his (admittedly chaotic) next move.

He picks a target, seemingly at random. It's a middle-aged man who's caught napping. He's slow to react – too busy watching everyone else. He starts to run but gets bunched up with the crowds and the panic, and the infected man catches the collar of his raincoat and pulls him back, stopping him getting away. The guy is screaming, pleading for someone – *anyone* – to help, but everyone else is just relieved it's not them and they're getting as far as they can, as fast as they can. And now the bubble of space has shifted. The dead man and his terrified prey are at the centre, everyone else at least a couple of metres away.

The sheer weight and unnatural physicality of the infected has taken his desperate victim completely by surprise. He's literally swept off his feet by the force of the sudden attack, and the dead man exhibits a further dramatic show of germ-fuelled strength in slamming him flat on his back on the rain-soaked ground and keeping him there.

A couple of seconds is all it takes.

The man on the ground does what he can to keep the infected's snapping teeth at bay, but it's not enough. He comes at him like a chatterer – *snap, snap, snap, snap* – and one particularly vicious lunge finds its mark. The dead man tears a bloody chunk from his victim's cheek and drools into the open wound.

Job done.

Suddenly disinterested, the infected rolls away then clumsily gets up and looks for his next target. The bitten man is still sitting on the ground, clutching his face, blood streaming. His mind's racing, his head so full of desperate thoughts that he doesn't even feel the pain. He knows the next few hours are crucial.

The dead man doesn't get chance to infected anyone else.

Salvation.

A clean-up crew has arrived. They were dealing with a similar disturbance about a mile away, but got caught in a traffic snarl-up and couldn't get here any faster. *That's the problem with our line of work,* Dale Harkness thinks to himself as he suits up again. *We're trying to get closer to the trouble while everyone else is doing all they can to get away.*

But it's okay. They're here now. That's all that matters.

It's a well-rehearsed routine.

The nine man crew all have their individual roles and are all aware what the rest of the team is supposed to be doing. They might only have been together for around seven weeks, but necessity has forced them to learn fast and learn well. They know they're on the front line here. They're the ones who are responsible for holding back the flood.

Three of the crew are on crowd marshalling duties, trying to restore some kind of order to this most fractious of situations while, at the same time, checking for bites and scratches, making sure no one else has been caught. Four more close in on the infected man and grab a limb each, then pull him out into a star shape as they hold him down. The crew medic attends to the bitten victim, giving him the jab he so desperately craves, then suturing the bloody gash on his face.

There's one crew member left to do his thing.

Dale's still not sure whether his is the easiest job or the most dangerous. He's the one who takes the lion's share of the risk, but the satisfaction he feels makes it all worthwhile. He's the one who grabs the germ-carrier by the neck then destroys what's left of his brain with a standard issue penetrating bolt gun.

Hiss. Clunk. Recoil.

And the second he's fired the bolt through the dead guy's right temple, the danger is over. Threat neutralised.

The clean-up part of the clean-up crew's work doesn't take long. They burn the infected body in the back of their heavily modified garbage truck, hose down the area and each other with a high-pressure water and disinfectant mix, then wait with the injured man until the secure ambulance arrives to take him into quarantine.

A couple of months ago, all this would have seemed like something out of a hokey science-fiction film, but *the condition* has blurred the lines between what we used to call fantasy and what is now undisputable fact. The dead are rising and are walking the Earth (but only if we're dumb enough and slow enough to let them).

In some ways Dale's pre-Rising life (as people have taken to calling it) felt as hazardous as today. In fact, being on clean-up has given him far more of a purpose than he had before, and with that purpose has come a wholly unexpected sense of well-being. It's also given him an excuse, a way to press a reset button he didn't know needed pushing. Like the guy who got bit this evening, it's hard to see things clearly when you're the one in the middle of the chaos. Before all of this happened, though, Dale was most definitely not in a good place.

It wasn't Helen's fault, though he blamed her unfairly and left her with the lion's share of the guilt he should have shouldered himself. Money was tight, the pressure was relentless, and neither of them could see an obvious way out. She thought about trying to find work, but baby Dylan made that uneconomical whichever way they looked at it. She'd have needed something full-time just to pay the nursery fees, not that there'd been anything full-time in the offing, not with the economy as screwed up as it was. They needed to do work on the house, the credit cards and bills were mounting up, Dale's work had switched him to a zero hours contract... whichever way they turned they faced obstructions. The pressure and stress was rising by the day, almost by the hour.

They both felt increasingly trapped. They'd struggled and argued and fought with each other daily, and until the world had been irrevocably changed by the emergence of the condition, they'd been growing further and further apart.

And it was just before the outbreak that Dale had made the ultimate mistake.

He'd known Amber for years, almost as long as she and Helen had been friends. He always struggled with the names of most of her friends, but not this one. Amber was something else. She was incredibly attractive and she knew it. Long, black hair, permanently tanned and flawless skin, legs that went on forever... he'd never dared admit it, not even to himself, but he'd wanted her from the day he first met her. She had no ties, appeared to be permanently single... Dale might have been an idiot, but he wasn't completely stupid. He knew what he was getting himself into, but he did it just the same. Helen didn't want to know about sex anymore; Amber definitely did.

Jesus, she was incredible.

She did things to him he'd only ever dreamed about, and let him do things to her he hadn't dared imagine. For hours at a time, several times a week over the space of a couple of months, she turned him inside-out and upside-down as they explored each other's vices and discovered new ones. She took pleasure to the point of pain and just beyond. But if he'd been able to plot his emotions on a graph, it wouldn't have made positive reading. There were brief but incredible highs when they were together, swiftly followed by crushing lows when he realised what he'd done. He'd risked everything of value for a quick fuck.

Amber, it quickly transpired, was predatory. She had history; a well-deserved reputation. When Dale tried to pull away, she dug her claws in deeper and pulled him back. When he finally plucked up courage to tell her he didn't want to see her again, she told him with equal certainty that he wasn't going to stop. In fucking her, she told him, he'd signed away all his rights and options. There were no get-out clauses, no escape routes... just her. Just *this*. And it wasn't like she was being unreasonable, she told him. She didn't want a husband, just a lover. She was perfectly happy to share him with Helen for now.

There was nothing he could do. Dale convinced himself the sex was worth the risk. Life became a balancing act, another tightrope walk. He couldn't change direction, couldn't turn around. Carrying on like the way he was going seem to be his only option.

And then the zombie apocalypse began, and everything changed.

Zombie apocalypse was what many folks – those conditioned from a slavish addiction to trashy films and books – called it, but apocalypse proved to be a little too strong. There's no doubt it felt that way for a while, certainly during those incredibly frightening early days, and how could it not have when the recently deceased were rising to feast on the living (as the tabloids inevitably put it)? But once the initial panic had died down and the scientists had done their thing, the storm clouds gathering overhead didn't look quite so ominous.

The golden hours.

That's what the press called it: that brief period between infection and death when a syringe full of drugs could counteract the effects of the germ that was doing all the damage before it properly took hold of its host. Four hours, on average, five at the outside. It wasn't an inoculation – you couldn't be vaccinated in advance – you just had to make sure you got your jab as soon as you were bitten or scratched or spat upon by one of the undead. Even a drop of contaminated blood or saliva would be enough. Leave it any longer and all the drugs in all the hospitals couldn't help you. You'd be fucked. Dead within twelve hours, back on your unsteady feet and out spreading the infection yourself before the day was done.

The chaotic fragility of this emerging new world order has come as something of an unexpected relief to Dale. The undead and the problems they present are the focus of everyone's attention now, and everything else seems to go by unnoticed. He thinks it's funny: old enemies have become friends now we've all got someone else to hate. Politicians are agreeing with each other on TV and, around the world, conflicts are pausing as soldiers on opposing sides all aim their weapons at the living dead instead of each other. At home with Helen and baby Dylan, things are almost starting to feel like they used to.

The end of another day, and it's good to be back in the bosom of his family again. Helen greets him as he comes through the door, and after she's given him a cursory look up and down and checked he's clean and okay, he reaches out for her and holds her like he used to, way back when. Back before the Rising. Back before he was a clean-up agent. Back before Amber.

They talk about their respective days as Dylan plays around their feet, blissfully oblivious as only someone so young can be. Dale can't help feeling a little envious of his son. He wishes his life was that simple. Toys, food, games, TV... no complications.

And speaking of complications... his phone vibrates in his pocket and he checks it fast, hoping it's work. Helen watches him intently, studying his face in the blue-white glow coming from his touchscreen. 'Trouble?' she asks.

'Yep. There's been an incident up by the station. All the night crews are already out. They want me back in.'

'You only just got home. Do you have to go?'

'You know I do.'

Helen smiles dejectedly, but she knows these things are out of his hands. He's over by the door already, putting his boots and jacket back on. 'It was hardly worth you taking them off,' she says. 'Be careful, won't you.'

'I will.'

And Dale holds Helen again, then says goodbye.

He hates himself for doing this.

That message wasn't from work, it was from *her*. 'Want U. My place. Now.' And he knows he has to go, because if he does anything to piss her off, she'll bring his whole world crashing down around him. One phone call is all it would take. And he knows she'd do it too. In a heartbeat. No hesitation.

He sends a couple of covering messages before he gets there, explaining to Helen that his crew has a couple of other call-outs to deal with now, and that he'll probably be a few hours, don't wait up. And even though he feels like shit for doing it, there's a part of him that's excited too. The nearer he gets to Amber's apartment, the more he's looking forward to being with her. Who knows, maybe he'll be able to keep this balancing act up indefinitely? The best of both worlds.

And he's not disappointed. She's naked when she opens the door to him, and he's undressed a few seconds later. And they fuck. Oh, Christ, they fuck... She's in a filthy mood tonight. She shackles herself to the bed's ornate iron headboard with a pair of handcuffs, and tells him exactly what she wants him to do. It's glorious. Incredible. Brutal. Insurmountable.

But the post-sex comedown hits him hard. What she says next hits him harder still. 'I've been thinking... we can't go on like this, lover.'

'What do you mean?' he asks. He's barely able to talk, throat immediately dry with nerves. Half of him wants to hear her tell him it's over, the other half can't stand the thought of being without her.

Then the sucker-punch. 'I want you to leave Helen.'

It's like he's been kicked in the balls. 'I... I thought you said...'

'I know, I know... I know what I said, Dale, but things have changed. The world's changed. I don't want to be on my own anymore. I want you here with me, permanently.'

'But what about Dylan? I can't just walk out on the kid...'

Amber rolls on top of him, still naked, and puts a finger on his lips to stop him talking. Despite the sudden shift in mood, with her so close he starts to immediately get aroused again. 'I know it's not going to be easy,' she says, sliding her hand down between his legs, 'and that's why I'm not going to be a bitch about it. I'll give you a couple of weeks to break it to her. Helen's been a good friend to me in the past. I don't want her hurt anymore than is necessary.'

'Okay,' he mumbles, not knowing what else he's supposed to say, distracted by the way she's stroking him now.

'But you will have to tell her, lover, because if you don't, you know I will.'

*

The days pass with alarming speed. There's a dark cloud hanging over Dale, but he doesn't feel able to do anything about it. He's full of excuses when Amber asks, always ready with a reason why he didn't do it today and why he can't do it tomorrow, but he knows her patience is wearing thin and his time is running out. He thinks it's strange that he can do all kinds of horrific things at work, that he'll fire the bolt gun through the forehead of any corpse no matter who it used to be, but he can't man up and face his wife.

The chaos of the clean-ups is by and large a welcome distraction. It's a particularly difficult one which has occupied him for most of the day today. They're not far from Amber's place; five crews struggling to contain the aftermath of a break out. Situations like this are few and far between, thankfully.

They call them break-outs, but maybe let-outs would be more appropriate.

Every so often someone will come across a pocket of infected undead who've managed to get themselves trapped somewhere. This time it was a homeless hostel right in the middle of town, alongside the cathedral. Places like this were among the first to be shut down when things went belly-up at the beginning of the outbreak. It's typical of the way our society works, Dale's always thought. The folks who need the most help are always at the back of the queue, and when the shit hits the fan, the queue inevitably gets longer and longer so they have no chance. They're the ones with the fewest alternatives too. So when the council boarded up their hostel, they kept on coming because where else were they supposed to go? More than fifty desperate men and women had crammed together in here, hiding from the chaos. All it took was for one of them to be carrying the infection. As it happened, three had it.

Some dick, either looking for shelter or looking for loot, opened the door today and let the hungry dead come flooding out. Fifty-three plague victims, all of them now existing purely to spread their disease, let loose in the heart of the city at the peak of the morning crush. It was never going to end well.

Dale has the bolt gun slung from his belt, but that's where it has to stay for the time being because the first task facing the clean-up operatives is differentiating the living from the dead and incapacitating those who are beyond help. You have to make judgement calls sometimes, and it's never easy. A decision you make in a heartbeat could have far-reaching ramifications. That blood-soaked figure coming at you right now is capable of speech so you know they're definitely still alive, but you can see they've got more than a few bite marks and gouges, and they've sustained a pretty serious injury trying to fight off the dead... so what do you do? Sure, you can get them injected, but is there any point? They're bleeding out; as good as dead, anyway. So the simple clean-up criteria is this: undead – stop them going anywhere; living but not mortally wounded – get them to the medics to be checked over and given a shot as necessary; everyone else – treat as per the undead.

There's constant screaming and untold levels of panic and fear, but that just goes with the territory these days. Dale works his way around the cordoned-off area along with other colleagues, doing what he has to do. Limbs are shattered, pelvises smashed, spines broken... whatever it takes to make them immobile. And then, as soon as he's able, he and the bolt gun operatives from the other teams work their way around again, ending lives or existences, depending on the mortality status of each individual.

Just don't look into their eyes...

It's exhausting. Heartbreaking.

Whenever Dale makes eye contact with any of them – living, dead, or soon to be dead - he sees the hurt, sees the pain. He also sees the pain he knows he's going to cause Helen when he tells her about Amber.

It's several hours more before the job's done. Those who can be saved have been saved. A mountain of bodies are being disposed of according to procedures. The streets are being hosed down and disinfected. Everything will soon be back in its right place.

This bitch of a day is almost over, but when Dale finally makes it home, things get even worse.

'Hi, Dale, how are you?' Amber says. What the hell's she doing here, sitting on *his* sofa in *his* lounge, reading a book to *his* kid? He panics, assuming she's here to tell Helen what he can't, but then he remembers she and his wife were friends long before she became his fuck-buddy. This might be completely innocent. But hang on, there's *nothing* innocent about Amber. He feels a momentary wash of relief when Helen appears from the bathroom with a grin on her face, genuinely pleased to see him home. He's safe, he thinks, for now.

'You remember Amber, don't you?' Helen asks. How could he forget?

'Of course I do. It's been a while. How've you been, Amber?'

'Just great, thanks,' she says, prolonging the illusion while giving him a knowing wink he hopes Helen hasn't seen.

'So what brings you here?' he asks, unable to help himself.

Helen answers for her. 'Amber's flat's out of commission for a few days.'

'Why?'

'A couple of those zombie-things got inside,' Amber explains. 'They don't know how, but one of them bit two of my neighbours downstairs.'

'That's bad news. They okay?'

'They're fine. They got their shots in time.'

'And the infected are still in the building?'

'Locked in safe, and no one's rushing to clear them out unfortunately. They're contained, that's what the council says. Low priority.'

'I said Amber could stop here for a while,' Helen says, and Dale hopes the sudden knot of fear in his gut isn't manifested in his face.

'Here?'

'She doesn't have anywhere else. She called asking for Gemma Taylor's number, and when she explained what she needed it for, I said she could stay here. We've got enough space. Is it a problem?'

'Of course not,' he says quickly.

'It should only be for a couple of days,' Amber says, smiling sweetly, cool as anything. 'You don't mind, do you? I'll try not to get in your way.'

'Of course I don't mind,' he says, trying to act equally cool, trying to play her at her own game and failing miserably.

'Great.'

The meal Helen's cooked is his favourite, but Dale's struggling to keep down even a mouthful. It doesn't go unnoticed, and he blames his lack of appetite on the hell of a day he had today, not the fact that he loves one of the women he's eating dinner with and fucks the other. Helen gets up to put Dylan to bed, leaving him in just the kind of situation he was hoping to avoid.

'What the fuck d'you think you're doing?'

'Were you not listening, lover? My flat's out of commission.'

'Bullshit.'

'It's not. There was a huge outbreak close to the building earlier today. You should know. You were there.'

'How do you know?'

'There's lots I know. You'd be surprised. I saw you, lover. I was watching.'

'You're spying on me?'

'I wouldn't go that far. Keeping an eye on you, maybe. I take it you haven't told her yet?'

'What do you think?'

'I was hoping you'd have grown some balls and done the decent thing. I've already told you, though, if you don't do it soon, I will.'

'Not yet...'

'When? It's not like there's ever going to be a good time.'

'Soon, then. I don't want to hurt her feelings more than I'm already going to.'

'So chivalrous, so considerate, so full of shit. We're both such lucky girls.'

'Fuck you.'

'That's something you're going to have to put on ice for a while. At least until we're back in my bed again.'

'Keep your bloody voice down.'

'And you keep your temper in check. Save all that energy and angst for the bedroom. You'll need it when I next get my hands on you.'

Helen reappears, and they both sit back and look at her, conversations silenced and expressions changed. 'Everything okay in here?' she asks, sensing an unexpected atmosphere.

'Just fine,' Amber says, voice as light as anything. 'Dale was telling me about his day.'

234

'Lucky you. He never tells me anything.'

'You said you were bored of hearing about work,' Dale grumbles.

'Bored of hearing you moaning about work maybe,' Helen counters. 'Anyway, let's forget about the real world for a while. I've got a bottle of wine in. Fancy a glass, Amber? It's been ages since we had a proper catch-up. I'm sure I've missed loads of gossip...'

'Oh, I could tell you some stories...' she says.

And Dale just sits there and watches as they go through to the lounge together, almost wishing he could trade places with some of the infected bodies he disposed of earlier today. But then he realises how stupid that sounds. Apart from the regrettable complication that is Amber, life is good... in some ways better than it has been for a while. He has his wife, his son, his health, their home... the last thing he wants is to throw it all away. And though he might feel safer around the dead than he does around Amber, he knows he's not completely out of options. Not yet.

She's doing this on purpose. It's early Saturday morning, and Helen and Dylan are sleeping in. Dale's up for his scheduled shift, and when he goes into the kitchen to get breakfast, she's already there. She's cooked for him. She's wearing an apron – just an apron, nothing else – and he doesn't know where to look. She thinks that's funny, and leans against him as she hands him his food. 'Don't know why you're acting so awkward, lover. You've seen much more of me than this before now...'

And Helen gets up because she hears voices, but all she finds is Dale sitting at the kitchen table, eating his omelette. Amber's long gone. *She's good*, Dale's forced to admit. *She's damn good.*

Another day and he can't take much more. The pressure's too much. It's like having the snapping jaws of one of the infected just millimetres from your bare skin, and no matter where you go, there they are, desperate to get you.

Dale thinks about the imaginary tightrope he's been walking since he first did what he did with Amber. The tension in the wire is starting to slip and it's getting harder and harder to keep his balance. He has to do something about the situation, but what? It feels like it's no longer a question of *will I fall*, but *which way will I drop?*

It's time to take control. It's time to man-up and sort out this mess once and for all.

As they sit and eat lunch together, Amber directly opposite, Helen and Dylan on either side, he announces his intentions. 'This is getting ridiculous,' he says. 'You shouldn't have to be shut out of your own home for this length of time, Amber. Your place should have been cleaned up by now.'

'I already explained this and you confirmed my suspicions. I'm low priority. I don't have the money to go private and the council aren't going to go in there and clean up because the risk of infection is contained inside the building. You said it yourself, how can they justify it when the clean-up patrols are over-stretched as it is?'

'I know... but I've been thinking.'

Both Helen and Amber are looking at him now. He doesn't know which way to turn, so focuses on his unfinished food instead.

'What?' Helen says, his pause overlong. 'Come on, don't keep us both hanging like this.'

'I was thinking I could do it. It's my job, after all. I can get the decontamination stuff from work, borrow a bolt gun... a couple of hours and you could be back home again.'

'You'd do that for me?' Amber says, false-swooning. 'I thought about asking, but I didn't think it would be fair.'

'Wouldn't it be dangerous?' Helen asks.

Dale shrugs off the threat. 'No more dangerous than a typical day at work.'

'But on your own...?'

'I'll suit up, get in, get rid of the infection, then decontaminate. I'll dump the body somewhere outside and call it in anonymously. It'll probably be my crew that gets sent out to clean it up anyway.'

'Sounds perfect,' Helen says. And to Dale's surprise, Amber agrees.

'Great,' he says. 'This afternoon then?'

'Sure.'

'It must have been so awkward for you staying here, Amber,' he continues, pushing his luck now. 'I'm sure you'll be looking forward to getting back to your own place.'

'Oh, I've loved being here,' she says, playing him at his own game.

'You've made me feel so comfortable. You've been very welcoming.'

'Then that's settled,' Helen says, looking from one to the other. 'I'll fetch us some dessert, then you can go and get Amber's place sorted out.'

Dale's not as stupid as she thinks he is. He knows exactly what he's going to do.

He finds the corpse on Amber's landing, prowling up and down outside her apartment. It comes straight for him the moment it realises he's there, and he lets it bite the sleeve of his protective suit. These things are always easier to deal with once they've got their teeth wrapped safely around something. He slams his arm – and, by default, the back of its head – against the wall, then grabs the bolt gun with his free hand and does what he has to do. A single squeeze of the trigger and the expected kick and hiss of air, and the retractable metal bolt shoots out then shoots back, having done more than enough damage to what's left of the dead thing's brain to 'kill' it again.

The rest of the building is empty and the clean-up is quick. Dale carries the body down in the elevator, dumps it outside where he knows no one's going to stumble across it and get themselves infected, then puts on a dodgy accent and calls it in.

He decontaminates, then showers and changes in Amber's flat. He knows this place well, feels strangely at home. Using her facilities without asking gives him a sense of power he'd thought he'd lost. It makes him feel like he's finally using her the way she used him (though few would argue they've both done more than their fair share of using each other recently).

He's ready and waiting for her when she gets back.

'Didn't expect to see you here,' she says, though she seems pretty pleased.

'Thought I'd welcome you home.'

'And how did you plan to do that?'

'How do you think?'

She senses a shift in his behaviour, and she's hesitant. 'So you think you can throw me out of your house, then just click your fingers and fuck me just because you feel like it?'

'Something like that.'

And she smiles, because she's a nasty piece of work, and because she likes this side of him. She hasn't seen it before.

'Fair enough. We fuck, then you call Helen and tell her everything. Right?'

'Right. It's about time. I should have done it sooner.'

She dumps her bags and goes through to the bedroom and strips. It's still cold in here. Her nipples are hard, but she notices he isn't. 'You not feeling the love yet?' she asks, running her hand along his length. She lifts herself up on tiptoes and kisses him, then touches him again. Something's finally stirring.

He tells himself that now's not the time, that she's not the one, that this isn't about sex anymore.

Dale distracts her with another kiss, then picks her up and lays her on the bed. He sits astride her, then reaches for the cuffs he left under her pillow: the same cuffs she's used to shackle him to the wrought iron headboard before now. She giggles excitedly as they click shut around her wrists, hands locked in position above her head, attached to the bedframe. 'You sexy fucker,' she says. 'You know I love this. You know how fired-up it gets me.'

He kisses her again, then moves lower and gently teases her right nipple with the tip of his tongue. 'I know exactly what this does to you,' he tells her.

For a moment longer they're silent, staring at each other. Amber's legs start to writhe with anticipation.

And then Dale gets up and walks out of the room. She's puzzled for a moment, but still too excited to care. His uncharacteristic unpredictability this afternoon is making her horny as hell.

The atmosphere changes in a heartbeat when he comes back.

Dale's no longer naked now, though all he's wearing is one glove. It's the thick, heavily padded glove from his clean-up suit, but Amber's barely noticed that because she's too busy trying to work out what it is he's carrying. He enjoys seeing the confusion on her face, and he takes further pleasure from showing her exactly what it is. It's a finger. A single, decaying index finger that he clipped from its owning hand at the knuckle. He's holding it with the nail pointing down, so as not to spill anything.

'What the hell are you doing?' she asks, nervous now. She knows exactly how dangerous that thing is. She kicks out at him as he gets closer, then shuffles as far up the bed as she can get with her hands still locked above her head.

'Tragic accident,' he explains. 'Seems I didn't do as good a clean-up here as I thought.'

'What?'

'I need you out of my life, Amber. It's been fun and all, and I honestly will miss you, but enough's enough.'

He grabs her throat and pushes her head back while he leans against her. And then he turns the dismembered finger upside down and squeezes it hard, making sure plenty of infected blood ends up in her mouth. She spits it out and tries spitting it at him, but he's already shifted out of range and he knows he's done enough. A couple of drops. That's all it would have taken.

'You bastard,' she sobs, still spitting, watching him as he paces up and down at the other end of the bed, just out of reach.

'Sorry it had to end like this, but you left me no choice. You were just using me, Amber. You'd have made me leave Helen, then you'd have dumped me when you got bored. You're a hard bitch. This is all you deserve.'

'Bastard...' she says again.

'A few hours from now and you'll be past the point of no return. The sickness will take you fast. You'll barely even feel it. Someone will find you eventually... naked and chained to the bed... undead. Who knows, it might even be my crew that gets sent in to clean you up.'

'I'm sorry... get me a shot, Dale, please... I promise I'll leave you alone. You'll never see me again, I swear.'

'Problem is, lover,' he says, mimicking her condescending tone, 'I don't think I can trust you.'

Dale freezes when he hears the door of the flat open. Shit. Has someone heard what's been going on here? But how could they have? This whole block's been empty for days since the infected got in.

Amber screams. 'Help me! Please, somebody help me!'

He'd put his hand over his mouth to shut her up, but he can't risk catching anything.

Dale's surprised when Helen appears in the bedroom doorway.

She, on the other hand, doesn't look surprised at all.

'Helen, help me,' Amber begs. 'He's crazy. He was going to rape me...'

'Oh, please,' Helen sighs, 'give me a break. Credit me with a little intelligence.'

'It's not what you think,' Dale says. 'She was blackmailing me.'

'And that's why you're naked, is it?'

Dale's about to say something else when his wife smacks him around the side of the head with a heavy glass paperweight she picked up from Amber's hallway. He's out cold. She drags him over to the bed then heaves him up onto the mattress, struggling with his unconscious weight. But she manages it, because she's a determined woman, and this is something she's been planning for a while now. She fishes a number of plastic ties out of her back pocket and secures his wrists to the headboard, leaving him lying alongside Amber.

And then she goes to leave.

'Don't,' Amber screams, desperate. 'He's infected me. Don't leave me here, please. This isn't what you think.'

Helen stops. She told herself she wouldn't do this, that she'd just walk out the door, but now it feels strangely appropriate. She thought this would be punishment enough, but the fact Amber's still playing games, still lying to her even now, just makes Helen want to hurt her more.

'You think I didn't know?'

'He infected me,' she says again, talking but not listening. 'Please, Helen, I don't have long. I need a shot.'

'I smelled your scent on him the first time you got your claws in him, long before the Rising or whatever they're calling it. He's just a dumb bloke, so bloody transparent. He was just after sex, and when I didn't give it to him, he ran straight to the first scrubber who'd have him. And you both thought you were being so bloody clever, didn't you? Both of you thought you were better than me, that I wouldn't see what was happening right under my nose.'

'It's not like that. I didn't want to hurt you, Helen. Dale came onto me and I just—'

'Oh, give it a rest. It's too late. The damage is done.'

'It's not too late. If I can get a shot I'll be okay and...'

Amber shuts up when Helen walks back across the room towards her. She stays safely out of reach; out of biting range and spitting distance. Next to Amber, Dale groans and starts to stir.

'You two deserve each other, you really do. Both liars to the bitter end. And this is the end, by the way.'

'What do you mean?'

'Those precious golden hours? All used up already. I infected you both at dinner. It was in your dessert and you didn't even notice. I got hold of some blood a while back when I let the infected into this place... I was just waiting for the right moment.'

'What?'

'Honestly, it's such a relief knowing this is all over at last. It's been such a balancing act... such an effort not letting either of you know that I knew.'

'But Helen...'

'I suggest you just lie back and wait now, 'cause you'll need all your energy. It's just you and loverboy now. Together forever... at least until you've both rotted down to nothing. I hope you'll be very happy together. But you won't be happy, will you? You won't be happy or sad or scared or angry... you'll just *be*.'

And with that she's gone. And all Amber can do is lie there and wait for it to take her. And even if Helen's lying and Dale's clear, she knows he won't be by the time she's finished with him.

MURIEL

I was asked to contribute an original story to a zombie special published by SFX magazine, and this is it. Writing within a very limited word count and for a broader audience than usual meant that I had to change my style (note the lack of expletives, the unexpected optimism, and the copious use of the 'Z' word), but I had a lot of fun with MURIEL. It's a quick and disposable little story which looks at the differences between surviving a TV or video game version of the zombie apocalypse, and surviving the real thing.

Chris Wilkins lay on his bed in his candlelit bedroom, stomach full of food, feeling safe and warm and isolated from everything that was happening outside. *Mum and Dad would be proud*, he thought to himself. *Their youngest son has survived the zombie apocalypse singlehanded.*

The zombie apocalypse.

It still sounded weird when he said it - weird, but undeniably cool too. All those years spent watching movies about the living dead thinking, *what if?* And then, eight days ago, those 'what ifs' had become reality. It was bizarre. It was frightening. It was spectacular.

It happened just like they'd always said it would: some kind of virus carried in infected saliva and blood, transmitted through bites. Textbook stuff. Outbreaks had occurred in major cities, and the infection had subsequently passed between so many people in such a short space of time that the familiar faces on the TV news hadn't even begun to talk about causes or cures before they were gone – a flick of a switch and they'd been replaced by the Emergency Network. Chris had actually started to miss the news. He'd got a kick out of listening to stony-faced newsreaders talking about the end of the world after having droned on for years about economic downturns, phone hacking, pointless wars, celebrity babies and the like. They'd rolled out all the apocalyptic clichés he'd never thought he'd hear used in the real world:

Stay in your homes.
Isolate the injured.

Do not approach anyone you suspect to be infected.

Along with the expected bullshit and lies:

The situation is under control.

And his all-time favourite (which could almost have been lifted word for word from any one of a hundred films):

It has been confirmed that the bodies of the recently deceased are returning to life...

Awesome.

Another long, quiet night, disturbed only by the occasional scream in the distance and the sounds of creatures scrabbling around outside, looking for food. Chris felt remarkably calm. He'd done well to stay alive against the odds. His parents wouldn't have been best pleased with what he'd done to the house (he'd have to do something about the gouge in the wallpaper on the stairs before they got back) but he was sure they'd understand. He'd removed a couple of the interior doors from upstairs and had used them to block the ground floor windows - hence the wallpaper damage - and he'd secured the exterior doors with crossbeams. Blocking the windows properly had been a key decision. He'd never understood why survivors in the movies always used individual planks. Had they wanted the zombies to smash the glass and reach in through the gaps? Bloody amateurs. It hadn't worked for the idiots in Romero's original *Night of the Living Dead*, and that was almost fifty years old. You'd have thought someone would have worked it out by now.

Hell of a week Mum and Dad had picked to go away, though.

They were hiking up around the Lakes. Chris thought they'd probably be safer there in their isolated, stone-built holiday cottage. They never watched horror films, and they'd only have made things more complicated if they'd been here, taking charge and bossing him around as if they knew what they were doing. Dad would have taken forever to do anything, accurately measuring the length of the crossbeams for the doors as if it mattered (*if a job's worth doing, son...*) while Mum would have been fussing around the house, vacuuming up the brick dust and making endless cups of tea and sandwiches with scant regard for their supply levels.

The day after everything had kicked off Chris had received a single, one word text message from Dad: SAFE. Did that mean they were safe, or were they telling him to stay safe? Whatever the meaning, the message had been incontrovertible proof that Mum and Dad were okay, but the longer time went on, the louder the silence which followed became. The network had failed altogether yesterday afternoon.

With his older brother Andrew on his gap year, travelling across Australia with his girlfriend, it was all down to him. Chris. All alone. In his bedroom. At the end of the world.

He saw some terrifying things from his window, but the house was warm and safe and quiet inside and he felt detached from it all, almost like he was watching TV.

The first zombie he'd seen (it still felt strange calling them that, wrong almost) hadn't initially looked much like a walking corpse. It had been a girl, probably his age, maybe a little older, and he'd watched her walking away from the house in much the same way he usually stared at girls from his bedroom window. She walked slowly like she was drunk, occasionally veering off course and tripping up the kerb. But then she'd stopped suddenly just a few metres down from his house, swaying unsteadily, auburn hair blowing in the gentle breeze, her attention caught by something unseen. And then she'd slowly pivoted around on leaden feet and dived out of view before he could get a good look at her face.

Chris sprinted downstairs and watched through the front door letter flap, desperate to see more. Beyond the gate at the end of his front yard he saw a pair of thrashing legs which almost immediately stopped kicking and became still. And then the dead girl stood up and lumbered back into view, chewing on a chunk of the poor sod lying twitching at her feet. Her skin was pale and taut, as if it had been stretched over her bones, and her eyes were dark and unfocussed. Black veins filled with poison crawled up her neck like spider webs, and her chin and the front of her grubby T-shirt were soaked with fresh blood, a startlingly vivid red against the lifeless grey of everything else. She walked away, chewing constantly, overfilling her mouth with flesh as if it was the first thing she'd eaten in years.

The shock of witnessing his first attack wore off surprisingly quickly, and the succession of nightmarish images he subsequently saw from the comfort of the house began to have less and less of an impact. The dead started hunting in packs, great hordes of them dragging themselves down otherwise empty streets like a scene from a Fulci film. Thankfully the proliferation of more easily accessible victims in the homes which surrounded his own meant that he remained unnoticed. The naïve idiots directly across the street, for example, were totally unprepared for Armageddon. They'd only moved in a couple of months ago, and clearly none of them had ever seen a zombie movie. When the dead caught their scent and began to gather around the front of their house in large numbers, one of them had gone to board up the window. Why they hadn't done it before he couldn't understand, because that, of course, had fired the vicious corpses up even more. Didn't these people know anything? If the zombies find out where you are, it's too late to start barricading yourself in. All you're doing is turning your home into a prison, not a shelter. Chris despaired. This really was basic stuff.

The people over the road hadn't lasted long. One of the windows had given way under the pressure of more than a hundred zombies trying to force their way inside, and Chris had watched them scramble through the broken glass like starving rats, trampling over each other to be the first to get to the living. One of the survivors had managed to escape – crawling out of a side door on his hands and knees as the dead flooded his home – but he too was quickly killed. He'd only managed to get a couple of metres away before those zombies at the back of the pack noticed and turned on him. Chris watched them tear the man limb from limb, stringing his innards across the street like bloody paper-chains. He'd wanted to grab a controller when the desperate survivor had first appeared, to try and make him move as if he was playing Xbox. Because if the man had just doubled-back on himself and slipped down the alleyway between his house and next door, he'd have been able to climb onto the dustbins there, then get over the wall and away. Easy. As it was it was game over, player one: no power-ups, no health boosts, no extra lives.

As each day ended and the next began, the street outside Chris' house gradually became quieter. In fact, he noticed that the whole world had become eerily silent. There were clouds of smoke on the horizon from buildings nearer to the centre of town and the occasional bird flashed across the sky, but other than that, nothing. No traffic. No noise. Zombies would, from time to time, wearily haul themselves along his street in search of food, but they were increasingly few and far between. Was it all over? Chris realised, with something approximating real pride, that he was close to becoming a genuine, *bona fide*, post-apocalyptic survivor. He felt like Robert Neville in *I am Legend* (the book, that was, not any of the film versions because he was nothing like Vincent Price or Chuck Heston, and he was *definitely* no Will Smith).

Chris' post-apocalyptic credentials seemed to be increasing almost by the hour. The Emergency Network eventually went off-air, and not long after that the power failed. The water supply reduced to a trickle, but he managed to fill the bath then put a load of buckets and pots out on the flat garage roof to collect rainwater like he'd seen them do in *28 Days Later*.

The house phone and his mobile network had long since been down, but his mobile's battery eventually gave up the ghost too. With no way of recharging it, it was useless. It had been bad enough when the Internet had died last week, but the loss of his phone had resulted in his total disconnection. The fact he hadn't had any communication with anyone else wasn't the problem, it was the fact he now *couldn't* make contact with other survivors, if there were any. That wasn't good.

Hungry.

He'd not eaten for a while, and his last few meals had been pretty meagre. He needed to find some food and get a few other essentials too. The toilet was backed-up, and the smell in the house was foul. And he had a headache that wouldn't shift. He decided a full-scale looting trip from the large supermarket a few streets away would have to wait until he was feeling better, and that a quick dash to the minimart at the end of the road would be enough for now. The front door of the store had been left open since last Thursday, and he'd seen no one go in or out. *Okay, so it's not the Munroeville Mall*, he thought, *but it'll have to do.*

Chris spent over an hour getting dressed and tooling up. He raided his dad's stuff: the boiler suit he wore when he worked on the car, gloves and boots from when he'd had a motorbike (Chris wished he hadn't sold the helmet and leathers), and a facemask and safety goggles from the garage. He took with him the golf club Dad kept at the side of his bed in case anyone broke in, and a long-shafted screwdriver, the best weapons he could find.

Feeling nervous and unwell, Chris let himself out through the side door and crept to the edge of the road. He moved at a painfully slow pace, so slow that he thought he might be overtaken by zombies if there were any of them left about. It was cold outside, and even through the facemask the smell out here tasted very different to the musty confines of home. Burning. Rotting. Dying. It made his stomach churn. And every step he took sounded disproportionately loud. He felt exposed. For the first time, he felt vulnerable.

Once he'd reached the minimart, Chris helped himself to as much food as he could stuff into the rucksack and holdall he'd brought with him from home. He was sensible, taking food that would give him energy and help him stay alive, not just the beer, snacks and magazines he craved. Despite all that had happened, he felt an undeniable pang of guilt looting the store, and he didn't want to come back in a hurry. *The longer I can stay safe at home*, he reasoned, *the better my chances*. He went deeper into the building to find more bags and take more stock. *Get as much as you can, then get out of here*. His legs felt weak with nerves and his pulse raced so hard he could hear it.

And it was in the storeroom that he saw her.

And it was in the storeroom that she saw him.

For a moment Chris remained rooted to the spot with fear, barely able to think straight, eyes locked onto the rotting shell of a woman which stood in the shadows less than two metres away, dripping with decay. He started to slowly back up, hoping she hadn't noticed, but then turned and ran when the foul thing lunged at him. He cursed his stupidity as he burst back out onto the street – the corpse had been safely trapped in the back room for days, and he'd just let it out. He tripped over the outstretched legs of a dead man (just the legs and about half of the torso, nothing else) and landed on his backside in the middle of the road. The zombie staggered out after him and it was on him in seconds, moving with predatory speed. He'd left the golf club in the shop along with his looted supplies, but he still had the screwdriver. He scrambled back up to his feet as the grotesque dead woman lumbered towards him.

Do it, he yelled at himself. *Kill it!*

But he couldn't. He couldn't move a bloody muscle.

Muriel?

A flicker of recognition caught him off guard. He had to look twice to see beyond the unnatural colours of decay and the dribbles of blood, pus and other muck which covered her rapidly disintegrating face, but he was sure it was her. Muriel Sparks. Mum's friend who worked in the minimart.

Dead Muriel, her unblinking eyes covered with a milky-white sheen, continued her unsteady advance, gaping black mouth hanging open hungrily, yellow teeth bared, ready to sink deep into his flesh.

He knew she wouldn't – or couldn't – answer, but he asked all the same. 'Mrs Sparks... is that you?'

He could see she had on her minimart apron now, the logo and her name tag obscured by crusty yellow-green seepage. The zombie moved again, one bare foot slipping in a puddle of dark brown gore, and he mistook her unexpected lurch forward for an attack and staggered back. He held the screwdriver high, ready to strike, but he still couldn't do it. He imagined sinking the long shaft into Muriel's skull like he'd seen in films, but he just couldn't move.

Another unsteady step forward from the corpse sent him tripping back again. She was backing him up towards the house. *Don't let her follow you home*, he silently screamed, remembering the family over the road and how they'd been slaughtered, and hoping Muriel's rotting brain was sufficiently decayed not to recognise him. He tried to stand his ground when she came at him yet again, but all he could do was grab her wrists, keeping his arms locked and at full stretch to put maximum distance between him and Muriel's constantly chomping, snapping jaws. Her greasy flesh felt like wet putty in his grip, flaking apart beneath his fingers and sliding off her bones, and the stench... Christ, her smell was appalling. Only fear stopped him from throwing up.

249

This is real! One scratch and it's over.

In blind panic, Chris shoved the dead woman away and she tripped over her own feet and collapsed before immediately dragging herself up again. He held out his screwdriver to attack, but he still couldn't use it because, through all the venom and rot, all he could see was Muriel. And suddenly this wasn't a horror film monster any more. This thing was Muriel Sparks. This was Mum's friend. The woman who'd looked after him and his brother that week years ago when Mum had been on nights and Dad had gone away on a course. The woman who'd been a dinner lady at his old junior school for as long as he could remember. The woman who'd been in the local paper for beating off an armed robber in the minimart last December...

And now Chris didn't want to be a post-apocalyptic survivor anymore. The corpse came at him again and he wished Mum and Dad were here to help him. He wished the power was still on and the TV and phones were working. Wished that all the people in this street were still alive, and that none of this had happened.

Muriel continued to lurch closer, one leaden foot after another, slow and uncoordinated yet relentless. Determined. Hungry...

'Muriel, please... It's me, Chris...'

She stopped suddenly as her head exploded, hit from behind by a rock fired at gunshot speed. Chris instinctively shielded his face as a shower of blood and brain splattered over him. He cautiously looked up and lifted his pebble-dashed safety goggles. Much of the left side of Muriel's head had been blown away: her skull smashed outwards, decayed flesh blown apart. She was still watching him with her one remaining glassy eye as she dropped to her knees, then she finally fell forward, her dead face slapping against the tarmac like a mouldy peach dropped from a height.

Standing in the middle of the road, a couple of metres behind the twitching corpse, was a small girl with a slingshot which she was already reloading with another large stone. She couldn't have been more than eight.

'Don't you know nothin'?' she shouted at him. 'That one almost got you. You don't talk to them, stupid, you *kill* them. Bloody hell, ain't you ever seen a zombie movie before?'

WISH I WAS HERE

Written specifically to close this collection, WISH I WAS HERE is a very short story which looks at the difference between the living and the dead, post-Rising. Although we usually think about zombie stories in terms of us versus them, there are no real winners and the lines between the two opposing sides become increasingly blurred.

It feels like it has always been this way. It's so long since it began now, so long since everything changed... Before these days her world used to always be filled with light and noise and people, but all that's gone now. All silenced. All dark. Stripped of all emotion and pared down to nothing.

Back then, back before it happened, she had a sense of purpose, a reason for being. She got up at a set time each day and worked her way through the things she had to do. She bought food and cooked when she was hungry, drank whenever her throat felt dry. Even those most basic habits have changed now. Now she eats like a dog: whatever she can find, whenever she can find it. No one knows where the next feed's coming from these days. No one knows if there'll even be a next feed. Most times you go hungry.

There's no aim anymore, no incentive; just an instinctive, inbuilt desire to keep on going. Every day is exactly the same as the one before and the one which follows. All she can do is what she's been doing for weeks now, maybe months: just keep moving, just keep walking, just keep trying.

Looking around, she struggles to remember what the world used to look like before the end came. Her eyes are tired, increasingly heavy. She thinks she might be close to home, but it's all so very different to the fragments she can still recall.

It's of little consequence to her or anyone else, but the reign of man ultimately proved to be a mere fleeting distraction in the overall scheme of things; a few brief moments of perceived control which felt like forever. Mankind's usurpation of the land happened gradually over many thousands of years and felt unassailable. Boundaries were reshaped, rivers re-routed, forests cleared. Apparently impermeable tarmac and concrete coverings were laid everywhere, burying the mud and grass, holding nature at bay with ease. Buildings stretched up into the sky, defiant.

Not anymore.

The decimation of the human race – their numbers now slashed from millions to barely hundreds – has proved to have an equally transformative effect on the environment. In a fraction of the time it took to industrialize the world, the fruits of all those centuries of effort are being steadily undone. Now when the grass grows, no one cuts it back. No one kills the weeds or does anything to arrest their virulent, unchecked growth. When insects and animals infest, they do so without fear of being impeded. Packs, hives and colonies of creatures which would previously have been exterminated without hesitation for fear of them encroaching into *our* world, are now able to blossom at extraordinary rates. Everything is changing. It used to be that the people fed off the animals and the land, but now the situation has largely been reversed and the animals and vegetation are nourished by the people, by *what's left* of the people. By the people who used to be people.

She walks on, tired feet dragging. There's no point her keeping going, but there's even less reason to stop.

Sometimes she sees things she remembers. It seems to happen increasingly rarely now, but this is one of those times. A familiar sight sparks a long-buried memory, bringing the dead world back into focus.

Do I know this place...?

It's changed, of course, almost beyond all recognition, but there's something about it which triggers scant recollection. Letters under lichen: *S A I N S B U R Y...* There are shutters over those doors which were permanently open, and it's dark inside where there always used to be light. But it's the silence and stillness that's strangest of all, even after all this time.

There are people that used to be people here, but they're ignoring this place. Way back when, she remembers this being a focal point: streams of people always going in and coming out, loaded up with things. Now it's no longer a destination, just somewhere else to pass along the way.

But she definitely remembers it.

She knows she used to come here with others, and they all used to be talking and laughing, and they did things because they wanted to and they made choices and they made plans...

Not now.

The rain starts falling hard again but she's used to it, hardly even feels it. And for a fraction of a second she remembers being caught out in a downpour near here; how she sheltered, waiting for the summer storm to pass, and how she worried about her hair and her clothes. And she wishes he could remember more than just a few snatched images.

She sees herself reflected in a grubby piece of glass, but she isn't even sure who she's looking at. There are others around – more people who used to be people – and they all look the same as she does. She knows everything must stink bad because of all the rain and the dirt and the rot and the germs, but she can't smell it because when you smell something so bad for so long, you get used to it. It gets everywhere. Coats everything. It's normal now.

Past the building she knows, and she starts to follow a long road she's certain she's walked along many times before. Sometimes it's like she's going round and round in circles, but seeing the long road stretched out ahead makes her think of trying to get to the other people who mattered, and she's frustrated because the harder she tries to concentrate on their faces, the less she can see. But she knows they were real. She *definitely* knows they were real. She thinks there are some things that get buried so deep in your head they can't be forgotten no matter what. They're sunk too deep to be taken away. Even when everything else has gone, you're still left with those few precious fleeting images that meant so much.

Another road, this one off to the side. Every so often she sees glimpses in her head of how things used to be, triggered by shapes and lines. Split-second images of everything clean and fresh and no one dead.

She keeps on walking and eventually reaches a place where four roads meet. The traffic used to dance with the lights here, but now it's all stopped: snarled-up and dead-looking. The only thing still moving is someone stuck in a car. They've been trying to get out since they died. She knows this. She thinks she's seen that dead man many times.

Something makes her follow one road and not another, and as she makes her way down a gentle hill, the world around her seems to take on a little more focus. It's like a fog is slowly lifting. She knows she's nearly where she used to be.

Home.

And seeing the place where she lived makes the mist disappear even faster, and now she can almost see the faces of the people who lived here with her. She pictures three of them at the window, watching her, calling to her. It takes her by surprise just how different they are to one another in her memory because everyone's the same now.

It's good to be home...

The front door's open, and she goes inside.

She doesn't know where the others are now. Doesn't know what happened to them. Familiarity guides her through the house to the largest room where she finds a body curled up on the ground, surrounded by stains. It's not moving like most of the others, but that's good. This used to be one of the people who mattered, but it became something else.

The body on the carpet is where she left it. She remembers doing something to it. Hitting it... hitting it again and again and again because she was scared... She doesn't remember much, but she remembers how fear felt.

And then she remembers the other people she used to live with standing in the doorway, all shouting at her and trying to warn her, crying for her. And she couldn't shout back then because she was scared and she can't shout now because her voice is gone.

And then she remembers the pain.

It was the bottom of her leg. Her ankle. She tries to look, but her body won't bend.

And she remembers even more pain now, can almost feel it, even though she can't feel anything. Her arm. This time she does look. Faded now, but the marks remain. Scraggy black lines. Half-moon cuts which never healed. Bites.

She looks down at the broken body on the ground again and thinks *I did that*, and she knows that she did that because it did this to her and because it was going to do it to them too.

That was when I stopped being me.

She knows the other people who lived with her here are long gone. She knows she won't see them again. She walks back out of the house but pauses in the hallway, rocking on unsteady feet. There's a picture she can barely focus on hanging on the wall. It's her before she died, surrounded by the others. She thinks it would be easier if she didn't remember, but some things are buried too deep to forget. That's why she keeps coming back here. That's why she walks the same back-and-forth route again and again, hour after hour, day after day, drawn to the same places, forgetting then remembering...

And as she stumbles out of the house, light flooding her dead eyes, there's one last recollection. Kissing them goodbye each day. Warm bodies held close.

She thinks, *wish I was still that person. Wish I was here.*

And by the time she's reached the end of the road and started the climb back up the hill towards the supermarket, it's all forgotten again 'til next time.

ACKNOWLEDGEMENTS

As usual a number of people helped get these stories from my head to the page. In no particular order, huge thanks to:

Wayne Simmons
Rebecca Stranney
Will Wright
Toby Bowman
David Shires

And not forgetting my brilliant team of beta-readers:

Dawn James
Niamah Malik
David McDonald
Jami Sroka
Mark 'Wally' Wall

Most importantly, thanks to Lisa and our girls for your patience, love and support over the years (particularly over *this* year). A dedication at the back of a book of zombie stories doesn't even come close to telling you how much I love all of you, or how grateful I am to have you in my life.

"Straight To You deserves to be ranked alongside such classics as The Stand and Swan Song." —*Ginger Nuts of Horror*

The sun is dying. The temperature is rising by the hour. The burning world is in chaos. Steven Johnson's wife is hundreds of miles away, and all that matters is reaching her before the end.

Every second is precious. Tomorrow is too late.

"An engaging and heart-breaking read – Moody is the go-to-guy for extraordinary stories starring ordinary people" —*Wayne Simmons, author of Plastic Jesus and Flu*

"Trust is a slow-burner and all the richer for it. The layers of characters and details of the story play out perfectly when matched with an ending you're not likely to forget. It's also an outstanding novel, delivers in more ways than one, and is worthy of a place on the discerning fan's bookshelf. 10/10."
—*Starburst Magazine*

www.trustdavidmoody.com

If you are the original purchaser of this book, or if
you received this book as a gift, you can download
a complementary eBook version by visiting:

www.infectedbooks.co.uk/ebooks

and completing the necessary information
(terms and conditions apply).

CPSIA information can be obtained at www.ICGtesting.com
Printed in the USA
LVOW07s1725151214

418939LV00006B/973/P

9 780957 656338